The End of the World…Again
or
Hitbodedut

Book One: A New Beginning

By: J M Dark

Credits to:

My wife, Linda, for putting up with me

and

Enya, for putting me in the mood

Inching precariously down the face of the boulder called "the dawn watch" by the men who stand guard over the camp, Chilcoat reached the niche etched into the stone by countless ancestors before him. Sweeping the surface with his hand, he removed a family of bugs that had taken up residence.

As he settled in for the short wait, he focused on the sun rising above the far hills on the distant horizon. Since he was taller than most, he had to slouch to fit his head into the saddle carved painstakingly into the rock face. As a master-hunter, it was his duty on the morning-watch to check for the season change. He knew it wouldn't yet be time, but one of the young men of the tribe might be watching, and he didn't want to be caught slacking, so he sat dutifully in the cold. His knee was starting to complain about his inactivity as he stirred slowly, swinging his feet around to the east.

A rat complained about the ownership of some morsel down by the trash dump at the base of the rocks. Tangar, the tribal Seer, sat in the darkness waiting for just such an opportunity. He moved quickly to better locate the varmint and threw a barrage of stones. There was a short skirmish and he emerged triumphant. *He has earned his keep, and is justly proud. He'll hold his head high at this morning's meal.*

Chilcoat reflected on his own age and the stiffness he felt in his knee. *I'm only in my mid twenties but the pain from a rockslide that nearly killed me as a young boy lingers still. The incident left my knee scarred such that I fear; I too will soon be hunting rats and grubs. It also scarred my memory with a bitter taste of an unfair god that stole my parents before I even knew them.*

He pulled his long dark hair back from his face and held his hand up to block the first full rays of the sun as it peeked over the horizon. *It's just to the left of the sighting hill. In a few weeks, it'll align and it'll be time to move the village to the lowlands.*

A cool breeze snapped at his cloak and cleared his path back to the village as a band of clouds gathered in the south. Passing the first hearth on the outskirts of the village, he smiled at Tangar sitting proudly while his daughter, Tarra, worked to prepare the rats he had provided. There were two large ones and a single small one, and the broth was rich with grains from the summer harvest. Chilcoat nodded approval to the old man who sat erect in acknowledgment and beamed with pride at still being the man of his lodge, able to provide for his families' welfare.

Chilcoat moved quietly to his own hut. His sister-in-law, Charona, tended the cooking fire near the entrance while he washed up and huddled under the blankets next to Caran, his wife. *I always enjoy this moment of warmth and union.*

He was nearly ready to doze off when she stirred gently to caress him before getting up to tend to her morning duties. Brushing her ample flow of brown hair back from her face, she wrapped her comfortable figure in her morning coat, and left through the drape that served as the door to their hut.

The village soon stirred and began to make too much noise for him to get any more sleep, so he sat up close to the fire and lit a pipe of smoking herbs. The familiar warmth swept through him and the prospect of the morning meal sounded good.

As he finished his smoke, Charona entered with a bowl of morning stew and a large piece of flat bread. The size of the bread spoke of a stew without body. *I need to hunt today even though I've been on watch most of the night. That usually doesn't work out very well, but I've no choice. The family needs meat.*

While the season started well enough, in the last few weeks, it's suddenly turned very harsh. The animals we depended on are skittish and hard to find. It makes teaching Chilton very difficult. We spend much time searching and little time actually hunting. Perhaps it's a blessing. I've had to teach the boy many tricks I didn't learned until I was much older. Hunting in the lean years is a much greater challenge and, perhaps, will serve the boy well.

The thin morning stew is only roots and grain, "dirt stew" the men call it when we're drinking around the fire. It's warm, but it isn't the meal I need. Maybe I should be hunting rats with Tangar.

She watched Chilcoat awkwardly as he stirred the thin broth. "Is there anything I can do? I'd like to..." She smiled slightly and rearranged her cloak exposing the warmth of her neckline.

"Ah... nah, I'm all right." He considered the chill of the day and the prospects of trudging around the hills searching for game as she continued to clean up the bedding. Her cloak loosened slightly exposing more of her ample charms. "Ah... a few moments of your time would be nice."

She knotted her long dark hair back from her face and burrowed under the blanket he had wrapped around himself.

As they lay quietly recovering, Caran called for her to gather more firewood. Charona knew they didn't need more wood, but it gave her an excuse to leave. She took the cue and left Chilcoat with a slight hint of a smile.

The ground swayed under him as he bent to the fire and lit his pipe. He hadn't felt such uneasiness since he had been sick last season. He steadied himself for a moment and realized that it wasn't his condition but that the earth itself that was gently rolling. He quickly joined his family gathered around the cooking fire. They looked to him as if he could explain the earth's unsettled behavior. The dogs skittered nervously around the group, cowering at the slightest movement or sound.

Rancon, their nearest neighbor, stuck his head out of his hut and called to him. "Did you feel that?"

"Yeah, it felt like I was still drunk."

Rancon wrapped his coat closely over his shoulders and picked his way across the clearing to stand barefoot in front of him. Sipping a cup of morning broth, he gestured toward the south. "Looks like a storm. It seems like there's always a storm when there's an earthquake. Kind of late in the season for a storm from the south though—must nearly be time to move to the lowlands and we're still having summer storms..."

Chilcoat followed his gesture and was surprised at how quickly the clouds had gathered. The gray blanket was just coming over the horizon when he finished his watch, and now it was nearly upon them. *It isn't going to be a good day for hunting and I'm not really in the mood for more dirt stew.*

He considered some alternatives. *Maybe someone will trade for some herbs or hides, or maybe Charona can serve one of the elders for a few days in exchange for some meat... I'll have to ask around. Larkon had a good hunt a couple of days ago and he has three sons that are always in need of a woman's touch.*

Just as he had convinced himself that things were going to improve the dogs started to dance around nervously and, again, the ground trembled. It started gently at first, and then a great wave caused a pile of wood nearby to tumble with cooking pots falling from their platform.

"Whoa! That was a good one." Chilcoat remarked as the commotion subsided. "Maybe it's a sign that we should leave the highlands early this year."

Rancon collected some of the wood that had fallen. "Maybe so, we should ask Tangar to divine the meaning."

"That's a good idea, sometimes you surprise me Ran." Chilcoat slapped his friend on the back. "It'll give the old boy a chance to lead again. He deserves a little boost... I noticed him hunting rats this morning. He's good at it, but it's a bit of a comedown for the clan Seer. I tried giving him some of my last kill, but the old bastard wouldn't take anything from the likes of me. You know how he is."

"You two have a falling out? You're his son man... make him take it."

"That's what bothers him. I'm not his son. I'm just the kid he pulled out of the rubble. The kid he wants no part of now that I've grown past his chants and prayers. I have no patience for his mumbo-jumbo and that pisses him off, I guess."

"That's pretty harsh isn't it? I mean, you used to tag along on his spirit-walks. What's changed?"

"I don't know. Him and a couple of his buddies dug up some old scroll and they think they've figured out some obscure crap that he wants me to buy into. He keeps calling me '*the man foretold*' that has some mystical path to follow, and I've got no time for such nonsense. That—and I started to show too much interest in his herbs. He got mad and told me '*You can't rely on them*'."

"Well, that much is true. You won't find me eating his poisons, even if it means you'll do my hunting for me."

"I'll do your hunting alright, just as soon as you make the pain in my backside go away." They had a good laugh while they finished their stew and returned to their families.

As the morning routine finished, Chilcoat approached Charona about serving the Larkon boys for a couple of days and set the rest of his family to work getting ready for the annual journey north.

Stopping at the edge of Rancon's clearing, he noticed that the storm had gathered strength and rumbled as it poured in over the hills.

He called out. "Hey Ran, are you going to come with me to talk to the old man?"

"Yeah, sure, give me a minute to get some shoes on." He finally emerged from his house and, after taking a quick look at the sky, returned for a moment pulling his raincoat over his head. "This looks like it's going to be a real mess."

"That's the spirit. I always like to hear that positive attitude when things look bleak." The old friends took the main path through the village and tried to attract as much attention as they could without being too obvious. They wanted everyone to know that they sought the wisdom of the Seer. "It never hurts to pump-up the old man's pride before you try to convince him to find in your favor."

As they stood at the edge of Tangar's clearing thunder rumbled in the south. Pulling the arrows from his quiver, Chilcoat quickly sorted through them and selected a dart from the cluster. He placed it across the flat stone next to the fire pit and called out for all to hear. "Tangar, I've come to report a quiet night with only the dogs being restless near dawn, and we would humbly ask your guidance."

Rancon pulled a rabbit hide from his belt and placed it with the arrow. "Tangar, we've come to ask your wisdom."

Larkon and a couple of others from the village approached from behind, tucking in their coats and pulling on their shoes, as they stumbled up the dusty path in front of Tangar's lodge.

Tarra emerged from her father's hut and quickly counted the number of people gathering in the half-light of morning. "What do you want? He's resting and doesn't want to be disturbed."

"Aw, come on Sis. You know you're going to have to let me talk to him. It's official business." Chilcoat goaded her.

"Don't call me that. You're not my brother, and your 'official business' can wait until he calls on you at the evening meal."

Tangar emerged wrapped in his ceremonial robe and pulled the hood to cover his bald head against the chill. He looked deep into the eyes of the two men standing at the base of the path and glanced quickly at the offerings on his hearthstone. "What have you come to ask? Can't you see I am resting?"

Chilcoat smirked slightly at Tarra's disdain and pulled his small hunting pouch of smoking herb from his belt. He tossed the pouch on top of the rabbit pelt. "We're sorry to keep you from your rest, Father, but we knew you would be disturbed, as we are, by the ground quaking. What does it mean, and why are we plagued with a storm so late in the season? Tell us if we should prepare to leave for the lowlands. Are the gods telling you what we should do?"

Tangar looked gravely at the gathering crowd and gave a quick nod before returning to his lodge. The two men followed and entered the hut as Tarra held the flap open. She quickly tiptoed across the clearing in her morning cloak and retrieved the offerings. Her hair was a tumult of ginger that she pulled back from her lightly freckled face as she closed the door behind them.

The men sat on the meager cushions scattered on the floor while Tangar assessed the offerings. The rabbit pelt was of good quality and met his immediate approval but it was of lesser value than the arrow. He pulled his hood back and rubbed his naked head twice, as was his habit when he had something to resolve. Turning his attention to the arrow, he smoothed the feathers skeptically and gave the remaining arrows in Chilcoat's quiver a quick glance.

Chilcoat considered the offering. *He'll need to replace the feathers before he can use it for bird hunting. His eyes have grown dim with the years and colored feathers make a missed shot easier to find than the dull brown plumes that adorn the shaft.*

Putting the arrow aside, Tangar turned to the pouch of smoking herb. Opening the small purse, he poured the contents carefully onto the flat stone near the fire. He was pleased with the quality of the herb as he took a small pinch and held it to his nose. Tossing the empty bag back to Chilcoat, he dug into his own pouch for his pipe. After burrowing through the leather purse for several moments, he withdrew the small clay cone with a great deal of satisfaction.

He tapped the end of the pipe on his palm several times and blew through the stained yellow barrel to be sure it was clear. He then took a pinch of the dried leaves and packed them firmly into the pipe. Making a loose fist, he wedged the cone between his fingers, lit a kindling twig, and held it to the pipe. Pulling his closed fist to his mouth, he drew a breath slowly through his fingers. With the practiced hand of an expert, he metered the acrid smoke with fresh air, mixing it in his fist. His lungs were also showing their age, and he found that he needed very little smoke and plenty of cool, clean, air to keep from choking.

He opened his hand and rolled the pipe thoughtfully between his fingers as the pleasant warmth of the herb spread through his body. He felt the comforting pleasure he had felt so many times before as he looked upon the young men awaiting his wisdom. He considered the pipe for a moment and then held it out toward each of them in turn. They both nodded acknowledgement, but didn't take the pipe from him. They knew that custom required him to offer it, but that it was also the custom to decline herbs given in compensation.

He placed the pipe carefully on the hearthstone and looked up at the two men sitting across the fire from him. "You're anxious to return to the lowlands? You know the season hasn't yet turned. Why do you think we should put the people through this hardship so early?"

"Father, please hear us out. You know that I've watched the signs of the season, and I know that it isn't yet time, but the time is near, and the hunting's poor, and now the earth trembles beneath our feet. I think it would be good to start our preparations and make the journey in an easy walk instead of running from the winds of winter as we have done so many times in the past. This storm is another sign..."

"Sign? Now you're reading signs in the winds. You know what the scrolls tell us… *'Look to the sky for your signs and know that God will give you no other sign than the knowledge that you live in heaven'.* You don't need me if you can read the winds. Perhaps you should take my cloak now..." The old man tugged at the decorative band around his collar.

"No Father. You know I have no taste for spirits and signs. I don't want your cloak now, or ever. I'm not trying to read the signs as you do. It just seems to me, and others, that the season has turned early this year. You know this happens and it makes the journey hard on the very young."

"Now you're telling me that I am too old to know the concerns of the young?"

"No Father. I ask only that you explain the signs and tell us what we must do. Are the gods telling us to leave this place before the ground falls away from under our feet?"

Tangar considered his words and knew that what they asked was on the minds of everyone. The tribe expected, and deserved, an answer to the meaning of the quake. For, while quakes are common in the highlands, they're always a warning from the gods. Someone had apparently done something that offended YodHeaVau and he needed to determine what to do about it. Usually he could find someone who had done something that offended the spirits, but that would take time to divine, and this request for a quick answer wouldn't give him time to find an infidelity or transgression to blame this on. The old man finally spoke. "Let it go. I'll consider your words. Now, let me rest."

The three men rose and passed through the door. Each stopped and looked at the sky as they emerged. The clouds streamed over ominously. Tangar spoke in calm measured tones loud enough for those gathered to hear. "You're correct to come to me with this. I'll need time to divine what Hea is saying, but it's best that you begin to prepare for the journey." The old man took a small scepter from his daughter and waved it, first at the clouds covering the sun, then at the men standing before him.

Tarra retrieved the scepter and held the door open for her father. She looked irritated at Chilcoat. "You can go now."

Rancon spoke quietly to Chilcoat as they left. "You seemed to have pissed her off too."

"Yeah, she doesn't think I show enough respect for the old man and his mumbo-jumbo. She's his understudy in all things mystical and thinks I should bow down to her, or something. I mean, I just can't see her that way. She's my little sister, sort of."

Chilcoat's family settled into the work at hand, but the children's reluctance grew as the weather worsened. The thunder became an almost constant distraction and the windswept rain made everything cold and heavy. By evening, their belongings were packed and ready for the long journey, but the weather was too dreadful to consider an evening departure.

Lannon, the eldest Larkon boy, had heard of Charona's offer of service and came around just after dawn. He was curious as to when they were going to leave and seemed to linger, showing undue attention to her. Despite the fact that he was a notorious flirt, or perhaps because of it, she appreciated his interest but he was a year her junior and was one of her own tribe so she couldn't really consider him as a mate.

It detracted from Chilcoat's objectives to have the doe-eyed lad hanging around getting in the way, but he was big for his age, stronger than most, and had been on several successful hunts. As the preparations continued, it became evident that he wanted to become an extended member of their party so Chilcoat pressed him for a contribution to the provisions. He stammered a little and left in a nervous shuffle of unsure bravado. He was glad that Chilcoat accepted him, and was proud to provide a man's share, but was unsure his father would allow him to take it.

Many of the less important details remained undone, but Chilcoat looked to the sky and felt an urgent need to get started. He stirred the fire pit looking for embers as he broke it up. The last official act was to put embers from the morning fire into a traveling pot and to piss on the fire to be sure it was out.

Lannon waited his turn and followed suit. He was proud to display his manhood and assume the position of "second man" of their little band.

Chilcoat struggled not to laugh and did his best to ignore the display as he hung the ember pot in its sling. He wedged the handle between two of the tent bundles and looked back on the camp. Chara, his daughter, complained but when everyone else left the campsite, she reconsidered her position and came whining up behind Lannon who gave her a knowing smile. He was still on his best behavior trying to convince Charona that he was a good fatherly type.

Chilcoat smiled to himself. *The poor fool is trying so hard to impress her and all he really needs to do is be here. Meanwhile, I'm glad to have the able young man in my family. He brought the hindquarter of a deer that's his share of the kill he and his brothers made two days ago. He's carrying more than his share of the load and he's keeping Chara happy. What more can I ask?*

As morning peeked gray over the distant hills, the small band made its way past the trash heap and onto the main trail. Tangar interrupted his hunting and stood to greet them as they passed. The storm buffeted the old man's overcoat and he called after them, "Be well my son. I'm glad you've taken this burden from me. Others will follow—perhaps tomorrow."

At the mid-day break, a small portion of the meat was prepared and eaten. The group had settled into a slow steady pace but they were ready for a rest. Everyone lay quietly huddling together amongst the bundles. Lannon pretended to fall quickly asleep and fitfully squirmed ever closer to press warmly against the curve of Charona's back.

She lay quietly and watched Chilcoat for signs of disapproval. With none coming, she enjoyed the firm cushion of his youth pressed against her.

A sudden bout of thunder roused everyone and the rain started to make everything cold again. The troop stirred without complaint and headed steadily down the path leading to the creek. Water flowed swiftly in the stream and the rain fell in a light mist making the stones along the bank slippery. *In good years, the streambed would still be dry and the walk would be less treacherous, but this storm's unrest makes every step more hazardous than the last.*

Lannon stumbled under the weight of his load and fell into the stream. He recovered well enough, but lost a great deal of his bluster. The children sensed his loss of stature and gave him room to nurture his bruised pride. He would recover, but it would be several days before he would regain his swagger.

By the third week, the slow march brought them to the lowland plain. The walking was easier, but the weather had improved only slightly in that time. The streams were impassable in many of the usual places but they eventually made it to the ceremonial "great-house."

The structure bulged from the hillside like a broad flat snout overlooking the sea. Its smooth curved dome forms a ceremonial terrace that hangs over a small clearing cut into the hillside. Chilcoat reflected; *the skill of cutting a single block of stone, such as this, into such a form has long since been lost to our people. According to the legends exchanged each year at the "gathering," the great temple has survived hundreds of generations without change.*

Those of the tribe that could no longer make the annual journey to the cool highland pastures used the structure as a sanctuary through the summer months. They would stay inside in bad weather and would otherwise fish and tend the gardens that spill down the hillside.

The only entrance is a tunnel under the terrace. The squat hallway passes darkly beneath the main floor of the temple with stone carvings and small altars set up in ceremonial alcoves along its walls. The tunnel emerges as a ramp leading up a gentle curving path into the central courtyard and through the sacred herb gardens to end in front of the main altar mound. The rain drifted into the temple grounds through the opening above the plaza and collected in neatly kept furrows throughout the garden.

Tradition demanded that Chilcoat and his family stand before the council of elders upon reaching the gathering. They were to offer gifts that would pass, in turn, to the elders who were unable to provide for themselves. The roof arching overhead held the storm at bay, but gusts of wind stirred through the open windows overlooking the sea and drove rain across the cold stone floor.

Chilcoat formed up his little band of refugees and tried to look as presentable as could be expected. They found their way around the garden mounds and up the stairway nearest the inner shrine. One last dusting and they stood proudly at the base of the altar.

One of the elders put aside the basket he had been mending and slowly made his way to the throne. With a couple of labored grunts, he pulled himself up the steps and sat in the chair.

Chilcoat stepped forward and laid a small packet atop the large smooth surface of the altar. *The platform always amazed and troubled me as a child. I would stare for hours at its smooth dark surface. It's like a highland lake when the moon shines on it on a still summer night. The deep black reflects light but is as dark as the darkest night. The elders polish it with great pride and reverence, but none of them has the slightest idea of where to find such a stone.*

As is the tradition at the annual gathering, the elders open the festivities by reading the sacred scroll and telling the story of how Vau, the mother of all life, had taken her children of Yod and imprisoned them for having spread lies on the face of the earth. "She put them in a house that was perfectly smooth on all sides. It had no doors, so they couldn't escape and spread more lies, but it had many windows, so they could look out upon the world and see the damage their lies had caused. When they refused to repent of their deeds, She flung the house from heaven into the sea and there it drifted for many years. When She finally asked them if they had learned their lesson, they smugly replied that they had been the teachers, not the students, and that She herself must answer the question. She was so disappointed that She called Hea, Her husband, and the father of all things, to send a great and terrible storm to carry the house to the farthest ends of the earth where it came to rest, stuck in the side of the hill upon which they now stand."

The people of the tribes were said to be the descendents of those children of Vau and, because She was punishing them for their lies, She made them forget the skills of how the temple had been built and scattered them among the hills. Now each year at the end of summer, the tribes from all over the island gather at the temple to trade goods and stories, exchange knowledge, and make and renew family bonds.

The elder on the throne inquired about their health and asked each person what they had learned over the summer. The children told warm tales that brought a smile to his eyes, and Chilcoat reflected on his unrest with the late summer storms. The elder nodded acknowledgement but offered no consolation for his concern.

The family left the high altar and wandered around the inner garden grounds for several minutes as the storm continued. The rain fell gently on the well-tended paths that curved through the garden. At the very center of the courtyard, a large boulder sat glistening in the rain. It had always seemed odd to Chilcoat that such an ungainly object should sit in such a place of honor. *It isn't a nice boulder, it's jagged and broken, and even with the shimmering coat of rain, its colors are drab and without life.*

Maybe I can talk some of my buddies into breaking it up and hauling it away this season. I'll have to see if I can make it a drinking game of some kind. He rubbed his hand across its rough surface and struck it firmly with his fist. *For all of its unattractiveness, it's distinctly solid. Maybe it isn't such a good idea to break it up. Maybe I can learn to appreciate its jagged beauty.*

I remember when I was about ten; I climbed nearly to the top of the boulder by shinnying up its northern face. It isn't anything I'd try again, but at the time, it seemed like a good idea. It earned me a scolding from one of the elders and I had to sit through a long lecture about the importance of the stone. I didn't pay much attention, but I'm sure there was something about it being a gift from Hea to remind his children of His might and glory. It had always seemed to me to be more of a sign of His random whimsy.

As punishment for my disrespect of God's gift, the elder insisted that I sit and visualize the face of God in the chiseled facets of the stone. Maybe that's why I dislike the stone and want to see it crushed. I missed many of the important games while I sat all day moving from side-to-side trying to see a face in the jagged crags and clefts of the boulder. I remember thinking. "If the face of God is to be found in the imperfections of this stone, He is certainly an ugly god."

The exercise concluded when I made up a story about a face I imagined in the cracks of the stone. While the elder seemed satisfied with my fabrication, I always felt cheated, having not really seen anything. Now, as I stand gazing at the same spot I pointed out so many years ago, I'm still disappointed. I'm not sure if the regret is with God for being so mysterious or with me for being so dim. All I know is that the beauty of the stone still escapes me and I still don't see the face of God etched in its rugged form.

The storm continued, off-and-on, for another week. At times, it seemed as if the sky would fall, at others, it was a pleasant autumn mist with no signs of thunder or wind. None of the elders could remember a storm that had lasted so long or a sky that had seemed so angry.

The storm had taken a grave toll. As other families arrived, he learned of births, deaths, injuries, and illnesses. The news that Teri, one of Chara's dearest friends, had fallen into the stream not far from where Lannon had fallen. She wasn't as lucky as he had been. The stream had risen considerably and she wasn't as strong as he is.

Chara was devastated. She had never known the death of anyone so dear and couldn't be consoled. "It's not fair! Daddy, make her come back. Make her well again..."

Chilcoat held her warmly, cherishing every breath she sobbed into his shoulder. "No. It's not fair. God has taken her to do something very special for him. She's looking down on you right now and wants you to be happy for her." He uttered the dogma he knew all too well. *I want it to sound honest and warm, but it just sounds hollow to me. I heard the same thing when my folks died. It didn't sound right when Tangar spoke the words to me then, and it still doesn't make sense now, but it's all I have.*

It was especially empty since the tears he was sharing with Chara were really for his own loss of Tangar. A tooth had gone bad making him weak with fever, and his stubborn refusal to become a burden had all but assured his demise. Chilcoat had hidden his grief when he first heard the news. But now as Chara wept openly it felt good to join her sorrow, to draw her close and feel her pain, to hide his thin facade of indifference in his daughters tears.

Chilcoat reflected on the gruff old man that had been his father. *He had had a good life, and falling on the annual trek was an honorable end for a good man, even if it was to an old man's disease. Perhaps it is even more fitting that he should fall to the nobility of an old man's illness. It's better than dying as a young fool at the hands of a challenger or under the hooves of a beast that established its supremacy. The old man had proven himself often, and lived his life wisely enough to succumb only to the greatest challenge of all: age.*

As the festival progressed, Chilcoat grew weary of the activities. *He knew the stories in the scrolls by heart and decided that the competitions were of less interest than they had once been. The adolescents found it great fun to wrestle and tumble about trying to get some ball, or bag, or stick away from everyone else. Now it all seemed to be just an excuse to grab and fondle each other.*

The ceremonies that followed the weeks of games revolved around matchmaking and always led to the wedding ritual and displays of commitment by the newly joined couples. While he enjoyed the confirmation rite, he still felt the burden of Tangar's loss and just wanted to be alone.

Grabbing what little smoking herb he had, he headed up the hill above the temple. He hadn't been on that particular trail for several years, and it seemed that no one else had either. He couldn't help but think of Tangar as he struggled up the narrow overgrown path. His knee complained and his chest didn't seem able to supply him with enough air. "So, Old Man you walk within me," he grumbled.

After an hour's climb, he sought refuge from the wind in a niche in the rock outcropping that broke through the underbrush high on the face of the cliff. *Far below, I can see the roof of the temple bulging from the side of the hill like a growth on an old woman's face. It doesn't fit the slope of the hillside, it just doesn't seem right.*

He sat quietly watching the clouds gather on the horizon. The storm appeared to be gaining strength again and a thick layer of gray blanketed the sun. The rock on which he sat poked him ruthlessly. *It must be part of the ugly boulder in the temple garden,* he thought. *It's the same drab color and shows the same disregard for my comfort. God must have cast this stone from heaven as well.*

He stuffed as much of his clothing as he could under his butt and added some dried grass from nearby. *The storm will soon be upon me, but I just can't bring myself to return to the gathering. I've reached a place in my life that the loss of so many, so close, has touched me deeply.*

He dug through his shoulder bag and found the ember pot he had carefully stashed amongst his other things. He plucked a couple of sprigs of grass from his butt pad and twisted them together so that they would fit through the feeder hole in the pot. Pulling the stopper from the chimney, he blew gently across it while stirring and feeding the embers with the shoots.

Before long, he had rekindled a steady glow and set to work filling his pipe with herbs. He lamented the remaining quantity. *I'll have to see if I can trade someone for more, or maybe I can take a walkabout to find some. Better yet, maybe I can walkabout the temple garden. The elders always grow ample herbs. They wouldn't mind giving me a little...* As he drew the first smoke deep into his lungs, he quickly forgot the issue and watched the clouds thickening across the sun.

Something stirred in the bushes to his left. He sat frozen and watched for signs of malice. *It wouldn't do to have a snake creep up on me.* The glimpse of brown fur darting through the lower branches of a nearby bush rewarded his vigil. He let fly with a stone and smirked as the rat squeaked and fled back into the underbrush. The old man again crept into his thoughts. *He had always been very fatherly to me in a tyrannical sort of way. We shared many an evening smoking and talking over the years, and now he's gone. Him and his damn rats.* The rain mixed with his tears and made his grief seem more fitting.

As he struggled to stand, the stone under his foot broke loose and tumbled down the hill causing him to fall back on his hands. From his awkward perch, he watched the rubble crash through bushes on its relentless search for stability. The stone ricocheted off the rocks and crashed through the wall of a small catch basin. It slowed for an instant and then seemed to gather momentum as it bound from side to side along the ravine lodging itself into a berm just above the temple roof.

Lying back, he looked to the gray sky in relief. *It wouldn't do to bury the temple under a landslide.*

The sun peeked through a thin layer of clouds catching his eye. The perfect disk glowed brightly behind the blanket of gray, but there were blemishes ruining its perfection. Two small unblinking eyes stared down on him as he sat in his little sanctuary. *It must be the herbs,* he thought, as he squinted against the glare. The clouds swept by quickly and formed a stern grimacing mouth. He shaded his eyes and felt naked as he sat wet and cold in the sight of such a displeased god. *For while I've, on rare occasions, been able to look upon the face of the sun and have, on even more rare occasions, seen spots on its face. I've never seen the spots form such a pronounced expression of displeasure.*

As he gathered himself for another attempt at navigating the slippery trail, it occurred to him that the alcove he had claimed bore more than just a casual relationship with the ugly stone in the temple garden. *At last, I've seen the face of God. It isn't in the rock. It isn't even on the hill from which it came.* He looked again at the sun as it peered through the clouds. The glaring face still stared down on him as he stood amongst the stones that had delivered His child to the shelter of the temple far below. *So, this is the way of God. This is His face; the subtle change of form and substance that leads to mysteries without answers.*

Tangar, I long for your wisdom. To ask you what these signs mean, to comfort me with your knowing confidence, to help me understand. His words from the scroll came back to him. *"Look to the sky for your signs and know that God will give you no other sign than the knowledge that you live in heaven."*

"Father—you've left, as you must, but I miss you so..."

A New Beginning

Chilcoat searched the jagged rock face seeking a small shelf with an overhang to keep the rain off. Displacing a bit of loose gravel, he selected a likely spot and spread his robe on the damp hillside in front of it. Lowering himself slowly to his knees, he dug into his pouch pulling a tightly knotted package from its depths. He held it thoughtfully, first in one hand then the other, weighing its contents. *It's all I have left of my father—his pipe and a small measure of smoking herb wrapped tightly in a patch of rabbit hide. The elders have taken his ceremonial robes and will pass them to an aspiring shaman at next year's gathering. For now, they rest in a place of honor on the elder's platform and, here I sit holding the remains of the man's worldly possessions in one hand.*

He took the dry grass he had used for his butt pad and made a small cushion on the cleft in the stone. Rolling the packet slowly in his opened palm, he tugged firmly on the knot holding it together and placed it carefully on the pillow of grass. Freeing the ember pot from its sling, he stirred the contents to life. When the warmth of the embers grew enough to make holding the pot uncomfortable, he looked to the sky, then to the packet sitting on its little cushion. His hand trembled slightly as he removed the chimney cap and dumped its contents onto the small pyre. Sitting motionless for several moments, he considered grabbing the treasure before the flames could consume it, then the voice of the old man drifted on the wind. *"Let it go. I'll consider your words. Now, let me rest."*

He bent slowly over the altar and blew the embers to life. *One last chance,* he thought as the flame began to devour the packet with the distinctive aroma of burning herbs and rabbit hide. *I can still pull it free and return to camp with something to cherish. No one would know, no one would care, and some might even think it noble to honor his memory with a memorial. Maybe a necklace made from his pipe would be fitting.*

The smoke stung his eyes and caused tears to flow freely as he drew the clutch of arrows from his quiver. He selected the longest, straightest, most colorful dart from the bunch and rolled it slowly in his fingers feeling the quality of its balance. *It took me three days to fashion the shaft, and I had to change the feathers twice to get it to guide true, but the result was worth the effort,* he thought, as he pressed his thumb gently on the fine stone tip. A drop of blood embraced the translucent edge of obsidian. He drew it slowly down the shaft forming a snake along its length. Considering the serpent for a moment, he snapped the shaft quickly across his knee and placed both halves on the flames. Grabbing another handful of dried grass, he sprinkled it on top of the offering. "Here, old man. Here's your damn bird arrow. May the sting of this viper serve you well in your quest."

The flames warmed his face and lifted his spirit as the smoke climbed over the top of the hill and joined the clouds. He watched the smoke play in the wind until the embers began to fade, leaving only a small pile of twinkling ash and the charred forms of the clay pipe and arrowhead. He thought again of salvaging these last remnants of a life well spent. *No. If I keep his pipe, he'll not rest, and I'll never be able to enjoy his company around the evening fire again.*

He struggled to his feet, with one last sigh of resignation, swept the ashes from the shelf and crushed the delicate stones under his foot. "Now you can rest, old man. You have your pipe and a good strong arrow to serve you. Your spirit is now with God... That's what you would have me believe... Well I hope you're right... I pray that you're right. You deserve it more than anyone I've ever known. You saved my body, but you couldn't save my soul... I was too stubborn, too proud, too young to listen to your foolish 'wisdom' of gods and spirits. Now I wish that I could listen just one more time—just to hear you scold me once again would comfort me so—would complete my grief so that I can move on." He looked briefly at the ash still clinging to his hand and then pressed it firmly on his chest, leaving a tribute of his mourning for all to see.

Slowly working his way down the path made slippery by rain and loose gravel, he lamented the opportunities lost with the only father he had ever known. The sun inched slowly beyond the sea and the clay under his feet seemed almost to bleed as the sunlight reflected red off the water that trickle from the fractured surface left by his unsure footsteps.

With the last glint of light, the bonding ceremony will begin. Tonight is the last night of the ceremonies so it's important to be there to make the official offering and to honor the old man's memory. I'm to act in his behalf at the ceremonies. Tarra has just come of age and will need to seek a mate. Tangar hadn't intended to let her pass over this season, but now that he's gone, she'll need to seek a new arrangement. Tarann, her mother, can't support her and will likely stay on at the temple.

Tarra will be one of the youngest offered this season, so she'll be in the first group. The girls in the first group normally don't wed, but they're included to introduce them to the ritual. They'll usually take a mate in their second or, more generally, third season. But, since her father is gone, she can seek attachment in her first offering.

I feel sorry for her since early pairings are not usually successful, especially if the boy is also young. Out of respect for the old man, I'll intervene if it looks as if she'll select someone too young. It'll mean that she'll have to move in with my family, but it'll only be for a season or two, and she can help with the harvesting. I'll have to talk it over with Caran, of course, but she's usually accepting of my decisions. Maybe Charona will find a mate and move out and everything will remain as it is, one woman too many in my tent. Still, I don't hold out much hope that Charona will find someone suitable this season. The gathering's small since some of the distant tribes haven't come.

The ceremony began right on schedule. The head priest appeared in the temple window overlooking the gardens, and just as the last rays of light winked out over the edge of the sea, he declared the ceremony open with a wave of his scepter. The youngest group of girls hugged their tearful families and formed into a short queue gathered at the end of the main path. The lane meandered through the ramshackle cluster of huts that sprawled down the hillside below the temple.

The youngsters had swept the path clear and a cable of twisted vines strung along the edges emphasized its importance. Some families decorated sections with garlands of flowers matching those worn by their children in the ceremony. The girls each went through a short supportive celebration with their families and ducked under the cable to enter the path in a symbolic separation from their past. Mothers wept, fathers hugged, and siblings scattered flowers. Some of the rituals were very elaborate, depending on the message their family wished to project.

Charona joined the senior group and displayed little of the trepidation shown by some of the others. She had been through the ceremony before and held small hope of finding a suitable mate. She wanted to show her support for the tradition and didn't want to look back and know that she hadn't even tried. There were only four yearlings including Tarra and five seniors with nearly ten midyear girls.

The women of the tribe began a rhythmic chant and hand clapping that soon grew as the young men joined in. The women of the offering joined the chant as they began to move slowly toward the temple entrance. The tempo built as the men began pounding on drums and the chant turned into an upbeat marching tune. The women of the offering danced and flirted as they kept time with the music weaving their way toward the temple. Many of the girls found family and friends to wave to and dance with while others caught the eye of would be suitors along the path with playful, and somewhat suggestive, gyrations. The last woman disappeared behind a cloth drawn over the entrance of the darkened tunnel as the chant gave way to general applause.

The young men now gathered a little less formally into similar groupings with the youngest forming up the lead. There were about ten in each group with the eldest casually swaggering into a clump near the edge of the clearing with much hand clasping and elbowing for the prestigious last positions. The families seemed less emotional about the possibility of losing their sons to the ceremony, but two fathers brusquely dragged their sons from the youngest group. Their families judged them too immature and removed them from consideration.

The matrons of the tribe soon surrounded the youngest group. Much whispering and conferring took place among the women with occasional poking and prodding of individual boys deemed unfit for serious consideration. Two more of the boys were eventually convinced to leave the count.

The more serious consideration of the older boys began with the men of the tribe gathering at the head of the path. Lannon survived the initial culling process with only a minor assault on his masculinity when one of the matrons probed his robe aside with a stick and laughingly exchanged whispers with the other women gathered for the ceremony.

Much of the conversation revolved around the inclusion of Bartan in the pairing ritual. It seemed he had lost his wife in the winter three years ago and had turned out his mate from last season's ceremony because she was not happy with his inability to provide for her. The men of the tribe measured, discussed, and considered his attitudes and contributions but decided he was not fit to participate. He argued his case and offered to work for the elders to prove his worth.

Santos, the prime-elder, intervened. "Bartan, we've known each other all our lives. You've been a good friend, but your lack of resources confirms that you aren't able to provide well for a family.

Despite your recent misfortunes, I must think of the tribe in these times of hardship... I'm not happy with your inclusion, but the tribe needs to consider all options. Our community will only work if each member is productive and cooperative. If you recognize this commitment, we will consider your request."

Bartan nodded slightly to his old friend. "Of course, I'll be happy to prove my worth to the community."

The assembly of men strode down the path with purpose, quickly gathering in a cluster at the temple entrance where they were ushered, pushing and shoving, through the tunnel. The passageway opened onto the garden grounds where the gaggle of youth timidly wandered amongst the elders that had already assembled.

The cleared garden mounds revealed their matching stone platforms. The podiums served as worktables during the growing season but now flowers and carpets of many colors disguised their form. Tangar's ceremonial regalia adorned a stick figure at the rear of the center platform where they stand in reverence over the proceedings.

The girls settled on their platform to the left of the main path while the boys gravitated to the mound on the right. There was considerable pushing and shoving as the larger, more dominant, boys found the most advantageous seating position around their platform. The elders meandered slowly up the third mound set between, and beyond, the others. The three hills formed a nearly perfect triangular arrangement of independently tended garden knolls.

As the elders climbed the last few steps to their hilltop, a small group of lesser status council members parted to allow them access to their privileged seating. The boys reshuffled their arrangement as they recognized that their positioning in relationship to the elders might be more important than posturing for the girls. The scuffling, pushing, and prodding threatened to deteriorate into earnest conflict but the larger boys quickly resolved the issue. While this display of macho brinksmanship seemed to serve some primal need within the hierarchy of young males, it had no impact on the pairing process itself. In the past, many a young warrior had gone home defeated and unhappy from the pairing ceremony after having done well in the athletic games leading up to the ritual.

The elders talked among themselves with only occasional gestures toward one or the other platforms. While the boys had been forming up outside, the girls had been seated in accordance to their age and given a lecture on process and procedures so they sat quietly only whispering occasionally to their nearest neighbors. The immediate families of the prospective pairs gathered around in an arc at the foot of the elder's mound. They also jostle each other for locations along the path.

Finally, Talbot, the high-elder, waved the ceremony to order and Santos spoke in a tone that echoed slightly in the upper reaches of the temple. "Who is the first daughter offered for pairing?"

A timid little voice came from the slender child standing in front of the girl's platform. "I am Tarra from the clan, Tangar."

Her hair was a striking flash of red accented with a wreath of yellow flowers and the dusting of freckles on her face gave her a boyish sparkle that betrayed her feminine charms. Tarra was the youngest girl in this year's ceremony and so had the dubious privilege of being first to stand for the offering.

"Who gives this child for pairing?" Santos again spoke to the world.

Chilcoat put his arm around Tarann's shoulder pulling her close and stepping to the front of the families gathered at the base of the hill. "I am Chilcoat, a friend of Tangar, the father of this—woman." He hesitated for a moment looking at the child. "Her mother, Tarann, and I offer her for pairing, but let it be known that she is here before her time and will not be given in haste." Tarann broke into tears and hid her face in Chilcoat's shoulder.

Santos spoke in clear tones un-phased by the emotions of the moment. "Who desires to pair with this woman?"

Two of the youngest boys jumped to stand at the front of their platform. A third stood but reconsidered after looking to his mother. The elder looked to Tarra who nodded that she was willing to consider these contenders. "How many elk have you felled this season?" He calmly asked.

The larger of the two boys quickly offered. "I've been on three hunts this season and one was successful."

"And how did you serve on these hunts?"

"I—I helped my father."

"What did you do to help?"

"I carried weapons and supplies, and I helped carry the kill. And, and I learned many important lessons." He struggled to bolster his case.

"Why do you wish to pair with this woman?"

"I am ready to—to be a man with a wife to care for me."

By this time, several of the older boys had begun to snicker and elbow each other in knowing gestures of having seen, or perhaps participated in, a similar discussion in previous ceremonies. It was inevitable that the youngest boys would make the biggest mistakes. Having them go first, built the errors into the process. Beside the entertainment value, it served to eliminate unqualified challengers early in the proceedings.

Talbot looked to Tarra for a sign of desire and with none coming, conferred for a moment with the high elders. Santos then spoke for all to hear. "You are not considered right for pairing at this time. Does anyone else seek to pair with this woman?"

The second young man standing at the front of the platform looked at his feet then back at his friends still seated at the platform behind him. He considered his options for a moment and, hanging his head, returned to his place near the far end of the platform. His nearest neighbor elbowed him mercilessly as he settled dejectedly amongst the others.

"Does anyone else speak for this woman?" Santos pleaded for others to consider her situation.

After several moments of silence, Bartan spoke from the back of the crowd. "I've had many successful hunts this season, and I'll keep her as she needs."

Talbot again looked to Tarra for consent. She appeared confused and disappointed at the prospect of this stranger's interest. A quick huddle between the elders culminated in Santos speaking clearly, "Does anyone object to this pairing?"

The muttering crowd erupted into full-blown arguments amongst the families. Emissaries from the various family groupings drifted in and out amid the uproar. Chilcoat stood with Tarann at the apex of the family arc and Bartan soon joined them. The two men greeted each other formally but remained silent for several moments.

Bartan spoke in measured tones. "I can care for her. I know she's young, but I'll not force her to do anything she's unable to do."

Chilcoat finally spoke. "Were those kills you had this season elk or rabbits? I've not seen you able to care for yourself and two other women. Why should I think that you could now care for one so young? She's my sister, and is welcome in my house. She can join my family and will grow to full age before she again joins the pairing."

The crowd erupted into heated discussions as various alliances formed then re-formed into factions. The elders gathered into a tight circle around Talbot's throne in the center of the platform. Tangar's robes hung nearby seeming almost to eavesdrop on the judgment. A heated conversation ensued with Santos directing priority order. After repeated cycles around the ring of point-counterpoint comments, Talbot finally spoke with a great deal of agitation. He gestured at Tarra and pointed his finger at individual elders around the circle. He finished his tirade and they cast their lots into baskets at his feet.

The basket on the left soon grew heavy enough to tip the scale on which it sat. Talbot was apparently satisfied with the outcome and sat back on his throne. Santos didn't seem as happy with the outcome but strode quickly down the steps that jutted from the platform.

He marched with purpose down the face of the mound leading to the central clearing and spoke for all to hear. "Both paths have been considered and argued. The elders have agreed that Bartan seems not well suited to this pairing but recognizes that in these times of poor harvest, we must all draw together to help when we can. Therefore, at this time, we don't condone this pairing, but if Bartan wishes to pursue her, he will need to prove himself to Chilcoat. Chilcoat, you, yourself, are perhaps not in the best position to provide for another. Has your son yet contributed to your clan?"

"No. He's yet unproven. But I am sure he will soon join the providers."

"Yes, I am sure he's a fine lad, but you have already burdened yourself with your wife's sister. Are you sure another woman is a good idea in your lodge? Perhaps your wife can speak to this."

"Caran, will you speak?" Chilcoat stretched his arm toward his wife.

"It's true my sister lives with us, but she provides many benefits to my young family. She is an experienced gardener and very good with my children. Besides, she'll soon wed, when a worthy man comes forward, and then she'll leave my tent. Perhaps this season will grant her desire. She's there on the platform. Ask her to speak, if you wish." Caran gestured toward the mound on her left.

Santos considered the offer for a moment and spoke. "She'll be heard in her time. My concern isn't with your sister. Your sister is fully of age and I am sure offers many comforts a woman can provide. I am concerned that this young girl will not fit well into this family with two women already tending to their needs. How will she fit if, as you said, Charona finds a worthy mate this season, or what if she doesn't find a mate for many seasons? Will you still welcome this young woman?"

Caran pulled close to Chilcoat and pondered the questions. "I think that my husband wants to help the clan of Tangar and has taken his daughter in loyalty. This girl comes as a sister to my tent and I welcome her."

Santos considered all the arguments and spoke to Bartan. "Do you still wish to pair with this girl?"

"Yes," was the only acceptable answer.

"And do you still claim responsibility for her?" He asked Chilcoat.

Again, "yes," was the reply.

"Tarra, the decision of the council is that you should join your brother's family. If you accept our findings, Bartan will join the clan of Tangar to prove himself worthy. If he proves himself to Chilcoat by this time next season, we'll again hear his offer. The people don't consider you paired, but you may correspond with him as a member of the clan during the year. Chilcoat, you are to help Bartan as you would a brother. Help him fit into the clan's needs. You're not to judge him or his actions. You're only to guide his efforts through counsel. If you find Bartan wanting, you will need to defend your assessment at next year's gathering. Each of you will be given an opportunity to support your position." Santos turned and began to trudge up the embankment toward the platform steps.

Bartan called up the hill after him. "This will leave my clan with only four skilled hunters."

Talbot called from the platform. "Your clan has always had only four skilled hunters. You haven't proven your worth for the past three seasons. You would do well to watch Chilcoat closely. You'll learn much from him... if you don't meet with an 'accident'."

A small chuckle emanated from some of the veteran hunters standing nearby.

The group that had gathered at the end of the path dispersed as Tarra made her way down the slope leading from the platform. She confronted Chilcoat and, pulling the wreath from her hair, looked scornfully at the handprint on his chest. She threw the garland, striking him squarely on the dusty tribute. "How dare you? You've ruined my life! Why do you shame me like this?" She then fled out the tunnel in tears.

"I'm just trying to keep you from making a mistake..." His voice trailed off as she disappeared down the tunnel. He looked at Caran for understanding and found only wounded resolve.

Similar family interactions consumed much of the next few hours as the pairing ceremony continued. None of the conflicts were as confrontational as the first had been but, on more than one occasion, the elders provided an opinion on the worthiness or advisability of alternative pairings. Most of it was standard agreements between tentative families with an occasional outburst of bravado or tears as family members discussed dowries.

As the ceremony drew to a close, Charona's time finally came. She offered herself for consideration with a small acknowledgment that, yes, she was indentured to her sister and would consider all for pairing, but that she was not desperate, or in need of a burdensome relationship.

The remaining male candidates nudged and prodded each other daring the older members to try it. Finally, two candidates approached the front of the platform. They were both younger than Charona and a bit small for their age. She looked disdainfully at the prospects and shook her head, rejecting their lustful assessment of her charms. Santos was dismayed at her response but knew it was of no avail to pursue the bond further.

The ceremony began to break up with the conclusion of the last offering but then Lannon stepped to the head of the path. "Father, I wish to pair with this woman." He spoke in clear tones for all to hear. The general din fell mute as people nudged each other pointing at the youth.

Santos turned to see who was speaking and readjusted the hood of his ceremonial robe as he approached Talbot. They spoke quietly for several moments with occasional gestures to various family groups and consultations with lesser elders. Finally, Santos walked slowly down the face of the platform mound toward the boy at the head of the path.

Standing face-to-face, he placed his hand on Lannon's shoulder and leaned in close to speak quietly to him. "Are you sure that you wish to pair with this woman? She is your senior and will not bend easily to your ways. There'll be talk of you being afraid to leave your mother."

"Yes, Father. I have a bond of many weeks with her and I wish to have her join my house."

"You have this bond because she's from your clan. It's not advisable for such a pairing. It may lead to much hardship and children that are unfit."

"I'm aware of the burden we'll suffer. We've talked about it and we wish to go forward with this pairing."

Santos spoke in clear terms. "The council has considered your request and cannot sanction such a pairing. If you wish to continue, you'll be scorned by your clan and unable to take your place at their table."

With the faintest of smiles, Lannon clasped the arm of the prime and turned his face away with eyes cast down.

Santos gave Lannon's shoulder a gentle squeeze causing him to look up. He gave an imperceptible nod hidden under his hood and turned to take the final trip back up the platform mound. Charona came running down the women's hill and fell quickly into Lannon's arms. They couldn't partake in the pairing ceremony, but they could stand at the edge of the clearing while the others approached the elders' platform.

The losing candidates returned to their families and soon left the temple grounds, leaving only those that had a stake in the remaining rituals. The elders descended from their platform and the sanctioned pairs replaced them.

Each elder, in order of rank, grabbed a small handful of flowers from the platform's edge and scattered them on the steps. The matrons placed gifts of remembrance on the steps of the platform for those that had been lost this year. A large cluster of flowers and a cherished doll belonging to Teri, the lost child, were set in the center of the topmost step and the stick-man dressed in Tangar's cloak stood guard blocking passage.

The elders proceeded down the face of the hill as a small group of council women gathered at the foot of the steps and chanted a blessing of consent and concern. The joined pairs began talking and gesturing to each other. Finally, they established some order, and one-by-one, the couples took up the central position with the others gathered around in a loose circle to witness the consummation of their vows.

The Robes

The relentless succession of storms and the eerie glow in the northern sky that pulsed and throbbed in iridescent sheets of green and violet lasted for months. The elders met many times over the winter to discuss the condition they decided to call "the cleansing." They had managed to consume nearly an entire year's supply of sacred herbs and still they had no answer that explained the misfortune that had befallen them.

As the gathering ended, Talbot took Chilcoat aside. "Tangar was a dear friend of mine and he spoke faithfully of your spirit. His robes should remain in reverence for a year while candidates are considered, but this year is an exception. It isn't good for a clan to be without a Seer in these times, so please take his robes and fulfill your duty."

"Duty? Tangar was a father to me that taught of responsibility and courage, not potions and chants. I know nothing of being a seer. I never really considered the idea. When a rockslide killed my parents, Tangar took me in until I was of age. It was a somber, healing, time but it wasn't a time of learning the spiritual dealings of a seer."

"Nonetheless, Tangar spoke of you as 'the man foretold' to fulfill his duty. He thought highly of you."

Chilcoat remembered the old man fondly despite his gruff veneer. He remembered, when he was young, how the old man had often said, "YodHeaVau has chosen you to walk a noble path." *I always figured it was just the old man trying to make a brokenhearted young boy feel better about his folks dying. I never considered that I would someday wear his cloak.*

"I always stayed away from his spirit stuff. It's just too weird for me. I mean—I'd sit around the fire with him and share a pinch of smoking herb, but I didn't like to see him on his spirit-walks. I know it's the Seer's duty, but it was troubling to see the man I loved and respected drinking and eating things that didn't seem wise—all to satisfy some old ritual. It just didn't set well with the things he taught me. He'd sit for hours staring at the fire not talking and when he spoke, he didn't make any sense. The clan needs a seer to settle big issues, but the cost to his health was too great, and the guilt he often bore when things didn't turn out well weighed heavily on him. He took it as a solemn duty, but he often found himself alienated and bitter with the obligation."

Talbot looked solemnly at Chilcoat. "It is the duty we owe to our people..."

***

Chilcoat sat quietly on the small rock outcropping just outside of the mountain village. He stirred slowly, thinking once again of the passing of Tangar. *The old man seems to talk to me in these moments of solitude. Your words haunt me. "It is our duty to guide the children in knowledge and faith."*

Chilcoat smirked. *The problem with your sanctimonious pronouncements was that you considered everyone your children.* "What am I to do to meet this duty?" He called to the wind. The only answer was the distant cry of a night bird.

The magnitude of the sky dwarfs me in wonder. I've never felt so small. I remember how you taught me of the movements of the night sky. They were lessons for a hunter, not a mystic.

The moon cast a cold light on the lake and drew his attention to the skyline beyond. *The weather's clear, at last. Maybe this is the end of the storms. It's been a long winter with endless storms and poor hunting. Would you have known what to make of it? No one else has a good answer.*

Chilcoat considered the ceremonial robes hanging in his hut. He hadn't worn them yet. He had told the elders that he would care for them and consider any candidates who may step forward, but the council admonished him that their ownership would be their decision not his.

The garish drape of layered cloth nags at me. There've been a few occasions, since the clan arrived back in the high country, that people have came to my door looking for resolution from the Seer. I turned them away to settle their conflict without my involvement, but people question me at nearly every meal. They want someone they can call on in times of conflict and doubt, and no one else has the stature to satisfy everyone.

Bartan came forward almost immediately to lay claim to the job, but the tribe quickly dispelled his desire with an open vote of no confidence. Rancon considered the office for a short time but decided that the toll on his family would be more than he was willing to make. *I know his concern all too well. I now understood why Tangar seemed so distant and cold at times.*

A single blue-green finger of sky-fire pulsed far across the horizon and seemed to almost point at him as he pulled his cloak tight around his shoulders and tended his pipe. *I need to settle the issue.*

Rancon has recently challenged the Larkon boys about their hunting etiquette and the friction between them is becoming a concern. The boys are trying to take a cat they've supposedly spotted and the regular hunting teams are suffering. I understand their youthful ambition to get the beast, but it isn't providing meat for the table, and their incessant prowling around in the bushes is frightening the real game away.

Chilcoat knew he was the chosen one. *Maybe that's what bothers me about it. I have no choice but to put on the robes and start acting like a leader. I'm OK with the duty of arbitrator, but Tangar taught me always to be uneasy about the herbs. I browsed through his medicine pouch when they first given me the robes, but I've no idea what any of it is, much less where it came from, or when to use it. If they expect me to act as a diviner of mystical things, I'm going to have to ask somebody what to do with all that stuff.*

He drew deeply on his pipe one last time and watched the last light of the moon slip behind the distant hill. The finger of sky-fire flared slightly and then faded to a deep black sky with countless stars blinking in silence. The image of Tangar sitting by the evening fire drifted through his thoughts. "I know, old man, I know. I should have listened to you closer. If you just hadn't been so damn—scary." He muttered to himself as he stirred from his spot and began picking his way along the path leading back to the village.

The robes hanging near the door moved restlessly as he held the entry flap aside. Cool air swept across the floor and stirred the meager flame, casting mysterious shadows around the room. He drew the flap closed and knelt to tuck it in to keep the pests out. As he finished he looked up at the robes that stood over him. They seemed to turn to face him in critical judgment as he took his place by the fire.

After the normal evening banter of gallant hunting efforts, Lannon and Charona retired to their sleeping space just off the living area. Tarra looked dismissively at them as she pulled her cover tight over her shoulders and twisted away from the family scene.

Chilcoat sat next to Caran watching the fire. "The old man came to me again."

"That's not surprising this time of year. He seems to like calm summer nights. Did he speak clearly?"

"No. Does he ever? It was just a gentle whisper about the robes. He wants me to wear them."

"Are you sure? You've never done that sort of thing."

"I think I have to. People keep coming around wanting counseling and it's starting to cause problems when no one steps in to resolve things. I'm just not sure of some of it. I mean, I watched a strong man shrink to a wisp of his former self with all his herbs and potions. Duty, or no-duty, I'm not ready to do that."

"Then, he taught you well the duties you must perform. People will come to you whether you wear the robes or not. People look to you."

"Yeah, but that's just advice from a friend, not spiritual guidance."

"Is there a difference?"

Chilcoat watched the shadow of the robe dance on the wall across the tent and rose to adjust the flap in the roof to meter the smoke out. He took the sleeve of the robe between his fingers and gently felt its fine-grain leather.

"The robes of a prince," Caran offered.

"A prince of fools," he added, as he reached behind the exhibit and dug out the medicine pouch. Soot covered the tightly bound satchel that was suffering from general neglect. Patting it gently over the flames, the dust turned to a shower of sparks that swirled and rose quickly through the roof flap. He prayed that they would rise to Tangar's spirit and that he would provide guidance for what he was about to do.

Untying the cord, he spread the contents on the floor in front of him and sat cross-legged sorting the bundles into several small piles. The larger ones were mostly sticks and twigs, the midsized bundles were dried leaves and flowers, and the smaller packets were seeds and powders of different colors and textures tied neatly with a stick holding the knot closed. He recognized some of the leaves, but the twigs could be anything, and the powders were obviously the result of grinding something up, but which leaf or twig they were was a complete mystery to him. He sniffed at a couple of the powders, but decided that may not be a good idea when he nearly choked on one.

"It's no use," he grumbled, packing the bundles into the pouch and stuffing it back in place behind the robes. "I'll let them be for now and ask one of the elders about them when we go to the gathering next year."

Morning came with a pleasant warm breeze from the east. The sky was clear and the sun glowed with a spirit of healing warmth. He had had a good hunt two days earlier, so the need to venture far from the village was less. The tall trees whispered with voices of the ancestors and the air smelled clean and fresh on the spring morning. He grabbed a couple of bird arrows and was just about ready to take his morning walkabout, when he once again thought of the old man, the robes, and the medicine pouch. Returning to his hut, he pulled the satchel out, and quickly sorted through the twig collection pulling one free. *It's one of several of the same type so it must be important. I'll see if I can find a source for such a highly valued stick while I'm out.* He wedged the twig behind his ear and returned the pouch to its storage place.

Rancon came from his hut and called out, "Where away, brother?"

"I figured I'd follow the shore around by the falls. Maybe I can scare up a pheasant."

"Sounds like a long walk for a skinny bird. I think I'll stay around camp today. Those Larkon boys have the kids all stirred up about a cat. Besides, I need to replace the arrow I lost last week."

"Sounds like fun, sitting around the fire scraping shaft-wood and telling stories to the kids."

"Yeah, well, somebody has to do it. You going to be back by evening?"

"That's the plan. I'll light a fire if I have any trouble." A group of children scatted as he approached. *It's odd to have them flee my path and stand timidly watching. It's those damn robes again,* he reasoned. *They know I'm the Seer now and don't want to risk drawing my ire.*

As he reached the lake, he considered the men fishing from the rocks. He could join them instead of taking the walk but he wanted some time alone. *Besides, I'm on a mission looking for a stick.* He reached up and pressed the twig against his ear to be sure it was still there. *Wouldn't do to lose it already,* he thought, as he rounded the last bend along the shoreline.

He headed out across the marshland that made up the western end of the lake and, once across the bogs, he climbed the cliff that formed the northern shore. Far around the ridge was a small waterfall that tumbled down the rock face in three faltering steps and eventually into the lake. He knew the old man had spent a lot of time at the falls in his younger days. *Perhaps he'll be there today and show me the right bush.*

Chilcoat leaned on his walking staff, giving his knee a rest, and reflected on the pleasant warmth of the sun after so much rain. *I remember when Tangar would take me on a walkabout as a young man. Both of us were young enough to make light work of a simple walk to the falls. Even then, my knee would stiffen by the end of the day, but it was a good pain that helped me remember my folks.*

I was only four when it happened. We were out picking berries along a cliff face. I don't really remember much about it other than it seemed like a party to me. There were people dancing and playing in the upper meadow. I remember that my dad argued with some man and then later, when we were busy picking fruit, the cliff suddenly began raining down on us. Mom grabbed me and threw me aside but, by the time I landed, my folks were dead. Both of them were gone in an instant. My leg was broken at the knee and would forever remind me of that day.

Chilcoat found his way around the ridgeline and was glad to rest under a tree. The dry grasses spreading up the ridge wafted a heady scent of buckwheat and hummed with life. He quickly ate a strip of dried meat and a fold of flatbread. *I'll be glad to reach the falls. A cool drink will really taste good.*

His hunting instinct took over as he sat quietly and listened for signs of life. A hawk boasted of its catch far up along the ridgeline but the whisper of the pines was keeping him from hearing any of the faint stirrings in the underbrush. The invigorating warmth of the morning had escalated to downright hot. The sun seemed unusually harsh in the clear mountain air. His skin had reddened noticeably and radiated with growing discomfort. As he sat in the shelter of the trees, he estimated the effort remaining on his journey and began to question the wisdom of his mission.

If I'm to return by evening, I had better get moving. Dusting the litter from his backside, he stepped from the shelter of the trees and raised his arm to block the glare. Quickly returning to the shade, he pulled his over-shirt from his pack and fashioned a head wrap that trailed loosely down his back covering his arms under its shelter.

Within the hour, he reached the falls and the amount of water pouring down the cliff astounded him. A cloud of mist rose from the rocks at the base of the cliff where it spilled into the lake. He stood open mouthed, enveloped in the spray. His skin screamed with delight at the cool nourishment as he took his shirt off and let the water pour down his back. He pulled the rest of his clothes off and spread them out on the stones so that the water could rinse the day's journey from them. He settled on the rocks and let the gentle mist bathe the dirt from his tender hide.

Refreshed, he gathered his things and wrung them out a couple of times before he moved them to a dry spot on the rock face. Grabbing his weapons, he moved into the shade of a large boulder where he did what grooming he could. His clothes would soon be dry and he could seek a more comfortable location, but for now, he was just glad to be cool. The hot breeze gusting off the surrounding boulders dried his skin leaving a tight dusty film and as he pulled his fingers through his hair, he realized that the twig was gone. He had lost the stick somewhere.

"Damn," he muttered and quickly searched the ground where he stood. After a quick inventory of his pack, he set out to retrace his steps back to his clothes. They were still a little damp, but they felt good against the redness. He carefully searched each garment as he pulled it on, but still had no luck finding the twig.

He turned his search to where he had taken his shower. Standing just at the edge of the wet rocks, he peered into the spray trying to see the sprig. There were three prospects but each was only a dark outline behind the wall of mist. The first was about three feet into the spray, but looked least likely to be fruitful. He considered the consequences of getting wet again and decided that it may not be a bad idea for the return trip anyway. He quickly stowed his dry goods, removed his pants, and carefully walked down the face of the gently sloping boulder. The mist soon dripped from the visor he had fashioned from his over-shirt as he shuffled in the general direction of the first twig.

Indeed, it was a twig, but not *his* twig. He bent and retrieved the soggy sprig, squeezing it absentmindedly in his left hand as he tried to locate the second objective. The rocks grew slippery as he edged closer to the falls. The second prospect turned out to be a root stitching along a crack in the rock face. He tried to envision where he was on the little plateau, and more importantly, where he needed to go to find the third prospect. He nearly pulled a muscle when his feet slipped and he had to go down on all fours, but he found the third twig by crawling down the rock face and inching out to grab it. It looked vaguely as he remembered, but it was dark and swollen from the water, and frankly, he hadn't spent much time memorizing its form, so he couldn't be sure.

As he emerged from the cloud of mist, he realized that he was still carrying the first stick as well. He stood dripping in the sun gazing first at one then the other. He thought about tossing out the first one but decided instead to put one behind each ear and move on with his hunt. He drip-dried for another few minutes before donning his pants and weapons and heading out in search of a good hunting blind.

A small scrub oak gave partial shelter from the sun but was of little help in preventing the birds from seeing him. He lay among the gnarled branches and tried to form as tightly as he could to their whimsy. Positioning his bow, he drew an arrow to its string and stood motionless against the trunk watching bird after bird explore the field. Finally, a small covey immerged from the edge of the field. A hen and four small squabs ventured toward a pool fed by the stream just before it poured over the edge. He remained motionless as the band wove its way single file toward its goal.

A large male took flight from the bushes just across the clearing. It shot up about thirty feet then banked and circled the pool in a large descending arc. He set the arrow and drew the bow slowly as it landed amongst the brood. He waited motionless as the bird settled into the business of drinking. The arrow found its mark and he relaxed watching the rest of the flock scatter and seek shelter back in the tall grass across the clearing.

"Thank you for the life you give." *It's a good kill,* he thought, pulling the arrow out carefully. He cleaned the shaft and inspected the tip as he washed it. Replacing it in his quiver, he prepared the bird for transport by draining its blood into a cool drink of water then bundled it amongst his dry goods. *Well, now if I can find a bush that matches the twig, I can go home happy.* He gathered his things and headed down the path toward the village.

Pulling the stick from behind his ear, he looked carefully at its form. *It still seems very unremarkable and, now that it's wet, it bears little resemblance to anything I remember seeing amongst the parched bushes of the highland.* He walked for several minutes along the trail tugging occasionally on nearby plants. *None seem to bear the slightest similarity to the now familiar form. Maybe the old man only came up here to be alone. Maybe he never found herbs up here at all.*

He rolled the twig gently in his fingers. Lifting it to his nose, he closed his eyes and tried to identify the slightly nutty smell. It wasn't strong, but there was a hint of earth from the damp sprig. A small gray bush caught his eye about twenty feet further up the ridge. It was unlike any others in the area. *"Maybe it's the prize I'm searching for."*

Picking his way carefully up the embankment, he eventually reached his goal. The bush turned out to be an old clump of crank-weed that was covered with a layer of dust that tinted it a pale gray. It was more puzzling than disappointing. *I've never seen a bush so oddly afflicted. Maybe that's what the old man would come up here for.*

He assessed the branches hoping one would bear some resemblance to his sample. Tearing a likely specimen from the trunk, he backed slowly down the dusty hillside. The sun bore down relentlessly as he retrieved his pack, stuffed his trophy in amongst the arrows, and headed off along the path home.

After the evening meal, Chilcoat once again spread the sacred herbs on the cloth and ordered them by type. He compared today's trophy with the likely samples spread before him and quickly concluded that it wasn't among them. Disappointedly he rubbed the gray powder from one of the leaves hoping that it would then resemble one of the samples. It didn't, and the powder left a film clinging to his fingers. He considered throwing the sprig into the fire but decided it was too green and would smoke the place up, so he tossed it across the room toward the door.

Tarra watched with some interest and retrieved the branch lying next to her. She inspected it carefully and remarked pensively, "Stanis."

Chilcoat rummaged through his pouch and retrieved his pipe and smoking herb. "What?"

"Stanis... This plant is called stanis."

"You know what it is? Well of course, you would know. You're his daughter. I should have guessed. Well, what's stenis? And what's it good for?"

"It's stanis, and it isn't good for much of anything. Dad used it to keep flies off by dusting himself with the powder sometimes, but it makes me itch."

"Well, thanks. It's good to know that I spent all day stomping around in the bushes getting sunburned and came home with itching powder."

"You asked." She smirked at his attempt at levity.

"Do you know what these other things are?" Chilcoat gestured to the bundles spread before him.

"Of course... I'm his daughter." She mocked his comment as she moved closer to the fire and began sorting through the various piles of bundles and pouches. "This is tennisin bark. You make a tea with it for headaches. These are coshin leaves. They're good for upset stomachs." She preceded to hand each bundle, pouch, and root to Chilcoat as she gave it a name and explained its use.

"I'll be damned. Here I am worried that this would go to waste, and you know all about it. Do you know where he found them?"

She looked scornfully at him and tossed a bundle of twigs toward him. "They'll tell you. It's the knowledge of the Seer."

Lannon and Charona had been sitting across the fire watching the exchange and whispered to each other in meaningful titters. "Maybe we should resize the robes to fit Tarra." Lannon offered, nudging his mate.

"Maybe we should." Chilcoat handed the bundle of twigs back to her. "Maybe we should."

She blushed as she packed the bundles and pouches into the bag. Chilcoat picked up the twig he had carried so vigilantly all day. "And what's this for? Can you grind it up and make sunburn lotion? I could use some of that."

Tarra looked up from her task in surprise and grabbed the stick from him placing it among the others like it. "It is a whisper of Vau. Didn't you ever listen to him?"

He sat questioningly across the fire as Tarra spread the medicine cloth on the floor in front of him. She carefully placed each of the sticks from the bundle on the cloth. "This one is for coshin, and this one is for bandas. I think this one is cena, and I'm not sure about this one."

"Whoa. What do you mean 'whisper of Vau', and what do they have to do with all this stuff?" He gestured at the cloth.

She sorted the bundle of twigs into two distinct piles. "These are for summer, and these are for winter. See, these are manzanta. You can only find it here in the high country of summer and see they're naked, like summer. These are syncmore. They are from the coast of winter and have bark to keep them warm.

Chilcoat noticed for the first time that indeed the twigs were of two distinct types. "I'll be damned." He took first one, then another, for closer inspection.

Tarra cleared the center of the cloth and carefully placed two twigs at the edge of the decorative sunburst. The broad end of each twig fit into a notch in the design. "See, this is the summer village and this is the path leading out along the lake shore, and this is the path leading out toward the woods."

"Yeah, I guess I can see that, but what about all of these others?"

"See, some of the sticks have flat ends that fit here in the design." She fingered the cloth. "This is the path toward the woods, and all of these sticks with a pointed end fit in this slot, and these with the blunt end lead out past the lake."

"Yeah, so? I mean, that's very clever and all, but why so many? They all go to one path or the other. Why do you need so many?"

"Look, each one has sections that are different lengths and have different branches. See this one, the first section is long, then it jogs to the right a bit and then it jogs again with a short section, that's where coshin is found."

"How do you know this stick is for coshin? It looks like all the others to me."

"See, the tip has these four notches cut in it. That is the symbol for coshin. Look, this one has two notches and a bar. That's the symbol for tersen, and it has two long sections, then two shorter jogs to the left along the southern path from the winter village."

He sat for several minutes carefully examining each stick and asking Tarra to give it a name. There were a couple that she couldn't make out and one, in particular, that was different from all the others. It had many small knobs and joints along its length. Chilcoat recognized it as the old man's talking-stick. *Tangar had a tale of adventure for every gnarled little section along its length. He would pull that old stick out and run his fingers over its bumpy profile for several minutes and then he would settle on one particular segment and regale his audience with a story that somehow related to the stick and usually ended up with a moral to fit the political issues before his audience.*

Tears filled Tarra's eyes as she placed the stick with reverence in the center of the sunburst. Chilcoat rose to his knees and held the young girl in a brotherly hug. She reluctantly allowed him to comfort her, but she resented his intrusion in her grief.

Caran stirred intolerantly at the vision and began putting the children to bed while the pair broke their embrace and began picking up the sticks and bundling them with care. Finally, the talking-stick was the last thing on the cloth. Tarra sat transfixed as he slowly picked it up and turned it thoughtfully from end-to-end. He focused on the young girl and held it out for her. "You should keep this and guard the wisdom it holds."

She looked for several moments at the stick but didn't move to take it. She searched his eyes for understanding then slowly reached with quivering fingers to take the wand.

He rolled the twig bundles into the cloth and packed it into the medicine bag then, as he was about to stuff it behind the mannequin, he stood and considered the meaning of the robes. They belonged to the Seer—the one who had wisdom about right and wrong. He turned to Tarra still kneeling near the fire holding the twisted little stick. He held the pouch out to her. "You should probably take this for safe keeping too. You're the only one that knows what to do with any of it. Maybe you can teach me so that I won't seem such a fool wearing these robes."

Tarra turned to face him and submissively took the satchel bowing her head in respect. He blushed in astonishment. He had never had anyone treat him with such reverence. It made him very uneasy. "Please, take this as a gift from your brother. I want you to have it."

"You've taken me at the bonding as if I was your disobedient sister, but I'm not your sister... I find it hard to treat you as my brother. I would rather take it as a free tribeswoman not as a sister." She looked quickly at Caran then, lowering her eyes, she turned to gather her things in preparation for bed.

He stood transfixed next to the robe for a moment then grabbed it by the lapels and stepped out the door pulling the flap closed behind him. The stars jumped from the early evening sky as he picked his way carefully down the path and stood alone in a small clearing. Holding the robe at arm's length, he began slapping it and shaking it to break loose any creatures that may have taken up residence. The dust irritated his eyes, and the commotion woke the dogs. "If you're to be mine, you'll have to fit into my life, not I into yours..." One last shake and he stuffed the bundle under one arm and began to pick his way across the clearing toward home.

A glint of white caught his attention as he surveyed the path ahead. A small object lay just off the trail. Carefully reaching in the darkness, he flipped it over on the ground and, judging it benign, delicately retrieved it. With only a blanket of stars to provide light, he recognized the shape to be that of an herb pipe. *It must've fallen out of the robe when I shook it. The old fool must have left it in the pocket. He was always losing things.*

After a quick glance to the north to see if the sky-fire had returned, he ducked back into his tent. Lannon and Charona had pulled their door flap closed and Tarra lay quietly in her bed next the children. Caran was by the fire looking questioningly at him as he stood next to the naked display horse. "I think I'll sleep better without the old man watching over me." He placed the bundle on a stack of house wares behind the display.

Turning his attention to the stick-man standing before him, he pulled the shoulder brace out of its bindings, folded the legs and trunk together, and tossed the whole thing out the door in a clattering crash that landed them just off the main path and disturbed the dogs again.

Caran sat quietly waiting to see if he had anything else to say. "I'm glad you've decided to own this thing for now. It'll settle the people."

"I'm not happy about it, and I'm not a seer. I have a hard enough time just dealing with my own problems. I don't need a bunch of drugs and potions complicating my life." He sat absentmindedly rolling the old man's herb pipe in his fingers.

"You have Tarra to help."

"I don't want Tarra to help." He grumbled in a low voice, glancing in her direction. "I don't want to be involved in any of this herb stuff. It's all too… strange. It seems like if I was supposed to take over as the Seer, he would've told me, or given me some training, or something."

"He trained you as his son. You know his wisdom better than anyone." Caran looked sadly at Tarra and moved to her bed pulling her covers into place. "Tangar also visits my thoughts and I see his wisdom in the sharing of duties he has given you. He knew the burden of conjuring potions, the duty of using them, and the temptation of abusing them. He has taught you to respect this duty and to treat the herbs with the highest regard. He taught Tarra the burden of the herbs and you should respect his wisdom in doing so... I think he separated these duties to keep you from falling to their seduction as he did."

Tarra pretended to sleep, not wanting to intrude on their warm exchange. She was jealous that Caran could have such an intimate bond, *even if it's with an oaf like Chilcoat.* A tear escaped as she realized that her jealousy was rooted in the pain she felt for her father. *I'm jealous that Chilcoat can talk with Daddy so easily and now even Caran says she has spoken with him. Yet I can't speak with him without so much pain. I can't accept his death and the thought that he wants me to serve as the herbalist for Chilcoat angers me. I can't see Papa in this way. He wouldn't abandon me like this.*

Chilcoat sat quietly for several more minutes and noticed the pipe as if for the first time. It was clean and unused. He sniffed it to be sure and was just about to make a comment when he realized that no one else knew of the pipe and probably didn't want to wake up to talk about it. *Why did you keep a new pipe in your ceremonial robes? Is there some spiritual meaning to it, or is it a gift for the one who will inherit the robes? More likely, you just forgot that it was there.*

He placed the pipe on the hearthstone and turned painfully to remove his cloak before sliding into bed next to Caran. The sunburn made things unpleasant, and the prospect of a long night dreaming of twig sorting didn't comfort him. He tossed and turned trying to find a position that didn't hurt, but ended on his back watching the stars through the smoke vent.

By morning, Chilcoat had managed to get a few moments rest but he didn't feel up to a full day's work. As he sat at the morning fire trying to clear his head, the pipe lying on the hearth drew his attention. He held it up against the morning light and marveled at its unblemished form. The simple cone was an exquisitely thin tube of white ceramic. It had several bands of texture along its length but the interior was polished smooth. *A skilled craftsman had spent considerable effort on creating it. Perhaps it was more meaningful than a misplaced trinket.* He looked to Tarra, but she was still busy talking Chilton into a morning scrub. He returned the cone to the hearthstone balancing it on end.

"It's a gift." Tarra spoke from behind him.

"What? How do you know?"

"Mom had me buy it for him last year at the gathering. She gave it to him for his birthday."

"Then it was very special to him?"

"He tucked it away in his robes saying it was too valuable to use, but I think he didn't want to give up his old pipe. It was a friend and he had no taste for finery. It made Mom happy to give him something, and that was all that was important to him."

Chilcoat retrieved the device and rolled it thoughtfully between his fingers again for a moment before slipping it into his smoking pouch. "Do you know of a sunburn cure? My arms are starting to blister."

She solemnly thought to herself. *I hate him confiscating the pipe. I hate his assumption that I'll do his bidding. I hate his arrogant attitude stealing any chance I had to make a new life for myself at the gathering. Now he treats me as a little sister he can command at his whim. I'm not his handmaiden and he can't boss me around. I'll not have it! I'm the daughter of Tangar, the Seer of the lakeshore tribe. I'm the one who knows the magic of the herbs, the one who can heal the sick, not because he says to, but because my father taught me this duty.* "Cure? No. I have no cure for arrogance. It's what happens when you don't respect Hea."

"I was…" He caught himself responding to her hostility and simply stopped.

Tarra retrieved the medicine bag and rummaged through it for a moment. Holding two small pouches, she sniffed each in turn. She returned one to the bag and busied herself mixing the contents of the other with a small amount of morning tea. A slightly acrid smell permeated the air as she sprinkled more powder into the cup and stirred the contents into a heavy paste. She put the cup on the hearthstone while she retrieved some butter from its storage bowl. The paste soon changed to a brown salve with the distinctive aroma of a wet dog. She finally picked up the cup and held it in offering to the spot where the robes had hung and then turned to kneel next to Chilcoat.

"This will help." She dipped her fingertips into the slime and slowly applied it to spots on his face, gently spreading it onto obviously sensitive areas. She started to apply the cream to his arm but was alarmed at the warmth as his firm muscles responded to her touch. Without saying a word, she quickly handed the cup to him and left the tent in a rush of loose morning clothes.

He could hear her dealing with the bundle of mannequin sticks he had tossed out and looked to Caran for understanding. She spoke solemnly. "She's still young, but she's very much older in some ways, and the loss of her father still weighs heavily on her. She'll get better with time."

He smiled gratefully at her consideration and left to see what all the commotion was. Tarra had gathered the sticks together and was working on lashing them into a bundle. He grabbed the nearest end and helped jiggle them into a more orderly cluster. She was startled and jerked the bundle away from him protectively clutching it firmly to her chest.

"What are you going to do with them now?" Chilcoat spoke defensively.

"I—don't really know. Why do you care? You obviously don't want them. You treat them like trash. You don't understand. You think you can discard him so easily. You want me to just burn them?" Her eyes clouded again as she stood clutching the bundle.

"You can burn them if you want. I'll leave that up to you. There may come a time when it'll be right to burn them. For now, why don't you see if you can make a hanger for the medicine pouch out of them? You know—a little rack we can stand near the door, so you can get to the pouch easily. Maybe it'll bring Dad to help me figure out all the stuff inside."

She hated his casual reference to her father. *It just isn't right for him to speak so personally of Daddy.* She turned indignantly and ran to the tent with her prize.

Chilcoat watched as Caran held the flap back for her and looked solemnly at him. He cleared his mind of them and turned to make his morning rounds. He hadn't gotten to the main path when he decided to return and find a hat to cover his tender hide.

Hesitating at the doorway of his tent for a moment, he made a commotion putting his gear down before calling to Caran through the flap. "Have you seen my hat?" He pulled the drape aside after a moment and entered knowing exactly where it was. "Ah, here it is." He tried to sound casual.

"You should cover your arms too." Tarra spoke coldly from across the room.

He stopped for a moment considering her words. Nodding and smiling, he retrieved a towel from the stack of laundry before he once again left the tent. He draped the towel over his head and fit his hat over it. With a few minor adjustments, he was able to fashion a reasonable sunshade for his shoulders. He felt a bit of a fool and had to listen to whistles and hoots from some of his hunting buddies as he walked past Rancon's hut but he didn't want to take any more chances.

He joined the men near the night watchman's hearth with only a few comments on his attire. It seemed that a couple of others had similar afflictions and told of eye irritation and fuzzy vision. The heat of the last few days was the primary topic of the morning, with minor diversions to address the cat sightings and related hostilities between Rancon and the Larkon boys. The conversation then drifted back to the weather and Chilcoat offered Tarra's services in mixing burn lotion for anyone who needed it.

As the group began to break up, Rancon smirked. "Your cape isn't befitting a man of your stature. Maybe an umbrella would better fit the Seer. Maybe you can have Tarra carry it for you, like a temple maiden."

"Not funny, but a shade cloth may not be a bad idea."

"Yeah, might make hunting a little awkward, but I sure could use some shade right now." They quickly sought cover under the nearest tree and continued to talk about umbrellas.

Chilcoat reflected solemnly as he joined the evening hunter's brief and pulled the hood of his sun cape from his head. *It was great to have the rain stop, but the months of the cleansing has stripped the sky of any protective haze and left us unprepared for this summer. Hunting and fishing during midday is useless since the creatures we're hunting are also seeking shelter from the blistering heat. Tending the fields is limited to early morning and late evening, leaving everyone with nothing to do all day but sit around trying to stay cool. The cluster of shade cloths set up in the lake shallows helps, but most people just "tough it out" in their tents. The nighttime hunting is dangerous and one of the Larkon boys reported a twisted ankle that will keep him from hunting for a while.*

"Larkon," Chilcoat called across the clearing. "Larkon, you got a minute?"

Larkon excused himself from his comrades and came quickly across the clearing shielding his eyes with one hand. He normally wouldn't seem so anxious to comply, but the sun made any exposure something that was best hurried. "Yeah, what's up?"

"Well, I'll tell ya— I'm concerned about the women. They're unprotected while they work the fields at night and they've asked that someone guard them. I think it'd be great if your boys would help us out there. They're always out looking for that cat, and I think we'd be better served if they kept the cat from coming to us."

"I'll talk to them about it. They have a big hunt planned as soon as Laot's leg gets better." He turned to leave.

"If it's for that cat again, I'm going to have to ask you to please consider what I've said. Your boys have brought it on themselves. If they weren't so boastful of their exploits, the women wouldn't be so upset and we wouldn't be having this conversation."

"We'll be expecting you on the hunt tonight." Rancon barked at Larkon who simply kept walking without acknowledgment.

Charona entered the hut pulling her cape off in exasperation. She had finished her morning duties and the sun was unrelenting. The cloth she had fashioned into a headscarf draped over most of her body and blocked any breeze from getting through so she was glad to rid herself of it.

The rolled up walls of the hut let the air circulate, but the heat was oppressive. Caran watched casually as her sister disrobed and began washing the morning's grime away.

Tarra had also finished her morning chores and entered performing much the same ritual of shedding clothing and starting a sponge bath. "That Bartan is such a jerk. He keeps sneaking up on me while I'm working and jumping out as if he just happened to be there. Then he wants me to go for a walk with him. I keep telling him I'm not interested, but he won't leave me alone."

"He's just a man. He thinks you're playing hard to get," Charona rinsed the cloth and handed it to Tarra.

"He's such a lazy drunkard. He smells of sour wine and why's he hanging around with women instead of hunting like a man?"

"He just wants a chance to talk with you." Caran tried to be diplomatic.

"He just wants to get me alone in the woods." Tarra shuddered at the prospect.

A cloud of bugs swarmed around the upper reaches of the tent and occasionally sent a scout to test the temperament of the residents. Tarra swatted absentmindedly at the intruder and used a fan she had crafted to cool her neck. Her gaze fell on the medicine pouch hanging from the little stick figure she had set up near the door. Her mind wandered back to her father and how he liked the heat of summer. *"It makes my joints work better,"* he used to say. She wondered if he would like this summer. *I've never experienced anything like it and I doubt he had either. I wonder if he'd have anything to say about it. Of course, he would. He always had something to say about everything.* She smiled to herself. The fly returned for another bout of swat-and-swipe.

She rose and, with a small bow of reverence, retrieved the pouch from *his* grasp. Sitting by the meager fire, she unrolled the medicine cloth and placed a few select pouches of herbs in the middle.

Rummaging through the bag, she found the mortar stone. It seemed foreign to her touch. *I haven't used it since before Daddy died. I did his bidding grinding and mixing herbs under his close supervision for years and then, as the end drew near, all I could do was simply comfort him. He spent nearly all of his waking hours telling me stories and doing little chants he said belonged to the herbs I was grinding. He guided me through some very complex riddles and fine mixing of special herbs that resulted in a concoction of muddy tea that made him sleep quietly for hours. I hope I'll never have to use the recipe again.*

Right now, I'm looking for something less complex. She put the grinding stone at a slight angle to her knee and picked up one of the pouches. Pinching a small amount of its contents onto the stone, she gently crushed the dried leaves in a motion that quickly became comfortable. After several minutes of alternately grinding and mixing pinches from various pouches, she was satisfied with the puddle of gray dust. She carefully dribbled a few drops of water on it and used a flat stick to make a thick paste that she rolled into a small irregular worm. Being careful not to touch it, she divided it into four equal clumps that she cautiously rolled into large gray pills that clung to the curve of the stone. Using the mixing stick, she selected a pill and edged it out onto the flat surface then pressed it flat into a wafer that stuck to the back of the tool.

She stirred the embers and gently edged a small branch in to keep the flame alive. "Sorry guys, but one of has to go, and I pick you." She held the mixing stick over the coals until the wafer fell free. It hissed slightly and burst into a steady stream of pale blue smoke. She stood and closed the chimney flap then sat watching the haze that gathered in the rafters of the hut. The flies quickly recognized the inadvisability of remaining and fled for cleaner pastures.

"At least that's something," Caran said, recognizing her effort.

Charona once again washed her arms and chest and retreated to her sleeping chamber. Working the night shift made the heat of the day a miserable sleeping partner. She would rest but probably not sleep.

Tarra was about to do the same and pressed the second pill into a wafer placing it onto the embers for good measure. She sat holding the mixing stick and watching the trail of smoke issuing from the wafer. The stick seemed to grow warm in her hand as she gazed at the ghost rising into the haze that filled the eaves of the hut. She put the stick aside and grabbed a washcloth to clean her neck and chest. She was just about to lay down when she glanced at Caran. She looked hot and tired. Soaking the cloth again, she approached her. "You look like you could use this."

"Thanks—I get to working and I forget where I am."

"I wish I could forget this heat. Here, take your shirt off and let me get your back." Tarra rinsed the cloth and began tugging at Caran's blouse.

"OK, OK, I'll get it." She pulled her blouse off and squealed as the cool cloth slid down her back. "Now let me get you." Caran turned, taking the cloth, she applied it gently to the slender child sitting before her. She reminded her of who she had once been: small, thin, and strong. Now she was none of those things and felt somehow less than this child.

Tarra turned to face her when she was done and looked deeply into her eyes. "I don't want your husband."

"That's good, but what does he want?"

"He's like any man. He wants what he sees until he has it, then he wants something else." Tarra rinsed the cloth and began wiping down Caran's arms. "He has a good woman and he knows it."

"I hope he remembers it." Caran took the cloth and began stroking Tarra's arms. She rinsed it several more times, as she worked her way up to her face. She paused caressing the child-like features for a moment as she watched her transform into a beautiful woman then into the child she had learned to love. She hugged her close feeling her breasts form against her. "I hope you remember."

Tarra timidly put the medicine bag away. She took the remaining bug repellent and pressed it into wafers that she placed on the hearthstones then dropped the mixing stick on the ceremonial cloth while she brushed the grist stones off and placed them in the embers to clean any residue from their surfaces.

The mixing stick lay across the sunburst pattern on the middle of the cloth. It reminded her of the game her father played with the guide sticks. He would drink a strong concoction of spirit tea, gather the sticks together, and chant for guidance from Thoma, his father. Holding them high above the cloth he would drop the bundle loose in the middle of the symbol and read the signs in the scattered twigs. He would repeat the process several times with fewer and fewer sticks each time. Eventually, he would select a single twig from the scattered pile and place it in the center of the symbol thanking Vau for Her wisdom.

She hadn't thought of Thoma for many years. She really only knew him as a gruff old grandfather who gave her nice gifts for her birthday, but she knew her father respected him and frequently called on him in his prayers.

Digging through the bag, she extracted the bundle of guide sticks and carefully separated them into summer and winter piles. She put Tangar's stick in the middle of the cloth along with the summer bundle and put the winter bundle aside. She then tossed the one that Chilcoat had brought back from the falls onto the kindling pile with more satisfaction than the gesture deserved.

Gazing at the story-stick for several moments, she picked it up and rolled it over in her hand. Nothing happened. *I don't really know what I expect, but I know I need to feel your presence and warmth again Daddy. This stupid stick is the only thing I have left of you.*

She thought again of Thoma and the times he had played make-believe with her and her dolls. *Maybe if I dress the stick up in a ceremonial robe, he'll talk to me, as my dolls did.*

She found the damp washcloth and wrapped it around the jagged little wand then placed it back in the center of the sunburst with the head peeking out of the cloth. It didn't speak. Again, thinking of her grandfather and her dolls, she whispered to it. "Daddy, please help me."

Caran had been watching with great concern. She had known the loss of a loved one and felt her pain, but she knew that she really had nothing she could offer to help her.

After several moments, Tarra dejectedly dropped her shoulders feeling a little childish. She turned to tidy up the things she had scattered around and considered Chilcoat's stick as it lay amongst the kindling. *Perhaps I can make a doll for Grandpa from it and then Papa would talk to me.*

She picked up the stick and inspected its defects. *It does rather remind me of Grandpa. It's short and stout and bent in the middle.* She held it to her heart for a moment and placed it next to the little robed figure on the cloth. *It looks like it belongs,* she thought. It warmed her to think that Papa and Grandpa are together again, and that they're watching over her. *It isn't as good as the real thing, but I know they'd like to play with me again.*

She took the two sticks, set them aside, and picked up the bundle of summer guide sticks. She tried to remember what her father had done. *If I can dance with the wands as he did, maybe Vau's whisper will tell me why Yod has forsaken us.*

She held the bundle high above her head and let them fall on the center of the cloth. All but three hit and bounced out of the sunburst design. She looked at the three remaining sticks and tried to remember what he would do next. She noted that one stick was lying across the others. *Maybe that's a sign.*

She gathered the outliers into a pile and then picked up the three winners. Holding them high above her head again, she spoke softly, "Papa, please help me understand." The sticks fell and bounced slightly on the ceremonial cloth. Two fell in and one landed just on the edge of the sunburst pointing toward the door. She decided not to consider that a sign and put it aside with the other discards. Again, the tanasin stick lay on the top of the other.

She picked them up and held one in each hand. *Should I throw them again or would that be tempting the spirits?* She held them up and called quietly. "Papa, Grandpa, show me the way."

The sticks fell with a quiet thump just as Chilcoat and Lannon returned with the children. They brought the day's catch and two buckets of fresh water along with several tales of adventure from the shoreline. The commotion was soon resolved with everyone settling in for a nap. The heat was relentless, and a new batch of flies had come with the latest arrivals. Charona listlessly rebuffed Lannon as he settled in next to her, placing his hand on her naked breast.

The tanasin stick had fallen atop coshin again. Tarra smiled to herself and timidly whispered. "Thank you, Papa. I don't know what I would have done if you hadn't helped."

Setting the tanasin stick aside, she collected the others and tied them tightly into the satchel. She then took Tangar's story stick and the one she had given to Thoma and rose to drape the bag across the shoulders of the mannequin standing near the door. She started to shove the sticks into the top of the bag and hesitated a moment considering the figure she had fashioned. The tightly packed bundle of poles made a long straight body with the remaining, smaller, sticks forming shoulders and arms tucked tightly against its sides. First defrocking Tangar's wand of its washcloth, she jammed it amongst the rods of the left hand. The spirit seemed happy to have *his* talking-stick back.

She remembered how her father would sit for hours talking of adventures and triumphs from his past. Many of the stories were about how his father had done, or known, something that carried some proverb and words of wisdom. He would twist and turn the stick pointing to knobs and joints along its length that he used to remind him of details and nuances about Thoma. It occurred to her at that moment that the twisted little twig didn't hold the spirit of her father. It held the spirit of Thoma, her grandfather. Her father had treasured it because it carried the wisdom of his father.

"Well, I hope this makes you happy." She whispered still holding the water worn twig that Chilcoat had brought back from the falls. She considered it for a moment and decided that if Thoma lived in the other stick, then perhaps her father would live in this one. It seemed more fitting than living in the bag-rack, she thought, gently wedging the twisted little form in amongst the body of the mannequin.

She wondered if Chilcoat would notice her little shrine. She hoped he wouldn't disapprove. *He'll have to understand,* she decided. *He'll have to let me keep the memorial.*

Tarra pushed the feeder stick into the embers and dished the third bug wafer onto the ashes. The smoke trailed up into the rafters and fed the cloud forcing the swarm to vacate the premises once again.

Why does Vau whisper of tanasin? She tried to remember the use of tanasin. *If I can remember the story Papa told me about tanasin, maybe I can figure out what I'm do with it.* She drifted to sleep listening to the gentle rhythm of the family and thinking of stories of Thoma.

Chilcoat stirred in the late afternoon when the bugs returned and wouldn't leave him alone. The last smoke balm had already been consumed so he had little alternative but to get up and start his day. Charona drew his attention as she moved listlessly. He couldn't help but admire her beauty lying quietly beside her mate. He missed their occasional intimacies and paused to remember her warmth.

Pulling his cloak over his head forming a tent, he turned to gather his hunting gear and noticed that Tarra was sitting up watching him.

She had grown into a beautiful young woman in the past months. She was no longer the little sister he had saved from suffering at the hands of Bartan. She turned to hide her nakedness while he quickly brushed past and left the hut. She couldn't rest either and rose to get her evening started. Once outside she remembered her ritual and the stick she had decided was a sign. She returned to her bed and retrieved the trophy. She couldn't help but look at the heart she had given the mannequin standing near the door. The twisted little wand nestled comfortably within the chest of the stoic figure.

She held the tanasin stick tightly and considered its secrets as she again stepped into the stark rays of the sun. She held her cape in place with a scarf twisted tightly around her forehead and peered through a small slit for her eyes. Underneath she wore as little as possible and relished the occasional breeze that would stir through and caress her skin. *They all look pretty silly,* she thought, as she joined the line of similarly dressed specters picking their way carefully down the path to the shoreline. It took on an almost religious aura.

Tarra arrived at the shade cloth Chilcoat had stretched across a small patch of sand and followed it into the lagoon several feet. She pulled her cape off and quietly settled waist deep in the water, then laid back and soaked her hair. As she scrubbed the last vestiges of sleep from her eyes, she noticed that Chilcoat was busy tightening the rope that held the cloth in place.

She turned to face his guarded gaze. "Do you think the heat will stop soon?"

Staring vacantly at her form for a moment he awkwardly looked away assessing her words. "No, I am afraid that Hea has other plans for us this season. We'll have to tighten down a little, but I think we'll be alright."

"I talked with Daddy last night."

He stood silently staring at the sky then turned to gaze at the young woman he hardly knew. "What did he have to say? Or should I ask?"

"I don't know. I danced with Vau, just as he showed me, and She gave me this guide stick." Her water-darkened hair fell in a rope across her shoulder as she extracted the twig she had used to pin it in place. "It's called tanasin, but I'm not sure what it's used for." She held the stick out in the palm of her hand.

"I noticed you gave him his talking-stick to play with."

"Ah… yeah, I didn't know what else to do with it. It makes me sad, so I gave it back to him. Maybe he'll be happier and speak with Yod for us."

"Maybe—maybe he will… " He chose his words carefully trying not to offend her.

"Maybe he has." She held the twig out to him.

"What does that stick tell you? You said you don't remember what it is, and I sure as hell don't know anything about it."

"Maybe if I saw some of it, I'd remember what he used it for. Maybe then we'll know what She's trying to tell us."

"Don't you have some in one of those little pouches?"

"No. The loose sticks are those things he doesn't have in the pouches. You must always dance with the loose sticks. They're special. They are the '*whisper of Vau*'. He used them only when he had to, and he had to hike in penance to get them."

"Hike… what are we talking about here? You want to go for a hike in this heat?"

She gazed over the early evening crowd that had now gathered in the lagoon. The excitement of the day's business filled the air as everyone readied for another night of toil. She looked down at the twig she held in her open palm and noticed the beads of water on her naked breast. "No. I don't want to hike in this weather, but I don't know what else it could mean. The stick is definitely tanasin. I know that, but it looks like a three-week walk according to the stick."

"How's that?"

"The stick, see here it has three sections. Each one is a week's journey. Then you get to where it's telling you to go and you should be able to find some tanasin."

"Oh, I see. Well, that's great, but we've got things to do here, and being gone for months is quite a commitment for not really knowing where you're going."

She twisted her hair and piled it on the back of her head jamming the twig back into place. "I know. I just thought you should know. Daddy said it's your job, not mine." She pulled her cape on hastily and peeked out from behind the slit adjusting the headband and smoothing the cloth against her still damp skin. It clung to reveal her firm young body and left Chilcoat wondering just who this young woman was.

"I'll think about it. You stay out of trouble." He called after her trying to sound as brotherly as he could under the circumstances. He doubted he had impressed her as she glanced dismissively over her shoulder and headed for the gathering of field workers that were beginning to assign tasks.

Chilcoat pulled on his sun cape and found Rancon down by the central hearth trying to mooch an extra bit of bread from the grandmothers. "Have you seen Larkon? He's supposed to come with us tonight."

"Nah… I saw him earlier with Bartan down by the lake, but I think they went to the trash dump. They have a batch of wine stashed up there. They'll be along soon."

"Those two aren't good together. I haven't seen much of Bartan lately. Where's he been? He used to hang around trying to convince me that he deserved to court Tarra, but lately he seems more interested in chasing that damn cat."

"Yeah, the whole Larkon bunch is trying to get that cat. They want a trophy to take to the gathering this year. They think they'll find honor at the men's ceremony. I think they're wasting their time. That cat's smarter than they are."

"I'm going to press Larkon to have his boys stand watch on the fields tonight. They need to start pulling their weight and stop all this cat nonsense."

"Yeah, well, good luck with that. They're pretty headstrong over it." Rancon leaned thoughtfully on his walking staff. "So Tarra's become quite a handful, huh? I mean she got rid of Bartan pretty quickly and now he just hangs around with the Larkon boys getting into trouble and drinking too much."

"She's full of surprises all right. She has her dad's medicine sticks, and says she can read them. She wants to hike up one of the valleys looking for some herb and she doesn't even know what it is."

"Wow, in this heat that'd be quite a quest."

"Yeah, but she has this way about her that makes me want to believe her. She's so—innocent, but I don't know—older. It disturbs me sometimes how clever she is."

"Careful there, pal. You're supposed to be her brother, not her—friend."

"Life's full of challenges alright, but right now I'm more concerned with our little hunting party. We need to get going or the game will take to the hills for the night and we'll miss our chance. Let's go see if they're up at the dump."

They made their way over the ridge that served as the backdrop to the village. It blocked the winds from the canyon beyond and separated the people from their refuse and the varmints that frequent it. They passed the dawn-watch station and went quickly down the other side to a sharp abutment that provided a drop point for trash. Just past the cliff, the rocks trailed up a small hill and formed a, sort of, amphitheater that the youngsters frequented when they wanted to get away from the 'old folks'.

The rough hollow in the stones provided seating for about twenty, but seldom more than a half-dozen would show up at one time. Their gatherings usually revolved around games, or in this case, because these guys had brewed up a batch of berry-wine and wouldn't be happy until it was gone. Bartan, Larkon, and his two younger sons were reclining on some of the flat boulders at the bottom of the bowl. They had a large wine bladder and a bit of leftover fish scattered around the large circular stone that frequently served as a gaming pedestal. Bartan sprawled across the platform staring at the sky while the Larkon boys passed a bowl of smoking herb.

Chilcoat stood judgmentally at the edge of the arena with Rancon behind him. "Evening, fellas. I thought we were going hunting."

Larkon handed off the pipe and turned to face Chilcoat while Bartan sat up on the platform but remained defiantly seated. "We were just talking about that." Larkon stepped closer to the pair. "We were thinking that maybe it would be better for us to split up into two groups. You go your way and we go our way."

Chilcoat considered his words carefully. "I think maybe you're right, we should probably split our efforts. A couple of us can go along the west wall of the canyon and scare the game toward the narrows and the others can cut them off. Bartan, you come with me, and Larkon you go with Ran. It'll give us all a chance talk out a few things."

Larkon swayed slightly from the wine as he tossed the bladder back to Bartan. "Well, I had more in mind that we can go any damn place we want, and you two can go any damn place you want."

Chilcoat stepped closer. "Larkon, you're a fool if you think you're going to get by drinking and bashing around looking for that cat. The people are in need of food and you and your clan aren't helping as much as you could."

"My clan gets by pretty well. My boys have brought in the last two kills. What more do you want?"

"I'm not saying you and your sons aren't good providers. I am saying the rest of the village needs their help. The community needs everyone to pull their weight for the betterment of us all. Our system won't work otherwise. You know that times have been tough, and well, I don't think it's going to get better any time soon."

"What do you mean? It's summer! As soon as this hot spell's over, it'll be fine. Everybody'll be back to drinking new wine and enjoying the growing season."

"Those two bucks your boys brought home have been gone for over a week now and no one else has been able to get anything bigger than fish and rabbits in that time."

"Well, we've been busy tracking that cat. As soon as we get her, we'll bring a feast to celebrate our kill."

"I know what you've been doing and I think it's foolish for you to continue. All this talk about a cat is scaring the children. That cat's too smart to let a couple of drunks catch it. If you boys are serious about getting that cat, you should stake out the fields where the women work. It'll come for the children, but it'll never get caught up here on its own terms." Chilcoat gestured to the pass above the village.

Lannon came up the trail behind them. "Besides guys, traipsing around in the bushes at night only gets you hurt. And if the women see you standing guard for them maybe they'll be grateful." He nudged his younger brother, Lon, meaningfully.

Lon considered the tactic and the possible benefits. He prodded the youngest brother, Laot, into gathering up their party favors.

Chilcoat hefted his spear. "Lan, it's good to see you. You and your brothers get set up at the fields. Larkon, you and Ran take the west side and Bartan and I'll go to the narrows to cut them off."

Bartan was less drunk than Larkon, so the sprint to the narrows was not too difficult, but his condition didn't make it a very quiet venture. As they settled in their lair, they rested and listened for the telltale rustling of fleeing game. "Have you given up on Tarra?" Chilcoat whispered.

Bartan sat quietly for several moments. "She doesn't like me. I understand that. She has no reason to, but someday, she'll realize she needs me."

"Perhaps... Maybe if you stopped drinking and spent some time tending the lines…"

"If she'll have me, she'll need to accept me the way I am."

"Then I don't think she'll ever have you."

"Maybe—maybe you're poisoning her mind. Maybe you want to keep her for yourself."

"That'll be enough of that! Your position in this tribe doesn't allow you to question me. You would do well to listen instead." Chilcoat pulled an arrow from his quiver and readied his bow. Bartan watched closely as Chilcoat positioned himself in ambush above the ravine. "You go over there and wait for my signal then scare the game this way." Chilcoat coldly ordered with the tip of his arrow.

Bartan pulled his bow to the ready and hesitated a moment considering his next move. Assessing Chilcoat's cold stare, he decided to take up his hunting duties.

Within a few minutes, they could hear a commotion in the distance as the drivers chanted an old hunting song. Soon the bushes down the gully rustled and a young doe emerged with a fawn in tow. They cautiously picked their way up the ravine toward them. Chilcoat held his hand up to stop Bartan as he began to rise. A second pair, and then a third, soon joined the herd. He again had to halt Bartan with emphatic hand gestures. The animals wound their way up the arroyo past them and quickly disappeared up the canyon. He gave Bartan a gesture to listen quietly.

The bawdy ramblings of the driving crew grew closer and then a strong young buck broke through the bushes at the mouth of the ravine. A second more mature male quickly followed. They seemed to sense the presence of the predators as they balked and drew up short sniffing pointedly into the hot summer night. He gave Bartan the signal, and he rose alarmingly at their flank. They hesitated for a split second and bound up the gully in bursts that carried them alternately from side to side of the narrow rift. Chilcoat waited anxiously until the mature buck was in range then rose and fired a quick bolt. It faltered and fell in two quick bumps.

Bartan fired at the younger male, but missed. As he drew a second arrow from his quiver, Chilcoat called out. "Let him go!"

Bartan drew a bead on the fleeing buck, but Chilcoat's arrow zipped past his ear and shattered on the rock behind him, distracting his shot. He turned his aim toward Chilcoat but met a drawn bow peeking over a distant boulder. Bartan considered his stance and dropped his aim as the young buck bounded over the last barrier and escaped further assault. "Why did you do that? I could have got him."

"Yeah maybe, and what would you do with him? We've enough to carry with this one. '*I thank you for your life and the life you give us*'." Chilcoat quickly moved to sever the scent glands from the fallen beast and held them up in bloody tribute to the stars.

The drivers joined the group and quickly went to work eviscerating the kill. A hasty meal of organs and blood filled their bellies and they quartered and packed the beast for transport as the morning light smeared the horizon. They would have to hurry to get back to camp before it got too hot. They had to leave some of the less desirable bits of flesh and bone, but they were able to cart the prime cuts on their backs in a gruesome division of bounty.

***

Chilcoat rested deeply as Caran sat up with the children in their normal family scuffles and Charona wrestled playfully with Lannon. It was a night like any other except it was midday and blistering hot.

Tarra went through her, now familiar, ritual of bug abatement and listened to the gentle rhythm of the lovers with more interest than usual. She finished her task and quickly retired to seek her own relief. She lay on her side for a few moments and watched Chilcoat's nearly naked form sleeping a few feet away. Turning her back to him, she could see the mannequin standing guard by the doorway. *I wonder if Daddy's happy with his story stick. Maybe he'll visit me tonight,* she thought. *Or, better yet, maybe he'll visit Chilcoat and tell him what a dolt he is.*

Boys Will Be Boys

Morning came early as the matrons declared the breakfast feast ready. Everyone devoured the venison in quick order, with accolades going to the hunters. The ceremony demanded that each man tell his version of the adventure. Chilcoat left his at "a job well-done" for his cohorts, but Bartan took the opportunity to expound on his critical role in the mission, and how he had missed a second kill by only inches. He had fortified himself with wine before breakfast and was willing to go to any length on the techniques he had used, and how Chilcoat had robbed him of a good shot. Most of the audience quickly showed disinterest in his tale, but thanked him for his effort, and returned to their evening's preparations.

It was still too early to start work, but it felt good to be out in the daylight with friends and family. Tarra wandered among the specters, clad in their ghostly apparel exchanging news and gossip, until she finally found Chilcoat. She callously pressed the tanasin stick into his hand. "Daddy said to give this to you."

He stood speechless for a moment then, as she turned to walk away, he called out to her. "What am I supposed to do with it? You're the only one that can read the damn thing."

She continued along her path toward the field-maidens with only a dismissive wave. He looked at the twig noting its smooth polished form had nicks and notches along its length. What at first seemed to be bud joints, now told the story of a careful artisan who had obviously spent many hours sculpting the distorted little wand. He pulled it in under his hood and stuck it behind his ear. It would have to wait. Right now he had to be sure Lannon was able to get his brothers setup to guard the fields.

It sounds like that cat is taking advantage of the carrion we left last night and has cornered a scavenger back up the canyon. Larkon and his boys will be anxious to get the beast and I'll be hard-pressed to stop them. It just doesn't feel right to me. Something bad will come of it.

He called to Rancon as he passed his tent. "Ran, will you join me?"

Rancon came pulling on his hunting garb and still eating. "What's up—we gonna visit the kids?"

"Yeah, I think a few things need to be said in front of the others." They suffered the short hike to the central plaza in silence. As they approached, Lannon was talking with his brothers. *That's a good sign,* Chilcoat thought. Larkon and Bartan were nowhere around. *That isn't a good sign.* He tried to get started on the right foot. "What's up guys?"

"They still want to go hunting for that damn cat. They won't listen to me," Lannon reported.

"I know it would be great to take such a prize to the gathering, but I really think it's a bad idea. I think someone will get hurt or worse… That cat is no threat to us if we protect ourselves. It'll be moving to the high country soon and we can go back to our normal routine. In the meantime, we need someone to guard the fields and the job fits you guys perfectly."

The boys stood silent for a few moments and whispered a couple of unintelligible sibling grunts to each other. Laot gestured to his swollen ankle and Lon looked longingly at the group of young women forming at the edge of the fields. "We have to go hunting. Dad's expecting us."

"Where is he? I want to talk with him anyway." The boys looked at each other and then at Lannon who gestured toward the dump. "You boys go to the fields and get set up. Lan, you come with me. Ran it's up to you if you want to come, but I would appreciate your support."

"Sure. I wouldn't miss it." Rancon hefted his spear.

They once again made the trek to the gathering circle and, as they neared the base of the rocks, Chilcoat readied his bow and cautioned the others to be alert. They both followed suit and slowed their pace. The group held fast and listened for traces of activity.

The scent of burnt herbs wafted over the boulder as the three edged quietly toward the opening in the blocks of stone that formed the bowl. This put them at a tactical disadvantage but it showed the boldness that must carry the day. Chilcoat drew his bow to the ready and led the way down the short passage. He motioned Rancon to guard the cross field while Lannon hung back as a third shot, should it be needed. Chilcoat edged up to peek around the corner and was satisfied that no one was sitting in ambush so he relaxed his posture and motioned the others to gather closer.

The three cautiously entered the central ring of stones. Generations of idle youths had left oddly sculptured boulders scattered across the floor of the arena. Larkon and Bartan sat on their usual wine-drinking platform. They looked up quickly, gathered their weapons, and ducked behind the stone.

Chilcoat called out to them. "Larkon, I need to talk with you."

"I've got nothing to say to you that hasn't already been said. Me and my boys are going to get that cat tonight and we don't need your advice on how to do it."

"Well, that's what I want to talk about. I have your boys standing guard on the fields, so they won't be able to join you tonight. I don't think your hunt's going to end well. Listen, you can hear the cat, it must've missed its prey and it's getting desperate."

"I hear it, and I think you're right. It's desperate. That means it'll make mistakes and that's why I'm going to get it tonight. I don't need to listen to your cowardly foolishness. I'm going to do you a favor tonight and you won't need to be afraid of that cat anymore. Lan, go get your brothers and let's get going."

Lannon stood defiantly looking at his father. "I've assigned them other duties tonight. If you insist on this foolishness, they won't be a part of it."

Bartan moved nervously repositioning his weapons. "We don't need them. Let them hide with the women."

"No! I want them with me learning how to get that cat, not hiding and waiting to become prey. Lannon, I want you to go fetch your brothers and you get ready for the hunt too. You can help."

The opposing groups stared at each other for several moments. Lannon finally broke the silence. "I mean no disrespect, but, I have a family that's become more important to me than your blessing. You've taught me always to do what I think is right, and I think Chilcoat's right. Times aren't good. We need to work together as a tribe... That cat isn't like any other. It seems to know what you're thinking. My brothers have hunted it for weeks now and they haven't even come close, so I don't think two drunken old men are going to do anything more than get someone hurt."

Larkon stiffened in defiance and slurred his words. He obviously had had more to drink than Bartan. "Soo, you really're n outcast. That ol bag has you twisted round her finger. Well, do as you want then... but I'll have *my* realsons at my side. I'll get'em myself."

Chilcoat confronted him. "I'm afraid I can't let you do that. I've taken the robes of the Seer and I've decided that your boys are better off doing what's best for the others. I'm sorry that your judgment conflicts with mine, but I'm trying to do what's best for the community."

Rancon stepped forward to stand beside Chilcoat with his bow at the ready.

Lannon did likewise, forming a line. "If you won't abandon this plan, you'll have to do it alone. I'll not lead my brothers into such foolishness."

Bartan fidgeted with his spear and looked to Larkon for assurance. "Come on, Lark. We don't need the blessing of the 'great and noble holder of the robes'. We'll get that cat and then we'll see who should be wearing them. Then maybe you'll stop meddling in other people's lives. Maybe then Tarra will be able to live her own life instead of being your—servant. She won't have to listen to your 'wisdom' anymore and maybe then she'll come to me as she should and not sleep with her brother."

Chilcoat drew his bow taut. "Bartan, you would be wise to not say any more. You're an outsider in this tribe and your position is weak in this matter."

"I'll decide who I sleep with." Tarra stepped into the clearing and stood defiantly facing the pair. "I wouldn't be your wife under any circumstances. You're a loser, and I'll not waste my time with a loser. And who I choose to sleep with is of no concern to you."

Bartan stood perplexed, looking alternately at her and Chilcoat. "We'll see about that. Come on Lark, let's get out of here before that cat dies of old age." The pair turned to gather their belongings and head out the far exit toward the dump.

Chilcoat barked, still on edge. "Tarra, why are you here? You should be tending your duties."

"I'm here because I want to talk with you. I think that Daddy has spoken with me and you have to listen to what he has to say."

"You listen to me. I know you had a special bond with your father, but he's gone now—we have to move on—without him."

"But he talked about you."

"I don't care. He visits me in the night too, but he has no answers to my questions. He only haunts my dreams with walks in the woods and pipes of smoking herb. Maybe I'm not right for this job because I don't know what he is saying or what to do about any of the things that have happened. We've had storms like never before and the fire in the sky, and now the summer—instead of a time of plenty, has turned to a harsh and bitter trial. Still Yod doesn't guide me—Dad doesn't guide me."

The clear hiss of an arrow ruined his little tirade as the dart struck the ground at his feet. It was the one he had broken the night before. The blunted tip gave the shaft an unbalanced flight and it lodged ineffectively in the dirt. Chilcoat and the others crouched, weapons at the ready, searching the tops of the surrounding boulders for targets.

"I figured you could use this!" Bartan laughingly shouted from beyond the farthest stones.

Chilcoat plucked the arrow from the ground, snapped it in half, and tossed it down in fury. "He's an ass…" He turned to face Tarra's disarming visage. "So what would Tangar have me do?"

"Listen to Vau's whisper... Papa knows that things aren't right. He had me dance with the Spirit to ask for guidance and She gave us this." She reached up, plucking the twig from behind his ear, and held it defiantly in his face. "I don't know what it means, but at least it's something."

Chilcoat recoiled slightly and gazed silently at the delicately carved implement. He reached up to grab it, more out of self-defense than desire to accept its importance. "Yes, it's something, but what? Is it truly the whisper of Vau or is it the wishful fancy of a young girl?"

She held her grip on the twig and stared deeply into his eyes as they struggled gently for control. Eventually they both recognized the tension and dropped it with a muffled click onto the splintered arrow at their feet. In a flash of awkwardness, he retrieved the jumble of sticks. They reminded him of the gift he had given to Tangar at his funeral. He clinched the bundle of twigs as he once again faced the young woman.

The distant scream of the cat echoed on the wind as Rancon intruded in their exchange. "Are we going to follow them, or what?"

"Or what." Chilcoat separated the medicine wand from the arrow. With one last flash of Tangar's company, he cast the splintered shaft onto the platform. "Let them follow their spirit. If they kill the cat, we'll celebrate. If the cat kills them, we'll mourn, but right now, we need to find some game. The stew will be thin if we can't find meat soon and with all the commotion those two are making they'll flush the game towards the falls so it should make our job easier."

Take the Damn Stick

The early morning light was just beginning to push the stars from view when the cat once again announced its dissatisfaction about something. Chilcoat stirred the fire to life and lit his pipe. As the comforting smoke relieved his tired body, the smoldering twig once again reminded him of Tangar and his silly sticks. Tossing the twig into the fire, he retrieved the tanasin wand from his bowl. He rolled its twisted form slowly between his fingers. The ends danced wobbling circles in the morning light. The thought of also tossing it into the fire crossed his mind, but he knew he couldn't do that to Tarra.

"What are you going to do about the stick?" Caran asked.

"I don't know. Tarra thinks it means something, but I don't know if the old man has spoken to her or if she's just a child making up stories."

Caran finished tucking their children into bed and gently touched his arm. "You know she's not a child—and I hate her for that. But I love you both, and if you love me, you have to listen to her, even if she hasn't talked with Tangar."

After an uncomfortable moment of silence, Caran spoke again. "At the gathering Tarann took me aside. She spoke of Tarra as a— 'keeper'. I thought she was just being a mother, but now I see she meant more... She cursed Tangar and his 'witch's scrolls' and told me she was sorry for 'the pain I must endure'. I thought she was just crazy with grief, but now I see she was trying to tell me that I... that we—are destined to bear her burden to its end."

Chilcoat tried to defuse the tension. "I wouldn't worry about the ravings of a grieving wife. Next fall we'll return to the gathering and talk with her about it. By then she'll be less upset and I'll bet she'll change her story."

He relit his pipe and watched in silence as Tarra returned from her nightly duties and began to prepare for bed. He sat smoking, thinking, and toying with the stick while she once again prepared the bug balm and retired. As she lay nearly naked in the morning heat, her chest moved in the gentle rhythm of sleep that touched him like a cool autumn breeze. It felt good and stirred his heart but left his mind unsettled. *What am I to do with this girl?* He put the stick aside and rested as best he could in the heat.

By midday, Bartan returned to the village with his sun-cape torn and his shoulders severely burned by the morning sun. He came begging Tarra for burn ointment. She wasn't happy about the early wake-up call, but hadn't really been able to sleep. She tended to his wounds and dismissed him with cold disregard when he tried to involve her in his tale of adventure regarding the cat. He said that he and Larkon had separated in the night and that he needed to gather a search party to look for him.

Chilcoat listened with cheerless resolve, not giving any sign of interest. After Bartan left, he sat smoking across the tent from where Tarra was cleaning up her apothecary. She had sunburn lotion in her regular consignment of concoctions, so it was a small favor to dispense an occasional batch to a neighbor, but she didn't like to have to rub it on Bartan. She knew he would try to make more of it than was intended and she didn't want to encourage him in any way. She draped the medicine bag over the shoulders of the mannequin near the door, and quietly resettled in her bed.

Chilcoat was about to do the same when he noticed the talking-stick jutting from the hand of the figure. He pulled the tanasin stick from amongst his belongings and lay on his back holding it up against the background of smoke drifting in the rafters. The simple form zigzagged in three distinct segments, each projecting at a different angle from the previous. Each section had notches and knots carved into it. *The old man was clever all right, maybe too clever.*

"I'll go with you." Tarra spoke from across the tent.

He flinched at the unexpected voice. "Maybe you'll have to." He twirled the stick between two fingers then tossed it to her. It landed on her naked chest where she let it lay as if she hadn't notice it.

Placing her hand flat over the stick, she sat up holding it. "When do we get started?" The bug repellent had thinned to the point that flies were beginning to make their presence known so she drew her legs up and sat cross-legged to address the fire. "I can teach you to read it if you want."

"Do you think I can learn? Maybe I am too dim to learn such tricks."

She smiled timidly at his attempt at wit and glanced self-consciously toward where Caran slept. She quickly busied herself tending the bug repellent. "You're not dim—just stubborn."

"What are you going to do with Bartan? He's becoming a problem without a woman to keep him in line."

She stopped her task and looked out the raised skirt of the tent, out beyond the clearing, toward the lake. "I don't think he's a very good man. He doesn't fit in. I mean, he's always busy doing something else when work needs to be done."

"Maybe he just needs your help to stay on the correct path."

"I don't want to have to keep him on the path. I want someone who's strong enough to stay on the right path himself." She flung the stick back at him striking him on the chest as she rose. She grabbed her cloak and left the tent in a flurry of smoke.

He followed calling after her. "Wait, I—I just want to be sure you're not making a mistake. I mean, I don't want you to feel pressured by me. I mean—I didn't want you to be mated before your time, but—well now that I know you better, well, I guess you're wise enough to make up your own mind."

"You guess? You're a pompous ass to think that you have the right to decide anything for me! I'm not your sister. I'm the daughter of Tangar. You've taken me at the joining ceremony, yet you don't accept me as your wife… What am I? What am I to do? What's to become of me? The boys my age are afraid of me and the women don't accept me as one of them… I'm alone. You've ruined my life." She stood trembling with her cape draped over her head partially covering her naked frame.

He pulled his cape on in a similar fashion to shield his shoulders from the sun. "I—we, Caran and I, love you as one of our own. We want you to be happy, to be part of our family, to be—one of us."

"Don't you see? I'm not one of you! I'm me... I'm not happy being just half of a person. I'm not a wife. I'm not a real sister. I'm not a little girl... Maybe the times have made me more than my age, but I feel like I need to do something to make things better... Papa haunts my dreams. He wants me to do something better with my life. He wants *you* to do something better. He doesn't want you to be just a hunter. He wants you to be the Seer of the clan of, Tangar. He had faith in you."

Chilcoat stared into her eyes. "You can't know that. He haunts my thoughts too, but I don't know what it means. He doesn't make himself clear and maybe it's just a dream. Maybe I'm just looking for someone else to do my thinking for me."

"I know—I know. I just feel it. I feel like I have to do something. This heat isn't right." She gestured at the shriveled brown stubble in the fields. "The crops are dying and we can't stop it. We water all night and each morning more plants are dead. We have to walk around all day dressed up like ghosts. It's just not right... I danced with the medicine wands the way he taught me. I want to believe that Vau whispered to me. I want to believe! That's all."

He stood staring at the young priestess. The baggy sleeves of her cape covered her arms and formed small wings as she pulled the tanasin stick from his hand. "You wear the robes. I'm only a child."

"What am I to do with you?" He drew her close and hugged her warmly. "I want to believe too... I just... don't feel it the way you do. I knew a different father than you. He taught me to doubt... to know... to demand proof... I'll take the stick, and I'll study it with you, but I'm not signing up for any spirit-walk or anything." He gently fought the stick from her grasp and considered it for a moment before sticking it behind his ear.

After a few hours' rest, Chilcoat stirred to wander restlessly around the camp. He clinched the stick tightly in his fist and tried to remember Tangar. *What would you have done?*

He didn't think of the frail old man that drank too much spirit-tea and talked to rocks. He thought of the strong young man that taught him to hunt and fish and to know right from wrong. *You kept it simple for me. You kept me from your herbs and spirits saying only that I would 'someday know their place'... Dad, would you now teach me of these things?*

Tarra soon joined him as he stood watching the parched fields stir listlessly in the heat. "Are you ready for a lesson?"

He looked solemnly at the young woman. "Right now I have to go find out what's happened to that fool Larkon. Do me a favor, go tell Lan to meet me at the clearing as soon as he can get ready, and tell Caran where we're going, and that I love her, and here—take this damn stick. I wouldn't want to lose it." He rolled the wand thoughtfully between his fingers once before pressing it gently into her hand.

He roused Rancon and met with Bartan, Laot, Lon, and a couple of others in the central clearing. When Lan arrived, Bartan quickly recounted the previous night's venture and they broke the group into small search parties each heading on different paths up the canyon.

By early evening, they had covered most of the likely lowland sites and were working their way up the canyon in short leapfrog bursts of activity. If the cat was near, they gave it plenty of room by making enough noise to give it warning of their approach.

The shadows deepened into night as the groups moved steadily up the valley looking for any trace of their lost companion. There were no signs of either Larkon or the cat. *That means the cat must have made a kill and has already taken to the high country with its prey. Everyone knew the signs and grew anxious with dread that Larkon was the reason for the cat's absence.*

Laot found fresh blood among the rocks of the western canyon but there was no sign of weapons or clothes, so the hope grew that the cat had taken a deer and would be happy for the time being. The trail of blood was hard to follow in the darkness and soon disappeared into the boulders.

The search continued into the early hours of the morning. Laot argued frantically. "We have to go further up the valley. He must've been chasing the cat. He wounded it and has it on the run..."

The others grew tired and frustrated with the lack of signs. They all knew that if the cat had him, it was already too late, and if she didn't, then it didn't matter, so they headed back down the mountain.

Lannon tried to comfort his brothers but it was a sullen group that trudged back to camp. Most of the clan was gathered around the central hearth and the information was shared with several future actions suggested but no real plans made.

Chilcoat addressed the group before it broke up. "Lan, you and your brothers are going to have to stand watch on the gardens every night until we figure out what that cat is up to. I know you don't want to hear this, but we have to face the possibility that your father is gone. If he is, that means the cat has tasted human flesh and will be bold about approaching the fields. If we're able to find your dad, we can relax a little, but until then we need to be very cautious. And some of you others may have to lend a hand. Work with Lannon to be sure none of the field workers or children wander off without protection. Do you understand?"

It had been a long night, and no one was in a festive mood. Chilcoat propped himself on one elbow while arranging his pillow and noticed that Tarra had tucked the stick in amongst his bedding. He had to smile at her tenacity as he looked across the tent where she rested.

He lay on his back and slowly rolled the crooked little wand between his fingers. Holding it up against the background haze in the rafters, he marveled at the intricacies of the design that snaked along its length. He, at last, turned to Tarra to ask her what the bumps and notches meant but found only her naked back. Not wanting to disturb anyone who might actually be sleeping, he simply watched her slow rhythmic breathing until he too fell asleep.

By late afternoon, the camp was beginning to stir and the bugs had grown bold enough to make rest out of the question. Lannon and Charona made their way to the lake for a few moments alone and Chilcoat played warmly with his children. The frailty of life weighed heavily on him, and protecting them from the loss of a tribesman seemed somehow more important to him as he helped Chilton win another round of cards over Chara's domineering ways.

Tarra couldn't endure watching the family scene to which she didn't belong, so she left with her washing tucked under her arm. At the shoreline, she joined the others talking mostly in mourning for Larkon and concern for his family. Someone suggested that perhaps Lan could now return with Charona as his wife to head up the family. Someone else said, "Since Bartan has moved in with them, he should head the household."

Neither option sounded very good to Tarra, but she joined in the speculative banter to try to fit in. "Charona would make a good addition to the family but, I doubt Bartan would fit in very well. He'd have to take Katlan as his mate and she's not likely to go for it. She's a few years older and has little use for a lazy drunkard."

The conversation quickly shifted to concerns of the cat when Charona and Lan approached. Tarra finished her laundry and joined the pair as they wandered toward their hut. They jostled and bumped along in a warm bonding of laughs and giggles approaching their hut.

"What's so funny?" Caran asked as they came bounding into the smoke-filled room.

Lannon scoffed as he shed his wet clothes. "Oh, nothing, the town has us moving in with my mother and Bartan now that my father's dead."

Caran looked solemnly at Chilcoat. They had also been discussing the situation, but not in such crass terms. "Maybe you should consider moving back with your family for a while… Until your dad comes back, I mean." Caran tried to sound optimistic. "Maybe they could use your help, just until things get settled."

He stood in naked silence considering her words. He didn't want to allow himself to think so absolutely about his father. *Moving on so quickly doesn't seem right. If I don't admit that he's gone, then everything's normal. I can go on in the warmth of Chilcoat's family just as before, and everything will be OK*. His hands trembled as he dressed for the night's guard duty. He looked to Charona for comfort as he gathered his weapons and stood in the doorway. "If I go back, you'll have to come with me."

She cast her eyes down knowing that she was not welcome by his mother. "I'll come, but it won't be easy. If you're to be head of the house, then the council is likely to make me the matron, and your mother probably won't go along with that easily."

"Let me worry about the council." Chilcoat spoke with confidence. "Lan, you should probably help your mother and brothers out until we get this matter settled. I don't think it'll be good to have Bartan's influence over those boys go unchecked right now. I think you need to be there to temper his control. You two knew you were taking a difficult path, but I think you can do it... You've proven yourself a good husband and now you have to prove yourself a good man. Besides, maybe your dad will turn up. Maybe he just twisted his ankle or something and needs a couple of days to get back."

* * *

Three days passed with extra caution at night and small search parties in the early evenings. Finally, one of the hunting parties found Larkon's bow. It had scars likely caused by the cat that settled any doubts about his demise.

As the eldest son, Lannon claimed the bow and held a small ceremony at the central hearth where he burned it, despite Laot's objections. As the third born, Laot had no claim on the weapons, but he was perhaps the most affected by the loss of their father. He hadn't yet recognized weakness in him, and burning his weapons in disgrace seemed too harsh, too final.

Laot fought back his tears as he confronted Chilcoat. "He was a master hunter and doesn't deserve the shame of a failed huntsman. I shouldn't have listened to you! I should've been there—we all should've been there. If I'd been there, we would've killed that cat. We'd be heroes—not cowards."

Chilcoat tried to put a good light on Larkon's bravery, but he hadn't condoned the hunt, and his words were somber. "He'll be missed by his family, and he was an able provider that will be missed by us all."

As the ceremony broke up, Lannon and Charona accompanied his mother and brothers back to their hut. Bartan attended, but he stayed in the background and tagged along behind the family like a concerned uncle.

They had found the bow in a place Bartan claimed to have already searched. Chilcoat grumbled as he watched the grieving family depart. "I'll have to talk with him about it." *His position will need to be clear if he is to continue as a part of Larkon's family. As matriarch, Katlan will have the last word, but his presence in the community is questionable. His goal of wooing Tarra has come to nothing because of her absolute rejection of his advances and his predilection to drink. Now with the loss of his drinking buddy, his position in the tribe is weak.*

Bartan pulled Lannon aside as he got ready for duty. "Lan, I've been thinking, since my weapon skills are a little rusty, it might be better if I stand guard with the boys. It'll free you up for more hunting, and give me a chance to do a little practicing."

Lannon had to admit that it made sense, but he hated to let him think he had put anything over on him. *I figure he's lost his nerve and doesn't want to go hunting while that cat's still around.* "Perhaps you're right. That cat smells your fear. And don't ever call me '*Lan*' again... That's the name my friends call me and you're not my friend." Lannon stood defiantly in the door of his mother's tent for a moment then pulled his hood into place and left.

It soon became clear that the cat had cubs and was desperate to keep them fed. The trio frequently checked on the gardens in the early morning hours. It seemed to be on their patrol list when they returned from the lake. A few shouts and well-thrown stones were usually enough to keep them away but, at times, the mother was willing to confront the challenger until the cubs were safely out of the way.

Chilcoat returned from a long night hunting and fell quickly into his normal bedtime routine with a short sexual excursion with Caran. As they lay quietly amongst the sleeping clutter, he thought again of Tangar. *The old man frequently quipped after some wine that, "sex was always better after a good hunt." I can't argue the point, but it bothers me that's the only thing you have to say to me. If you're going to visit my thoughts, why don't you bring some words of wisdom, not just some prurient interest in my sex life?*

He turned on his side in an effort to rid himself of such diversions. Tarra lay a few feet away in the bedchamber vacated by Corona and Lannon. He couldn't help but notice that she too struggled restlessly to reach a sexually charged release into slumber.

He rolled over to face away from her and once again thought of the old man and how he had always doted over the child. *Now she's a woman and I don't know what to do about her. She's great to have around the house when it comes to medicine and babysitting, but she isn't happy.* He closed his eyes and tried to think of other things but, as his hand reached under his pillows, he thought of the stick that she had put there before and wondered vaguely where it was as he finally drifted off to sleep.

A Pleasant Walk

By midday, the heat was unbearable and the children were insistent that they go to the lake. Caran relented and dragged the morning laundry down to the shore. The water felt good and the children finally stopped whining. She was in bliss for a few moments. Tarra also stirred early from the day's rest but decided against a wake-up dip in favor of a quick sponge bath and a few moments alone.

Chilcoat finally stirred and celebrated the solitude with a quick smoke sitting by the morning fire. As he finished, he lamented what little herb remained and considered where he might be able to find more. *That's another thing I miss about Tangar... He always knew where the best herbs grow. Maybe the tanasin stick leads to some smoking herbs. What the hell is tanasin anyway?* He rummaged through his collection bowl but didn't find the stick. Looking up, he noticed Tarra tending to the breakfast dishes. "Have you seen that stick you've been poking me with?"

She stopped her scrubbing long enough to pull the twig from her hair and toss it to him. The light caught her hair in scarlet profusion as it fell silently across her shoulders and tumbled down her chest.

He caught the stick and smiled in response to her questioning gaze. "The old man's been with me lately. He has nothing to tell me, he just comes around to remind me of how things used to be… What does the stick mean? Has he really spoken to you?"

"I don't know. It's like a shooting star. He's gone before I can be sure he's there. I did the dance of the wands as well as I know how. It seemed important to him. He spent a lot of his strength teaching me, just before—he died."

She dried her hands, pulled the medicine bag from its hanger, and approached to kneel next to him. Spreading the cloth flat in front of them, she took the tanasin stick from his hand, and inspected the blunt end carefully twisting it in her fingers to look at all sides. She then scanned the sunburst painted on the cloth and placed the stick down flat, lining it up with first one notch, and then another in the sun's sculpted surface. "I think it fits this one best," she gestured.

The stick lay angled from the sun's face like a twisted little antler protruding from the otherwise regular border of flames. "I think that's the southeast trail that leads over the low hills. See, it has bumps here in the middle of the first section. That means that in a couple of days you'll reach some hills. That seems about right doesn't it? I mean if you took the southeast trail, you'd get to some hills in a three day walk, right?"

"What? Yeah, I guess so. So you're telling me that this stick is a map I am supposed to follow?"

"Yes. It's the wisdom of the Seer… Papa was clear. 'The sticks whisper to the children of Yod, telling a story you must follow to seek wisdom from Hea, the father, and bounty from Vau, the mother'."

Chilcoat reached out almost touching the twig. "What else does this tell you? So far you have me lost in the hills and we're only partway up the stick."

"See how it forks to the right just before the end of the segment. I think that must be a branch in the trail. The second section seems to be flat, but it has lots of little bumps and notches along its length. I think that means the second week has many rocks, but at least it seems to be flat. The last section is shorter, maybe only three days walk, and branches back to the left. Then it finishes up a sharp kink right at the end."

"You're telling me I'm supposed to walk for two and a half weeks out, and two and a half weeks back in this heat, just to find out if the old man's pulling my leg?"

"Yeah, I guess so…"

He sat silently gazing at the crooked little stick lying in front of him. Picking it up, he looked carefully at its intricate notches, bumps, and bends. A warm vision of Tangar sitting solemnly at his hearth carving the stick flashed across his mind. "Tanasin, huh? What the hell is tanasin?"

She timidly whispered. "It's a spirit-herb… I think."

"A what? A spirit-herb... You mean if, and when, we should find it, it'll be some kind of poison that's going to screw with my head? This just keeps getting better and better."

"I don't know for sure, but Vau's herbs of knowledge demand tribute."

Chilcoat stuck the twig behind his ear and waved at the cloth. "You better pick this stuff up for now. I'll have to think about it for a while."

She hung the medicine bag around the shoulders of the mannequin. "I'll come with you if you want." She offered timidly as he got up to leave.

"That cat has a mate and he's probably staked out the oak groves in those hills you have me going through. If I go, I want somebody who can guard my back not do my dishes."

"I want to go. I think I can help." She defiantly grabbed the twig from his ear and jabbed it into the rope of her hair she quickly twisted together.

***

Chilcoat ask Rancon to take over for him while they were gone and filled him in on the quest, just in case he needed to send a search party. Lannon was eager to join the adventure and since Bartan had volunteered to take over his guard duty, he was free. Charona didn't like him going on such a silly mission, especially with the aspiring priestess tagging along. "She's so young, and so is he."

Caran was somber but knew Chilcoat was determined to do something to help the people. *If that means following the duty of the Seer, then, that's what he'll do.* She pulled Tarra aside. "I know you feel you're doing what you should, but I ask you to think carefully about it. You'll be alone with two men for many days. There'll be no privacy and much danger. If things go badly, you'll be a burden on their ability to protect you. Are you sure you're ready to accept the responsibility of hurting another?"

"No. I don't want to hurt anyone, but I don't know what else to do. You know as well as I, that things aren't right. The heat is killing us slowly. The eyes of many of the old have faded long before their time. They've become burdens on their families, and the hunting is bad, especially with that cat around. Daddy would know just what to do. He'd perform the duty of the Seer and take a spirit-walk. But, he's gone... and Chilcoat resists his ways. I know it's not my place, but I want to help."

"I know. I know. But, there's a pain in my heart that begs you not to go. I've grown to love you dearly, and I am afraid that I'll lose you. Or maybe I am afraid that I'll lose him—to you." The two embraced softly and lingered for several moments in silence.

Tarra finally broke the spell. "You've nothing to fear from me. I love you too dearly to ever hurt you." They kissed gently and held each other tight. The two stood alone amongst the scattered bedding and explored feelings that left both of them a little aroused and confused.

"I'll tell him that he must be careful. I don't want either of you hurt."

"I'll be careful." Chilcoat offered from the doorway as he entered. He stepped forward and held both of them warmly lingering for several moments holding Caran. "This'll be a simple walk in the woods and we'll be right back. If we find something... great... if not, well maybe then we can put the old man to rest." He turned to Tarra. "Let me see what you are going to bring."

She stood perplexed for a moment thinking first of clothing and food then considered the medicine bag. She quickly rummaged through it, made a small first-aid kit, and dumped the remaining contents behind the mannequin. She stood a quick muster in front of Chilcoat and asked if he could think of anything else she should take.

"Water, we'll need lots of water, and some jerky just in case."

Lannon and Charona arrived and made last-minute preparations for the long trek. Chilcoat considered waiting for the cool of the evening but decided that they should get started while they could still see the trail clearly. Final goodbyes were made and they were just about to leave when Chilcoat paused by the door. He looked at Tarra skeptically and then at the mannequin standing next to him. Grabbing the tallest rod sticking out of the head of the figure, he wrenched it free. "Here," he held it out to her. "You'll need this. Do you have the damn twig?"

She nodded timidly patting the bag she had slung over her shoulder. The three specters skirted the edge of the village not wanting to attract any more attention than they already had. Their cloaks swished and rustled in the dry grass that had overgrown the seldom-used trail.

Chilcoat stopped their progress early in the evening, reasoning that while it would take them longer than the stick metered, it would be a lot safer to wait for daylight. They sought out a stony clearing amongst the tall weeds that choked the shallow valley.

By first light they were ready, if not anxious, to resume their trek. Tall reeds closed on the stream that trickled along the gorge and blocked any breeze that might try to stir the valley. The soggy hallway meandered along the valley floor where signs of snakes and small game marked the path. The undergrowth smelled of summer and hummed with insects but it also blocked the view of any predator that might be lurking.

The men grumbled and growled a familiar guttural chant and frequently struck out and slashed at the bushes with their spears. Tarra didn't know the hunting song but she occasionally interjected a shrill screech that she figured would serve to alarm anything hiding in the bushes. Each time she did it, Lannon gave her a dismissive groan, but she went ahead and did it anyway.

By midweek, they reached the first of many hills scattered before them. Lannon quickly trudged to the top of the first hill and surveyed the scope of their challenge. From the crest of the knoll, he could see the trail continuing along the low pass toward a small cluster of oak trees. From there, the hills continued in golden profusion in all directions. The oaks spilled down the face of the hills giving the distant vista a mottled appearance. "It looks like it'll be days to get through these hills at the rate we're going. There are some trees up ahead about a mile. Why don't you guys go set up a camp and I'll see if I can scare up some game back in the hollow?"

Chilcoat was a little dismayed at their progress, but was relieved that the stick had been right so far. "You be careful and don't take long. If that tom's around, he may have the same idea."

"Yeah, I won't go too deep. I think I spotted a rabbit run a little ways back. If I'm lucky, we'll have fresh meat."

They loosened their clothes to fit socially acceptable policy while they waited for Lannon to return. The shade of the oak grove was a relief and the rest was welcome as they reveled in the coolness of their naked forms. Tarra pulled the stick from her bag and puzzled over its contours again. "This section is just straight, so I guess that means we stick to the trail. But, right here, just before the end of the hill section, it jogs to the right. I think the trail must split there and we're to take the right fork." She poked at a particular bump on the twig.

Chilcoat grunted indifferently raising his head to gaze out to the horizon. Checking his water supply, he measured out a small sip. "You need to drink. Not too much, but you have to keep wet."

Lan finally returned with a rabbit that he presented to Tarra in a dismissive gesture dropping it at her feet. He then proceeded to remove his cloak and loincloth, settling in for a well-deserved rest. His speed in meeting a socially correct level of cover was slow and animated as he paused to drink and wipe his brow before sitting and covering his semi-aroused state.

Tarra watched the display with some note. She had never really been the target of such a preening exhibition. It was a little flattering, but not really of interest to her. She quickly set to work preparing the rabbit and refused to return his gaze.

The trio spent the hottest part of the day under the oaks swatting flies and trying to stay out of the sun. As the afternoon began to cool, Chilcoat stirred and roused the others. Again, Lannon was slow in donning his cloak with plenty of time to exhibit his masculinity to the young girl.

"If you wave that thing in my face one more time, I'm going to cut it off while you sleep and feed it to the dogs." Tarra pulled her cloak into place and turned to retrieve her walking stick.

Lannon stood speechless with his cloak loosely draped over his shoulder and his loincloth hanging limply from his hand.

"Ha! She's got you there." Chilcoat scoffed as he headed out from the protective cover of the oak.

Tarra was quick to follow, letting out one of her now familiar screeching howls, as she hurried to catch up. Lannon groaned and quickly finished getting ready. He lingered a macho distance back as the troop wound its way among the rolling meadowland.

By the evening of the eighth day, they found a fork in the trail and reconsidered their options. They could continue for a few more hills and get a glimpse of what tomorrow's trek was going to be, or they could make camp in the pleasant comfort of the oak grove. They decided to just set up camp and try to get some rest. Lannon ventured to the top of the nearest hill while hunting, but reported that he couldn't see anything, and didn't catch anything either.

As the night progressed, each stood watch listening for the cat and letting the others rest. Their meager fire was probably enough to keep it away, but Tarra gathered a couple of tumbleweeds just in case. *If I can't scare it away by waving them around, I'll light them on fire while the guys get up.*

As soon as there was enough light to make out the path, they started their walk. It was as cool as it was going to get, and they wanted to make the best of it. Lannon quickly reconnoitered the path to the left and returned with a report of more hills. The fork to the right led them past the final hills and out into a stony basin. It looked as though the rains had channeled through depositing the austere landscape with scrub brush and rugged water washed stones.

Chilcoat gestured toward a ravine that was still deep in shadow. "The trail will be hard to follow in all of this rubble. Does the stick tell you anything that will help?"

She quickly retrieved the implement and held it up in the early rays of the sun. The second section of the twig was straight and flat with an intricate snakeskin pattern etched into it making a series of textured patches. "I guess that means beware of snakes, other than that I don't see anything. The bumps are sort of like little rounded stones, but there's no hint of a trail mark."

"Here, let me see." Chilcoat took the stick and held it up at arm's length rolling it slowly in the light. "You know if you role it like this, the lines zigzag back and forth. Maybe the trail zigzags?"

"No, I think the trail is straight like the stick, but straight where? It could head off in any direction across this wasteland. No, wait, the final little tip jogs back to the left and tweaks up a little at the end. There must be some mountain or ridge or something, maybe you can see it from the hilltop." Tarra turned pointedly to Lannon.

"Yeah, alright, but I warn you it might make me hot." He smirked at her frown and jogged off toward the nearby hill. Chilcoat couldn't help but smile at their adolescent flirtations but hoped it wouldn't lead to too much friction.

Lannon returned in a few minutes and unconvincingly said, "There might be a rock outcropping off to the left just over that way." He gestured with his arm as he took a drink of water. "But I can't be sure. It's pretty far away, and the light isn't good. There're still lots of deep shadows. It may just be a boulder or something, but it is the only thing sticking up on the horizon. The rest is just rocks, nothing but rocks and scrub brush."

Chilcoat turned to Tarra. "Are you sure you want to go through with this? I mean, my trust in the old man and his damn sticks is starting to wear thin. The more I think about walking all over the place looking for some weed, the more I think he was wrong to have faith in such things. We could head back, spend a little time hunting in the oaks, and go home as heroes with a deer or a pig."

She clutched at the stick thoughtfully running her thumb up and down along its length looking deeply into his eyes. "You're the Seer. We'll do as you wish. It's only a stick." She twisted her hair into a tight rope, piled it on the back of her head, and pinned it in place with the wand.

Chilcoat flinched at her challenge. "Alright, we'll go on, but if we don't find water today, we'll have to turn back. This heat has taken a toll." Gathering up his things, he headed off in the general direction shown by Lannon. "It seems to be a little downhill this way so there might still be some water down there."

The trail meandered among rocks and boulders weaving a rough arc toward a low point in the gully that sheltered a small pond. The water was a pale shade of yellow but it was usable when boiled and a welcome encouragement to the troop.

The harsh landscape offered little except snakes and lizards to eat, so by the end of the second week they had nearly exhausted their supplies. They were happy to, at last, reach a sandy embankment leading up to a large grassland. They could make out a small gray rock outcrop in the distance standing defiantly against the monotonous flat skyline.

A spit of terrain jutted into the arroyo making a convenient backdrop for their evening camp. It gave them a safe boundary on three sides so they quickly built a fire, and Lannon provided a large snake for dinner. He thought about taking advantage of the serpent when he presented it to Tarra for preparation, but decided to respect her boundaries, electing simply to drape it over the hearthstone.

Tarra diced the snake into bite-sized pieces and rummaged up some skewers from the surrounding bushes. When it was ready, she prepared to offer the first piece to Lannon as was the custom in honor of his having provided it. She took the uncooked tail and impaled it on a skewer so that it draped as a limp little sausage from the end of the twig. She then divided the remaining pieces carefully distributing them with the largest pieces shared evenly between the men. She held the tail in one hand and the hunter's share in the other as she walked awkwardly toward Lannon holding the tail in front of her loins. She wiggled it as he turned to accept the meal.

He hesitated a moment trying to think of some way to retaliate then took the skewer rattling it toward her. "Ah, just what I was hoping for, a piece of tail from the priestess." He stabbed the skewer into his hair so that the limp little appendage dangled in front of his face. "What do you think? The other guys will be jealous that I was the first to get such an offer."

She clinched her teeth and shoved his food into his hand turning quickly to get the other servings. "Dream on, Lan... you'll need more than that to convince anyone you're worthy of my favors."

She sat reflecting that it had been years since she had called him 'Lan'. *When we were kids, he was the eldest of our playgroup and everyone called him Lan. I was Tar. Kids can't be bothered with full names or titles of respect. I had always looked up to him since he was the oldest and wisest of our little band of ruffians, but now he seems no older or wiser than he was then.* She watched as he laid back to enjoy his meal with the serpent tail dangling in front of his face.

The stars winked indifferently at her frustrations until she felt his strong young hand gently squeezing her shoulder. At first, it seemed a comforting caress but quickly transitioned to an irritation as she regained full consciousness. "Get up, it's your watch." Lannon's familiar voice grated the still night air. She groaned meekly as she stirred from her bed.

"I think there's a pack of javelina scouring the gully over there, but they shouldn't be a problem. It's a good sign the cat isn't around." Lan settled on his back and pulled his cloak over as a bug guard. "You might keep an eye out toward the savanna though... I think there may be some ground apes watching us." He gestured dismissively toward the grassland that spilled out to the horizon.

She couldn't be sure he was serious, but she would stay alert anyway. She checked the fire and noted that he had tended it just before he retired. *Maybe there's hope for him after all,* she thought as she sat cross-legged holding her walking stick and watching the stars. Chilcoat snorted and grumbled and was soon joined by Lan in a sort of conversation with first one then the other growling threats into the night. She watched the goat-herder march imperceptibly across the heavens and listened for any noise in the bushes.

The apes, if there were any, didn't present themselves and eventually it was time to rouse Chilcoat for his turn at watch. She knelt next to him and hesitated watching his rhythmic breathing. As she placed her hand on his shoulder, his arm seemed so much more massive than she had ever noticed. She nudged him gently pulling her hand back at the first sign of movement. After two more attempts, he grumbled and acknowledged that he was awake. She lingered for a moment still feeling the heat and dampness of his body. "It is your watch."

Tarra wiped her hand nervously on her cloak and settled in for some rest. Her hand fell near her face as she tried to find a more comfortable position. She could smell his scent. It wasn't like her father or any of the boys she knew. She didn't bother moving her hand. She simply closed her eyes and drifted into a half-sleep.

By morning, the bugs from the grassland were humming and the camp was quickly broken with both Chilcoat and Lannon peeing on the fire. Tarra ignored their display even though Lannon coughed and choked loudly as the smoke from his effort drifted in her direction.

She busied herself once again consulting the stick. *The final section—at last,* she thought, as she held it up in the first rays of the sun. It jogged to the left and was flat and smooth with a fine web of grass etched into its surface. Just before the end, it bent upward crowning the nub with a crooked little finger. "Since there're no hills to send Lannon up, we'll have to figure it out from here." She smirked at Lannon's obvious irritation.

A dull haze hung on the plain giving the grass a slight gray tint in the morning light. The trail leading away from their camp meandered aimlessly across the grassland and promised only ticks and thorns.

After three days of growing anticipation, they reached the base of the cliff. Their disappointment was palpable since there was no apparent trail or fabled reward of tanasin for their effort, just a massive granite crag rising abruptly out of the grassy plain. The heat was relentless and Lannon balked at Tarra's suggestion that he climb the cliff to reconnoiter.

They skirted the edge of the rock face looking for something that might provide a hint of their goal. Tarra was paying particular attention to the plants growing along the cliff face but found nothing of interest. She was familiar with most of the scrub-brush clinging to the rocks and none of it was anything special.

By early evening, they had searched a little over a mile to the south and returned to where they had started. This time the conversation was more philosophical. They found nothing that they considered worthy of the weeks of toil and hardship. She found some conche growing near the edge of the rock face that she needed to replenish her supply, but it wasn't tanasin, and it wasn't on the cliff.

The rock face caught the light from the setting sun and amplified it into pulsing waves of heat. As they rested and ate, Chilcoat thought cynically of Tangar. *Is this just one of your jokes, a fool's errand to teach your foolish children one last lesson? Whatever value you found in your sticks and stories is gone...* He plucked the twisted little twig from Tarra's hair.

"Ow!"

"Sorry."

"You could ask."

"I said I was sorry." He slowly ran his finger along the length of the stick. Thinking back over the last couple of weeks, he remembered the hills, the rocky gully, and the grassy plain. *I can't help but admire the old man's attention to detail in carving the wand. He had captured the spirit of those places in astonishing detail with only a few strokes of his knife blade, but now the stick doesn't speak to me.* He sat in the sandy clearing and held the stick up to the sky studying the details of the final little quirk at the end. It jigged back and forth irregularly and ended abruptly with a small blunt tip. *I wonder if maybe it's broken and missing a piece that has more information on it.*

The cliff face glowed orange in the failing light and provided a flaming backdrop as Tarra stood over him expectantly. She had pulled her cloak up to expose her torso and stood with her arms spread to capture the slight breeze that whispered in off the savanna.

He held the stick up to her. "You got any ideas? We seem to be at the end of it and I don't see anything."

She stood with her hair aflame and her sleeves forming small drooping wings against the orange glow. "Maybe we should just make camp and think about it for a while."

"Maybe… Lan, how about doing a little scouting for us again? When you've rested, you can go on around the next bend before the light fails and see if there is anything worth looking at. If you find something we'll check it out tomorrow, if not, well—we'll have something to talk about when you get back."

"I'll see if I can scare up something to eat while I'm at it." He pulled his hair back and wiggled the snake tail at Tarra as he inserted the skewer along his scalp. He had taken to using it to hold his cape off his forehead and took advantage of the opportunity to irritate her before setting off in a slow jog toward the next rock outcropping. She turned away without speaking and studied the silhouette of the stick against the orange background.

Chilcoat watched her for a moment then jumped to his feet. "Let me see that." He once again took the stick and held it at arm's length. Using the glow of the cliff as a background, he remembered how Tangar had told him stories when he was a child. *I vaguely remember a story of great adventure with flaming cliffs and magic people that lived in great stone houses. I wonder if these are the flaming cliffs. I don't remember the moral of the story... There was always a moral to his stories. Maybe that's why I didn't listen as well as I should have. I always felt cheated when the old man would drag me into a good story of adventure and then ruin it with some moral that just seemed to confuse the ending. I could never know when he was telling the truth and when he was making things up to fit his lessons.* The flaming cliffs had always been one of those he had chosen not to believe. "Flaming cliffs," he muttered. "Damn you, old man, and your flaming cliffs."

"What's that? Flaming what?"

"Oh, nothing, just trying to remember something. Here, why don't you see if you can get something flaming." He took the ember pot from its place and handed it to her. Sticking the twig behind his ear, he set off looking for stones to build a hearth.

By the time the fire was built, and bedding material gathered, Lannon straggled back with a single plump quail hen that was quickly prepared and eaten. "I covered nearly a mile further along the cliff but I didn't see anything very promising. There's a place that I might be able to climb, but the light was pretty bad by then so I'll need to look at it again in the morning to be sure."

Tarra looked up from her task. "Did you see any tanasin?"

"How the hell would I know? There are lots of bushes, but I don't know which one you're looking for."

"Wishful thinking, I guess. Does that mean we stay another day?"

"Yeah, I guess so." Chilcoat spoke after thinking for several moments. "Since the hunting's been good, we can stay another day. Maybe we can stock-up for the trip back."

The watch schedule was set and Chilcoat sat by the fire with weapons at the ready. He smoked a pipe full of herbs and watched the sky for signs, but only an occasional shooting star drew his attention. The absence of the sky-fire still haunted his thoughts. *The weather over the last months has been horrific. The rain and wind with storm after storm of relentless lightning etched my memory. Day and night, the conflagration had hissed and pulsed like a living creature while the rain fell relentlessly. The coming of summer and the absence of the sky-fire was such a welcome blessing at first. The clouds cleared and the sky was quiet. Everyone hoped that life would return to normal and the warm summer months would bring their bounty, but instead, the heat's killing everything.*

It was odd, he thought. The night was frightening when lightning ruled the heavens, and now, it's the daylight we fear. The night has become a friendly shelter from the heat of the sun. In the clear night sky, the stars seem closer and brighter than they ever have.

A skirmish in the grasses beyond the edge of the clearing drew his attention as he grabbed his spear and watched the darkness for movement. A second scuffle, a bit to the left, showed a rabbit fleeing. *Probably a snake,* he guessed. He absentmindedly stoked the fire and watched the sparks rise to the heavens. The radiance of the cliff drew a light breeze in off the grassland as the heat rose up the face of the rocks. *That's good,* he thought. *Our scent won't draw any unwanted attention drifting across the savanna. I haven't seen any cats, but I'd be surprised if there isn't a couple nearby.*

The goat-herder is fully above the horizon now, so it's time to wake Tarra for her watch. He tended the fire one last time and readied his bed before reaching to wake her.

She had her cloak drawn over her slight frame as she lay with her back to the fire. He touched her gently on the arm and felt her moist warmth soaking through the fabric. She soon rose and left him to his rest as he lay quietly thinking about the warmth lingering in his fingers and the commitment that he felt for Caran.

They enthusiastically greeted the coolness of the morning as they broke camp. Lan and Tarra went through their usual bickering about who should carry what, while Chilcoat gathered embers and put the fire out. When he was nearly done, he noticed that Tarra was timidly watching him. She peeked out from the cloak draped over her head and acted as if she was adjusting her load, but her eyes lingered on his form until Lannon joined the ritual. That was enough to break the spell and send her marching toward the cliff face. "I want to see if that bush is anything I can use."

The trio made their way along the rock face continuing north until midmorning. They ruled out Lannon's possible climbing route from the previous day but found a second more promising site further along the cliff.

Lannon peered skeptically at a crack in the rock face. "Looks like those bushes might make footholds, but the other branch might be more direct."

Chilcoat deferred to his judgment. "You're doing the climbing so it's up to you."

Tarra wanted to continue further along the wall looking for her herbs. "I don't think you can climb that, so let's just keep going."

Lannon climbed easily up the escarpment for the first ten feet but found a thorny little bush to be a formidable barrier. He took his knife and began slashing aimlessly at the resilient little specter. Bits and pieces rained down on the bystanders, but he gained little headway. "I don't suppose this is what you're looking for?" He called down from his perch.

She called back to him. "No, it is just some sort of tersen, I think. I can make you some tea out of it if you want, but it'll just make you pee and you do enough of that already. Just try going around it."

He considered the alternatives and decided that perhaps he could step over it now that he had trimmed some of the top branches. The awkward exercise rewarded him with scratches along his inner thigh and a near fall from the narrow shelf. He was able to sidle along the ledge for several more feet before he confronted another bush of similar extraction. He tried simply pushing it aside while he stepped in amongst its brittle branches but his leggings quickly became entangled in the thorns. He tried pivoting his weight, but the stone he was standing on crumbled and he fell with a resounding thump onto the sandy clearing at the base of the cliff.

Lannon grumbled as he determined that only his pride was hurt. "It's almost like those weeds are growing in just the right place to make things tricky."

Chilcoat tried to sooth his pride. "Maybe you're right. Maybe we should move on a little further. If we don't find a better spot, we'll rest and head home tomorrow."

For the remainder of the afternoon they walked along the edge of the savanna keeping a respectable distance from the flaming cliff. By evening, they reached a large flat stone that had fallen from the crag making a convenient resting spot. It was a couple of feet thick and roughly rounded from rolling the last few hundred yards down the rubble pile that buttressed the rock face. The channel it had gouged in the rubble had long since lost any distinctive edge as it swept out a gently curving arc that ended at the base of the cliff.

Lannon was anxious to end the journey. "This'll make a good bed for tonight. We'll be up out of the bugs for a change."

Tarra continued to hope the whole trip hadn't been in vain. "We still have an hour of light. Maybe it's just around the next bend."

Chilcoat considered the rocky outcrop another mile down the cliff and the stone platform before him. "Let's call it quits for today. I think Lan's right. This is as good as we are going to get for tonight. We can think about our next move after we've had some rest."

The failing light again set the cliff ablaze in orange profusion with dark scars and pockets where shadows had already taken hold. He relaxed and considered their plight. *We've already spent weeks on this silly venture and have found nothing. The old man has had the last laugh after all,* he thought, pulling the stick from the clutter Tarra had gathered near the fire. *Even as you slumber in Yod you mock me. Are you teaching me something I don't yet understand? Father, you know you must speak plainly for me.*

In frustration at Tangar's indifference, he was about to use the stick to light his pipe when he caught a glimpse of Tarra tending her cleanup duties. She was kneeling on the platform silhouetted against the blaze of the cliff face. Her skin glowed with the moisture of a long day and her hair fell to cover her shoulders. She pulled it back, twisted it into a bun, and began searching the clutter for the stick. He reconsidered his use of the twig and held it out to her. She overlooked him at first then recognized his offer with a dismissive droop of her shoulders. She took the stick and twisted it through her hair before returning to tend to the cooking of leftover meat.

He watched her delicate form for a moment then turned his attention back to his pipe. The acrid smoke of the freshly picked herb burned his throat but a full stomach comforted his mood. The cliff glowed in the last rays of the sun and the crags and cracks formed a web of dark shadows on its face. As he lay there watching the growing complexity of the design, it struck him as something very familiar. *I can't put my finger on it, but it reminds me of something. The cracks in an old cooking pot or the cliff face at the falls...* He closed his eyes and rested his thoughts as the jagged pattern faded on his eyelids. "The stick," he called out! "Let me see the stick."

"What? Why? You aren't going to break it are you?" Tarra pulled the twig from her hair and held it protectively to her chest.

"No, no, I just want to see it for a minute." He held it up at arm's length silhouetted against the pale orange of the cliff. He moved it slowly from side to side squinting with one eye. "There! You old bastard, there it is." He twisted the twig slightly adjusting the last little crook to match the outline of one of the jagged shadows on the cliff face. "That's our path. See, it lines up perfectly. Well OK, maybe not perfect, but it's a good match."

She leaned close to him and tried to see his vision. Putting her hand on his, she steadied it for a moment then wrenched the stick from his grasp and tried doing her own matching exercise. "I don't know, maybe that one, or this one." She moved her arm and tilting her head.

"Let me see," Lannon said. "If I'm going to have to climb it, I'd better get a good look at it before the light fades." He skeptically moved the stick back and forth at various arm lengths then it occurred to him that he could use the platform to steady his hand. He jumped down off the backside of the stone and moved to the far edge, bending down to put the blunt end of the twig on the smooth surface. He crouched behind the stone to see if he could find a match in the crags.

Tarra watched his antics for a moment then jumped down beside him. She brushed the stone surface and blew dust from the cracks and crevices along its edge. "Here, let me see it." She blew several more times to clean out a distinctive dimple in the stone surface. "The guide stone... I remember him talking about a guide stone, but it was all jumbled up with a bunch of gibberish about houses of stone or people of stone or oceans of grass. I just figured he was delirious."

She carefully wedged the blunt end of the stick into the hole and crouched to view the cliff. Moving her head back and forth tilting it slightly, she began brushing the rock surface again. With some considerable effort, she uncovered distinctive smooth spots on either side of the borehole. She put a hand on each spot and lined up her sight with the twig against the now dull brown cliff face. "I think that's it. Look quick." She grabbed Lannon by the hand and dragged him down. "Put your hands here and here and keep your arms straight."

"I guess I can climb that. I'll have to get past those weeds, but maybe it won't be too bad."

"What weeds? You're looking at the wrong thing. Here, get out of my way." She bumped him aside with her hip and leaned over to reassess the view. "There, see? Put your eye right here so the bottom section lines up with the trail left by the guide stone. See where it broke away from the cliff up near the top. It hit that ledge and looks like it bounced about halfway down and rolled along that ravine until it got here."

"Hmm, yeah, I think I see what you mean." He put his hands on her waist and leaned in close to her, sighting along her point of view. "You mean that first ledge leading to the left?" He casually ran his hand along her side and pressed against her legs.

She suspended her effort and straightened up. Plucking the twig from its nest, she casually pressed her heel on his toe and ground it firmly as she turned to leave. "I guess you can figure it out from here then."

He grimaced but didn't say anything until she was well clear. "Yeah, I guess I have it figured out."

"Good!" Tarra twisted her hair and used the twig to pin it in place as she climbed back onto the platform. "Tomorrow we'll find out for sure."

"Yeah, sure... If there is anything to find, I guess I'll find it."

The night swept in with the wind gusting up the cliff and stirring the grass in waves of excitement. Tarra chanted a woman's song, softly mocking her culinary duties, as she finished storing the dried meat for the long walk home. The smoke from the fire had a heavy scent of meadow-brush, and a continuous trail of sparks streamed into the night sky. The platform served well to keep them above the bugs, but it was a little small for the three of them and the demanding fire.

Dawn ushered in a pack of dogs yelping in the distance. Lannon rose to better judge their approach but decided it wasn't worthy of further concern. He stretched in the first rays of the sun and jumped down from the pedestal moving stiffly to the edge of the clearing to take care of personal issues. He returned with some kindling and stirred the fire to life with a cloud of sparks. Chilcoat and Tarra began to stir but remained in their beds trying to eke out the last few moments of rest.

"You two are missing the glory of the dawn's Graces." Lannon jibed from within the shower of smoke and sparks.

"The Graces can wait a few minutes since they were nice enough to bring me a stack of morning wood." Chilcoat grumbled and rolled away from the dawn horizon burying his face under his arm. Tarra simply pulled her cloak up to cover her face.

After a quick meal, they decided that Tarra would remain at the guide stone and use the medicine stick to direct his path and Chilcoat would relay her hand signs at the base of the cliff and help if anything went wrong.

"What am I looking for? I know it's a bush, but what does it look like?" Lannon asked as he cinched his legging tight around his calf.

"The stick has three notches on the end. That means the plant has three leaves on the end of each branch." Tarra held the stick out for inspection and drew a rough outline in the sand.

He looked at it dismissively and turned to face the cliff. "And which path am I to take?"

"I thought you said you had it all figured out."

"Just checking to see if you changed your mind." He pulled his cloak into place and headed toward the cliff with Chilcoat in trail.

"Never." She called out to him as she took the stick and wedged it in place in the guide stone. She draped her cloak over her head forming a loose tent along her outstretched arms as she leaned on the stone and sighted the path on the cliff. "Just head up the gully on the right, I'll let you know when you've gone too far."

While the path was not the one he would have chosen, his progress was steady with only minor detours around thorn bushes and rock-falls. Tarra called out course corrections and pointed her spear to signal direction changes. Chilcoat, in turn, called up the cliff to make sure he followed the guidance and wasn't in any trouble. A couple of times he called back down the cliff to be sure of her path selection since, from where he stood, there seemed to be better alternatives. By mid-morning, he had made it to a ridge that let him rest and reconnoiter.

Lannon gathered his things and turned to the cliff resuming his climb along the narrow ledge. He was soon behind a rock outcropping that was beginning to calve away from the cliff. It blocked his view down the mountain, but it sheltered him from the heat of the sun and served as an easy path cut into the rock face. By wedging himself against it, he easily scaled the last several yards until it opened onto a large plateau. There were clumps of bushes and a cluster of trees that blocked his view toward the south and a wide expanse of low shrubs scattered across the vista. He turned and waved to the specks at the base of the cliff before cautiously walking out onto the flat terrain. *It's all very odd... It's quiet, yet I sense the presence of something, maybe a cat.* He pulled his knife to the ready.

After several minutes of walking, the bushes changed variety in a gentle curve leading away to his left as if they were chasing a stream. He followed their arc until it intersected a different type of bush trailing a similar curved path leading back toward the cliff's edge.

The clay under his feet was smooth and unbroken with only occasional vines and runners obscuring it. *People have obviously been here and have left their mark, but not recently. It doesn't look like anyone has tended these gardens in years.*

As he rounded the curve, he noticed a cliff edge horizon ahead. He approached carefully while still scanning for signs of attack from the bushes. He stared blankly for several moments as he looked down into a courtyard hidden from the savanna below. A huge triangular gallery of windows and doorways two levels deep stretched out before him. The walls followed the same gentle curving arc of the gardens and formed a terrace with three well-worn stone stairways that led down into a plaza in which a large round platform stood. He walked around to the closest stairs and cautiously descended into the courtyard. Pausing at the first level, he peeked into the nearest doorway.

Moving down the second run of stairs, he wandered around the courtyard for several minutes peering into doorways. There were remnants of recent animal habitation, but no signs of people.

He used a second set of stairs to return to the plateau and immediately recognized a path branching out across the flat terrain. There were feral crops scattered in sparse clumps and patches across the landscape.

He wandered the curved paths amongst the segmented garden undergrowth and eventually found a small spring that trickled into a pond, but he still hadn't found the stupid bush he was looking for. He hesitated for a moment and decided that it didn't warrant further consideration. He quickly found his way back along the path to the cliff face and onto the ledge overlooking the savanna. He stood waving and yelling to his companions. "Come up here, you won't believe this!"

Chilcoat curtailed his hunting foray and stood questioning his perception. "What's wrong? Do you need help?" He shouted back up the cliff.

"Come up! You have to see this. I found a palace." He stood waving his arms.

"What? You found what? Bring it down so we can get out of here."

Tarra joined Chilcoat and they tried to make sense of what they heard. They decided it didn't really matter. Lannon apparently had found something and wasn't coming down, so they would have to go up. The camp was broken down and they began the long trek up the cliff. The path was more treacherous to negotiate than either of them had anticipated. It gave Tarra a newfound respect for Lannon's rock climbing prowess and Chilcoat an envy of his youth.

By late afternoon, they stood bewildered in the courtyard. Lan spent the time harvesting a sample of the plants he found growing in the fallow garden and created a display on the platform in the courtyard. "Well, what do you think? Are any of these the bush you're looking for?"

Tarra ran her hand along the carvings that lined the edge of the stage. "Are you kidding me? Look at this place, and all you can think about is plants?"

Chilcoat spoke to Tangar as he wandered slowly around the courtyard peeking into doorways and probing piles of refuse. "You crafty old bastard... What have you gotten us into now?"

Lannon sat on the edge of the platform. "This place gives me the creeps. It's like it's haunted or something."

"This might be it." Tarra offered as she sorted the bundles of herbs into accept/reject piles. "I think you can eat these, but I'm not sure what this is. I'll need to test them. Where did you get this?" She held up a short branch.

"Up there." Lannon gestured to the edge of the cliff dwellings over his shoulder. Tarra dropped the stem she was holding and started up the nearby stairs.

"You be careful up there." Chilcoat called after her as he ventured into what looked like the main social hall. It had two large doorways and three windows low on the wall facing onto the courtyard. The doors led into a spacious room with more doorways at the rear leading deeper into the mountain. "What's back in here?"

"Beats me. I spent most of my time picking weeds for the princess."

"Hmm… Smells like rats and probably a snake."

"Yeah, what do you suppose this place was? Who lived here, and where did they go?"

"Or, more importantly, why did they leave? I don't see any signs of war so maybe they just ran out of food."

"I don't think so. There seems to be lots of food and water up on the roof and it's so hard to get here I can't imagine an enemy forcing anybody out. Maybe they all got sick and died."

"Maybe, but then there should be bodies or something. There isn't anything left. If they left in a hurry, they would have left things behind. There isn't anything. The place is empty."

"Maybe it all rotted away."

"Yeah, maybe, but it seems like there would be something left."

"Maybe that's what all this is." Lannon poked at a pile of refuse with his staff.

"Well, I don't know, but I guess we should find Tarra and get this over with." They returned to the central plaza and made their way up the stairs to the garden. They found Tarra tugging on a large plant near the far end of the garden. "Have you found it?"

"I think so. But I need help pulling it out."

"Here, let me." Lannon elbowed her aside and leaned into the task.

She cut the root from the stalk and washed it in the nearby pond. "There, I think this is what we came for, the little man from the Sky Temple." She held the small tuber up by its trunk.

Lannon grumbled as he washed his hands. "Little man, huh? Well, it doesn't look like much considering the pain in the ass we've gone through."

"No? If I am right, it is a spirit-herb and you should respect it. We need to burn these branches and offer prayers for taking him from his home."

Chilcoat recollected, "Sky Temple? Yeah, I remember Tangar telling stories about a Sky Temple. That was all just a bunch of fairytales about magic little people flying around in the clouds with wings on their feet."

"Yeah, well here's one of those little people." Tarra held the root with its two legs hanging down from its body. "See, it has arms and legs and it even has a penis just about your size." She pointed out the small nub between the leg branches to Lannon.

He looked to Chilcoat for guidance but with none coming decided not to bother acknowledging her assault. "How long is all this praying going to take? If we have the damn thing, can't we just go home and worry about oblations later? This place gives me the creeps."

"No! The little man needs to know we have taken him for a good cause or he'll haunt us with bad spirits."

Chilcoat stood gazing across the feral landscape. At the far side of the plateau, the sun was setting near a large rock that he was sure must have some astronomical significance to some ancient people. "Again with the spirits... That old man is going to drive me crazy with his stories and spirits and crap. What are we supposed to do now?"

"The rest of the plant needs to be offered in thanks before the sun fully sets and then the root needs to be prepared and the Seer is to take the gift meal with the Spirit."

"That's it? That should be easy." Lannon assessed the pile of branches.

"Yeah well, then the Seer walks with the Spirit."

"Why doesn't that comfort me?" Chilcoat knew the answer.

"Well, you wear the robes." Tarra looked contemptuously at him.

"Yeah, don't remind me." Chilcoat bent to retrieve his weapons. "Well, pick them up. That pile of rocks looks like a likely spot." He gestured first at the pile of branches then to the far edge of the plateau.

The group wound their way across the garden landscape and approached what appeared to be a crude altar of some sort. It had a large hearth bed nested in the front and a chimney stone near the edge of the cliff. A hint of soot from some ancient fire still clung to the face of the stone. The hearth needed clearing of displaced stones, but the dead leaves made a good start for their ceremonial blaze. They soon added the green branches, and the three of them sat quietly chewing on dried meat and watching the smoke drift across the garden. Tarra had trimmed the tips off the extremities of the little man and placed the root standing near the hearth as if it was watching the blaze.

"That's a little silly, isn't it?" Chilcoat scoffed at her actions.

"It's cooking. You want to eat it raw?"

"I don't want to eat it at all. What's it going to do to me? I don't think poisoning myself is such a good idea, you know?"

"Daddy often walked with the Spirit."

"Yeah and look what it did for him. He was always talking to himself and making up stories and who knows what all."

"He knew about this temple. He brought us here, didn't he? Just because you didn't listen to him doesn't mean he didn't know what he was talking about."

"Yeah, yeah… I know, I just don't like being out of control, and talking with spirits is just a little too weird for me."

"I'll be with you." She held her hand out to him.

"Oh, you'll be with me all right, and you too Lan. I don't want to fall off this rock." He peered over the nearby edge onto the savanna spreading in all directions below.

Tarra plucked three young leaves from the last branch before placing it on the fire. She rolled the leaves into a tight bunch and tucked them into her pouch as the fire crackled and hissed its complaints. The smoke rose up the chimney stone and quickly dissipated into the evening sky.

"Well, at least there aren't any cats to worry about." She gingerly turned the root to cook on the other side.

"We'll see... I think there're snakes, and a cat could get up here if it wanted to." Lannon offered.

"Yeah, I guess it could, but why would it waste its time?" Chilcoat tried to sound confident.

After several minutes, Tarra plucked the root from its perch and dropped it quickly on the hearthstone. Small trails of steam rose from the tips where she had trimmed it. "Are you ready?"

"No. Don't you have to do some kind of song and dance or something?"

She peeked at him from behind a veil of unruly hair as she cautiously considered the small tuber placed before her. She carefully measured the legs of the little man and couldn't help but snicker at the shriveled little member where the legs joined the trunk. She held it tightly to the stone and cut the feet off then solemnly took the remaining body and held it out toward Chilcoat. "The strength and wisdom of Yod is within you. May He whisper ever gently on your soul."

She turned and laid the body gently on the embers of the fire. It smoldered for a few moments before bursting into flames. It burned brightly then settled into an even glow of coals, occasionally flickering a greenish-blue flame. "He lies quietly. That's a good sign. His spirit is happy to be a part of the sacrament."

She diced the remaining 'feet' of the little man into smaller and smaller pieces then mashed it into a paste that she scraped into a small ball on the edge of her knife. "Well this is it. You want to eat it or put it in some tea or something?"

Chilcoat took the knife and sat looking at it for several moments in the flickering light of the fire. *I've seen Tangar contemplate similar prospects, but I never considered that I'd be on this side of the decision. It had always just been an evening of light entertainment watching the old man chanting and talking to plants and rocks. Sometimes he'd be ill or wander off and need help finding his way back, but I was always just one of the guardians who witnessed the ceremony from behind a cloud of wine and smoking herb. The old man and his spirits were nothing more than a trivial sideshow during an evening of games and stories with my hunting buddies.*

He poked his finger at the little ball of paste clinging to the kitchen knife then tasted his finger. Shrugging his shoulders, he scraped it onto his tongue and wrinkled his nose as he swallowed it. He sat expectantly waiting for rejection. It didn't taste very good, but it seemed as if it was going to stay down, so he sat back and waited for something to happen.

Tarra smirked as she cleaned her knife and stoked the fire. She had tended her father for many years while he performed his priestly duties and she had witnessed this sort of response many times. "Let me know if you want anything."

"Hmm? Yeah sure."

"Yeah, me too," Lannon chimed in.

The three sat quietly for several minutes enjoying the clear night air. The plateau raised them above the ground haze that perfumed the savanna so the sky was majestically pure. Chilcoat stared at the flames and said, "I wonder who used to live here."

"Maybe it was the children of Yod," Tarra ventured.

"Yeah, that'll make the story better in the telling," Lannon offered. "Whoever they were, they were here a long time. The stones are worn from use and the sheer size of the place must have taken generations to build."

Chilcoat prodded the fire into a shower of sparks that danced up the chimney stone and winked out of existence. "If this isn't the Sky Temple, it ought to be. That crafty old man brought us here for something, but I don't know what… Well, old man! What do you want? Tell me what I'm to do. The heat now, the storms of winter, the sky-fire—what does it all mean? I've taken your damn poison, so speak to me, or leave me alone!"

"I doubt that threatening him is going to work." Tarra looked scornfully at Chilcoat and added, "What was the story of the lost tribe and the Sky Temple?" She asked more as a prompt to herself than expecting an answer.

Chilcoat reflected on how Tangar had charmed the children with his easy smile and colorful stories. "The only thing I remember is that the old man would chant a climbing song and make all the kids pretend to climb great ladders to the temple. Once they got there, they'd get a reward of fruits and honey. We should look around and see if we can find any of those ladders. It would sure make the climb easier, and maybe we can find some of that honey too."

Lannon tried to defuse the suggestion. "Yeah, well, let's wait for morning to do any looking around in this creepy place. If the spirits of the Shanare want us to find their ladders, they'll do it in the morning."

Chilcoat burst out. "Shanare! That's it. The Shanare would climb the ladders to the temple! How did that song go? 'Climb, climb, climb oh children of—something, something, Shanare. Climb something, something—temple.' It was something about learning to climb the straight ladder to the rewards of heaven. I just figured it was a way to scare us into doing our chores and gave us a dance we could all do together. I'm proud of you, Lan. I didn't know you remembered your school days so well. How about you, Tarra—do you remember the song?"

"No. Most of my schooling was herbs and potions. Daddy spent most of his time hunting and was too tired for dancing by the time he got home. We would study songs and chants but dancing wasn't usually part of it. I think I remember him talking about the lost tribes of the Shanare though. That's what they always say when they find something they don't understand, 'the Shanare did it'. I don't remember much except that the lost tribes wandered the wilderness in search of 'the light of Yod'."

Chilcoat reflected on his youth. "Yeah, yeah, 'the light,' I remember. He was always talking about the light as if it was something you could actually find. I just figured it was more of his spirit crap and nobody could ever really find it." *The stories taught by Tangar were a jumble of bittersweet memories and morals that always left him wondering what was real and what was just an old man trying to seem important to a bunch of kids.*

Tarra rose and walked to the edge of the plateau near the far side of the altar. From there she could see to the horizon beyond the savanna. The moon had turned the landscape to grays and blacks, but she could make out the hills at the far edge against the field of stars. "Maybe they found the light and that's where they went." A tear escaped as she remembered her father and his teachings.

Chilcoat rose to stand by her. He put his arm around her shoulder and marveled at the feeling of warmth that seemed to radiate from her as they watched the goat-herder peek above the horizon. Lannon had dozed off by this time and the little man had lost all form as the fire glowed in a simple pile of embers.

"Look. Is that a fire?" Tarra pointed across the grassland toward the distant horizon.

Chilcoat followed her gesture, but his vision flickered with sprites from the herb. "I don't think so. I don't think there's anyone out here but us." He pulled her close as the fragrance of her hair captivated him.

She turned to face him in a brief embrace. "You're wrong; Daddy watches to be sure we follow his ways, and Caran watches over us through her love." She turned to tend the fire and arrange her bedding by pulling her cloak neatly across the grasses she had gathered into a mat. "You should try to get some rest."

"Hmm? Yeah. I guess so. I don't think the old man is going to talk to me tonight—herbs, or no herbs."

Chilcoat lay trying to come to grips with the concept of being the newly ordained 'Seer' of the lakeshore clan. His stomach rumbled from the poison Tarra had given him. *It all seems so contrived and unnecessary to have to eat her damn spirit-herb after finding this strange temple, and besides, the herb isn't doing anything except keeping me awake and upsetting my stomach.* He fought with his bedding trying to settle his robust frame on the meager pile of leaves and grasses she had gathered for him.

She was also keeping him awake. Her delicate figure played erotic mischief in his thoughts as he struggled to find a better position. The churning in his stomach brought him back to reality as the duty he felt for his family overpowered his lustful dalliance.

He opened his eyes and was startled that the stars overhead connected in a web that created figures across the sky. He knew the poison was playing tricks on his mind and wondered what Tangar would've said about it. "Is that why you've brought us here, to show me the web of heaven?" Chilcoat grumbled to the spirit of the old man.

Tarra stirred sleepily and spoke from behind a screen of auburn hair fallen across her face. "Are you OK ?"

"Yeah sure, just wondering why we're here."

"Mmm," was all she said before reclining on her mat.

He watched her settle into a comfortable contour that started him again thinking of things best left alone. He considered taking a walk, but decided it would just upset his guardians. He was curious about the abandoned temple they had found, and the people that must have lived here, but he didn't trust his perception so he just closed his eyes and waited for dawn. He was disappointed that Tangar had not seen fit to speak with him as he drifted into an uneasy sleep.

Tarra stirred Lannon to take the dawn watch and reclined to try to sleep. She cried quietly watching Chilcoat's fitful slumber. Tangar's words echoed in her thoughts. *"Cry the tears of the heart. They are the most sacred prayer."*

By dawn, Lannon managed to snare a rabbit that had taken up residence in the gardens and Chilcoat rose early to take care of some pressing personal needs. Lan quietly tended the fire, giving Tarra a few extra minutes of rest, but as soon as the light allowed, he roused her to start cooking.

"YodHeaVau, thank you for what we receive." She offered the entrails in a smoky profusion of sparks and sizzle. "Well, how was your night?"

Chilcoat sat quietly with his pipe by the fire staring blankly at her for a moment. "OK I guess—not what I expected. I think that we need to explore this place better today and then we need to get home."

"How much exploring?" Lannon looked uncomfortable. "I'd like to get home as soon as possible. I'm worried about my brothers and that cat and all." He glanced at Tarra for support.

"We know why you want to get home." She rearranged her cloak to cover her torso. "Did you dream?"

"Oh yeah, I dreamt all right! I have no idea about what, but I dreamt all night. I don't know if I was dreaming when I started thinking about why Tangar brought us here. I prayed to Yod for guidance, for the people, and He brought us to this place. I think we need to know a little more about why."

"Yeah, I know. I just want to know how long we're going to 'explore', that's all. I've already looked around and it all seems pretty empty."

"Where does the water come from?" Tarra queried. "This is a big place—lots of people, lots of plants. Where do they get all the water?"

"Yeah, there are a lot of questions I'd like answered." Chilcoat drew lightly on his pipe. "The Shanare, if that is who they were, were a mysterious people."

They answered the water question in quick order when they found a large cistern along the eastern edge of the garden. The winter's rains had filled it to overflowing, causing the pond they had found earlier. They split up and went from room-to-room with spears at the ready. Tarra was at a disadvantage since her staff had only recently been fitted with a crudely pointed stone. They quickly confirmed the company of rats and snakes, but the lack of any recent signs of people was disappointing.

Chilcoat found a workshop off the plaza that had a ladder that seemed to be in a state of repair, but there was no stack of ladders or scaffolds. "That means the ladders must be down on the savanna so they must have left on their own."

Lannon added. "Most of the places I went in had another room or hall leading further into the cliff. A couple of them smelled musty, maybe plants."

Tarra poked at a pile of straw collected against the stage. "Well what do you want to do now? Do we make some lamps and go further, or do we go home?"

Chilcoat considered her questions and gazed around the courtyard. The sun was nearly overhead now and the heat was starting to become uncomfortable. "Let's go in here. It's cooler inside." He gestured toward the large social hall they had first explored. He quickly searched the pile of sand near the doorway for snakes and spread it evenly to form a smooth surface. Using his staff, he drew a bulging triangle. "This is the plaza out there; this is where we are in this hall." He drew a box off the side of the shape. "Here are the stairs." He scribbled quickly in the sand. "Let's see, the cistern is over here, and the gardens are all around here. The altar stones are over here some place, and the path up the cliff is here I think."

They made some minor adjustments of size and orientation until they all agreed on the basic layout. Lannon continued to sketch the map. "The workshop is over here, and what looked like it might be a bath area was over here, I think."

Tarra added. "There's a kitchen hearth here and some kind of altar or something over here. Basically, everything you need is all here in one little cave."

"How many rooms are there? I went into about ten on the second floor and each of them had a second room and most seemed to have more beyond that. If we each went into about the same number of rooms, that's enough space for nearly fifty families. It's not enough for the whole tribe, but some may not want to come."

"Whoa, wait a minute. Are you saying that the whole tribe should move in here?" Lannon gestured toward the courtyard.

"The sun doesn't feel so harsh here among the stones but I don't think all of them should come. When we get back, and tell the people of this place, there'll be many who will want to see the Sky Temple. Some will want to move here to be with their ancestors, and I think it will be good to reduce the strain on the lakeshore gardens. I think this place is an answer to my prayers, but you know how people are, they'll want assurances I can't give them. Either we can make a pact never to speak of this place again, or we'll have people asking us for directions. Times are hard, and the people are looking for relief. Do we tell them of what we've seen, or do we hide it as just a spirit-walk gone wrong?"

Tarra combed her fingers through the cool sand spread on the floor. "I think we have to tell them, and I think you're right, there'll be those that'll want to come. I want to come."

Lannon stood guard looking out onto the plaza. "What if the Shanare return and want their temple back?"

"We'll give it back. We're not here to take what isn't ours, but I doubt that anyone would care if we use this place for a while. It doesn't look like anyone has cared for this place in a long time." Chilcoat rose and placed the butt of his staff in the middle of the drawing. "Then it's settled. We'll rest another night, and start for home tomorrow. Maybe we can find those ladders down on the savanna so it won't be such a pain to get up here next time."

Tarra drained the last bit of sand through her fingers. "Does that mean that you're coming back?"

"I think I'll have to. It's the Seer's duty to lead the people. I mean, I ate the poison, I saw the light, and I have a vision."

The trio spent the afternoon going on small excursions to far off points on the plateau and into some of the more accessible inner sanctums. They found a second cistern and Chilcoat confirmed the sanitary facilities through frequent use. The figures carved into the central altar stone drew much speculation. *They seem to be ceremonial pornography with a pair of chubby people intertwined in various highly contrived positions.*

They plotted an alternate route back across the savanna, but the trail quickly became a familiar struggle of dust and bugs. As the sixth week ended, they made their way to the outskirts of the village. The dogs and children greeted them as they found their way to a quick bath in the lake before going home.

They told the adventure briefly around the evening fire for all of those who cared to listen, but most had already gone to work and considered the whole thing a frivolous waste of time. They would discover the mysteries of the Shanare on the re-telling at the morning meal. For now, the three adventurers were out of cycle and needed to rest while the others were hard at work trying to salvage their lives.

By morning, rumors and exaggerations had grown the tale to include a monstrous cat and several evil spirits. When Chilcoat arrived at the morning circle, Lannon had dispelled some of the embellishment but couldn't speak to the evil spirits.

"Look, it was a long walk with many dangers. Lan was vital to our being able to be here today and Tarra was equally important for what we did. I'm not saying I think it was the smartest thing I've ever done, it was just something that I owed my father—Tangar. We went to a place that will sound strange to you. I want to say, up-front, that I am not sure what this place is or what it meant to the people that once lived there, but I think it's important to our people now."

"What sort of spirit-walk did you have?" Bartan called from across the fire. "It sounds to me like you've fallen under the spell of that witch-child."

Chilcoat snapped around to glare at him. "I know some of you will question what I say. It's important that you do. I wear the robes of the Seer and I fulfilled the ritual as I should, but Tarra had nothing to do with it. All that happened was that I had a crappy night's sleep. I didn't see visions or hear voices, other than my own. That's not the important part. The search for the herb led us to a temple from some ancient time. No one lives there now. It's just a big empty lodge on a mountaintop far away. I know it sounds like I've walked with evil spirits to believe such a thing, but Lannon and Tarra can attest to what I say."

"We don't care to hear from your son or your consort. We know they'll back up anything you say," Bartan challenged.

"Bartan, I know you don't like me, and that's OK. You don't have to like me. All I'm saying is that times are hard. The crops are poor, the heat is unbearable, and the loss of Larkon has tainted the hunting. I think it best to let that cat forget the scent of man. I've spent a lot of time considering this, and I think that if half of the clan stays here in the meadow by the falls, they can stay clear of the cat and stay cool enough to get through the summer. The other half of the clan can move to the old temple with me and see if we can get the gardens to grow. Look, I don't want anyone to misunderstand. I'm not saying this temple-place is some kind of miracle garden in the sky. It'll be a lot of hard work and danger. It's a long hard walk and some may get hurt, some may even die. It's not a choice anyone should make lightly."

"And who is to lead this half of the clan?" Bartan demanded.

"There are many strong men who will step up to the challenge. The one that people respect and follow will be their leader. If you think that's you, you'd better check with the people that you think you're leading. I, for one, don't think you're the man for the job. But, I'm not part of that decision. I'll be going with my family and anyone else who is willing to suffer the hardships to move to the old temple. We may come running back begging for mercy, but I think we have to do something."

"I have a sick kid, so I'll be staying here by the falls," Rancon offered. "If anyone wants to stay here at the lake, I'll be here with you."

"I am sorry to hear about your son, but it's good that someone with some sense will stay here." Chilcoat tried to encourage his old friend.

The conversation deteriorated into a general chatter as the family groups wandered off toward their waiting beds. *Any decisions about going or staying will need some behind-the-scenes negotiations.* Lan gladly returned to Charona but that left Chilcoat and Tarra alone while the rest of the village slept. They ended up spending some of the afternoon reclining in the shallow water of the lagoon.

"When do we leave?" Tarra absentmindedly arranged her hair and forced a wooden pin in place to hold it off her naked shoulders.

"Probably by the end of next week, if I can get people moving."

"How are you feeling?"

"Shaky… I keep thinking about Tangar and his damn herbs. It all seems like a waste of time to me. I could've done without the loss of sleep, and I don't remember anything worth screwing up my stomach for."

"Vau whispered to you and now you see Her wisdom."

"That's easy for you to say. You didn't have to spend all day sitting on the fool's throne."

"It was a noble duty you performed well."

"You aren't using the tanasin stick anymore." Chilcoat gestured at her hair.

She blushed at his observation. "No. It's back with the others. I figured I should respect his tools. We may need it again."

"What for? I'm not going to forget that walk anytime soon."

"For our children's children."

"Can you see that far?"

After a moment, she rose, pulled her cloak over her slender frame, and turned to leave. "They depend on you. 'The Man Foretold'."

He laid back in the water and dropped his head in to wash away the thoughts of the old man, his sticks, and his daughter. The job of organizing people for the trip, and what to do about ladders, occupied his mind. *The tall grass of the marshland worries me. With children and old people in tow, the snakes will be a concern, and any stragglers will certainly draw the interest of a cat.*

By the time he returned to his hut, Tarra was busy reassembling her little mannequin in tribute to her father. She removed the stone tip from her walking staff and replaced it in its central position in the bundle that made up the figure's torso. She removed Thoma's story wand from its hand and the heart stick she had placed in its chest. They lay awaiting their inclusion while she cinched the binding straps tightly around the bundle.

She spent considerable effort positioning the various sticks to mimic human proportions and was intently tying the legs in place when Chilcoat entered. He only vaguely acknowledged her presence and dismissed her undertaking with a small shake of his head as he settled into his place by the fire. Caran and the children were still sleeping, so he helped himself to some tea and drew quietly on his pipe.

The talking-stick drew his attention. Tangar had used the twisted little stem to tell stories and enchant people, while the stick Tarra had given to the mannequin as a heart, was stark in comparison. It had dried completely during their absence and had taken on a reddish-brown hue with a gray patina left by minerals from the water. He picked them up and considered their worth.

The talking-stick, with its intricate patterns, is now simply scratches meaning nothing to anyone. It was the prized possession of a man no longer able to appreciate its value and the other is a worthless token from a fool's errand that another now treasures.

The stone now drew his attention. *The spearhead is a crude example of hasty stonework that needs more delicate dressing to be worthy of a real weapon. In the fashion of a woman's blade, it has a single sharp edge. It served Tarra to scrape the few hides they had gathered on their quest, but otherwise only vaguely resembled its intended purpose.*

He used the edge of the stone to scrape the surface of the little gray stick. It left a pattern of irregular brown stripes that vaguely resembled flowing water. *Interesting,* he thought. With a little more care, he was able to whittle the stubby end of the stick leaving serrated grooves that reminded him of the falls where he had found it. He then made three simple bands ringing the shaft below the water symbol. He started to etch his mark in the lead band and, considering the mission for a moment, put Tarra's symbol followed by his own in the second band with Lannon's in the third. He was then able to squeeze in three little notches resembling the tanasin symbol before he ran out of room at a branching joint on the twig. He admired his handiwork blowing loose shavings from the grooves and looked up to see Tarra disdainfully glaring at him from across the room. He quietly returned the stick to its former place on the hearth and casually used the spearhead to tap the residue from his pipe.

She resentfully retrieved the sticks and returned them to their positions within the sculpture. As she replaced the heart stick, she paused for a moment to note the symbols he had etched into its surface. *I don't understand why I feel as I do, but it bothers me that he has imposed on my fantasy.* She seated the stick deep within the chest of the figure. "Why did you put my mark first?"

"You started this madness with your spirits and sticks and now we're committed to a new world. So maybe it's credit for starting this whole thing, or maybe it will turn out to be blame. If that damn spirit-walk wasn't part of it, it would all seem more sensible. I mean, if I'd just stumbled onto that temple while hunting, I wouldn't think twice about using the ruins, but with the stick, and spirits, and all... I just don't know if it's the right thing. "

"You want to ask Daddy?" She held up the medicine pouch.

"No. We'll let the old man rest for a while, he deserves it." Chilcoat drew deeply on the last bit of herb in his pipe and settled in next to Caran. She flinched from the sunburn she had gotten while they were gone but nestled in next to him.

Tarra finished her project by placing the medicine bag over the shoulders of the little figure and then settled in for some rest. She lay sweating amongst the bedding and tried not to watch while Chilcoat and Caran took some discreet marital privileges. It usually didn't bother

her, but the heat made the little sounds and smells particularly irritating. Despite her resentment, she couldn't help but peek when it became obvious that it would soon be over. She was surprised to see Caran watching her. Caran gave her a faint smile as Tarra blushed and pretended to sleep. The interlude was soon over and Chilcoat quickly fell to sleep.

Caran took advantage of the respite to cool her reddened skin with a sponge bath and rearrange her bedding. As she settled in again, she touched Tarra on the arm and gave her a gentle squeeze and the hint of a knowing smile.

The discussion of alternatives animated the evening meeting. Some people quickly decided that the lake had comfortable advantages over the concept of moving anywhere in the heat. Others were sure they couldn't pass up the "temple-in-the-sky." Many of the undecided wanted some assurance or sign that they were doing the right thing.

Chilcoat simply stated. "I have none. I don't want anyone to feel that I know more than they. I didn't get a big flash of light or voice from the sky or anything like that. I just feel that we are too many to live off the crops we've been able to grow this season. There'll be those who will not have enough. If some of us move to the temple—village," he corrected himself. "We may be able to get by for another season. It may be that we'll do well, or we may starve so that those that remain here may live. If we're able, we'll rejoin the clan at the harvest gathering. Maybe by then the weather will be back to normal and we'll all be happy to tell stories of our adventure."

Bartan stood with Laot and Lon and put his arm around Katlan. "I, for one, will be happy to remain here and gather the crops we've worked so hard to keep alive."

Laot spoke contemptuously to Chilcoat. "Besides, we still have a cat to kill."

Chilcoat started to respond but reflected on his own childhood and the loss of his parents. He remembered how he hated everyone for letting them die. He silently spoke a prayer for the boy. "*Yod, please help him to someday understand.*"

Rancon spoke from behind the fire pit. "You'd be wise to leave that cat alone and move to the falls with the rest of us. We'll return at night to tend the crops and stay away from that cat and her cubs. They'll soon be as formidable as she, and then we'll really have our hands full."

Chilcoat tried to ignore Bartan's obvious bluster. "I think Rancon's right. If everyone leaves this place and lets that cat alone, maybe she'll forget the taste of man and move back to the high country." He noted that, in their absence, Bartan had endeared himself to the grieving widow and her sons and now stood as the man of their household. *Maybe that's a good thing. The boys can teach him to hunt and maybe he'll benefit from a mature woman set in her ways.*

Chilcoat wondered if Lan would come with him or stay to try to defend his family. "Anyone who thinks they'll be coming to the new village, please think carefully. The trip will be very difficult. Our carts won't fit on the trail in places, and there are many miles of stones. We may have to leave things behind, and once we get there, there'll be more work and no guarantee that there are enough crops to feed us all."

Bartan pulled Katlan close for assurance and challenged Chilcoat. "It sounds like a bad idea to me. I think we stand a better chance together here as the clan should be."

"I'm not asking anyone to come who doesn't want to come. It'll be a great sacrifice, but it's a sacrifice that must be made for the betterment of us all." Chilcoat turned and left the clan to argue their points without his involvement. He went to the lagoon and sat quietly in the shade dressing the stone he had taken from Tarra. The voices from the arguing crowd rose and fell almost in a chanting rhythm in the background as he diligently struck at the stone. Small flecks and splinters fell through his skilled fingers as the rock slowly took on a more lethal aspect. *"It's a good stone that Lan found and deserves a hunter's edge."*

Rancon stood at the lakeshore behind him. "You're going to get waterlogged sitting in a puddle like that."

"Yeah, I just wanted to finish this before the light's gone."

"Nice work. Where'd you find the stone?"

"Lan found it in the ravine on our little adventure. We should check it out sometime. It could be a good source for tool stones. It's too bad you won't be joining us." After a short hesitation, Chilcoat admitted, "I really could use your help."

"Yeah, I'd like to come, but I just can't move my son. The heat's taken a lot from him. He played too long in the lake a week ago and he hasn't recovered from the burn."

"Maybe Tarra knows of a cream that'll help. I'll ask."

"Thanks, that'd be great... She's turned out to be quite a surprise. She seems to have learned a lot from that crafty old geezer."

"Yeah, she's quite a handful alright. I thought she was going to poison Lan a couple of times."

"She's more than a handful. She's a woman to be reckoned with. People are talking, you know. They say you've taken her away from Bartan, but won't take her as a wife as you should."

"People should mind their own business."

"I'm just telling you what happens when you run off into the bushes together for weeks... and speaking of Lan, has he committed yet?" Rancon tried to change the subject. "In case you didn't notice, Bartan moved right in while Lan wasn't around, so I don't know how welcome he's going to feel at home."

"Yeah, you better keep an eye on Bartan. I don't trust him. It was kind of odd how he claimed to have already searched the place where we found Larkon's weapons."

"Yeah, he's a character alright. He got drunk the other day and bragged about how you owed him for taking care of things for you, 'before Larkon had a chance to finish off what his father started'. I think he's full of crap but Katlan seems to like him. Her mourning was short."

"Oh really? Well, that changes things a little I guess. If her boys accept him, maybe he'll straighten out."

"Yeah, it's been working out pretty well with them guarding the fields at night. I think he likes the authority and he's not so pressured to show his hunting skills."

"Just the same, I think you need to keep an eye on him."

Lannon spoke as he approached. "I think he's a coward and I doubt he'll ever challenge you. He's weak and not good with weapons, but you need to watch your back. He might poison your wine like a woman."

"Lan, it's good to see you finally managed to crawl out of bed," Rancon jibed.

Chilcoat wanted to get to the point quickly. "How are things at home? Have you decided yet to go or stay?"

"I think that I'll be coming with you. Things between my folks haven't been good for quite a while. Few feel Dad's absence deeply. He was a good hunter and taught his sons well, but he was a mean drunk and didn't treat us good." Lannon spoke apologetically. "Bartan seems to make Mom happy, and my brothers treat him as a friend. But

Charona and I aren't comfortable there. If we're welcome back in your house, I'll be thankful to join you."

"Of course, I am happy to have you, if you think your brothers will be OK without you."

"I've talked with them about Bartan and the cats, and think they'll be OK. They've changed their thinking now that there are three cats on the prowl. And I think Lon has found girls more interesting than the cats lately, so he's content with guarding the fields and keeping the women safe."

***

Lannon returned at midday with Charona and their meager belongs. She dropped her bundles and hugged Chilcoat warmly. "It's good to see you, old man. I've missed your smiling face." She kissed him on the cheek.

"OK, you two break it up, I'll get jealous," Lannon chided.

"You should be jealous. If he wasn't married to my sister, you wouldn't stand a chance." Charona kissed Lannon and swept up her bundles in a flurry of exuberance.

Caran was glad to have her sister back in the family. They hugged and began a quick sibling-speak conversation that resulted in giggles and laughter that gave Tarra an uneasy feeling.

"I'm glad to be rid of that Larkon clan. Lan's the only normal one in the family." Charona confided in Caran.

"I'll move my stuff." Tarra said as the two women continued their cryptic bursts of dialog and gestures. Tarra gathered her bedding and dragged her things out of the sleeping alcove.

"Here, let me help. It's the least I can do." Charona grabbed the edge of the bedding and helped position it near the hearth where she had been before. She had to move Chilcoat's bed a little since it had expanded into 'her territory' during her absence. "It'll be just like old times," Charona smiled and tried to put a good face on the inconvenience.

"It's only for a little while. Soon we'll be on the trail and no one will sleep well," Caran reminded everyone.

Charona pulled up next to Tarra and helped smooth out some wrinkles on the far edges of her bed. "So little girl, you've really started something."

"I'm not a little girl—but yes, I guess I have. I am sorry, I didn't mean for any of this temple stuff to happen. It was just supposed to be a simple spirit-walk. I've watched my father do it many times and nothing like this has ever happened."

"Don't be sorry, child. It's the best thing that could've happened to us. I'm rid of that horrible Larkon bunch and I'm back with my family, and we get to go on an adventure. What could be better?" Charona hugged her gently. "I just hope it all works out. I sure would hate to die right now." They laughed and hugged again quickly.

"I'm glad you two are getting along. I love you both, and really need your help getting through this." Caran gathered the children's laundry.

Chilcoat entered dripping from his bath carrying his clothes in one hand and the finished spearhead in the other. The women all fell silent and looked up as if he had interrupted something. "All right, if you're going to talk about me, at least wait until I get some dry clothes on."

"Don't flatter yourself," Caran chided. "We were talking girl stuff that doesn't concern you in the least." They all giggled at his expense.

"Yeah, well, I'm not sure that's any consolation."

By now, Lan had joined the group and was also wet from his bedtime bath. As the two men struggled to recapture some dignity, the women giggled at their awkward attempts of modesty.

"Oh, here, I almost forgot." Chilcoat dug the spearhead out from under his pile of clothes and held it out to Tarra. "I finally put the finishing touches on it."

She sat silently gazing at his outstretched hand. It was the most beautiful thing she had even seen. He had transformed the crude gray stone into a sleek amber blade sculpted to a fine point with uniform serrated teeth running along the length of both edges. It was a killing blade not a kitchen knife. She admired the workmanship and commented. "Yes, it's very nice."

"No. Take it. It's yours. You've earned it." Chilcoat pushed it into her hand and turned to look for some food.

She sat silently gazing at the stone and looked up at Caran and Charona for disapproval. They both sat bewildered at the transaction. They had never seen a killing blade given to a woman before.

"What am I to do with this? It's a great honor, but I know nothing of its use."

Chilcoat looked up from his plate in surprise. It had never occurred to him that it was a social blunder. It was just a gift to someone he cared for. "It's yours. You've already proven that you know how to use it. It just needed a little sharpening." He dismissed her concern.

The Real Reason

The sun beat relentlessly on the tent and limited sleep to fitful twists and turns. Chilcoat sat up and looked to Tarra. Touching her gently on the shoulder, he smiled at her blinking response and whispered quietly to her. "I almost forgot, Rancon's little boy, Randa, is sick from sunburn and it would be good if you can help him."

She sat up to face him. "I'll go see him now, it may be serious." Quickly measuring herbs into neat little piles on a cloth, she worked diligently at the hearthstone. The rest of the family dozed as she measured and remixed different concoctions. Finally satisfied, she distributed the herbs into small pouches, bundled them in the cloth, and rose to venture into the midday heat.

As evening approached, Tarra finally returned from tending Randa. She was tired and sad. He was not doing well and the herbs had helped only slightly. She sat quietly staring at the fire considering her options. Pulling the medicine bag from its hook, she rummaged through the ointments and potions considering what she could mix. None of them seemed to fit the need.

She pulled the bundle of sticks from their pocket. *Maybe I should dance with them again and beg Papa for help.* The tanasin twig was still on top where she had put it. She set the bundle aside and dug into the recesses of the bag pulling out the tanasin leaves she had hidden away. They were limp and had turned a dark shade of grayish-green. She considered them for a few moments and sniffed at their apparent degradation then pulled out her herb knife and chopped the damaged tips from the leaves.

She couldn't help but think how sharp the tool was and how different it was from the gift blade. Looking up from her work, she noticed that she was alone except for Chilcoat lying close by trying to get a few moments of rest. She watched him sleep and thought of her father's faith in him. *I don't understand your devotion to him. When I was growing up, Chilcoat had always been a weird cousin who hung around with you. By the time I was old enough to figure out who he really was, he had moved out, and started a family of his own so I didn't really know him. I remember how you always said he was, "a special man foretold." I don't know what that means... You would only laugh and cuddle me saying, "You're my special girl foretold."*

When I cried to Momma, "Dad's teasing me," she would cry with me and tell me, "you are—a very special girl."

She diced the leaves into a fine residue on the back of the new hide she had gotten on their trip. The pigments stained the skin dark green and bled to purple at the edges. She heated some vegetable oil and dusted the ball of paste with a variety of other herbs then stirred it into the oil. It took on a pale green hue and smelled lightly of pepper.

She readied herself to return to her patient and then thought of Rancon. *He would be happy if Chilcoat shared his concern.* She leaned close and touched him gently on the arm. Her prodding eventually roused him. "It would be good if you would help. If it doesn't work, the boy will soon be lost and you should be there to comfort your friend."

***

She spoke softly to Rancon's family. "He's very sick. He'll sleep now, to help him recover, but he may not awaken. God has chosen to test us mercilessly. Hea has punished him harshly for his carelessness. It should be a lesson to us all. I pray that the Vau finds grace in your son, Randa."

She applied ointment to the boy's burns but he was only vaguely aware of an angel gently stroking his flesh. Tarra chanted quietly for several minutes while the boy drifted off to sleep. "When he wakes, get him to drink honey-water, and apply more oil if he suffers, but it's very important that you never do it more than four times a day."

"Ran, I'm really sorry about this... Tarra's right, we're being tested harshly and your son is one of those tests... He'll be all right. I hope you'll tell others that this has happened and that we all need to respect the sun more."

"I will, and you're free to do the same." Rancon resumed his vigil over the boy.

The concerned pair excused themselves from the family and returned to their own hut, carefully draped in their hooded sun cloaks. They didn't speak until they reached the doorway. "He's very sick," she offered.

Chilcoat held her warmly. "I know. You've done what you could."

"I just hope Daddy guided me well. I've never used tanasin in this way."

"What? You used that weed on him. I thought you made up some regular sun cream."

"No. He's too sick. I had to find something stronger. I know the elders use tanasin leaves as a lotion for spirit-walks. It makes them sleep for many hours, so I thought that it might work to help the boy rest. If he can rest, he may recover."

"Wait a minute. You made me eat that thing and spend two days on the throne and you knew all along it was the leaves that you are supposed to use?"

"No. The root's the important part. I'm sure of that. The leaves are very dangerous and used only rarely—as penance for the lustful pursuit of Vau's pleasure. I just grabbed them on a hunch that maybe that was why Daddy took us to that place."

"What? You think he knew the boy was sick and that hike was just a way to get the right medicine?"

"Maybe."

"Well, for the boy's sake, I hope you're right, but in the meantime, I have half of the village ready to abandon their lives and go to a temple in the sky that I saw on a spirit-walk. Woman, you're going to kill me!" He pointed her into the hut and pushed gently.

He stood looking at his half-finished cart upgrade for a moment then gauged the stars pondering if there was enough time to do any hunting this evening. *I need to lay-in more meat before we'll be ready, but perhaps the cart's more important. On the other hand, maybe I should forget the whole thing. If the real reason for this silly escapade was to get herbs for Randa, maybe the rest of it is just a bad idea left by the drugs and that crafty old man.*

I beg the stars of Hea for a sign, but no, that would be too easy. They simply wink in somber indifference. The thought of Tarra and her sticks, potions, and prayers haunted him as her chanting softly drifted from the hut. He grabbed his knife and began cutting segments of wet cord to reinforce the joints on the cart.

In the morning, he and Lan dragged the cart to the top of the hill near the outskirts of the village and pushed it backward down the grade toward the central clearing. As the three of them hurtled out of control down the little arroyo, the cart jumped and rattled over the stones. At the bottom of the hill, the event ended with the cart turning on its side and both men stumbling to a stop, panting and laughing out of control.

A crowd from the breakfast gathering collected as they righted the cart and inspected it for damage. Chilcoat went into detail explaining his knot-work and structure modifications to anyone who would listen. He suggested that anyone who wanted to come on the trip would have to prove his cart could survive the same test.

Occasionally someone, attempting to meet the performance goal, broke the tedium of the next few days. No one got hurt but some carts, and their owners' pride, suffered disastrous setbacks. By the end of the week, a simple wheeled platform won out as the hardiest design. Everyone quickly realized that the real test would be figuring out how to pack an entire family onto the simple flat pallet.

Chilcoat's cautions went largely ignored with everyone, including his own family, showing up on the staging day with everything they owned piled high on rickety little wagons. "We'll try it as we are, but the going will be very slow. When your neighbor breaks down and needs help, stop and help him. It does us no good to get separated and strung out along the trail. We must stay together and help each other."

The first day's walk seemed extra hot and slow. They barely cleared earshot of the village along the eastern trail. The ground haze that hung in the arroyo muddled the night sky, but the moon provided a majestic backdrop for stories of hope around an early fire. Chilcoat reminded everyone of Randa and asked them to pray for his recovery.

By the end of the third day, they were at the entrance of the long narrow hallway leading through the marsh grass. Chilcoat's admonishment now made sense to everyone as they tried hacking at the grass to widen the trail. The morning brought no solution other than teams of cutters and haulers who needed frequent relief.

The stack of cut reeds mounded higher near the camp yet the headway into the marsh seemed minimal. The process was tedious and those not involved in clearing the path had little to do but sweat and complain. Chilcoat assigned Caran to oversee the weaving of ropes from the grass cuttings. "It won't be as stout as hemp but with good weaving discipline, they should be a real asset when we get to the cliff."

A Chance to Say Goodbye

The oak hills were a welcome sight as the first carts finally emerged from the swamp. Everyone gathered and made camp early in celebration of passing their first trial. They spent the evening commiserating over bug bites and heat issues that plagued the group, but the prospects of heading into the luxury of the rolling oak meadows buoyed everyone's spirit.

It had taken over a week to get through the marsh, and while the oak glen was less confining, it wasn't any faster to traverse. The continuous ups and downs of the hilly terrain proved to be a challenge as they banded together to drag their carts up the long slow grades and then were confronted with trying to prevent them from running out of control on the downhill leg. By the time they finally got to the fork in the trail, they had exhausted their provisions and elected to camp for a few days to allow the hunters to try to stock up for the next leg of the journey.

On the second night of their respite, Tarra had a bad dream and wouldn't stop crying. She and the other women had conspired to have their cycles and wanted to be alone for a couple of days. Chilcoat left Lannon to watch over their needs and returned along the hard fought trail they had blazed through the marshlands. He was surprised that the swamp was already showing signs of recovery and would soon forget their passage completely.

He had briefed the congregation on how arduous the next leg of the journey would be and offered to return to the village with anyone who had had a change in heart about continuing. It also gave him the opportunity to replenish their water supply. The three families that elected to return with him quickly reunited with their friends and relatives and told tales of the unspeakable hardships they had endured. Chilcoat remained only long enough to load his cart with fresh water and to check on how Randa was doing.

As he approached Rancon's tent, he knew that things were not well. There were wilted flowers strewn about the closed door. Randa had fought bravely for many days, but the burn wouldn't leave him. His eyes clouded and his skin peeled and bled as he got weaker each day. He rested only when the lotion was freshly applied and then only for a short time. As the ointment ran low, Rancon wept and applied all that remained—to let him sleep.

Rancon was devastated and hadn't eaten for days when Chilcoat arrived. They talked quietly but Chilcoat had nothing to offer to console him. *I know Rancon will eventually heal, but a big part of his life is gone, and he isn't yet ready to move on.*

None of the remaining villagers wanted to join his venture, so Chilcoat struggled alone with his overloaded water cart. He thought of it as penance for his grieving friend as he looped the harness over his shoulders. *The loss of a young one is far worse than this modest struggle with a rickety cart.*

He needed to bring as much fresh water as he could, but every container made his task more difficult. It hadn't taken long for snakes and other varmints to claim sections of the freshly mown meadow, so frequent negotiations over territorial rights slowed his progress. The long green hallway seemed endless in the heat as the damaged plants bled a pungent haze into the meandering path. He considered waiting until the cool of evening, but quickly discarded the thought. *The local residents would make it too dangerous.*

He dragged the cart steadily along the path pausing frequently to breathe deeply and fan the air under his cloak. He was about to resume his mission when he heard the unmistakable snarl of an angry cat. It was still at a safe distance but it changed his whole perspective. He had several hours of hard work ahead before he would emerge from the corridor and the company of a predator at midday troubled him.

The next few minutes were torturously slow as he tried to gauge the location of the occasional outbursts. *The brute must be involved in a skirmish with a fair-sized opponent,* he thought, as the snarls grew more resolute over the ownership of some contended morsel. *As long as I can still hear it, it's busy with the disputed meal and is of no danger to me. Still, the prospect of having a hungry cat lurking about puts a new tone of urgency in this effort. There's no place to flee... The narrow channel we cut through the reeds is inflexible, and the soggy ground makes maneuvering slow.*

Why is a cat out this time of day? It must be desperate or threatened, and that isn't good. It may do something reckless and I don't want to be a part of it. The cart frequently bogged down in the moist stubble and grew heavier with his slowed progress. His forced breathing made it hard to hear the subtle changes in the cat's location as the beast broke off its dispute and ventured closer to investigate the new noises.

He stopped for a moment to ready his spear and remove his cloak so he could see. *I'll just have to suffer the sun until I can get past the cat. I feel oddly naked without the cover, but I need to be on equal terms with the beast.*

Grabbing the cart firmly, he started jogging quickly along the path of reeds. *I'll just have to risk disturbing a snake and hope that I can stay ahead of the beast. In my mind, I can see the end of the tunnel growing closer, but the view ahead doesn't match my wishful delusion.*

He knew the cat was moving among the reeds to his left and redoubled his effort but quickly realized he was no match for its speed. He hastily shrugged off the harness and crashed the cart into the reeds between himself and the cat. His bow tangled in the harness webbing and left him with only his cloak and spear as he moved cautiously away from the hulk. The only thing he could hear was his own breathing. Even the bugs seemed to be silent as he scanned the reeds for movement. At last, he spotted a slow displacement as the beast stalked him. He wrapped the cloak around his left arm and began waving it rhythmically in large sweeping circles. To this, he added a growling roar and a ready spearhead.

The cat replied in kind by snarling and stepping forward into the path. Its sleek golden form contrasted with the background of the reeds, but its cunning transition from light to shadow made it difficult to judge its approach. It skulked silently toward him shifting its head from side to side measuring its prey. Its eyes continually shifted between him and the cloak. As it got within range, Chilcoat lunged and tried to stab him with his spear. He was surprised that he was able to get in a good jab without any attempt by the cat to block his staff.

It withdrew in surprise, but immediately returned to its hunting crouch shuffling its feet getting ready to spring. Chilcoat shouted and snapped the cloak several times then braced for the assault.

He dodged as the cat sprang and he thrust his spear again. The beast swatted the assault away and spun to resume its attack. For the first time, he realized that the cat was very lean and was having a hard time seeing. *Its eyes have the, now familiar, haze of too much sun. It never occurred to me that the weather is just as hard on the animals as it is on me. The cat's having a hard time making a decent living so it's out hunting in the daylight. It's desperate and I just happen to be next on the list of possible prey.*

The cat circled slowly slinking along the edge of the clearing. It crept behind the cart and out of sight. Chilcoat moved to try to get a better view and draped his cloak over his staff forming a flag. The cat leapt onto the cart and the load jiggled and sloshed under its weight. Its claws punctured a couple of bladders as it panicked, leaping quickly at him. The flag draped over its face and added to its confusion as Chilcoat dodged its attack. The cat screamed at the specter and tore madly at the cloth, shredding it along its length and catching Chilcoat on the forearm. His spear flew from his hands as the cat spun to re-attack. The thump of a well-placed arrow stunned the beast and a second bolt, moments later, killed him. Chilcoat stood panting in disbelief at the carcass at his feet.

Lannon swaggered down the corridor. "Sorry old man, I know you wanted to make that kill, but I owed him one."

"Bless you boy, I thought I was a goner," Chilcoat stammered.

They laughed in relief; poking at the beast to be sure it was dead. "It's a big male but has seen better days. He's skinny and has lesions on his back. He was desperately hunting strictly on instinct. I think he's better off now. He was a noble challenger but Vau has seen fit to leave him and spare me."

Chilcoat retrieved his spear and started to assess the damage to his cart and cargo. He grabbed the two nearly empty skins and tossed one to Lannon while he held the other up to form a small fountain from which he drank. As the water dribbled down his face and chest, he rubbed it in and enjoyed the exhilaration of living another day. "What in Hell are you doing out here anyway? Don't get me wrong, I owe you my life, but I am surprised to see you here."

"Tarra... She had another dream and insisted that I had to take this cream to Randa." Lannon pulled a pouch from his cloak.

Chilcoat took the pouch and stared at it for a moment. "Randa doesn't need this now. He's gone."

"Well, it looks like you might." Lannon poked at Chilcoat's tender pink shoulder. "I'm sorry to hear about the kid. How's Ran taking it?"

"He'll live, I guess. What else can he do? He still blames himself, but he'll learn to live with it, and in time, he'll understand—I hope." Chilcoat retrieved his shredded cloak and ripped a sleeve off to bind the wound on his arm.

They righted the cart, resettled the load, and considered the cat. "It's your kill and you can bring it you want but it'll add weight and we need to get moving."

Lannon assessed the hide and elected to simply pull the fangs and leave it for the scavengers.

They each took an arm of the wagon yoke and set out at a fast trot. By early evening, they emerged from the passageway and basked in the dry air of the oak hills. They were exhausted and quickly ate their provisions before lying quietly watching the stars emerge. Chilcoat dressed his wound with another segment of his tattered cloak. He burned the blood-soaked rag and tied what remained of the garment into a vest that partly covered his shoulders.

Tossing fitfully from the sunburn and the wound, he thought of Tarra and her ointments. He wondered what sort of weed she had put in the cream Lannon had brought but decided it didn't matter. He spread the salve liberally on his face and shoulders and in a soothing flush, he drifted off to sleep.

Near dawn, Lannon stirred the fire to life and shooed a dog away that was sniffing about the camp. The causeway echoed with cries and complaints from all sorts of varmints that were celebrating the loss of their overlord. He rolled the two fangs over inspecting their condition in the morning light then rubbed them in the sand to clean them. *I'll give one to each of my brothers and ask them to forget hunting the mother and her cubs. I've taken their father just as she has taken ours. I wonder if I'll ever see them again.*

***

By the end of the week, they made their way back to camp. The two men told their tale of adventure to the crowd and Lannon proudly displayed the fangs to all who would listen. Chilcoat embraced his family and told Caran of the loss of Randa.

"You need to tell Tarra. She'll be hurt. She's had a hard time the past few days. Her dreams are troubled and she chants most of the day praying for him."

"It'll be hard." Chilcoat dreaded the task.

Tarra approached from the tent. "What'll be hard?"

"Randa is gone." Chilcoat whispered as he reached out to pull her close. "I'm sorry. Ran was grateful for what you did for him. The boy slept only with your lotion, it made his last days peaceful, and allowed his parents the time to say goodbye."

"When?" She pulled away from him indignantly.

"What?"

"When did he pass? A spirit that I don't know visited me. He sang to me and scattered leaves at my feet."

"It must have been weeks ago, I guess. He was gone before I got there," Chilcoat said, trying to comfort her.

"He was a brave little boy, and he was happy to be free from the pain." She began a quiet song of mourning with Charona and Caran chanting softly in well-practiced harmony.

Chilcoat was always amazed at how the timid little company of women could rip his heart out with their songs of love and loss. *I don't need such a release right now. I'm tired and I've served my penance. I just want to relax with a bowl of smoking herb and maybe some wine if I can find some.*

"What have you done to your arm?" Caran grabbed him as he tried to leave.

Chilcoat dismissed her concern. "Just a little cat scratch, it'll be OK in a couple of days."

"Let me see." She tore at the bandage he had cinched tightly around his arm.

"Ahh! Take it easy. It's still a little sore."

"Tarra, come and look at this. Is there something you can do for him?"

Tarra grabbed a lamp and peered at the swollen flesh. "Just a little cat scratch huh... You're lucky you can still walk. Take your clothes off and lay down."

"Now wait a minute. I just need a little rest, I'll be fine."

"Lay down or I'll knock you down!" She put the lamp aside and grabbed what remained of his cloak ripping it off his shoulders. "Burn this." She tossed the bloodstained garment to Lannon and began sorting through her medical supplies. "Caran, I'll need your help. Get his clothes off and get plenty of clean cloth."

Chilcoat wearily succumbed to their insistence and soon lay naked on his bed. Caran gave him a quick sponge bath and Tarra instructed her on how to cool damp cloths by waving them over his body before applying them. "Put one over his face, and wrap another around his neck. We have to keep his head cool."

In the meantime, Tarra boiled a cloth and applied it to his swollen arm.

"Ahh! That hurts."

"Of course it hurts. Here chew on this." She pulled a stubby little stick from her bag and shoved into his mouth.

He clamped his teeth onto the stump and grimaced. It tasted like dirt and released a bitter sap down his throat that made him wretch as he spit it out. "Is all this necessary? I just need to rest for a few minutes and I'll be OK."

Tarra grabbed the little stick and shoved it back in his mouth. "Quiet!" She mixed a batch of drawing-slave and applied it to the wound then wrapped it with a hot cloth. "Keep applying cool cloths to his head. I need a sling..."

Tarra sat for a moment thinking of what Papa would do. She looked to the stick figure standing by the door for several moments. Grabbing it roughly, she tore three of the shortest stick from the bundle, and tied them together to make a tent frame. She wedged the legs into the ground around Chilcoat's arm and pulled his wrist up to hang from the structure.

"Ow! Take it easy."

"Quiet. Here drink this." She quickly prepared a muddy brown tea and poured it hastily down his throat. "Keep changing the cool cloths. I need to apply another hot one. We need to keep him cool."

The tea soothed him, but the fever raged on as their vigil of hot and cold cloths continued. For the next few days, he slipped in and out of consciousness lying naked on the floor of their tent. Caran refused to sleep as she stroked his flesh and fanned him. Tarra solemnly changed his bandage and tried to get him to drink. It wasn't going well and she had done everything she could think to do.

She searched her mind for something she had missed, something that her father would have done. She scanned the clutter of medical supplies scattered around the floor. Visions of her father toiling over injured people came to mind. *Papa, is there something else I should do? Please guide me. We need him... I need him.*

The words of one of his prayer chants drifted across her mind as she collected some of the unused herbs and stuffed them back into the medicine pouch. Toma's talking stick and the crude little stick Chilcoat had fashioned found their way into her hand. She considered them for a moment and returned Toma's wand to the pouch. She began to chant the verse softly as she caressed the crude little wand. As the song finished, she scattered incense on the fire and spoke plainly to the smoke that rose through the vent. "Papa, please help us. Please speak with Vau... beg Her to whisper gently on this man. If he is the man foretold, Vau must spare him. She must..."

Chilcoat's breathing became shallow and rapid as he convulsed and chocked on his vomit. He tossed his sweaty head back and forth trying to rid himself of the visions that fought for his mind. Tarra struggled with his arms trying to keep the sling in place and Caran sat back in terror that her husband would soon be taken from her.

He opened his eyes but couldn't see. He tried to pull the shroud from his face but couldn't move his arms. He could hear Tangar's voice scolding him. "*How many times do I have to tell you that you can't hunt alone?*"

It wasn't the old man's voice. He was still young and strong. "*You know I'm busy with Mom. I don't have time for your tricks and games right now. She's brought you a baby sister and I have to be with her.*"

"*But Papa, I killed a pig.*" Chilcoat *proudly announced that* he *had made* his *first kill.* The scene danced vividly through his mind. *I was only seven at the time, and I was practicing with my bow, when the beast appeared near the practice range. I did my best to remember all of the things Dad had taught me as I snuck up on it. I let fly with my first shot and was shocked that the beast dropped to its knees and fell over. Papa will be so proud... I killed a pig and I'll be a hero at the evening meal.*

"*How many times do I have to tell you that you can't go hunting alone? That pig has a family. You're lucky the whole passel didn't eat you.*"

"*But Papa, it was alone. There weren't any others.*"

"*That's what I said. He was alone and he died. Aren't you smarter than a pig? If you walk this world alone, you'll die, and no one will know, no one will care.*"

I was crushed. My real dad would've been proud. My real dad would've been with me practicing, not doing women's work. Besides, she's not my real mom. She's not my real sister...

I remember how Tangar chanted quietly welcoming Tarra into the world. The song praised the glory of Vau and the wonders She provides. He whispered softly as he cradled the child. "Could I dare to think that this child fulfills the sacred scrolls? Should I wish such a thing on this precious gift?"

I was surprised that he mocked the old women that had cursed the child with doom saying. "Tarann is too old to have a baby. The child will be a burden on us all. She should know better than to bring such a child into the world."

Tangar's ghost spoke clearly, as his form began to dissolve. *"Old women be damned. The scrolls speak only the truth. If I've been blessed with this burden... I accept it gladly. 'YodHeaVau please whisper ever gently on her soul'."*

The shroud on his eyes lifted slowly. He could see the ghost of Tangar drifting silently over him. The ghost writhed and twisted in the wind as it sought freedom through the vent. Caran mopped his brow and prepared yet another cool cloth. "Wait. I'm OK I just need a little rest."

A smile spread across her face. It had been three days since the fever claimed his mind. He had tossed and turned mumbling incoherently and thrashing about trying to free his hand from the restraint. "Tarra, Tarra... He's awake." She called across the tent.

"Really, awake or just trying to get free?" Tarra sat up wearily across the room and looked bleary eyed at him.

"No, really awake. I think. He says he's OK"

"I've heard that before." Tarra stirred from her bed and knelt next to him. "Let's see if you know what you're talking about." She unwrapped the cloth around his injured arm and poked at the puffy flesh. "Hmm... yes, you might be right. How do you feel?"

Chilcoat looked irritated at all of the fuss. "I'm fine, if you'll let me out of this contraption." He tugged at the sling.

"OK, but you'll be sorry." Tarra unhooked the sling and carefully lowered his arm to lie beside him.

"Ahh! It's throbbing like hell."

Tarra smoothed some yellow salve along the scab that had formed. "Sit up and see if you can drink something."

"Drink what? Don't tell me you have more of that devil's brew."

"That devil's brew has saved your life." Caran grabbed him and rocked him lovingly. "You've been asleep for three days with fever. Tarra saved you. I couldn't have done it without her."

"Three days! No. You drugged me with that tea just last night. I remember... You gave me some tea and started screwing with my hand. Which, by the way, still hurts like hell."

"Poor baby..." Tarra began cleaning up the mess.

"I'm sorry dear, but it's true. You've been out for three days with Tarra tending you."

"With your wife tending you." Tarra timidly smiled at Caran.

"You almost died... Your fever made you crazy and you almost died. You almost died..." Caran pulled him close and squeezed until he finally returned the gesture.

The cart needed some repairs after their adventure, and the loading of household goods needed serious consideration if they ever hoped to get through the boulder field. The makeshift hut they had thrown up for the past few weeks was adequate for their needs and left several of the tent panels and poles unused so Chilcoat collected them into a pile.

Lannon ambled up eating his morning stew. "What's up, Pop?"

"Yeah… Just trying to figure out if we can lighten the load a little…"

"Maybe we can leave some stuff and come back for it later."

"Yeah, that's what I was thinking, but what?" Chilcoat stood for several minutes assessing different items and moving them from one tarp to the other. When he was satisfied, he called to Caran to pass judgment on his selections.

She considered the prospects, occasionally nudging an item with her toe. She eventually moved a couple of things from one pile to the other and settled on her preferences. It all seemed fairly well settled when she noticed the stick figure and robes lying amongst the clutter. "Has Tarra agreed to this?"

"I don't suppose you'd talk to her about it."

"Oh no… This is between you and her. You know what she is going to say."

He nudged the bundle with his foot. "Yeah, I suppose so." He rolled it awkwardly onto the 'move tarp' with his foot. "I guess it won't hurt, besides, maybe we'll need it for firewood."

"I'll carry it if it is too heavy for you." Tarra scornfully pulled her ceremonial clothes from the 'leave pile' and placed them with the bundle of sticks.

"Yeah, I know you will." Chilcoat tried to lighten the mood. He gathered the 'leave' articles into a tight bundle. "Lan, Give me a hand." He struggled one handed to gather the loose ends under a rope.

Together they lifted the bundle onto the back of the cart and used it as a platform to drape it over a branch high in a tree. After a quick assessment, they decided to use the last bit of hemp rope. *It's a gamble that we won't need it for cart repair, but safeguarding the household goods is worth the risk.* As they finished the job, some of the other families gathered around to watch.

"It would be good for each of you to find another tree and do the same thing," Chilcoat offered.

"And if you leave any kitchen things, be sure they're clean so the animals won't be attracted." Caran struggled onto the cart and sprinkle ground pepper on the package hanging overhead. "That should keep them away for a little while."

They spent the next full day hoisting overloaded bundles into the oaks scattered around the glen. Some of the trees were not very receptive to their new duty and rejected their load in bouts of cursing and comic relief. Many of the decisions of what was to go, and what was to stay, turned into shouting matches amongst the family groups.

Chilcoat tried to remain uninvolved telling them, "It's your decision, but it would be best to take as little as possible for now, and come back in a couple of weeks to pick up the remaining things."

As morning arrived, the village gathered at the fork in the trail. Some of the young men hiked to the top of the nearby hill and gazed out onto the boulder-strewn gorge extending to the horizon. Chilcoat pointed out the small knob silhouetted in the haze. "That's where we need go, and I don't see any good way to get there. If there ever was a trail, the rain seems to have washed it away long ago, so this gully is as good a place to start as any. We just need to keep that ridge in view and pick our way as best we can."

A snake-crew took up the lead and the heavily burdened carts followed their way winding along the sandy riverbed. A gaggle of children excitedly drew up behind in a long staggered line of grunting sweating families.

Breakdowns became more frequent as the creek bed narrowed and hardened to fist-sized stones that eventually turned to impassable boulders. The men formed teams hoisting each cart, in turn, over the next obstacle until everyone was exhausted and they found a relatively flat section of ground. The hastily assembled tents clustered in a windswept channel and the young women set up as alarm watch.

The next few days were near repeats of the previous. The long hard hours of dragging, less-and-less capable, equipment across the unforgiving landscape was taking a toll. By the time they finally reached the savanna, everyone was done with the purgatory of stone.

Waves of brown grass spread to the horizon, broken only by an occasional cluster of trees. The incessant wind diminished to a gentle breeze and brought with it the heavy bouquet of plants and bugs. The camp was again hastily set, and a very tired community resigned themselves to rest fitfully on the edge of a new adventure. The arroyo made a reasonable barrier to the west, but the savanna teemed with beasts of fair size, and ill intent, so the night was not without alarms. The young women performed their sentry duty well, and on two occasions had to roust the young men to deal with dogs and a possible cat sighting.

There was no apparent trail, so they headed off at a gentle angle across the plain guided by a clump of trees that generally aligned with the direction they wanted to go. Chilcoat struggled with the sling on his arm and pulled his cloak back over his head sweeping a couple of bugs out of its shelter. "We need to keep that bunch of trees to our left, and it's probably a good idea to give them a wide berth since they undoubtedly harbor a den of cats. The pond probably still has a little water in it, but we'll have to time our visit to avoid predators. Lan, you take a hunting party and a cart to get water."

Tarra called to the crowd. "We've walked this path before so wear your leggings tied tightly and rub this bug repellent on your chest and arms. The grass is sharp and will scratch and the ointment will help to keep some of the bugs away." She held out a large pot of yellow salve.

The group looked unsurely at her so Chilcoat dipped his fingers into the pot and drew his arm into his robes and began rubbing it onto his chest. Tarra set the pot down and roughly yanked on his cloak, pulling it over his head. As he stood in his under clothes, she dipped her fingers in the ointment, spun him around roughly, and began rubbing it in. Others in the group began doing likewise and the anointing turned into a giggling grab-fest with everyone trying to be sure they applied an ample amount to all of the hard-to-reach places.

They quickly struck the camp, and the first carts began to make their way slowly southward. The grasses were ripening early in the heat and the pests were taking advantage of it. Dust rising from their movement mixed with the heat to make the miserable walk even worse. They began beating their walking sticks and utensils rhythmically on the carts and chanted threatening guttural conversations punctuated from time to time by yelps and screams. The song boosted morale and served to announce their passage to any territorial beasts they may run across. While their progress was slow and unpleasant, it was steady and less laborious than the past weeks had been.

Spirits improved after the sun went down, and everyone had had a chance to recover from the day's exertion. The central fire burned brightly with showers of sparks rising to the stars. The men gathered to smoke and discuss tomorrow's plans, and the women drank tea and resolved political issues.

Tarra tried to join the young women on watch duty but soon found they considered her too old to join their alliance. *I know I'll be the eldest in the group, but not by much. I'm too old for the kids, and too young for the grownups.*

She returned to the tent and once again sat in the doorway watching the night sky and listening to the family exchange going on inside. "Lan is only a little older," she complained to the sky. She absentmindedly began grinding herbs to make a new batch of bug repellent and chanted softly.

Lannon came and sat next to her. He nudged her shoulder with his own. "We're almost there."

"Yeah… I hope we don't have any more trouble."

"I hope we can find some more water tomorrow. The grass doesn't look like it has had much rain lately, and we could all use a drink."

"Are you going to lead a party to look for it?"

"I don't know, depends on what *he* says, I guess." He gestured at Chilcoat's slumbering hulk lying nearby and looked doubtfully at the spear she had fashioned. "He may need me here."

"Yeah, or maybe Charona will need you."

"Yeah—maybe she will." He rose rattling his snake tail necklace at her. "Maybe she will."

Tarra renewed her effort grinding herbs and fought back tears of frustration. After a few minutes, Caran came and sat in his place. "He's still a boy in many ways, just as you're still young. I know you feel alone here and for that, I'm sorry. It's—unfair that you were unable to wed at the gathering. 'Unfair' isn't the right word... I now see the wisdom of your father in what Chilcoat did. I was mad at first, but now I see that he meant only to protect you as your father would. It wasn't to hurt you, it was his love for you, for your father,—for whom you are to become. You're important to who we are. You've saved him for me and I'm forever grateful. You're welcome here, we love you."

"Welcome as what? Am I your sister? I don't feel like your sister."

"No—you know we haven't been able to treat you as a sister. You're—one of us." Caran drew her close for a long hug. "We're a family, and you're part of it. Just how you fit in is up to you. You can choose to pout and feel sorry for yourself or you can enjoy our offer to be one of us." The hug turned into more of an embrace as they held warmly together. "I need to tell you something, and I don't want you to tell anyone." Caran whispered in her ear. "Will you promise?"

"Of course, I have no one to tell." She peeked over her shoulder at Chilcoat and considered the warmth she felt for them.

Caran whimpered quietly. "My eyes—trouble me. I am afraid that I'll soon be blind and that I'll be a burden on you and the others."

"I'll stay close by you and help you see."

"No! That's exactly what I don't want. If Vau has seen fit to give me this affliction, I'll suffer it as best I can, but I don't want you, or anyone else, to be troubled with it."

"It isn't trouble. It's what we are. It's what we've become. I'll stand by you in everything you do... Well, maybe not *everything*," she glanced at Chilcoat. She knew she didn't hate him for what he had done. She understood that he had acted from the duty he had learned from her father. *Perhaps that's why I resent his authority. I know it's Papa speaking. He left me too soon... I want to punish someone, and I know Chilcoat's strong enough to take it.*

"We'll see…" They laughed knowingly and once again hugged warmly.

Lannon led a crew to look for water but, by evening, they returned with only a few casks filled. The water they found was murky and tasted flat even after boiling. They would try again tomorrow, but they didn't hold out much hope once they moved beyond access of the central basin.

The weeks dragged on and the ridgeline along the horizon slowly grew closer. The bug repellent ran out, but the bugs didn't, so the last few days were a challenge, especially when they decided to not thread-the-needle between two clumps of trees. By going around, they avoided a possible run-in with a pride of cats, but it added an extra day to their journey. When they finally reached the guide stone, it was late evening and everyone was ready to rest. The warm evening breeze swept across the savanna and rushed up the cliff that loomed over the camp.

Chilcoat felt considerable satisfaction that no one had been lost on their venture. *There are many pulled muscles, sunburns, and strained backs that will need time to recover, but everyone is in one piece.* The guide stone seemed familiar and somehow comforting to him has he leaned on the crude slab.

Tarra approached quietly placing her hands on the sighting handles. "Do you want the guide stick?"

"No. I don't think we need it. I think we can find the path again after all the damage we did to it last time we were here."

"We should celebrate or something? I feel like we should do something to mark the occasion."

"Yeah? Everyone's too beat to do much celebrating. Besides, maybe praying is a better outlook to have right now. Will you do it?"

"If you wear the robes, I'll help."

"Robes? You don't make anything easy do you?"

"I'll make it as simple as I can." She left to get her things.

Chilcoat kindled a fire in the center of the guide stone where they had rested before. He was just about ready to call everyone together when Tarra approached chanting softly. She was wearing her ceremonial robes and carrying a neatly folded package with Tangar's scepter lying across it. People stopped their evening duties to watch as she approached and laid the package on the platform at his feet. She bowed submissively and backed away spreading her arms with her robe forming wings hanging nearly to the ground.

A chill ran down his spine as he watched the angelic figure. He had never really paid much attention to her ritual duties when Tangar was around. She was just part of the show, but now that he was also part of it, he saw her graceful gestures as if for the first time. She was beautiful, and gave a somber reverence to what otherwise would have turned into a quick pep talk with his hunting buddies. He retrieved the robe, shrugged off his sling, and quickly pulled the robe on. By the time he was ready, she had joined him near the fire and held the scepter out to him. He took a deep breath and accepted the twisted little staff, quickly dropping it to his side.

"Can I have your attention?" He spoke in clear tones for all to hear. "I want to thank you all for your cooperation in getting here. You've done well and we've grown together helping each other, as we should. Tomorrow we'll enter the new village, and we'll have even more hard work ahead of us, but tonight I want to ask that we all thank YodHeaVau for preserving us in our quest and Tangar for his guidance." With that, he raised the scepter toward the moon as it peeked over the horizon in the east and then pointed it at the cliff standing before them. "Praise to the oneness of us all."

Tarra chanted softly and scattered incense on the fire causing a swirl of smoke and sparks to rise into the starlit sky. Everyone joined in the song and seemed somehow more settled in their preparation for the evening. He handed the staff back to her and quickly shed the robe to her waiting hands. He considered his sling for a moment but didn't put it back on.

"Very nice." She smiled timidly as she folded the robe over her arm and took the sling from his grasp. "Thank you for remembering Papa."

He sat for a few minutes smoking his pipe and thinking of the old man and his daughter as the crowd broke up. *I have to admit that she wears the robes well, but I still don't feel right about my involvement. It all seems too foreign to me. There's something there, but I'm not sure what, and that makes the warrior in me uncomfortable. It's like the feeling I get when I know a cat's around, but I'm unsure where. If I knew more, maybe I wouldn't feel so uncomfortable, but right now, I just wish I could get the vision of her out of my head.*

Caran drew close in reassurance and Tarra brought their bedding so they could sleep in relative comfort on the platform. She had changed out of her robes, but she carried a small packet of herbs and the bundle of medicine sticks. She sprinkled the powder on the fire causing it to give off a fragrant smoke and an eerie blue-green light while she organized the sticks into groups.

"Now what?" he goaded. "Are you going to send me on another quest already?"

"No. I just wanted to let Papa dance with the wands again. He deserves it for bringing us here. Maybe he has something else to tell us." She collected the bundle together holding them warmly in the smoke for a moment and dropped them on the medicine cloth. The jumble of twigs scattered lightly into a random pattern with some falling out of the center cluster. She gathered the outliers and set them aside then collected the remaining sticks and repeated the process twice more. On the final drop, only four twigs remained in the center.

"He really likes that tanasin stick." She laughed pointing to the twig lying on the bottom of the pile. "I guess that's a good sign. Maybe the other three sticks are us laying here on the guide stone." They sat quietly watching the stars for several minutes leaning on each other for comfort and enjoying the warmth of their growing bond.

Chilcoat rose at first light and couldn't help but feel a little confused as he watched Caron and Tarra adjust to his departure by cuddling closer to each other. The camp began to stir in fits and starts as he pulled his cloak into place against the bugs.

Lannon soon joined his solitary breakfast. He too had donned his cloak and huddled against the guide stone. "Any ideas on how to proceed today?"

"I know everyone's anxious to get started, but I'm afraid they'll kill each other trying to scale that cliff." Chilcoat pointed at their nearest neighbors as they packed their tent for the day's travel. "I guess we should have a meeting to get organized."

"Does that mean you and the priestess are going to put on another show?"

"No. I think we can do without the theatrics for now." He finished his meal and lit his pipe while he watched others begin to pack for the final leg of the journey. They all seemed a little confused since they didn't really know where they were going to go from here. They just wanted to get started, and packing came as second nature to them by now.

He climbed onto the guide stone and called out for all to hear. "Can I have you all gather around again? Don't bother packing your tents. We'll need them tonight if we don't get up the cliff. I want everyone to bring your best ropes to the base of the cliff where the trail comes off that incline." He pointed to where the guide stone had carved its path in the stone rubble. "The first group to climb will need to carry the ropes so we can set up ladders and guide lines for the others to use. We'll have to make many trips, so this camp will serve us for another day or two while we move things."

By mid-morning, a pile of ropes had grown at the base of the cliff and they begin weaving ladders from the somewhat frayed reed cables.

Chilcoat was disturbed to find that Caran was not feeling well and that Tarra would not leave her side even to care for the children's meal. Charona took up the burden without hesitation, but it put an unsettled edge on the day. He was puzzled at their indifference to his concern but resigned himself to the day's tasking and figured that things would be better when they were finally able to get in out of the heat.

Lannon led the first team of young men to begin climbing the treacherous route to the top. They strung ropes against the cliff face in short, staggered, sections making the climb somewhat easier, but the project took longer than anyone expected. The stone was an unforgiving master, frequently rejecting their attempt to drive anchoring stakes and resulting in sections of rope dropping callously back to the base of the cliff.

They rigged over half of the cliff with ladders on the first day and a small scouting party ventured into the temple to dispel the rumor that Chilcoat had fallen under the spell of the young witch. They returned with some ripe fruit and stories of wonder and amazement speculating on who had built such a fortress. Everyone generally agreed that it must have been the Shanare who had built the temple and that they were entering into the *Promised Land*. Chilcoat reserved judgment on the issue and merely acknowledged that it was an amazing bit of stonework.

By the end of the next day, the rigging was complete, and the first group of residents entered the temple. The fit youngsters were, of course, the first to reach the top so they just wandered around in disbelief and explored the far reaches of the gardens eating their fill of fresh fruit and drinking cup after cup of cool water.

Chilcoat returned to the camp to fetch Caran and the children. He energetically bound into the tent ready for squeals of glee from his brood, but instead, found Tarra still tending Caran with damp cloths and cups of cool tea. She looked up from her nursing with somber concern and assured him that they would be ready in a few minutes.

"Take the children and the kitchen stuff and we'll follow with the bedding in a few minutes." Caran struggled to appear normal.

He did as she desired, but was unsure why she excluded him from her infirmity. *She normally seeks my comfort and relies on me to tend her needs in times of illness. Maybe it's a good thing that she has taken Tarra into her confidence in this matter. They've grown close enough to feel they don't want to burden me with women's issues in this time of celebration.*

The children were a handful climbing the ladders. They had to stop to rest many times and allow others to pass them as they inched their way up the precarious rungs of makeshift rigging. The ladders had begun to show signs of wear and the children were the first to recognize it since they didn't like being so high to begin with.

Chilcoat grabbed Lannon as he passed on his way down for another load. "Put some of the older guys to work on repairing the ladders before somebody gets hurt. It'll make them feel like they are part of it."

"Yeah OK, if you say so, but it'll take twice as long." He agreed to the tasking but didn't think much of the crew selection.

"Yeah, I know, and see if the women need any help while you're down there. They seem to be having one of their 'quiet times'." He turned to urge the children up the next section of ladders.

They finally reached the narrow path that cut behind the cliff face and opened onto the plateau. The children shrieked in delight as they spilled out into the bustle of villagers exploring the myriad of gardens, rooms, and terraces scattered around the structure. They each ran in different directions and joined the fray of people hurrying from place to place poking their heads into doorways and windows and calling to each other, "look at this."

"Don't run, and stay away from the edge," he called in vain.

There were discarded bundles of household goods and tools scattered wherever their owner's had dropped them around the plaza. Chilcoat walked directly to the workshop alcove he had noticed on their previous visit. Someone had put a bundle of tools in the doorway apparently making a claim to the location. He hesitated a moment in disappointment then realized they were his tools. *Lannon knows me well,* he recognized, as he stepped over the pile and added his load to the heap.

The interior of the shop was empty except for the work platform in the center of the room. The windows high along the front wall cast columns of light onto the stone table where the unfinished ladder rested in crumbling atrophy. A layer of dust covered everything except where they had disturbed it on their previous visit. The rooms in the rear of the shop were dark and mysterious with their earlier footprints disappearing into the blackness. He brought his staff to bear and approached the first doorway. His eyes slowly adjusted to the darkness, and he could make out another doorway in the back wall that led into an even darker room beyond. His eyes strained to adapt, but the gloom only hinted at possible outlines and shadows.

Again, in the shop space, he grabbed some of the tools and utensils from the pile and placed them on the work platform. The stillness of the stone swallowed the noises they made and startled him slightly. *It's as if I didn't complete the task because the clatter of the tools just isn't there. It's an eerie artifact of the temple that will take some getting used to.*

He used his staff to write his name in the sand on the floor and restacked the remaining heap to form a barrier across the entryway. As he stepped into the stark light of the central plaza, his eyes strained to adapt to the evening glow. Everything blended into surreal monotones of red from the setting sun as he searched the scurrying populace for his children. He had to judge, largely by size and stain patterns on their cloaks, but he eventually spotted them running up one of the stairways with a group of their friends.

"You guys be careful. I am going to go fetch Mom, so be good, and don't get hurt." They flapped their cloaks in a flying gesture and resumed their play.

He found his way past other families that were starting to stake out homestead claims around the central plaza and quickly snaked his way down the cliff coordinating his descent among loads of people and things. He found Caran and the others nearly ready to start their passage but they were moving frustratingly slow. Lannon had bundled the remaining household goods in the tent tarps and was puzzling over what to do with the poles when Chilcoat arrived. "Bring them along; we can use them as skids to drag the bundles over the rough spots."

The women climbed the ladders one section ahead and waited for them to raise their load and exchange the ropes for the next section. They dragged the tent poles up behind and repeated the process again. The slow progress suited the women and gave them plenty of time to socialize with others moving up and down the rigging. They left the poles in place for others to use on the last section and wrestled their load down the stairway and into the central plaza. Chilcoat directed them toward the workshop he had selected for their home and lugged their bundles around the ceremonial platform.

Caran was mesmerized by the temple. She felt her way slowly along the smooth surface of the platform delicately tracing some of the carvings with her fingertips. Tarra and Charona hovered nearby urging her toward the workshop alcove while still marveling at the complexities of the temple.

The evening meal was quickly prepared with vegetables and fruits from the gardens and everyone's spirits were high. As soon as the meal was complete, Charona rummaged through the bundles scattered around the workshop floor and found two small lamps that still held a meager amount of fuel. Tarra joined her in a giggling, whispering, exploration of the dark interior of the mysterious rooms. The children also joined as rear guard carrying hunting staffs made from Tarra's mannequin at the ready. It was eventually resolved that the mysterious inner sanctums were probably larders or closets of some sort. There were niches etched into the walls that likely carried shelf supports.

Chilcoat dug out his pipe. *It's been yet another long hard day, but the relief of finally being in the temple makes it all worthwhile. It bothers me to call this place a temple. I'm not sure what this place was, but I don't like calling it something religious. It's more of a fortress or palace in my mind. I'll have to start calling it Fort Chilcoat. Maybe then they'll find a better name and stop calling it the Sky Temple.*

Caran staked out the bedroom on the left and turned the closet into a nursery, leaving the children with a lamp and freshly made beds for the first time in weeks. She too retired leaving the others to chat and speculate about what the future held.

Charona rose and gathered up their bedding. "We'll take the other room, and Tarra, you can use the closet if you want."

"Ah, yeah, no. I'll be fine out here. I can sleep on the table. It'll be kind of fun." She gestured at the massive platform.

Chilcoat sat quietly considering the girl and her recent devotion to Caran. "You're welcome to share our room if you like. There's more space than we had in the tent, and you can help with the kids." He tried to defuse any suggestion of intimacy.

She considered the offer and looked fleetingly at Charona. "No. I'll be all right. Thanks anyway."

"Don't let me bother you, kid. You can sleep anywhere you want. You're part of the family." Charona stepped into her bedroom with Lannon in tow.

The small lamp sitting on the table flickered and sputtered consuming the last drops of fuel. Chilcoat and Tarra both rose on impulse and stood inches apart as the lamp died. "You're welcome to join us." He spoke quietly as he brushed past her.

She stepped back feeling for her cloak. "I know." She spread her cloak on the table and started groping for bedding materials. The fire on the ceremonial platform outside cast pulsing orange beams of light onto the ceiling that danced with mystery and hinted of unknown specters. Charona and Lannon decided to celebrate their new apartment and were noisily involved in *"child's play,"* as Charona called it.

Tarra found most of her bedding and spread it atop her cloak on the platform. She lay quietly for several minutes considering her position in the family. *I've grown to love them all, but I'm afraid that I'm causing strife.*

Chilcoat soon began snoring in a low growling rumble and after a few moments, she thought she could hear Caran weeping softly. She sat up silhouetted in the flickering orange glow and wondered if there was anything she could do. The passions of the younger pair had subsided leaving only the gentle rhythms of sleep and pain. *Caran has hidden her malady from Chilcoat well, but she won't be able to continue the ruse much longer. Her eyes are getting worse and she's showing other signs of the sun-sickness. She has burns that won't heal and she can't eat well enough to keep up her strength.*

Tarra quietly stole into their bedroom dragging her bedding along. She spread her things next to Caran and settled close.

Caran took her hand gently and squeezed it whispering, "You take care of him."

"Don't talk of such things," Tarra whispered.

"I'm not asking you, it's the truth. You take care of him. For that, I'm grateful. I live the only way I know how, but it just isn't good enough. I couldn't stay in a tent all day and work all night. I had to be in the light—when I got blue, you know? I would steal away when everyone was sleeping and walk in the sun by the lake. It made me feel alive to feel Hea's warmth. It felt like I wasn't hiding from life. I just couldn't stand to be inside all day. My spirit needed nourishment."

"Yes—don't talk. I'll make you a lotion. Maybe if he hadn't been in such a hurry..."

"No! Don't talk that way. I'm all right for now. I just don't know what's to become of me. My eyes are useless, and now here in this strange place, I won't be able to get around."

"You'll do fine. I'll make you a lotion and you'll get better, and the people here know you and they'll help you find your way until your eyes heal."

Caran took her hand and held it to her cheek. "I dreamt of you while you were gone. I was doing the laundry and I scolded you for staining your robe. You know—the pretty white one you wear for ceremonies. You stained the sleeves with blood and I couldn't get it out. You argued with me that it wasn't your fault. You said '*you had to do it*'. Well, now I'll do what I have to do for as long as I can, but I don't think your potions are going to help me. I hurt deep inside." She gripped her stomach. Tarra held her close until she slept, then she too wept in pain.

Rising early, Tarra went to the gardens. The sun was still below the horizon, but she could easily navigate the network of paths weaving across the plateau. The exuberance of the people had carried into some very callous weeding and harvesting and the tailings cluttered the path. *I wonder if any of them are the medicine I need.*

At the far end of the garden, she could see the chimney stone outlined against the horizon. She picked her way around the vines that besieged the cisterns and approached the rocks cautiously. With her spear at the ready, she circled the structure looking for any signs of threat hiding amongst the loosely fitted stones. She drew near the hearth clutching the bundle of Tangar's guide sticks still wrapped in the medicine cloth.

She held the bundle close to her heart for a moment then slowly placed it in the fire pit just as the sun's first rays began to creep over the horizon. "Father, I don't know what to do with the things you've given me. Yod has forsaken us and your stories of potions and magic don't serve me well. I can't help as you did—I think it would be best for you to take this burden from me." She covered the bundle with dried leaves and kindling and turned to find the ember pot.

Chilcoat stood at the edge of the clearing. "Are you sure you are ready to do that?"

She turned suddenly, dropping the pot. "…I don't know. I can't help—I'm not him. I can't do this…" Her eyes swelled but she had already spent all the tears she could offer. "I just wanted to help and now people are dying."

"Who's dying? You did everything you could for Randa. He was just too sick."

"I'm not talking about Randa. Haven't you noticed some of the others? The eyes of many have faded, now they're getting sick, and I can't do anything for them. These herbs and potions are useless against the wrath of Hea. He burns the sky and punishes us without mercy."

"I don't know if I'd go that far, but you're right... Times are hard. We need all the help we can get and without you, and your sticks and herbs, we wouldn't be here... I wouldn't be here."

"That's just it. I brought us here, and now people are dying."

"No one is dying! Some of us will have to deal with bad eyes for a little while, but we're out of the sun now... It can't hurt us in this fortress. We can live here sheltered from harm." He drew her close and held her as the sun climbed on its relentless journey. "I'm all for burning the damn sticks if they are going to be as much trouble as the first one. But, what if that just makes him mad? Maybe it would be better to wait awhile before you chuck them out."

She pulled away from his grasp indignantly, retrieved the ember pot, and returned to the hearth. She brushed the leaves away exposing the bundle of brown cloth. "They don't work here anyway."

"Sure they do. You just drop them and read their stories. Right?"

"No. Remember, they all fit into the symbols on the cloth. The symbols are of the old villages, not here on this cliff. The sticks tell us of paths that are of no use to us here."

"All right. Have it your way, but I think it's a mistake to discard the old man too soon. He led us here, not you. You've served him well, but he's the spirit that has brought us here. He loves you and wouldn't see you harmed." Chilcoat turned and left her on her own.

She finally returned to the shop with the bundle tucked under her arm and several small clutches of limp plants in her hands. She quickly stuffed the bundle into the medicine bag and considered where to put it. She hadn't reassembled the mannequin since the children had absconded with some of the sticks to make hunting spears. *Daddy's happy that the children are using his bones to hone their skills but now I have no place to hang the pouch. A recess carved into the shop wall near the door seemed like a logical place of honor.* "Papa, I hope you have fun playing with the children."

She put the plants she had gathered on the workbench and sorted them. She recognized one as a mild painkiller and another was a likely digestive remedy but the others were unknown to her, except of course the tanasin. She had ventured to the far end of the plateau and found a bush near where they had found the first one. She took only a few new leaves and three small blossoms. "Guide my hands, father. You're one with Yod. I beg you, please be with me now."

She placed her mortar on the table and began grinding some of the leaves and chanting rhythmically to accompany the chore. She considered the texture for a moment then added the blossoms, one at a time, until it thickened to a dull gray paste. To this, she added a small measure of kasis she retrieved from the pouch. She carefully scraped it into a bowl and added some tea and the last bit of cooking oil. Satisfied with the concoction, she turned to the alcove where the medicine bag rested and offered it in reverence.

Her solemn mood concerned Chilcoat. He looked to Lannon and Charona for an explanation as Tarra knelt next to Caran and began gently applying the lotion to her arms and chest. "What's going on? Are you still not feeling well?" He asked.

Tarra paused for a moment but didn't speak.

Caran finally answered. "I have the sun-sickness—I'm sorry."

"Sun-sickness, what do you mean? Are you burned?"

"It's burning within," Tarra interjected. "She's very sick."

"What? You're fine! You walked for weeks with no problems." He looked around desperately at the others. "Am I the only one who doesn't know that you're sick?"

Lannon avoided eye contact.

"I didn't want to worry you. You have the others to think of," Caran offered.

"What? I don't care about the others. I care about you. You should've told me!" He dropped his breakfast and went to her side.

"It wouldn't have made any difference," Tarra added. "She's been chosen."

"No! I won't accept that. We have to do something."

"We're doing what we can," Caran confirmed. "I won't leave you until I must."

"Don't talk like that. You'll be fine. You have to be. I need you. We need you!" He gestured around the room.

"You have to rest now," Tarra interrupted. "The medicine will comfort you."

Chilcoat knelt close and held Caran's hand until she slept. "How has this happened and why didn't I know?" He whispered harshly to the group.

Lannon defended their silence. "She wouldn't let anyone tell you. She wanted to help you. She wouldn't be denied in this."

"Nor will I be denied in treating her," Tarra added. "We'll do all we can. You know that, but it may not be enough. This sickness does not answer to medication, as it should. Hea challenges us beyond my knowledge. It changes people, to teach Yod through their sacrifice."

"Sacrifice… You've made her sleep as you did for Randa… Will she wake?"

"She'll wake, but she'll be weak, and we'll need to watch her carefully. If we can get her to drink, she'll have a chance."

"What can I do? There must be something. How do I battle with something I can't see? If it was a cat or a bear, I could fight... I would gladly do it, but I'm helpless here. I want to do something."

"Find some honey. It'll help her strength if she has some honey in her tea. And stop the people from pulling up all of the plants until we figure out what they are. Those fools have pulled things up that may be useful to us. Just because we don't recognize them doesn't mean we can't use them."

"I'll go talk to them." Lannon sprang to his feet and fled the tension of the room.

"And I'll see if anybody has any honey." Charona followed her mate out the door.

Chilcoat sat silently for several minutes searching his mind for something he should've done, something he could do now. "I have to— go." He slowly stroked Caran's hair. He gave a guarded look to Tarra and took his daughter by the hand. "Come on, you guys, we'll go find some medicine to make Mom feel better."

The next few weeks were an endless parade of sick people seeking help from Tarra. She set up an infirmary in the shop space and had as many as three people at a time on the table. Caran stayed in her room while others came and spent time lying on the table basking in the care of Tarra's gentle hands. Some got better, but many did not.

Tarra collected plants and seeds from everything she could before the gardeners pulled them up. She then set about trying to figure out if she could use it for anything practical. Those that the rabbits wouldn't eat she treated with additional reverence drying and grinding them into teas and poultices. Most didn't do anything except make her skin red or upset her stomach. It was a slow process of trial and error, but it kept her busy while Caran recovered. Tarra wouldn't leave her company except to gather samples and disposes of rejected research.

As the months passed, the gardens slowly came under control and the ailing among the villagers eventually found a way to be productive. The savanna provided game and the gardens supported the village sparingly, but the sun continued to punish their days relentlessly.

After much haggling over ownership, nearly everyone agreed to use their tent panels to cover the central plaza making a twilight patio for communal gatherings. The shade was welcome but it blocked air circulation, so fires were a tightly controlled proposition. In time, a more stable set of ladders and hoists leading up the cliffs were rigged and life became a settled regimen for the villagers.

***

Caran sat on the work platform weaving a basket. "You should go and visit your friends. I am fine here with my work."

Tarra arranged a couple of trinkets she had set in the alcove near the door. "I have no friends to visit. They all think I'm some kind of witch because of the herbs and things. They treat me differently now. They like it when I help them, but they don't treat me as a friend."

"You've chosen a difficult path. I think your father prepared you as well as he could, but it won't be easy. If you continue on this course, you'll have to make new bonds with these people. You've grown into a beautiful woman. Perhaps one of the young men would please you."

"No. I don't want a boyfriend. I am fine here with you."

"Suit yourself, but I don't want you to stay here just to tend me. I get around pretty well here in my shop. As long as no one moves anything without telling me, I'm fine." She rearranged the pile of weaving strips and resumed her task.

"Did you mean it when you said I was pretty?"

"Child, you're probably the most beautiful woman I've ever known. Even without eyes I'm stunned by your beauty." Caran put her basket aside and turned to drape her legs off the table. She stretched out her arms. "Come here."

Tarra hesitated a moment but went into her arms. They hugged tightly for several moments. "I may be blind now, but I've seen you. I've seen the way the boys look at you. You were a very pretty girl and now you're a beautiful woman." She held Tarra's face in her hands and gently traced her features. They kissed tenderly and remained silently transfixed. Caran ran her hands down her neck and shoulders then squeezed her arms firmly drawing her close. "You've given me this time, and I'm grateful, always."

"I wish I could do more." She spoke softly after several moments. "You've—completed me."

"Oh child, I wish that were true, but I'm afraid you still have much to learn. I'm sorry that I'll not be a part of it."

"Don't say that, you'll always be part of my life." They hugged again quickly and Tarra stepped away from the platform pulling her robe into place. "I think I'll see what's going on in the plaza. The sun will be down soon and people will be gathering for jobs."

"Good. I'll be fine here. Remind Chilcoat, if you see him, that he has the kids."

Tarra wandered around the plaza greeting people and checking on patients. Everyone seemed to be on the mend. No new cases were reported and everyone was stabilized and coping well with their afflictions. The weeding and cultivating was underway and new social bonds were starting to form. Her status as a witch had grown among the children to the point that the young ones stopped and stared at her when she walked by, and the older children pointed and whispered. The young men treated her like a priestess and the young women treated her as a threat, but everyone treated her with a new respect that rested uneasily on her. *I know these people. They've always treated me as a little girl and now they only speak to me as a physician.*

She walked slowly around the central platform tracing her hand along the carvings. The little figures danced and played in strange erotic puzzles. *I wonder what they represent. Did Papa ever talk about dancing figures? I don't recall anything, but maybe Chilcoat or Lan will remember something.* She looked carefully at the figure under her hand. *I'm not sure, but it looks as though a short fat man is enjoying a one-way conversation with a shorter, fatter, woman. People spend a lot of time thinking about sex.*

"Got it figured out?" Lannon approached dressed in his hunting gear.

"What's to figure out? Men are always carving statues of naked women."

"Well, it's better than naked men." He poked at the little fat man.

"You going hunting?"

"Yeah, there's a bunch of us are going to give it a go... You want to come?"

"No. I don't want to get caught with you bunch of hooligans stomping around in the bushes at night. I think I'll work in the gardens like a good girl."

"Is that you—a good girl?" He scoffed. "I always had you pegged as a troublemaker." He stroked the snake tail on his headband and headed out across the plaza toward the group of intrepid hunters gathering near the stairway.

"Don't do anything foolish!" She called out to him.

"Yes Mom." He mocked her concern.

She traced the carving again and moved on toward the social hall. The long counter along the far wall was usually where all the '*leaders*' gathered. It was a good-old-boys club where the old men would talk, drink, and gamble. To her surprise, Chilcoat wasn't among them. *I wonder what he's found that's more important than hanging out with his buddies. He must be hiding up in the gardens.*

She found him just as the first stars peeked through the gray evening. He was standing out in the middle of one of the fields poking something with his walking staff. The children were kneeling at his feet tugging on some vines.

"What's up?" She called from the nearby path.

"The kids found a hole."

"A hole—what kind of hole?"

"That's what we're trying to figure out. It's square; I've never seen anything like it. These vines have choked it. I hope they're nothing you want because I don't see any way to save them and still clear the hole."

"No. They're just gourd vines. We have plenty of them growing around the cisterns. Caran asked me to remind you that you have the kids tonight." She shouted as she turned to leave.

"Is she OK?" He called back, trying not to alarm the children. He poked his spear down the hole to distract them. Tarra didn't answer so he continued involving the children in exploring the mystery.

He wondered at the size and shape of similar shafts they found scattered around the garden. *They, like the stonework at the winter temple, are beyond anyone's ability.* "The Shanare were an amazing people," he spoke to no one, as he worked to clear the vent of his own house. He and the children made quick work of it and were soon in the kitchen cleaning up the debris and building a small fire.

On Her Own

As Caran recovered, Tarra grew unhappy with her place in the family. Although she loved them all in very special ways, the tension between her and Chilcoat had grown to the point that something had to change.

Caran hugged her warmly and tried to assure her that she still needed her, but Tarra decided to move into a nearby apartment. The loss of so many had left several dwellings vacant, and she felt ready to have a place she could call home. Chilcoat stood by in silence. He cared for her dearly, but knew that it was best that she not be too close. The suffering of so many had transformed her into an independent woman of considerable stature, and he found a restless place in his thoughts for her.

She entered the doorway of the vacant apartment with the medicine pouch over her shoulder and a small bundle of sticks she had fashioned into a rack for it. She decided that Thoma and Tangar could rest for a while and that a simple utility rack served her needs more effectively. She set the rack up near the doorway and draped the bag over it. As she placed the two talking-sticks in the nearby alcove, Lannon dragged the remainder of her possessions callously into the sleeping chamber. He stood in the naked kitchen and watched her position the sticks in different settings.

"Are you sure they care?" He goaded.

"No, but I do." She fidgeted with the stick Chilcoat had carved. "You can go. Thanks for your help." She set the stick down and held her arms out to pull him close.

"You going to be OK? I can hang around for a while if you want. Maybe I can help clean up or something."

"I'll be fine, and if I'm not, I know where I can find you."

"Has Chilcoat said anything about you moving?"

"No. We, sort of, have an understanding. He doesn't talk to me and I leave him alone. I'm happy working the fields and he has more important things to do."

"What about Caran? You two seem to get along pretty well."

"She's the one who asked me to move. Not in words—she's old and wants to be alone when the end comes. She thinks it'll hurt less."

"What are you saying? She's not that old and she seems to be better now, except for her eyes, she gets around pretty well."

"I've seen this many times now. She has the sun-sickness. It will take her soon and she doesn't want me to be a part of it."

"No! That can't be right. She's strong. She'll be alright."

"For now... She wants this time with her husband—alone."

"Does he know?"

"No. He doesn't want to know, and you had better not tell him. It's between them."

"How can you be so calm about it? Isn't there something you can do? Some kind of herb or spell or something?"

"You're such a fool. Do you think, like the children, that I'm a witch? Don't you think I would've done something already if I could? Vau will soon leave her just as She will leave us all. Until then, I'll do what I can, what Caran will let me do. I'll give her herbs and I'll sing prayers for her."

Lannon shuffled quietly through the door and stood looking back at the young woman. "I don't know how you can face him."

"The same way you will. I'll work and I'll pray and I'll avoid them as much as I'm able." She spread her arms gesturing at the apartment.

He left without speaking and she returned to her stick arrangement, crying quietly, and praying for her family. *The apartment seems so big and empty. I've never lived without a whole gaggle of people milling about.*

She found a small table in one of the sleeping chambers. The previous tenants, the Tornas couple, had left it. *I only knew them briefly before they succumbed to the illness. I treated them for three days, but it was of no avail. The strain of the journey and their age was too much to ask of Vau.*

It isn't much of a start, but somehow it feels right. She considered the table's placement, it was really too short to sit at, but it provided a convenient podium as she settled in. She spread some of her bedding nearby and sat facing the little platform. It had a simple pattern of interlocking rings inlaid in its surface that seemed oddly familiar to her. She spread some of her medical supplies out on it and inspected the quantities of each. *I have enough leaves for two of the important* herbs, but I've only a small amount of the most critical component. It's already the powder I need, but there's only enough for three measures. I'll have to find more. She took the twig tied to the little bundle and inspected it.

It's kasis vine. I know that. But, what I don't know is where to find any close by. I haven't seen it among the plants growing on the plateau, and the guide stick tied to the packet references the winter village so it doesn't point to anything close by.

Spreading the medicine cloth on the table, the sunburst of summer glared up at her. I know that it's nearly time for the seasons to change but we're miles from the path that leads to the seashore. I wonder if Chilcoat has decided what to do about the gathering.

She turned the cloth over where the sunburst was less dramatic with small even flames radiating from the large circular disk. She looked at the image for a moment before she realized that the disk was a caricature of the winter temple with its central garden and ring of outer structure. She had never really paid much attention to it before. She confirmed that the kasis stick fit the path leading north along the shore. The stick shows only a weeklong hike out of the temple, but we're too far from the winter village. I'll need to find some closer or maybe I can find another herb to use instead.

She looked critically at the symbol lying before her. It was so useless here in the citadel. She searched the room and noticed her father's talking-stick resting near the door. "Are you speaking to me again? Am I to follow another whim? No— I have to stay here where people need me. Caran will need me soon, and I don't think either of the guys would be up for another hike. Besides, you've brought us here. Show me a better way. Show me the way of God." She gathered her implements and packed them tightly into the medicine bag returning it to its rack. She kept the kasis stick out as a token. "I'll have to tell Chilcoat about it. That should be worth a couple of laughs."

Mixing the remaining kasis into a batch of lotion for Caran, she cried as the last of the ingredients blended into the salve. It will give her three days of relief and then it will be between her and Vau to find comfort. Her father's words again haunted her. "Cry the tears of the heart. They are the most sacred prayer."

I want to do more... I hate you Papa. You didn't give me the potion she needs. You brought me here and gave me these people to love and now you abandon me with this potion. It's too dangerous to

use and too weak to cure her. I hate myself for the part I must play.
Pouring the salve into a jar, she set it aside. *I dread the moment I know will soon come... the moment when I'll have to go to Caran.*

***

She walked along the outer path of the garden as the sun set. The workers began strolling toward their plots. *This is where I've seen the circles etched into my table. They're the same design as the garden paths.*

She stopped at the shadow cast by the chimney stone. The long silhouette stretched across the garden as the last few rays of the sun bled from the far horizon. Watching the edges of the shadow soften into the general gray of dusk, she followed it out across the garden to its source. The sighting stone stood in complete darkness at the eastern edge of the plateau. A shadowy figure stirred from the base of the stone. She could tell it was Chilcoat by his swaggering gait. He teetered stiffly as he wove his way back across the unkempt ground outside the garden paths.

"Is it time for the seasons to change?" She asked as he passed.

He stopped and turned to look at her as if he hadn't noticed her. "It'll be soon."

"Are we going to the gathering this year?"

He gazed at the woman before him. "You always have the easy questions… I don't know. It's far, and few are healthy enough to make the journey. Maybe we can have a gathering of our own this year to celebrate our new home, and maybe next year we'll have had time to prepare."

"Will you offer me for pairing this year?

He spoke after a moment's hesitation. "Of course, if you want me to."

"I'll think about it." She resumed her walk toward her garden duties. She thought about the kasis stick but decided that it wasn't a good time to broach the subject.

As the days passed, she tended her small plot of herbs and joined the regular gardening crew harvesting and tilling.

"Tarra!" Charona called from across the garden. "Tarra, Caran is calling for you."

She dropped her task and rose slowly to stand silently staring into the heavens. The stars were startlingly clear and a crisp breeze out of the west spoke of autumn. She prayed softly to the evening sky. "YodHeaVau, please whisper ever gently on her soul."

She collected her tools and bid farewell to her coworkers. They simply lowered their heads and resumed working knowing the task she had to perform.

Caran was lying in her room quietly with Chilcoat sitting nearby. "She's in pain and asked for you. She said you would know what to do. What's going on with her? She was fine a week ago and now she can't get out of bed."

"The sickness has changed her. She has pain deep inside. I've seen it many times now. There is nothing I can do except try to make her comfortable and pray with her. I'm sorry... I wish I could do more."

"No! You have to do something! She can't leave me." He wept openly.

"Be brave." A frail voice trailed up from the bed. "I told you I won't leave until I must, but now Vau pleads for release from this tired shell. Now, you alone are destined to bear this burden to its end."

Tarra began massaging the lotion along her arms and Caran winced as she spread it on her belly. Tarra chanted softly until she slept then gathered her things and packed them into the pouch. "You can use the lotion four times a day. There's enough for three days. After that, she'll be in great pain."

"Well, make some more."

"I need an herb I don't have, and it is too far away for her. It'll take weeks to find it."

"Can't you just use the stuff you gave to Randa?"

"This is the stuff I gave to Randa and it needs kasis vine to make it work, and the closest kasis is a weeklong trek outside of the winter village."

"I thought it was tanasin..."

"It is, but it needs kasis or it will kill her."

"There must be something else you can use that will do the same thing."

Tarra handed him the jar of salve. "You stay with her, get her to drink sweet tea, and listen to her wisdom."

"Will you stay with us?"

"No... This time is for you."

Chilcoat did his best to follow her directions, but he found himself sitting silently staring at the nearly lifeless form of the woman he loved. The children sat with him occasionally but they understood that she was very sick and they didn't really want to be a part of it. *Maybe they understand it better than I do. They accept that she'll pass while I relive the years of pain and struggle that she endured for me.*

"I told you I don't want to do this." Tarra sat stubbornly in her ceremonial robes with her arms crossed over her chest.

Chilcoat resignedly stood dressed in his robes. "I don't want you to do it either, but Caran insisted that you preside. It meant a lot to her."

Most of the village attended to show respect to him but a couple of the old women grumbled about the young witch "...*having him all to herself now.*"

At the chimney stone, the cold ashes of Caran's pyre sat on a small cloth near the cliff's edge. Chilcoat approached with his children in hand. He knelt slowly, pressed his hand firmly on the ashes, and transferred them to his chest. He nodded to his children to do the same. Chara understood the tribute she was expected to perform and did her best to mimic her father, but Chilton was too young, simply grabbing a handful of ashes and letting them fall back to the cloth. His father tried to guide his hand, but he was confused and embarrassed that he wasn't doing as expected. He began rubbing his eyes with tears made worse by the smudge of ash.

Tarra drew her head up and marched confidently across the garden with her ceremonial robe flowing boldly. She knelt next to the boy and comforted him until he stopped sobbing. She then pressed her hand into the ash and defiantly made the mournful tribute on her chest. The handprint seemed almost to caress her breast as she stood and faced the crowd of expectant villagers. "Caran was a dear friend of mine. I know some of you say I have plotted to take her place, but I am Chilcoat's friend, nothing more. We have grown together as a family over the years and now we grow apart. Caran was a good woman and I'll not have your wicked tongues spoil it for her. She loved me and she trusted me. I did what I could to save her, but Vau has left this dust and released her to join her family in Yod. I pray that she finds comfort in their blessing."

Tarra chanted a short song of summer that had been one of Caran's favorites. It was a bright cheerful tune that didn't seem to fit the somber mood but created a fitting release as she bent over to grab the cloth and fling it open off the edge of the plateau. The contents tumbled down the face of the cliff flowing in a cloud that wafted on the evening breeze sweeping up the face of the mountain.

Tarra walked gracefully through the crowd with her arms held open to exaggerate the fluttering wings of her ceremonial robe and expose the dusty handprint of mourning tribute. The crowd parted and let her pass as she made her way to stand in front of Chilcoat. "You've taken me in the bonding ceremony, yet I'm not your wife. I've grown to love you and your family, but I am, like you, alone now that Caran has left us. I'll join in the bonding ceremony this year at the gathering and I'll find a mate who fits my needs."

Chilcoat sat resolute. He had spent all of the tears he could over the past few days and felt only emptiness as he watched the angel spread her wings and fly away from him across the garden. Caran's words haunted his thoughts. *"Now, you alone are destined to bear this burden to its end."*

One of the throng called out. "Are we going to the gathering?"

Chilcoat looked somberly over the cliff where the ashes drifted as he rearranged his cloak to shield himself from the sun. He couldn't help but feel disgust with a god that would take his wife so easily and not even allow him to mourn respectfully as he pulled his cloak over his chest covering the dusty handprint. "I've watched the signs of the season and it's not yet time to concern ourselves with the gathering. I'll consider your thoughts at the morning council."

He gathered his children and returned to his shop. It was a lonely place. Charona and Lannon had also decided that they would move into one of the abandoned apartments. The children moped around their bedroom and Chilcoat tinkered with minor repairs on some gardening tools. Occasionally friends and neighbors would stop by and leave gifts of food and flowers. *The place is beginning to look like a garden. I wonder if Tarra can use any of them.*

Even in his misery, he couldn't help but think of Tarra. *I don't want to see her ever again. I don't want her floating in and out of my life. She didn't mix the herbs correctly for Caran. She should've saved her, not killed her.*

I wonder if Tarra will find a mate and really be out of my life. The pickings are slim and it wouldn't be good for her to marry too close to her kin. I hope I don't have to interfere again, but I can't let her do something she'll regret.

Tarra entered the shop and went directly to greet the children. She had brought a map of the garden with little people carved from pieces of wood. She spread the cloth on the floor of their room and made up a game of tag that they could play with the little characters running around the overlapping garden paths. She contrived some simple rules and the children were happy for the distraction. They wanted to show it to their friends and quickly gathered it up and ran out the door. She followed them to the door cautioning them not to lose any of the pieces as they scampered up the nearest stairway.

Chilcoat tried to be sociable. "Do you want any of these flowers? Maybe you can use them for something,"

"No, they're mostly just tea and garnish."

"Well, at least take some of this food. It'll spoil before we can eat it all."

She looked deeply into his eyes for some sign of relief. There was none. *He still hurts too deeply to find comfort in another's concern.* She took the package she had tucked under her arm and placed it on the shop bench while she ate a piece of overly ripe fruit. "How long until the seasons change?"

Chilcoat looked up from his work. "The signs are not yet aligned."

"What are we going to do when it does?"

"I don't know. Nothing I guess. I don't think we're ready to go to the coast village this year. It would be too much of a hardship, and I don't think this place will get as cold as the lake, so we should be OK here."

"What about the gathering? How will we form new bonds?"

"I guess we can do a small ceremony here. It won't be as good as the real thing, but we can have some games and maybe work out some new relationships. I know you want to move on, and that's good. I'm glad you feel you want to—grow." He paused hoping that he hadn't already said something he would regret. "Next year we'll prepare early and be sure we're ready to carry the news of this place back to the clans. Maybe you can wait another year. I know it's a lot to ask but I don't want to see you paired with someone who isn't right for you."

"And you know who's right for me? You're an ass!" She picked up her package and headed for the door.

He grabbed her by the shoulders. "You shouldn't talk to me like that. It'll give the others a bad impression."

"Others? Who? You and I have something. I'm not sure what it is, but I have the right to tell you you're an ass when you're an ass."

He looked into her eyes but saw only the pain that he felt so deeply. He loved her like a precious jewel: too valuable to let go, but too costly to keep. "Well—at least don't do it in public."

"Deal... I have something to show you." She un-wrapped the bundle she had brought.

"Oh, let me guess—you have one of your sticks, and you want me to hike to the ends of the earth."

"See, I told you we have something. You know me so well. Yes, here is the winter village." She spread the medicine cloth flat on the workbench. "See, this is the guide stick for the kasis vine I need, and it fits right in here." She positioned the stick protruding from the sunburst. "See, this is the path leading north out of the coast village."

"Please—how important is this weed? That's over a month's journey each way, and now we don't really need it. Besides, it doesn't work anyway. You didn't—save her." He flashed at the recognition that Caran was gone.

"No—I couldn't. I did only what I know to do. I have no cure for Hea's wrath. I can only take the pain for a short while. We don't need it right now, but we might if someone else falls ill. I just wanted you to know. It's a need that we have." She quickly bundled the stick into the cloth and headed for the door.

"I'll keep it in mind and—thank you for the game for the kids."

She paused for a moment looking at his cheerless form then stepped out into the afternoon glare pulling her cape into place as she headed home. *It's odd to think of the stark apartment as home, but it's beginning to feel that way to me. It offers comfort I've never felt living with my family. The mess I left on the table making the game is still there untouched. The medicine bag is still lying open near the door. My bed is still unmade and my robe's crumpled in the corner with my dirty laundry.*

Sitting at the table in her living room, she started to clean up the mess. The broad blade of her kitchen knife lay with a pile of wood shavings left from her carving job. She still had two partially completed people pieces from the game. Each was a chubby little barrel onto which she had started carving a head and legs, but each had an imperfection of dark wood where a bud sprout had been. She set them aside, standing them on their incomplete feet, and swept the shavings into a basket for kindling.

The tabletop mocked her with its interlocking circle design. It had served well as the inspiration for her game but now it seemed frivolous to have such a showy trinket. *I wonder why the Tornas' had such a thing and why their relatives haven't claimed it. It's exceptional workmanship,* she thought, *much better than old Mr. Tornas was capable of, and it really makes no sense that he would have spent his last days creating something so dedicated to the citadel's gardens. I'll ask around to see if anyone else has discovered such a thing.*

She placed the two little figurines on the table and chased them around the paths following the rules she had contrived for the children.

The Game Begins

The table turned out to be less than unique. It seemed a few others had discovered similar pieces but hadn't spoken of it for fear of offending the social committee. All of the tables were different in some details but all had the same pattern etched into their surface. Most people thought that it must have something to do with gardening assignments, or perhaps it was a game, as Tarra had imagined.

She retrieved the medicine cloth from the pouch, where it had been hastily crammed, and spread it on the table. Taking the kasis stick from the bundle, she absentmindedly twirled it in her fingers thinking of Caran and the emptiness she felt. Her eyes again clouded as she sat alone on the floor of her living room. She finally realized that the stick was still in her hand and put it on the table in the center of the sunburst design. It was the summer village and the stick didn't really belong there, but it gave her a feeling of closure to think about how the cloth had played such an important part in her life.

She placed her hands down flat on either side of the stick. "Father—please show me the way. YodHeaVau, I'm humble before You. I need Your strength... Chilcoat needs Your strength. He has slipped from Your warmth in his time of pain."

She retrieved the talking-sticks standing by the door, and placed them on the cloth. It didn't feel right. The skinny little guide stick looked odd next to the intricate carving of Thoma's wand. She gathered them up, turned the cloth over smoothing it into place, and then replaced the sticks in the center of the winter village sunburst. She shuffled their order several times but it still wasn't comfortable.

"Papa, I don't want to keep you from your peace in Yod, but I'm alone. I have no one else now." She leaned on the table and cried until she slept.

Startling awake, she scattered the cloth and sticks across the floor. She had a kink in her neck and her face was red and sore. People were beginning to stir in the central plaza and she needed to take care of a few things before her gardening duties. She looked bleary-eyed at the garden map etched in the tabletop and her eyes immediately fell on the sector where her herb garden is located. She gathered some of the junk from the floor and rose to get ready for work. In a painful tribute to its existence, she soon found one of the half-finished game figures with her bare foot. Limping across the floor, she grumbled about her housekeeping needs and tossed the little figure onto the table next to the sticks.

By morning, she had gathered several ripe herbs from her garden, but the yield was poor. *The soil on the plateau isn't favorable for many of the seeds we brought from the old village so it's a struggle keeping up the supply of some very critical plants. Vau hasn't smiled favorably on this hilltop. It's a great fortress, but it isn't a good garden.*

***

The seasons changed in an endless progression of heat and cold that were unprecedented in anyone's memory. Hea punished the people relentlessly. Everyone spent daylight hours indoors and nights tending to social needs. It wasn't easy, but everyone eventually grew accustomed to the schedule.

Tarra spent months nurturing different strains of plants and compounding different concoctions. She eventually found some effective lotions and teas that satisfied all but the most critical ailments. She tried to keep up on her religious duties, but found it difficult to put on her robes and call people together to chant and pray. At first, people were demanding that she do her little song and dance, but now that things had settled into a routine, no one wanted to spend time worshiping such an unfeeling god.

People made and broke social bonds, children were born, and people got old and died. Tarra matured into a young woman who demanded respect as she performed her duties. With the passage of time, the tribe had evolved into mostly young, mostly healthy, people. A great deal of wisdom was lost and many of the young grew impatient with the old ways. Chilcoat retained leadership through confrontation and bluster, but he had grown older and knew that a younger, more active, warrior would soon replace him. Lannon was his choice, of course, but others had formed factions that would not be ignored in the selection process.

Chilcoat sat at the sighting stone once again and watched the sunset. Another summer was ending. He knew the signs well by now. He had confirmed that indeed the stone placements around the plateau were seasonal beacons. Autumn would soon be on them, the harvest would be in, and it would be time to prepare for the journey to the winter village. The tribe hadn't been to the gathering since they had moved to the 'temple in the sky'. *That's funny,* he reflected. *Very few ever thought about the temple stuff anymore. The citadel has lost its aura of divine presence and is now simply a difficult climb after a successful hunt.*

"I think we should go." Tarra said, interrupting his reminiscing.

"What? Go where?"

"To the gathering. I saw you watching the signs. I know you."

"Yeah, I know. It'll be hard. Not everyone can make it."

"I think there'll be those who won't want to go. It's a long walk and unless you've something important to resolve, it's not worth it."

"Do you have something important to resolve?"

"I still need some kasis and there are a couple of other things I want." She placed her tools against the stone. "You may be able to find something you need as well."

"Maybe I'll be one of the ones to stay behind."

"You know you can't pass up another chance to lead. Besides, who's going to know the right path?"

"Speaking of right path, you haven't been holding any services lately. Is something wrong?"

"People just aren't interested. I got tired of getting all dressed up and not having anyone show up... not even you." She looked coldly into his eyes.

"Yeah, well when you didn't help Caran..." He caught himself making excuses to the girl.

"Yod knows your pain, yet you turn away from Him."

"He doesn't care for me, and I don't care for Him. Besides, I didn't want people to talk about—us."

"People talk about us whether we're involved or not. The witch has your heart, haven't you heard?"

"That's just what I'm talking about. You're not..."

"I'm not what? And how would you know?" She drew a small pouch from her purse. "Here's a potion I've mixed for you. It'll take all the bad memories from you and you'll do my bidding without question."

He stood speechless as she grabbed his hand and stuffed the packet into it. Turning quickly, she headed out across the garden without looking back. He sniffed at it cautiously. It was just some tea she had brought for break time.

He gathered his hunting gear and headed out. Several of the other men were already on their way down choosing bands to venture onto the savanna. He soon found Lannon and headed off toward the western trail that led out to the watering hole. *Hunting's always good there but it's dangerous and a long walk.*

Chilcoat finally spoke as they made their way across the savanna. "It's time to prepare for the gathering."

Lannon adjusted his grip on his spear. "Gathering... Are we going to the gathering this year?"

"I don't know. I'm just saying it's time. I've seen the signs."

"I'm not sure I want to go through all that. Charona and I don't have much of a place at the gathering, and that's one damn long walk just to play grab-ass with a bunch of cousins."

"I figured you might feel that way. Tarra wants to go and so do some of the others."

"Oh, I see. You're doing her bidding again?"

"No! I'm not—I'm..."

"Relax; I'm just busting your chops. I heard her talking to you. She's still quite a handful."

"Want some witch's brew?" He pulled the tea packet from his belt and offered it to him after taking a small pinch and placing it behind his lip.

"I'll pass, that spirit-walk stuff isn't for me."

Chilcoat hadn't thought of Tangar and the spirit-walk for quite a while. He remembered how disappointed he had been that nothing had really happened. *I didn't get great wisdom or insight. I didn't talk with God. I've only a vague memory of a bad night's sleep and a deep-seated resentment for all things mystical, including Tarra and her herbs. Whenever someone gets sick, I can't help but think of the old man and his herbs. Maybe he could've saved Caran. Maybe his daughter doesn't know what she's doing. Maybe the old women were right. Maybe Tarra poisoned her. It doesn't matter now. Caran's gone, the old man's gone, and I'm not ready to deal with all that has happened.*

He resented how the old man and his witch-daughter had brought them to this strange place and then ignored his prayers. "Him and his sticks and herbs…" he grumbled.

"How's that?"

"Oh, nothing, just lamenting my lot…"

"Are you going to go?"

"I'm going to try. There's a lot of planning that needs to be done, and I need to convince the right people to go along."

"Right people? Got anyone in mind?" Lannon adjusted his bowstring.

"I think there are a few who need to get away for a while. This'll give them the excuse they need."

"There's a couple I'd like to be sure make the trip."

"We'll compare notes. In the meantime, I think we'd better get some meat on the table."

Chilcoat stood on the edge of the cliff facing north in the morning haze. In the distance across the savanna, he could see a hint of the rocky arroyo and the hills beyond. *I don't look forward to the walk. A couple of people have tried to make the trek in years past, but all of them either returned after a few days or never returned at all.*

Tarra approached with a bundle of herbs in each hand. "Well, what's it going to be, you and me alone, or the whole gaggle?"

"Neither. I think only a few should make the trip. I don't want any unnecessary risks, and we need to keep this place going, or there'll be nothing left when we return."

"Will we join the others?"

"Others?"

"Rancon and the rest of the summer village?"

"See that pass?" He pointed across the savanna toward a small dip in the hills. "That's the way we came from the lake. I think the winter village is more over in that direction." He gestured further west along the horizon. "If we can find a pass over there, we may be able to cut weeks off the journey, but we won't be able to join the others."

Tarra sorted through the plants she had gathered. "Sounds good to me. I'm all for keeping the hike short."

"It would be good to see how the others are doing."

"We'll see them at the gathering."

"Maybe... For now, we need to gather everyone and ask for guidance."

"Are you going to dress the part?"

Chilcoat winced at the thought of dragging his robes out, but a vision of Tangar flashed through his memory. *The old man always made a big deal about getting ready for the journey. Maybe that's what I need. A little more formality might shore up my position.* "I'll do it if you will."

"It's a date. I can be ready in about a half hour."

"You bring the stick. I'll meet you on the pedestal."

He returned to his shop and dug out his ceremonial robe patting it and sneezing from the cloud of dust. As he pulled it on and smoothed it into place, he could feel a lump in the breast pocket. He cautiously extracted the delicate gift and again thought of Tangar. He was about to replace it when he heard Tarra's voice calling everyone to service. The lilting chant echoed around the courtyard as she slowly descended the stairway from the garden fully draped in her robes. She now filled the garment in a heavenly visage of warm freckled flesh peeking seductively from the pristine white cape. She waved her arms in slow beckoning motions trailing wings of sheer fabric in a rhythmic flow. The normal morning commotion soon stopped as everyone watched the specter float down the stairs and up onto the central platform. He took a pinch of smoking herb from his pouch and carefully filled the pipe.

I haven't smoked since Caran passed. It never felt right, but, if I'm going to wear the robes, I'm going to be prepared. The new pipe flowed quickly nearly choking him. The herb was a local concoction that smelled slightly of damp socks but it left a pleasant flavor and a light feeling of well-being. He emerged from the shop just as Tarra finished the last refrains of the call to service. She stood in the center of the platform with her arms held out offering the scepter her father had wielded for so many years. Most of the township gathered in silent wonder at the apparition. It had been years since they had seen anything so formal.

Chilcoat solemnly approached the platform and stood for a moment staring at the flaming hair of the angel before him. He accepted the scepter with both hands and she backed away bowing slightly as he turned to face the crowd. Raising the scepter in the direction of the rising sun for a moment, he spoke clearly. "I've watched the signs for many seasons now and it's time that we prepare for the journey to the gathering. I know that some of you are not able to make this trip and that's OK. It's good that we have those who can stay here and tend the crops. We'll offer those who are of age for bonding if their families wish. It'll be a hard journey, but I think it's time that we try to join the other clans and tell them of this place."

The crowd rumbled with excitement. There had been some suggestion that Chilcoat had no desire to undertake the journey, but his theatrics and confidence carried the day. There was little doubt who was in charge and who wore the robes of the Seer.

"In future years, when the trail is well set, others can go for less critical reasons, but this year, only the fit and able are welcome."

Tarra sang a hymn of closing and the meeting broke up before the sun's rays grew too harsh. Some of the crowd lingered to see if they could catch Chilcoat for a side discussion, but he followed the ritual strictly and returned the scepter bowing respectfully to her station before he quickly adjourned to his shop.

Tarra likewise maintained protocol and majestically ascended the stairs returning to her apartment in a whisper of flowing gowns. She quickly hung her robes away and sat silently at the table dressed in her sleeping clothes. She was still excited from the ceremony and confused about what to do. *I've convinced myself that I want to go, but now that it's going to happen, I'm unsure that I'm ready. I know that if I find a mate from one of the other tribes, I'll no longer need to hear the whispers of the old women, but I really don't want to leave my people. I'll have to find a mate who's willing to leave his tribe and come to stay with me in the temple. I like the idea of calling it a temple again.*

Looking at the collection of trinkets that cluttered the alcove next to the door, she noted the spirit sticks standing stoically with the two incomplete game pieces. The spearhead lay at their feet. She gathered the little diorama together and brought it to the table placing the two sticks in the center.

"Will you speak with me Papa, Grandpa? We need your guidance. Hea continues to punish us. Will you speak with Yod for us? Show us how we are to understand our place." She ran her fingers over the intricate carving of Thoma's wand as the words of her prayer hung in the air unanswered. A tear formed but she wouldn't allow herself to dwell on it.

What little carving Chilcoat has done on his wand seems simple and dull next to the complex carvings Papa spent so much time on. She picked up the spearhead and considered embellishing the carving but knew it wasn't her place. The blade felt cold in her hand, its translucent amber beauty misleads its purpose. *I'll need to mount it on a good strong shaft for the trip.* She remembered the words Chilcoat had quoted. *"It's an unfeeling sliver of Hea that can kill a beast, or even a man, without the slightest remorse or blame."*

The game pieces now drew her attention. She stood them up and decided that the one with a little brown stub protruding must be Chilcoat and the one with the equally unattractive little brown dimple must be her. She played with fitting them together but decided that it wasn't a very good fit. She chased them around the design on the tabletop making little squealing noises but soon grew tired of it and picked up Thoma's wand again. She used it to push Chilcoat's figure along the garden path making rude comments about how slow and awkward he is.

She remembered how her father would take a stick from the fire and draw maps and figures in the sand when he was arbitrating an argument. *He would sometimes take a spirit-walk and call the conflicting parties together around the fire while he spent hours considering circles and lines. He would ask them questions and move stones and twigs in and out of the different figures he had drawn. I watched him whenever I could, but it never made much sense to me.*

She suddenly realized that the figures from her childhood were the same intersecting circles etched on the tabletop. She tried to remember what he had said about them, but she could only remember vague chants about the harmony of YodHeaVau and arguing with people about the placement of sticks and stones within the symbol. She moved everything to the center of the diagram and went to bed.

***

Lannon spoke from the doorway as she pulled her work clothes into place and headed out for the evening labor. "Good show this morning Slim."

"Are you coming with us?"

"Nah, I don't need the aggravation."

"Do me a favor and see if you can find me a good staff for a spear."

"There's another reason I don't want to go. I don't want to be on the wrong end of that blade. Here, let me have it. I'll see what I can do."

"What are the others saying?"

"Do you care?"

"Not really. I just wondered if the rumors are starting."

"They never stopped. '*The witch has enchanted him and is going to lead our children to their doom*'."

"Maybe they're right. He wants to take a shortcut."

"That should make it more fun. You can add a new notch to his story stick."

"What do you know of…? Oh never mind." She felt strangely violated that Lannon knew of the wand.

Chilcoat assembled a scouting party and ventured across the savanna to the northwest. The trail wasn't difficult but it led through lion country and the hills beyond were monotonous possibilities of alternative routes. They got close enough to locate two good prospects but would have to let the selection go until the actual journey. *It's too far for the scouting party to go without better preparation, and if we're going to go to all of that trouble, we might as well make an attempt at the journey.*

When they returned, Chilcoat climbed the stairs with purpose and walked along the causeway straight to Tarra's apartment. He had never actually been there, so as he approached the door, he turned to see if anyone was watching. He scanned the windows and doorways of the dwellings and, spotting a curious onlooker, waved acknowledgement. He didn't want to seem to be hiding his actions.

"Tarra—are you awake?" He called into the gaping doorway.

"Please come in." She called from the sleeping chamber. She was getting used to the protocol that the townspeople showed her. She liked being able to invite people in to visit but was glad that she could un-invite them just as easily.

"I'm going to call a meeting. I'll need the stick."

"It's a scepter, get used to it. What's the occasion? I might need something."

"I'm going to start the selection process, so I figured I'd make it official. I don't think we need a big ceremony or anything, I just wanted to sort of bless it, you know."

"I'll get ready."

"Ah—can you just give me the 'scepter' now and I'll handle it from here."

She looked coldly at him. "You said we needed guidance. If you want YodHeaVau to smile on your quest, you need to do His bidding. You need to follow *His* ways."

"Woman, you are to do my bidding and not argue with me."

"I'll not give you the scepter in this way. It is over there, you'll have to take it." Tarra turned away and busied herself by covering the table with a scrap of cloth. She smoothed it into place and put her collection of trinkets on it. "Well—if you have what you want, you can leave."

"Look, I'm all for a little show, but I just wanted to keep it simple, that's all."

"I'll be discreet if that's what you want. I just think it's important to keep the traditions."

"You and your damn sticks, I don't suppose you have a guide stick that tells us which pass to take through the hills?"

"I have this." She picked up the stick he had started to carve and pressed it into his hand.

True to her word, Tarra kept the ceremony simple. She wore her robes but somehow seemed less ethereal as she walked to the platform chanting her call to prayer.

Chilcoat, also, was less formal as he casually accepted the scepter and dropped it to his side. "As I've said, only the fit will make this journey and we'll return as soon as the bonding is complete."

"I want to stay and visit my sister." A voice called from the group along with supporting jeers and grumbling.

"I'm sorry, but you'll have to wait for another season. We're going to mark a trail and let the young form bonds, but we'll be unable to visit family and friends. There'll be times for that soon, but not now."

"You can't deny me! I want to see my family and join in the celebration. I've listened to you long enough with all of your doom saying and witchcraft. You're not a true seer and you've led us only into hardship and suffering."

Chilcoat walked slowly across the platform to confront the distraught man standing amongst his supporters. "You're right. I am not a seer as Tangar was. I sat at his knee and I learned many things from him, but I don't follow his ways of herbs and spirits. For that, perhaps I'm wrong, but I am who I am, nothing more. I'll lead you for as long as you'll let me. After that, I'll pass and another will take my place. That's as it should be. I'm sorry you feel that way, but I'll not endanger any that I don't have to, and you're not eligible to join in this passage. If we can find a suitable route, you are welcome to lead the journey next year, but until then you'll have to stay here."

He turned with a flourish of his robes and raised the scepter to the setting sun. "Hea, bring us the life force of Vau to nourish the humble children of Yod, but please spare us Your wrath. We've suffered greatly under Your merciless cleansing and ask only that You find us worthy."

Tarra took the cue and sprinkled incense on the brazier that stood in the center of the platform. The sparks wafted on the evening breeze and disappeared into the darkening sky.

Her action distracted Chilcoat for a moment. "For now, I'll count on two hands those men who will come with me, and I'll count on one hand those women who will join us. Tarra, bring a stool and I'll sit here and listen to all of those who think they are in need."

He selected a band of young people who were of bonding age. The mix included several of the young bucks who were beginning to form factions of disruptive influence. *It will provide them a challenge to prove their manhood and serve to break up some ill-considered relationships.*

When the selections were complete, and everyone had had a chance to speak, Chilcoat rose from his stool and looked wearily at Tarra handing back the scepter. "Lannon has served me well and will assume my duties while I am gone, and Tarra will remain to nurse any who become ill."

"No! I need to gather herbs, I have to go." She made her position clear for all to hear.

"You're too valuable here with the elders, they need you more than we will."

"You don't know that. My knowledge may be of more use to this bunch of children on the trek." Some of the older 'boys', that had been selected, stirred in discomfort at her dismissal but decided they didn't want to get between them. "I have to restock some very special herbs, and unless you think you're up to the task, I need to go. These people need these things."

"You can come to seek your herbs then, and you're free to enter the joining ceremony. I'll be happy to offer you if you wish." Chilcoat smiled slightly with relief that he was able to make an open display of their relationship.

"I'll decide that when we get there. In the meantime, I need to get ready." She bowed respectfully offering the scepter up in reverence before she turned to leave in a purposeful display of flowing robes.

"Yes, that goes for all of you. Both those selected, and those who will remain behind, must make preparations. Each will have added burdens they must accept. I think it's important that our young take part in the bonding, we must keep the bloodlines pure, and it's important for these men to find their position in the tribe." He gestured toward the young men that had recently risen in defiance. "I want you all to understand that none of you are being forced to go. There's no shame in waiting for another season. The trail will be better set and you may have fewer doubts about your desire to enter into bonding. It's a reckless venture that'll be dangerous for everyone involved. Those who remain will have to pick up the duties of these healthy young bucks, and those who come will have to do only what I tell them to do, and only when I tell them to do it. If you don't agree with that, you can come to my shop and we'll resolve it, otherwise, I want you all to prepare in the way Lannon instructs you. Bring nothing more nor less than instructed. We'll leave at first light in three days. Be at the guide stone, and be prepared, or you'll not be allowed to come." He straightened his cape and left the platform.

No one came forward to decline the mission, but many of those not selected took every opportunity to ask him to reconsider their worthiness.

***

On the third morning, Chilcoat arose from a fitful rest atop the guide stone. He questioned the wisdom of the venture as he rubbed his knee into action. *The day is the marking of the seasons. The sun's aligned with the chimney stone and I lament not sitting comfortably at the dawn watch drinking my morning tea and smoking my morning pipe. I've grown soft living in the citadel and grieve the loss of my bed.*

Feeling for the lion's fangs hanging from his neck, he glanced up the cliff face and watched the stars fade. *Lan entrusted me to take them to the gathering for his brothers. He's a good strong leader and will get much-deserved honor when he makes the trip himself and tells the story, but for now, the fangs will go to his brothers in memory of their father.*

Standing on the edge of the platform, he called out across the small encampment. "Everyone rise and shine. It is time to get started." Tarra soon stood beside him and began a light melodic chant meant to cheer the uneasy mood.

The trip was uneventful except for a snakebite that took one of the cocky older boys that had become complacent. Chilcoat had cautioned him more than once, but the lad knew more than the master, and wouldn't listen.

They had to double back on three separate occasions, but they eventually found their way to the coastline and were soon standing in front of the temple. Everyone welcomed them to the festivity and the storytelling began. All of the stories were pretty much the same except for the citadel, of course. Everyone had tales of suffering and hardship with many deaths mourned and few births celebrated. Chilcoat sought refuge in the men's tent and quickly found a cup of wine and a pipe full of herbs amongst old friends.

The joining ceremony grew more important in everyone's thoughts as the day drew near. Chilcoat found Tarra talking lightheartedly with the shaman. They had questioned her ruthlessly for many hours at first, but they eventually warmed to her charms and welcomed her into their alliance. She brought a young tanasin plant for the elder's gardens and asked to understand its use better. She learned that she had been correct about the leaves, but there was much risk with their use.

The high-elder approached Tarra as she gathered up her things getting ready to leave. "You probably don't remember me. I'm Talbot and this is Stafon, the Seer of the western tribe. We were friends of your father and wanted to say how sorry we are for your loss."

"Thank you. Yes, I remember you both. I'm glad to see you again."

"You flatter us, you were so young. I'm sorry we were unable to talk with you on your last visit. Things were a little hectic. We would like a moment of your time, if you don't mind." Stafon gave a quick hand gesture to a young monk standing nearby who moved to intercept the approach of a couple of council members. He led them away with congenial gestures and feigned interest in their issues as Stafon led Tarra into the inner sanctum of the high-elder.

"Forgive us for intruding on your time, but we have only a few moments. We are of the 'old-order', just as your father was, and must guard what we say. The 'enlightened' council doesn't agree with our teachings and will oppose what we are about to tell you." Talbot moved quickly to uncover a stack of scrolls buried within a pile of carpets. "Your father's passing has touched us deeply, not only because he was a dear old friend, but because his passing fulfills a prophecy foretold in these scrolls." He gestured at the dubious looking pile of rags.

"These are the lost scrolls of the Shanare." Stafon pulled his hood off exposing his bald head and thin, somber, face as he caressed the scrolls lightly with his fingertips. "The monks of the new-order have forbidden their use. They claim the enlightenment has made them useless to the new ways."

"Ah—they don't look very lost to me." Tarra bent down and nudged the rolls aside counting them.

Stafon could hardly contain himself. "Well, the council has, sort of, lost track of them on purpose. That's not the important thing. The important thing is that you are here. You are to read them. To fulfill the prophecy foretold: 'the Keeper of the Word and Warrior of Truth'."

Talbot placed his hand on the shoulder of his old friend. "Let's not get ahead of ourselves. You see Tarra, these scrolls are very important to your future, to everyone's future. They are yours to keep. The Keeper 'must receive the scroll of heaven, freely given by the one foretold' to fulfill the prophecy."

Stafon addressed the young monk that entered the room and nodded meaningfully. "Shadoc, this is Tarra. I want you to stay close to her. The council will be upset if they discover we have spoken with her. I want you to be sure they don't suspect our involvement."

Talbot covered the scrolls and quickly left the room with Stafon closely in tow.

Tarra stood a little bewildered as Shadoc directed her to leave by way of the side door. They stood in the shadow of the tent for a moment then ventured nonchalantly into the traffic flow of people headed for the gaming fields. He put his arm around her shoulder and pointed out various team members as they moved casually past a cluster of shaman that had gathered around the high-elder.

Tarra shrugged his arm off as they rounded the corner. "Was that really necessary?"

Shadoc smiled confidently. "I don't know for sure, but it seemed like a good idea."

"Well, next time ask."

He stopped and faced her solemnly. "Tarra, can I put my arm around your shoulder?"

"What do you know about all this stuff? Talbot is the high-elder—can't he just 'find' the scrolls and make everybody read them."

"The new-order is very powerful and only tolerates him because they think he's going to die soon. The irony is that they're probably right."

"You don't know that. Besides, who are you anyway? What makes them think I need your protection?"

"It's not really protection. It's more of a diversion so you stay out of the council's view while you learn what you are to know."

"And you know what that is?"

"No. You're to teach me."

***

The pair spent many hours pursuing the other shaman and asking questions about their trade. Their relationship was flirtatious and a little arrogant as they gathered seeds of wisdom scattered amongst a good supply of fertilizer provided by their mentors. They talked of the joining and participated in their own little bonding ceremony, but they both realized they could not seek joining without one or the other tribe suffering from their loss. There were too few practitioners to allow them to live in the same tribe.

The shaman's tent was an honored place just outside the main courtyard. Several young monks scurried about tending to mundane tasks a Chilcoat stood awkwardly outside and addressed Tarra. "Do you want me to take you to the ceremony?"

Tarra introduced Shadoc and proceeded to avoid the question by simply changing the subject. "We're going to get the kasis vine tomorrow, you want to come?" She waved the guide stick at him.

"Ah—no, I'll pass if you don't mind. You two go and have a good time. I'll nurse my sore muscles here and see if I can catch up on a few personal things."

"Suit yourself but I'll miss your smiling face." She smirked at his pained expression. "The stick shows a week, so we'll be gone for a while."

Shadoc finally spoke. "It's along the shoreline north, so if you need to come and get us, we'll stick to the shore as best we can."

Chilcoat looked sternly at him assessing the flimsy little bow he carried. "How are you with your weapons?"

"I'm fair. I guess."

"And I have my spear." Tarra flashed the delicate amber blade into Chilcoat's vision.

He winced upon recognizing the familiar form. "You'll miss the joining. Are you sure you want to do that?"

"I've seen the pickings and I think I can pass for another season. Besides, it's important that I make this trip. I'll be back soon, and we can start home."

The slender lad tried to stay in the conversation. "Same here... I have things I want to do before I'm ready to take on being a husband." Chilcoat looked at him dismissively and turned to leave.

The next few days were an odd combination of celebration and mourning. Chilcoat and a couple of his old chums tried to fit in with the games by competing in events they hadn't taken part in since they were adolescents. It was a mixture of sweet memories and comic relief as he and his drunken friends tried to match the youngsters. The mourning came when he collapsed laughing and sweating on the sideline and realized that he had no one with whom to share it.

He worried about Tarra and asked around about the young man. Shadoc turned out to be a perfect fit for her. His fellows considered him more-than-fair with weapons, but he was an odd mix of warrior and shaman in a very young package that many had a hard time dealing with. *They are reflections of each other,* he thought.

Rancon had brought a small group from the highlands last season but said they would not have anyone of age for this season and would probably not come. Chilcoat was glad to hear that he was doing well and had taken command of his tribe. He handed the lion's teeth off to the elders in a public recounting of bravery shown by Lannon in saving his life. He asked that they pass the fangs to his brothers and tell the story to them if they should return next season.

Strangers approached him and asked questions about the 'temple-in-the-sky' and the wonders of the Shanare. He tried to be patient with them but couldn't help but get short with some of their fantasies. When the elders finally called their general session, Chilcoat took advantage of his position to demand time to speak. He was glad Tarra wasn't there to insist that he wear his robes.

He spoke so that all could hear. "I know you've all heard of our great fortune—what some of you call the '*Sky Temple*'. It truly is a place of wonder, and I invite you all to come and visit, but I must warn you, it's a place of great hardship. The crops don't grow well in the poor soil, so we can't support large numbers. I know some have said that it is the promised temple of the Shanare. I don't know that. No one knows that. If you think you have proof, bring it forth for all to judge. Until then, it is simply a stronghold provided by Yod. It has saved many of our tribe from the fury of Hea, but others are blind, and many have died from the cleansing. So I'll leave it up to the elders to show wisdom in how to deal with this new tribe."

As expected, the elders needed time to consider their stance on the issue and adjourned to their meditation hall. They would burn many bowls of herbs before they would come to any agreement, but Chilcoat was sure they would opt for the non-committal... *"Let's wait and see how it all works out."*

As far as new people wanting to come to the citadel, the bleak prospect of the long walk discouraged most of them. All of the women and two of the young men that had come with him elected to join their mate's tribe, but the others brought new partners back with them offsetting their numbers. *People are not as fussy as they used to be and everyone feels the need to do what's right for the good of the clan.*

Tarra returned with her bounty of leaves from far off lands and told stories of miles of endless sand and sheer cliffs rising from the sea. She wasn't happy about leaving her newfound companion, but they both understood the need to return to their people. Their parting was warm and promised of future commitment that tore at Chilcoat. He resolved to be brotherly about it, but their apparent intimacy disturbed him. *I hate myself for thinking she poisoned Caran but can't get it out of my head and now, she has so easily found another. I feel cheated that I've lost her.*

The Change

On their way home, Chilcoat spent extra time exploring and marking alternative paths over difficult patches of terrain. Everyone's spirits were high, and one of the disgruntled challengers from the group had elected to move to his mate's tribe, so the tension was less.

Something had changed in Tarra. She no longer talked to him as she had. She was more formal and distant. She was cooperative but not the spirited sister he had known. In the evenings, she sat by the fire drawing figures in the sand and chanting prayers to the stars.

"Are you OK? You seem kind of distant." Chilcoat approached.

"I'm fine. I just have a lot on my mind."

"Anything I can help with? I mean, if there's anything I can do, let me know."

"No—thanks. I'll let you know if I can think of anything."

"You thinking about home?" He gestured at the circles she had drawn.

"Sort of, the scrolls speak of the symbols we've found at the temple. They explain a game using the symbol, and it has me scared."

"Why are you scared of a game? You made a game for the kids with the symbol. How is that any different? Just because some old scroll has some mumbo-jumbo in it, you shouldn't get all worried about it."

"Maybe scared isn't the right word… I'm concerned about what it means to the ways of our people. I feel changed by it, but I don't know how."

"You've met someone who's touched you. That's good. You should treasure it."

"It's not Shadoc. We have an understanding. No, I'm talking about the teachings I—we've been given," she corrected herself. "I've learned new things and I am trying to understand it all."

"Would it help to explain it to me? Maybe talking about it would help."

"I have to think first. I'm upset by it, that's all."

"Did those old geezers give you drugs? I'll go back there and kick their asses!"

"No. The only herbs offered were known to me, and I didn't take any." She suddenly felt like a sister again explaining a mistake to her big brother. "No, they've given me a great burden. They told me of fables, and witches of the past. That's what they called me, a '*witch*'. They said there've been witches in the past, and they were special, a sign of good fortune. Can you believe that? I'm a good luck charm."

"I'm not surprised. I'm surprised they didn't anoint you queen of the festival or something."

"Well, they sort of did. They said I'm the '*Keeper of the Word*' and a '*Warrior of Truth*' that is to bring a message from Yod."

"Those old bastards, I'm going to kill them. They shouldn't be filling a kid's head with such nonsense."

"I'm not a kid, and it isn't nonsense. I've read the lost scrolls. Shadoc and I studied them when we went in search of the kasis herb. Most of it makes sense. It's just very... disturbing." She looked down at the symbol she had traced in the sand. "I'll be OK. I just need time to think."

"What lost scrolls? There's the wedding scroll and the funeral scroll. They're not lost."

"No, there are others that Talbot showed me. He said I'm to keep them."

"Talbot? You're on first name basis with the high-elder? Did he give you the scrolls?"

"No. He said, '*the council must give them in acceptance of my station*'. I don't know what that means and I'm scared."

"Well, the offer still stands. You can talk to me anytime. Besides, we'll be home by tomorrow night, and you can sleep in your own bed. That'll help." He suffered a kink in his back as he rose to leave.

She traced the symbol one last time then slowly erased it, one segment at a time. As she did, she chanted hauntingly to the stars and shed tears of grief for those who had passed. Chilcoat watched from a distance and grieved from his own sense of loss. *She's grown into a big part of my life but now she's shut me out. She's gone just as completely as Caran.*

The tribe welcomed the returning heroes. Everyone participated in a ceremony of grief for the boy lost to the snake and they held a small feast to praise the rejoining of the tribe. Chilcoat gave a quick overview of his political dealings and each of the newly wedded pairs introduced themselves and pledged their intentions for all to hear. It wasn't as good as the gathering, but it served the purpose.

By the time the third couple was introduced Tarra had already managed to get to the top of the stairs and wandered slowly around the garden paths. *I've never experienced them in this way. They've always just been convenient trails through the gardens. Now they're tied to the stars and to life itself.*

Everything she had learned swam through her head as she scanned the skyline and found the chimney stone. *That means I'm on the path of Vau; the path of 'life'. I wonder if that's a sign.* Passing the intersection that belonged to Hea, she followed it as it slowly arched through the gardens. The vegetables changed to beans and peppers and eventually she came to the intersection with the path that belonged to Yod.

She stopped and stood at the juncture for several moments thinking and watching the stars. *My patch of medicinal herbs is out at the far end where it joins with the outer path of God. I never realized I have such a prime piece of real estate. It's always just been the plot assigned by the gardening committee where nothing else will grow.*

She wandered along the path and checked on her plants. She knew the committee had taken care of them while she was gone, but she wanted to feel the presence of the herbs she had nurtured so carefully. *They speak to me in a warm fragrance as they rustle in the evening breeze. I'll soon harvest the remaining crop and start the cycle again. For now, I'm happy just to stand quietly feeling the warmth of the soil on my feet and watch the stars pour the light of Hea upon us.*

Charona approached from the other direction. "How's it going?"

"Fine, I was just checking on my plants."

"You're a big girl. You can be up here alone if you want. I just wondered if you wanted to talk. I know you and Caran had sort of a thing going and I wondered if I could do anything for you. She was my sister, we shared a lot."

"Did Chilcoat send you?"

"Him? No. He's clueless. He's cute, but a little thick most of the time. Maybe that's why I like him."

"The high-elder told me that I'm the *'Keeper'*. He said it's written that it's my destiny and I have to do it or the tribe will vanish forever."

"Oh he did, did he? Well, that slippery old bastard... It sounds to me like he doesn't want to get blamed for all the crap that's going on and found a girl to blame it on."

"I don't think it's like that. He showed me the ancient scrolls, and said that 'a witch will speak with Yod and bring forth the people of heaven on the true path'."

"Oh is that all. Well, don't you go letting those old frauds talk you into anything. I know you're kind of—special... Your dad was one of them and all, but wouldn't you rather just be one of us? You can let God take care of himself. I mean, you're great with the herbs and things, and everybody appreciates what you do, but I'm not sure anybody is ready to accept you as the shaman."

"No, it's different than that. It's not being a shaman the way Papa was, it's being the keeper of the knowledge—the one who will speak with Yod and who will bring the true faith to the people."

"Well, it sounds like a line of crap to me. Say, I hear you found a guy at the gathering. Why didn't you bring him home to meet the family?"

"Shadoc is the shaman for the western clan. He can't be away from his people. Besides, he's not my *guy*."

"That's not what I heard. I heard you ran off with him for weeks at a time."

"I went with him to gather herbs—oh, never mind. It's none of your business anyway."

"Ha... That's my girl! You tell 'em." Charona laughed and continued her walk along the path back toward her apartment.

Tarra stood thinking about what she had learned. The moon rose in waning reverence to the season and cast a cold gray light on the paths. She wandered from intersection to intersection along the route the scrolls spoke of and tried to remember the writings. *It would help if Shadoc were here to talk to. He remembers things effortlessly. He'd know exactly what the writings say."*

Their brief relationship had fulfilled her. She no longer felt that she was a little girl. She knew now what it was to be a woman and felt confident in it. She knew they would always be close but that they would seldom see each other. *That's OK. I carry his baby and admire his knowledge, and that's enough.*

Tarra returned to her apartment as the field workers began to arrive to do holiday schedule maintenance. She cleared the table, spread a cloth over it, and aligned the edges with the table. She smoothed it and stretched it several times to align the weave so that the pattern etched in the table showed lightly through the cloth. She then prepared a thick ochre paste and carefully inscribed a stylized sunburst following the outer circle of the symbol. As she worked her way around to the top, she pressed the crooked little tip of the tanasin guide stick into the design. On the northern edge, she took a tanasin twig she had brought from the garden and made a notch for it in the pattern. She completed the ring in uniform little flames that she could easily modify when they found a new path. In the center of the sunburst, she traced the circles that showed through the material. By the time she had finished, the cloth was a thing of beauty with blazing yellows and reds smoothed into interlocking rings of perfect symmetry and proportion.

Her fingers looked like bloody stumps and she had apparently rubbed her face giving her an exaggerated rosy complexion and a bright red mustache. She moved the table to stand in the first rays of the sun as dawn crept over the far edge of the courtyard and onto her living room floor. She had worked all night, as if possessed, and now stood exhausted in the morning light. She cleaned up as best she could but was obviously going to have to suffer snickers and whispers for the next few days while her bloody mittens faded. *I'll have to come up with a good story,* she thought.

Chilcoat stood in her doorway in the morning glare. "You've been busy I see. I missed you at the party last night."

"I had some thinking to do."

"So I see. Anything you can tell me about?"

"Sure. Everything you thought you knew about God is wrong, and I'm going to set it right."

"So you said. Does that mean you've spoken with Him and you're ready to amaze us with your wisdom?"

"No—yes—maybe, I don't know. It means I'm scared, and I want your help."

"Sure. What'll it be? You want me to dress up and wave my stick around?"

"Don't be crude. No, I want you to listen to me." She seated him across the table from her and proceeded to explain what the scrolls said about her, the symbol, and the legends of the Shanare. She explained how the scrolls revealed the use of the symbol to invoke the wisdom of God. "I watched Papa do it when I was young, but it's banned by the new-order. It takes a very strong mind to use the symbol and not fall to its seduction." She traced her blood red fingers gently over the patterns on the table. "Daddy grew too dependent on herbs to help him see its wisdom." She looked wistfully at the spirit sticks she had placed on the table. "None of the new-order use the symbol. Daddy, Talbot, and Stafon were the last holdouts, and even they don't use it except for dire situations."

"What are you talking about? It's just a bunch of circles on a table."

"They're the paths in the garden of the Sky Temple."

"Yeah, so it's a bunch of paths. Personally, I think it would have been better to use straight lines. It wouldn't be such a long walk to the cisterns."

"They're the paths of understanding. They take the long route because that's the way of life. Here, see this is the circle of Yod and this is Hea and this is Vau." She traced each circle in turn. "Each is a part of the whole of God, and each has a critical part that it must play."

She took a half-finished game piece and handed it to him. "Here, this is you. Put it in the circles of life where you belong and explain to me why it's there."

"What are you talking about? You said these were circles of God. I don't fit into any of them."

"Don't be dense. You're a part of God. Where do you fit in His plan? Are you more Yod or more Vau?"

"What's this all got to do with me? It's a silly game and a waste of time." He placed the figure down in the center of the diagram. "There. Are you happy?"

"Why did you put it there?"

"Because it's right in the middle. How can that be wrong? Not one way or the other."

"Is that you? Right in the middle, not one-way or the other? Is that where the leader of our people should be?"

"Are you questioning my authority?" He rose to leave.

"It's not I who must answer the question." She grabbed the little figurine and pressed it into his hand.

At the evening meal, Tarra surprised everyone by wearing her sun hood. At first, she tried to hide her hands in the long sleeves, but then she decided it was of no avail, and proudly flaunted the discoloration of her hands. She accentuated the blaze across her face by wearing the hood open at the neck with her hair deliberately tousled around her face. Everyone had seen shaman with painted faces and hands from time-to-time, but it was usually for a festival or some special occasion. To have the young witch appear this way stunned the children. They were sure she had just murdered one of their friends and was out looking for more blood.

After the meal, a small group of children hovered around her, curious to see if she was going to do anything else. She finished her meal and proceeded to walk slowly through the crowd to the main platform. She pulled the carefully crafted medicine cloth from under her cape, rolled it out on the stage, and began an evocative chant. She accentuated certain verses by casting incense into the dwindling ashes in a shower of sparks and smoke that soon had everyone's attention.

When she finished her song, she opened her eyes and gazed onto the crowd. "YodHeaVau has spoken to me." She gestured at the cloth spread on the platform. "He has spoken of the old ways of the Shanare and the Sky Temple. He has brought us here, to this place, to help us learn."

Someone from the crowd scoffed. "Are you telling me that you've spoke with God? Not even Tangar made such outlandish claims and you're only a girl, not a real shaman."

"You're correct... I'm not a shaman as my father was. I am the *'Keeper of the Word'*. I've been entrusted by the elders to bring the word to the people and this is the word." She gestured again at the cloth.

Another voice joined the rumble of dissension. "Somebody go get Chilcoat and tell him that his consort is trying to take his job."

"I'm no one's consort! I speak only for my ancestors and myself. I've been given this burden without choice and I intend to carry it out with, or without, the support of Chilcoat or any of you so-called leaders."

"What do you know that your father didn't? Why didn't he bring us this message?"

"He did. He's the one who's led us here and he now whispers the will of Yod to me."

"Oh, great, the witch is talking to the dead now. That's all we need, no wonder Hea is punishing us so."

"No one speaks with the dead! I speak only with Yod, the spirit within us all, the spirit of my father, and his father before him. That spirit has spoken to me. He has told me that Hea isn't punishing us. He's cleansing the weak and foolish from His flock. When He's done, we'll be born into a new world of stronger, wiser, people who have learned the ways of God."

"And only you, a child, have this wisdom? That's just great." The exasperated crowd began to disperse.

"I don't expect all of you to listen to me. I can't teach any that don't want to learn. I'm only to bring the word. It's up to you to learn what you will. If YodHeaVau finds favor in that, perhaps He will spare you. If He doesn't, you will follow your ancestors to death and never know the light of God. It's up to you."

"You've been drinking more of that spirit juice haven't you? It's all a bunch of mumbo-jumbo you and those freeloading shaman have cooked up to fleece us out of our earnings. Let me guess, you want us to bring a share of our crops and give it to you, so you can spend all of your time in the 'nobility' of teaching us your *wisdom*."

Chilcoat approached from his shop. "That will be enough of that! No one will go idle. She'll work just like the rest of us. If you don't earn your keep, we'll cast you out of the clan to fend for yourself. We can't support an elite class and neither scholar, nor politician, nor priest is above earning his, or her, own keep."

"What about all her talk of God's word? Are we to listen to her?"

"That's between you and God. I can't tell you what to believe. All I can tell you is that she's divined many things for us. She has helped to bring us to this place. Without her, we wouldn't be here today. We would still be back at the lake starving, but I don't know how she does it. If it's talking with God or simply her good fortune, all I know is that I want to believe, and that's good enough for me."

He looked warmly at the young woman and the cloth she had spread on the platform. He slowly opened his clenched fist and exposed the little wooden figurine to her then placed it slowly on the cloth deep in one of the outer circles.

Tarra looked solemnly at his gesture. "Yod has spoken with you. You see, this place truly is a temple. Anyone who will listen will hear His voice."

"Tarra child, I know you feel this. But I, and others, must grow to it. I know that you feel things I don't, but faith is something that has to come because you've looked for it. Some people will come to it and some won't."

"They'll come. It's you that I am worried about."

"Am I so corrupt?"

"You're our leader. It's important that you believe."

"I'll come to it when—when I know that you..." He couldn't find the words to accuse her of poisoning his wife, but he couldn't get the thought out of his head. "I need some reason, some excuse, some answer to why God took Caran from me."

"Yod will answer your doubts, not I."

She turned her attention to a couple of young people that had gathered to look at the cloth. She explained the circles and the shapes and gestured at the garden above. She moved the little figurine Chilcoat had left to where the chimney stone would be and explained the path names she had learned. The small audience slipped away as she tried to explain some of the more cryptic details of the Shanare and their worship using the symbol. Her bright red fingers wrapped around the cloth like the claw of some demon as she grabbed the treasure and left the plaza in quiet dignity.

There was much whispering and prodding as the crews formed up for their evening labor. Tarra joined the others and tended her sections of the garden just as before. Some people passed by during the night and nodded respectfully while others scoffed at her attempt at normalcy. A couple of the youngsters she had spoken with earlier stopped by nervously to confess that they wanted to hear more.

"Come to my house after work, we'll talk."

The winter sky afforded little relief from the relentless rays of the sun. It dipped lower on the horizon but seemed even harsher in its punishment. The air grew cooler as the days shortened, but the cloudless sky provided no relief. Everyone continued their nocturnal ways with only brief excursions into the daylight cloaked in sheets.

She was beginning to show signs of her pregnancy. The robes hid her from public view, but she knew she was going to have to face up to it soon. She was happy that she and Shadoc had this special bond, but she wasn't sure how the others would take it.

***

"I'm pregnant." Tarra spoke plainly to Chilcoat as they sat quietly at her table. "Vau has smiled on Shadoc and me, and we're happy."

He finally spoke after the shock wore off. "How will he provide for you? Are you to leave us?"

"No, we know we can't be together and I'll provide for myself."

"You're a fool to think that you can bring a child into this world alone. The women will talk. They'll call you a harlot and no self-respecting man will have you. Do you know that? Do you know that the child will forever be a burden on the clan? He'll be an outcast."

"He'll be the savior of our people. It's written in the scrolls…"

"Don't you dare blame this on that nonsense! This is your fault and no one else's. You should know better than to have sex with some boy just because you read something in a fairytale. Didn't your father ever tell you that boys only want one thing and then they'll leave you to fend for yourself?"

"My father was your father too! He took in a boy that was left to fend for himself when his parents were killed. He wasn't afraid of women's gossip. He raised him to be the leader of our clan and to follow the word of YodHeaVau. He saw you in the scrolls just as he saw me and my baby."

"You twist my words. I'm worried that you and the child will be hated by those who are hungry and feel you'll burden them in these times of want."

"Will you hate us?"

"What do your scrolls tell you of that? Do they tell you of Caran and how I loved her and how *you*—took her from me?"

"The scrolls tell of our lives and how they intertwine. I know you blame me for the loss of Caran but I can't do anything about that. I can't replace her and I don't want to, but the scrolls speak of a long and fruitful bond between us."

"The scrolls—is that all I am to you, a fairytale to be played out at my expense?"

"No... I'll be your consort. Not only am I a witch, I'm a harlot, and the old women will claim the child is yours."

"The old women be-damned." His mind searched for a way to resolve his conflict. *I'm responsible for all that has happened. I listened to you when I shouldn't have, and now I have nothing. My wife's gone, my tribe's divided, and I'm no longer able to hunt like a man.*

He sat gazing around the room as if it could somehow provide an answer. "I'll claim the child as my own and raise him as my son to save you from their wicked tongues. I'll lie to the world for you because—because I love you." He grabbed her by the arms and held her tight. "But I must know... Did you poison Caran?"

She looked coldly into his eyes. "Will you believe me if I say no?"

"I want to believe you. I want—I want you." He pulled her close.

"You want me to make your life full again. I can't do that. If you'll take my son as your own, I'll be your consort as foretold, but Caran will always be between us."

The child was soon common knowledge, as was their relationship. The townsfolk accepted that the witch was part of their community and was not apologetic for who she was. She was the daughter of Tangar, and would not accept grief from anyone.

Chilcoat held his head high ignoring the grumblings of the old women and began spending extra time with his own children. They seemed to be growing away from him as they matured. He longed for Caran's guiding hand but dealt with them as best he could.

"Why doesn't Tarra come by anymore?" Chara pestered her father. "It's always more fun when she's around."

"She's grown up and wants to live on her own, just as you soon will."

"But we needed her to help us win. The other guys have Burwin and he cheats. We need Tarra on our team to keep him from cheating." Chilton bewailed their conflict.

"Maybe we can talk her into coming over more often. She's very busy with her classes, you know. Say, there's an idea. Why don't you start going to her classes."

That was all the children really wanted, they just needed the old man to suggest it. They ran off squealing in delight and he knew they had taken advantage of him. *It'll do them good to hear the word as she tells it,* he thought.

He found the kids on the central platform with Tarra and her disciples. They all seemed to be very busy cleaning the dais with brooms and water. She wore a ceremonial robe she had fashioned from colored cloth. It flowed easily with her rhythmic song and accentuated her hands. She had stained them an iridescent blue for the occasion and had matching stripes slashed across her cheeks. It seems she had discovered that the platform itself had the symbol etched into its surface. A slight discoloration peeked through years of dust and neglect, and looped to the edge of the platform merging with the trim tiles that accented the little nude figures marching around the rim.

The cleaners shooed a couple of people away and scrubbed every inch of the surface. The gray stone deepened to near black under the sheen of water and a band of pink intersecting circles sprang to life across the disk. Tarra called the group together and chanted softly as the morning sun peeked over the temple wall and touched the far edge of the platform. "It's time to seek shelter. Hea is still cleansing the world and will not allow His children to play any longer."

Chilcoat gathered his family and walked slowly toward home. They were still excited from the diversion and begged Tarra to join them for dinner. "You're welcome anytime, and it would mean a lot to the kids. It's Caran's birthday. I promised them that we could celebrate like we used to."

"I'll join you after I clean up." She wiggled her blue fingers at him and pulled her hood into place.

As she climbed the stairs, a small entourage of her followers talked and laughed with her. He watched with puzzled awareness that she was very special to him and his people. *It's like nothing I've ever seen. Everyone always respects the shaman, but usually it's just a cautious awareness that he knows mystical things, but with Tarra, it's different. Those who know her are enchanted and those who resist her feel her disarming charm.*

Tarra's appeal to the young folks grew with the season. The winter provided more hours to work the gardens, so the daylight respite became more prized. The precious few hours that remained for recreation became a great sacrifice that her followers made for her. Each person stood in different sections of the "great symbol," as they come to call it, and explained why they thought they belonged there. Their discussions were sometimes funny and sometimes very somber. Tarra guided the dialogue to areas that ranged from stardust to her pregnancy. *There's no forbidden topic, but the explanation must include the symbol's influence.* Occasionally, a small crowd gathered to watch their antics. Some were just curious while the games troubled others.

Chilcoat remained politically indifferent but he could see that there would soon be open conflict. He tried to sound gruff as he warned her. "You and your troop are starting to upset the town's folk."

"I know. I'll try to keep it down. They're kids. They just like to showoff sometimes."

"Tell that to their parents."

"I've spoken with Papa…"

"What did the old boy have to say? Are we going on another adventure?"

"Don't be mean. No. He told me that what I'm doing is right. He spoke of YodHeaVau."

"Are you putting words in his mouth or did he really visit you?"

"I don't know. You know better than that. He's gone before I can be sure he came. But now, I remember some of his teachings from when I was very young. Papa would take me along to his meetings and let me help set things up. He, Stafon, and Talbot would talk for hours about YodHeaVau. I realize now that they were talking for my benefit. I was really too young to understand much, but now I'm remembering some. Now I know what they were talking about."

"Careful, now, venturing into such thinking is heresy in the eyes of the council. Claiming to know more about their game than they do will get you into trouble."

"No. Don't you see? I was being trained as the Keeper. It's part of the prophecy. The scrolls say that 'A witch will be born as keeper of the word, and she will learn from birth to awaken the people…'."

"From birth?" Chilcoat looked at her skeptically.

She hesitated thoughtfully. "I can't remember a time that I wasn't tagging along with him. He was always chanting to me."

"Still, it's going to be a hard sell to the elders. Did the scrolls say anything else about this Keeper?"

"Yes, but I'm not sure I should tell you. They say, 'The Keeper is to bring forth a child to lead the tribes in heaven'."

"You're kidding. They don't really say that, do they?"

"You can read them the next time we go to the gathering. Until then you'll just have to take my word for it." She left the shop in a flirtatious swirl of flowing gowns.

He lay quietly wondering at the turmoil in his head. *She's beginning to consume much of my thinking. I need to find more to do. I seldom make the long trip down the cliff to go hunting anymore. My buddies made it clear that they no longer need my efforts. "You're slowing us down."*

***

As the season dragged on, he busied himself in the shop and tended to the children and the gardens. He hadn't taken up rat hunting yet, but he frequently thought about it. He could see Tangar proudly sitting at his hearth watching his meager catch being prepared. The vision haunted him as his knee complained about his inactivity.

He spoke to the empty room. "So you come to me again? You crafty old buzzard, you've got her all stirred up and you tell me I'm too old. What are you up to now?"

Charona stood in the doorway. "Need a hand there brother?"

"What? No. I was just getting ready for work."

"So I heard. I thought I'd stop by and see if you needed anything before work." Tradition demanded that Charona perform the sisterly obligation of checking up on him from time-to-time.

"Ah—nah, I'm alright thanks. I appreciate the offer. You need anything?" He offered after a few moments.

"I thought you'd never ask." She pressed close to him.

The episode was brief and left him a bit shaken. He and Charona had had a long-standing arrangement, but since she had bonded with Lannon, it had been only an occasional flirtation.

"I hope your consort understands." Charona straightened her hair and pulled her robes into place.

"She understands all too well. Right now I hope she's more concerned with how to keep her flock from getting too rowdy."

"Yeah, I've noticed the game she's made up has people arguing. Maybe that's a good thing. It keeps them on their toes."

"As long as they stay off mine, I'll be happy."

"That's the old Chilcoat I know." She gathered her things and headed to the garden for her evening chores.

He found Tarra in her patch of herbs. She was pulling up the last of the summer crop. "There isn't much left I can use, but they still need to be handled with reverence. I have to sort and trim the plants into bundles for drying or burning. I can't allow any of the dangerous ones to fall in with the garden refuse. I have to burn them before the morning sun can break their spell. The herbs willingly provide their healing gifts, but their sprits demand that they be set free before Hea can look upon them in their shame."

It all seemed silly to him, but he was glad to help her get rid of the toxic residue before the children had a chance to play with it.

They celebrated their final demise in a cloud of smoke and sparks that chased all but the hardiest souls from the area. Tarra finished the ceremony with a somber chant of thanks and humility while he took the opportunity to leave and clean up before bed. He carried a couple of bundles of herbs and left them at her door.

Looking quickly around her apartment, he noticed the little altar she had erected in the alcove near the door. He marveled at the intricacies of Thoma's wand and then grabbed the second stick. He considered it for a moment and tried to imagine how he could add new carvings that would tell the story of how Tarra had saved so many with her father's ways. He decided that he would have to think about it and was about to leave when he realized that Tangar had whispered to him again.

"You old bastard, you haunt me with stories of the past, but you don't tell me what you want."

"He wants you to leave my stuff alone." Tarra chided, as she entered with her clutch of branches.

"Oh, yeah, sorry. I was just thinking and sort of lost my way."

"Here, this will help." She dropped her load and handed him the little figurine from the shelf.

He clenched it in his fist and looked longingly at the young woman. "The kids would like it if you would come by more often."

"The kids?"

"*We'd* like it if you would come by more often."

"I'm right in the middle of testing some new plants. I'm not sure if it's them or the baby, but I haven't been very good company lately. Maybe in a few days it'll pass."

"Are you sure it's a good idea to mess with herbs while you're pregnant? Can't it wait until you're—done?"

"I'll not be 'done' for five more months and the herbs won't wait. I need to catch them before they dry completely."

"Still, it seems like it would be better to have someone else do that for you. Maybe Charona could help."

"No, she's pretty busy helping you."

He caught the edge in her voice and tried to avoid the subject. "What can be so important that it can't wait?"

"I've made a new sun cream. It seems to toughen the skin so you can stay in the sun longer. The only problem is that it upsets my stomach a little and makes my skin shiny. See?" She shrugged her robe from her shoulders exposing her arms and back.

"Yes I see." He reached out almost touching her firm white flesh but changed his mind, as the subtle discoloration of her freckles seemed almost to laugh at his lustful assessment. He paused at the little shrine next to the door as he left and placed his figurine next to the others. "I think he'll be happier here."

The gardens needed only occasional attention during winter. They prepped the ground and planted the seeds, but there was little else to do. Tarra spent more time experimenting with her concoctions and mentoring her flock of followers. The baby grew possessive of her thoughts and began to interfere with her every action. It would soon be due, and she could hardly wait, as she prayed that Yod would help her be a good mother. *A mother without a father,* she lamented that Shadoc was not here to join with her—*with us.* She caressed her belly feeling the presence of their child.

As summer approached, she found less time for Chilcoat and spent most of her time perfecting her salves and creams. She discovered that the kasis vine not only tamed the tanasin but was, in itself, a soothing herb. She would spice it with various different pollens and berries and make colored ointments that soothed her muscles and left warmth in her loins that helped her sleep. The baby also seemed to enjoy the relief and tumbled playfully before she slept. The only drawback to the cream seemed to be the rust color it left on her skin. It would linger for a day or two before eventually fading. She applied a liberal amount to her legs and arms after a long night's work and was about to retire when Chilcoat bound into the room.

"Someone's coming!"

"What? Is someone sick?"

"No. Someone is camping far to the west, about two day's journey near the foothills."

"Is it the tribe? Can you tell?"

"No. All I can see is a small fire just at the edge of the savanna. I'm sending a team to greet them, so we should know in a couple of days."

"What if it isn't them? What if it's the Shanare coming back to take their temple?"

"Then we'll deal with that. Lan will lead the team and be cautious about their approach."

"Lan? What's the matter, brother, getting too fat to make the climb?" She tried to evoke their old relationship.

"Yeah, something like that. Besides, I wouldn't want to leave you in such a delicate condition."

"Yeah, don't blame me just because your knee hurts. I gave you some lotion, use it."

"You and your creams... Has the baby been treating you good?"

"Yeah, he's a doll." She patted her tight belly and looked longingly at it.

***

They spent the next two days preparing weapons and food in anticipation of either a battle or a feast. By noon of the third day, Lannon and his band of warriors climbed the ladders with some game they had taken on their venture and word that the visitors were from the western village.

Tarra's heart raced at the thought that Shadoc would be among them. She had prayed to Yod to call him to her but she feared that no good would come of it. *The temptation of Yod's power pulled at me in selfish allure that is the greatest of all sins.* "Please forgive me, please, please... " She begged as she caught sight of him crawling over the edge of the plateau. Watching wistfully as he dusted himself from the journey, she resisted running to him. *I dare not diminish Chilcoat in the eyes of the clan by revealing our relationship.*

Chilcoat, and a large group of townsfolk, stood by greeting the travelers as they each scaled the last few rungs of the scaffolding and stepped onto the plateau for the first time. Their reaction was the same as it had been for everyone. They all wandered around in disbelief and wonder. Relatives from the tribe greeted some of them and others simply followed a friendly face to explore the citadel.

Tarra finally dragged Shadoc to stand in front of Chilcoat. "You know each other, and we're family, so act like it."

Shadoc solemnly extended his hand palm-up. Chilcoat hesitated a moment and covered it with his own. Chara and Chilton joined the trio as they toured the village. Shadoc repeatedly grabbed at Tarra's hand as they explored the signs and symbols that adorned the structure but she self-consciously avoided his familiarity when others were around. They were in a world all their own as they queried and resolved all sorts of teachings they had received.

Eventually the group broke up and everyone sought shelter from the sun. Chilcoat took his kids and went to his shop while Tarra acted as courteous host to the shaman. In her apartment, they laughed and cried over their predicament. She demonstrated some of her recent lotions for him, and they rested quietly in a warm embrace. As evening approached, she rose to her regular routine leaving him to recover from his journey. He would need a day or two to get on the night shift. In the meantime, she gossiped with the rest of the townsfolk about their fate. Some wanted to get off the plateau and join them when they returned to the western village and others wanted to make them part of the tribe. *We need new blood and the excitement of new, and rekindled, relationships is a welcome diversion.*

Tarra reserved her opinion and repulsed several inquiries about her new friend. The baby was coming soon and she felt the need to ready her nest. She cleaned and scrubbed things that didn't seem to deserve the attention, but it kept her mind off the stirrings she felt. As morning approached, the baby came while Shadoc held her tightly. They prayed and thanked Vau for bringing the Spirit to life. It was a perfect boy with a firm grip and skin the color of amber.

"Chilgar," she whispered to him. "*Child to the man foretold, fulfillment of the word.*" She chanted gently rocking him to sleep for the first time. They lay in naked bliss enjoying the miracle that had changed their lives.

Shadoc gazed lovingly on the pair. "He's an odd color, don't you think?"

Tarra placed him on his pillows. "There's nothing odd about him. He's perfect."

"Sure, but people will talk. Who do you know with skin so— warm?"

"He's yours, dummy, just as the scrolls prophesy, he's '*the one foretold',* the golden child that heralds the second coming. Personally, I think it's the herbs I've been using. It'll probably go away in a couple of days. It usually does." She held her palms out exposing the lingering rusty tint.

"Will you come home with me?" Shadoc pulled her close.

She looked solemnly at the child. "We'll talk. Now I just want to be alone with him."

Shadoc pulled his sun-gear on and ventured into the plaza alone for the first time. A couple of his clansmen were sitting on the edge of the central platform talking. They too were still off schedule and found comfort in seeking out their friends. He surveyed the temple walls.

"How long are we going to stay? Our presence is a strain on our host's hospitality. We have to either become productive or leave."

"We, kind of, want to move into one of the vacant apartments." One of the young couples looked nervously at their leader.

A second pair scoffed at the concept. "I'd rather get back on the trail as soon as possible. We've seen the temple and I want to get back to my life."

Shadoc was torn—he wanted to stay with his wife and son, but he needed to get back to his village just as Tarra needed to get back to her life. He climbed onto the platform and wandered around the symbol playing the game of souls from the scrolls. He chanted rhythmically calling upon YodHeaVau to comfort his thoughts. Some of his clan joined in the mantra they frequently used to ward off unwelcome spirits.

Shadoc addressed the group as it broke up. "We'll stay for three more days and those who will return with me, will meet here at this time." He gestured at the shadow that crept across a band etched into the plaza wall.

Climbing the garden stairs, he wandered the paths trying to get his bearing. As he rounded the squash patch, he spotted the chimney stone in the distance. He immediately headed for the altar and stood gazing into the distance looking at the sun and then across the plateau to the sighting stones. *This is truly a magical place, Tarra and the boy are lucky to be here.* He then realized it was not luck at all. *They must be here. I know that I can't ask her to leave. She has an important duty here and I was lucky to have played a small part in it. I know all of that, but I still want them with me.*

He wandered to the western sighting stone and gazed out across the panorama toward home. He tried to pick out the pass they had come by, but the haze made the hills a simple gray ripple along the horizon. *I wonder if everyone is OK. I left enough medication for the time we allotted ourselves, but that's only good if no one new gets sick or hurt. I have to leave. I know that. I just want it to be different.*

***

Chilcoat slept fitfully dreaming of Caran and wondering what was to become of him. *My knee keeps me from being an effective hunter and the sun-sickness has taken years from my eyes.* He saw

Tangar hunting rats again in his dream and startled awake. He was sweating even though the weather was cool. The children were still asleep and he couldn't help but think of the women in his life. The pain and loss he felt for Caran was blending into a dull emptiness that he accepted as *"times-gone-by." Tarra is now a part of that emptiness. She has changed so much in the past few months that I don't recognize her anymore. She too is an empty longing for the way things used to be. The comfort I find with Charona helps fill some of the void, but she also is a different person now that Caran is gone.*

Have I grown too old and don't realize it? My children need me only to resolve conflicts and provide food, and my hunting buddies need me only at story time... I'm not yet ready to leap from the cliff, but I understand how some people have taken that path. Maybe it's just their bad eyes, but more than a few have 'fallen' in the darkness over the years.

He pulled his sun cape on and headed out to see if he could catch a rabbit in the gardens. He took the stairs that led past Tarra's apartment, but there didn't seem to be any signs of life, so he continued up to the garden. He noted there were a few stragglers wandering around tending to irrigation needs, and then he spotted Shadoc over by the sighting stone. "Only works in the morning."

"What's that?"

"The stones—they only line up at dawn."

"Oh yeah, I know. I was just looking out toward home. We'll be leaving in a couple of days, and I was just seeing if I could pick out the trail."

"Will Tarra be going with you?" Chilcoat spoke uncertainly.

Shadoc hesitated a moment. "No, she and Chilgar have bigger things ahead of them."

"Chilgar?"

"Our son... Oh, I'm sorry. He was born last night. Oh, maybe she wanted to tell you... I know I'm not supposed to let on that he's mine, but you know..."

"You're the father. No one can take that away from you. The lie we live is for him."

"Yes, well, we have a son. His name is Chilgar, in your honor, and he is golden brown, and I'll have to leave him on his third day of life." He stood solemnly facing the western skyline.

"Does she know?"

"That I'm leaving? No, she's still living the dream of childbirth and thinks we can somehow be together."

"We can find a place for you here. We don't have much, but we can fit a few more people in if we have to."

"I'm needed at home, just as she's needed here. We knew this when we met. We knew we could never be together, but we know the parts we are to play. It isn't much, but it is all we have."

"No. Now you have Chilgar. He'll grow into a fine lad. She'll be a good mother, and I'll teach him all that I know."

"I'm glad you'll take the boy. I prayed that you would. But, I must warn you, he'll not be an easy child. The scrolls have told of many trials he must face."

"You people and your scrolls, he's a child and he'll learn like any other. If he's to be a prince among men, he'll have to earn it."

Tarra and the baby slept and played most of the day with a great deal of learning going on by both. As the news of the birth spread, many visitors stopped by to see the golden child and leave gifts of toys and food. By the third day, the coloration had faded to baby-pink but the story would live on for years that the child was born as a sign of good fortune.

Shadoc pled his case one last time. "I want you to come with me, but I know you can't. You have your people, and now you have him, but it doesn't change the way I feel. I still want you to come to my home and be my wife."

"I'll come to visit when I can—when he's strong enough for the journey." She cuddled her treasure. "We'll meet again at the gathering next year. You can tell me what you've learned and maybe someday we can move to the winter village together."

"When we're too old to care about our bond—that's not much to look forward to."

"Maybe I can teach someone to take my place and then I can come to stay with you."

"You know what the scrolls say. You and he are destined to grow strong in the ways of YodHeaVau here in the temple."

"The scrolls are just a bunch of stories. I'm not the 'Keeper'. Look at him—he's not the golden child. We're just a couple of pretenders who got caught up in a bunch of hooey."

"You know that isn't true. You called to me through Yod and I heard you. That's why I am here, but I'm only a small part, and I do only what He tells me. He told me to come to you, to meet the boy, to learn what you've found. I'll take the knowledge of the Sky Temple back to my people, and we'll strengthen our bond through Him. You can call to me again if you need me."

"Daddy taught me never to call on Yod for my own gain. I'm afraid it's a temptation I've fallen prey to, and now bad things will come of it."

"Nothing bad will happen. Tangar and the others of the old school protected those who are too weak and call on the Spirit for all things. 'It's a weak spirit that calls on Yod for daily bread and then does nothing to care for the grain'. Vau provides for all who will follow the way. You are Yod. You have no need to fear calling on the One."

"But Daddy said He would tempt us, and that no good can come from it, and now I've fallen by begging for you to come."

"Yod embraces the spirit of both good and evil for His own purposes. If you call on Him with selfish desire, selfish spirits will hear your prayers and draw from you. You didn't call to me for yourself. You called me to complete the prophecy, so everything will be OK."

"How do you know that? The scrolls don't speak of such things."

Shadoc lowered his voice and looked around for any who might be listening. "Of course not, the elders are very powerful and have spent many years 'preserving' the scrolls."

"Are you saying they changed the writings?"

"No. You remember the scrolls we read, the lost scrolls? They speak of many things that don't fit the vision of the new-order so the council doesn't use them. The 'enlightened' few select only those verses that give them power over the weak."

"Then where did you learn all of this? I need to come with you to learn from your master."

"It sounds of heresy to me." Chilcoat entered the room and interrupted.

"Yes, it may be—it is what I know, and it has served me well."

"Well, we're of Tangar's ways and have no need for another."

Shadoc bristled in defiance. "Did Tangar teach you of the child, or the symbol, or of the second coming?"

"No. He taught us of stars and seasons—things that are real. He dealt with spirits and symbols in his own way to keep us from straying into harm."

Tarra stepped between them. "He taught me of the symbol."

"He taught you in a dream. You have to keep what's real from what's not. This is real," he gestured at the baby. "This is not," he grabbed the figurine from the altar. "You're a mother now, with responsibilities and duties. You can't spend all of your time playing games."

"You're an ass! You have no idea what we're even talking about. Just get out of here and leave us alone."

"I'll not have you listening to this charlatan. You can't leave us. You have to stay with me." Chilcoat desperately pled his case.

"Get out!" She grabbed the little statue and threw it at him. "I'll go with my husband if I wish. You can't keep me here." The baby started to cry and Shadoc stepped forward to stand between them.

"We'll see about that." Chilcoat tried to save face by stepping back out into the light. The morning shadow was creeping down the western wall and the visiting clan was beginning to assemble on the altar stone. *It'll soon be time for them to leave and I need to find some way to convince Tarra not to go with him. My mind is a jumble of desperation... I can't let him steal her, yet all I can think of is to appeal to her sense of duty.*

As the shadow reached the designated band etched into the temple wall, Shadoc and his people checked their preparations and left the altar stone. There was much fanfare and celebration as the visitors formed up into traveling pairs. Two of their flock had decided to stay and three families joined their band.

Tarra arrived with Chilgar and was obviously not planning on leaving. Chilcoat breathed a sigh of relief since his only plan was to sic his children on her in desperation. She followed Shadoc closely talking and laughing. Despite the disapproving glares from some of the old women, she let him nuzzle the baby as they neared the scaffolding leading down the face of the cliff. Shadoc spoke softly to the pair. "We've had this time together, as we should, and I'll miss you both. YodHeaVau, please whisper ever gently on their souls."

He then turned to Chilcoat. "I made this for you. It's a guide stick that leads to the western village. You're welcome to visit us at your leave. I thank you for letting our tribes join in your temple."

Chilcoat swallowed his pride and stepped back into his political role addressing the group of travelers. "We have little, but you and your people are welcome to visit whenever you can."

Everyone was saddened as the last face disappeared below the edge of the cliff and the visit officially ended. A small band of hunters accompanied them onto the savanna to be sure they found the trail leading west.

Chilcoat handed the guide stick to Tarra and tried to be pleasant. "I see you made the right decision. I'm glad you are going to stay with me."

"I'm needed here and nothing more. I would leave if I could, and you couldn't stop me." She looked coldly at the stick and headed home. *I know he's just being who he is and that everything he said is true, but he's so damn arrogant about it that I just can't let him get away with it.*

***

Chilgar grew strong as the seasons passed. He was soon walking and getting into all sorts of mischief. Tarra took him along while she tended her plants, and he excavated paths and tunnels in the soft soil. He seldom wore clothes of any sort, despite his mother's objections, and his skin turned a shiny harvest brown with the summer. She held lessons for him and any of the other children who would listen, and they learned of plants, animals, spirits, and demons. She spoke of YodHeaVau but didn't dwell on it for the children.

She proved to be an able mother but could only gather a few of her loyalist followers to her meetings. Chilgar attended these sessions, since he couldn't avoid them, but he generally just busied himself with games and paintings. His paint covered, naked, form punctuated some of her most poignant lectures by sprinting across the ceremonial platform to jump into her arms with squeals of glee about some rock or lizard he had found.

When the weather continued to be harsh, her explanations of Hea's purification grew thin. They had done everything she had asked, and yet the cycles of heat and rain continued. She struggled with her teachings and found that she couldn't remember some of what she had learned. A vague jumble of dreams and haunting memories gnawed at her. *If I could read the scrolls again, maybe I'd have an answer.*

At times like these, Daddy would take a spirit-walk and come back with an answer. I just can't do that. I've seen my father ravaged by the toxins of the spirit-herbs and I can't do that to my baby. It just isn't right. It's the job of the Seer, the one who must guide the people, and that's not me. I can't even keep my own son in line much less the whole tribe.

She pulled her ceremonial robes from storage. She hadn't worn them since before Chilgar was born. They were dusty and creased in places they shouldn't be. Spreading them on the floor, she crawled over them tugging and pressing them back into shape. She was finally satisfied that they were as good as they were going to get on short notice and pulled some herbs from her supplies to make a thick black gruel that she carefully stirred into a small bowl.

She looked for a moment at Chilgar sleeping quietly in his bed and then stripped her clothes off and stood naked before the little altar she had made for the spirit sticks. She offered the bowl to them and then dipped a single finger into the mixture touching it to her cheek. A single deep blue tear rolled down her face. She did it again on the other cheek and then dipped her whole hand into the bowl and held it up over her head. The dye ran down her arm in purple ribbons that stopped just before her breast. She did it with the other hand and stood transfixed for several moments while the dye dried into a web of translucent blue lines radiating down her arms.

She carefully pulled her robes into place and woke Chilgar. He was groggy but compliant as he dressed for the occasion. He immediately noticed her blue hands and wanted some of his own. She was about to deny him when she decided that he too deserved to join in the ceremony. She showed him how to let the dye drip down his arms and helped him mark his face with three slashed lines on each check. "It's war paint and we're going to do battle."

He was more than happy to comply since he often played warrior games with Chilcoat. She tried to get him to wear a shirt, but he refused to cover any of the markings. Her robe fit a little more snuggly than it had before. The sleeves still flowed delicately in wings as before, but now her torso showed the ample cleavage of a mother.

She grabbed the scepter in one hand and Chilgar with the other and they made a grand entrance down the stairway and across the plaza to stand on the middle of the altar stone. The usual gathering of townspeople were milling about waiting for the evening's job assignments and were somewhat taken aback by their appearance. She chanted the call of evocation and floated around the platform for all to hear.

Chilcoat was busy with one of his old friends when he noticed the commotion outside his shop. He looked out and saw the specter from his past. He was just about to go see what she was up to when he returned to his room and pulled his ceremonial robes on. *If she's going to make a fuss, I'll show her that I'm still game.*

He marched to the platform where she calmly finished the last refrain of her song and ended by submissively offering the scepter to him.

"Anything in particular you want me to do with this?" He whispered to her.

"Tell me why Hea is testing us."

"Again with the easy questions… I thought you had it all figured out."

"I do—the Seer must walk with the Spirit."

"Whoa, that's not going to happen. You poisoned me for the last time."

"I poison no one." Their conversation got louder and started to draw attention from the crowd. "The Seer must talk with Yod to beg understanding. That's you, not me! I'm just the Keeper, I just hold the word, and you are to see that it's done." She pressed her hand against his bare chest and left a blue palm print.

"Can't we take this inside?" He grumbled under his breath.

"The Keeper can't hide the word. Everyone should hear what I say." Chilgar was growing impatient with the exchange and began to pull the scepter from his hands.

"You'll take this from me soon enough." Chilcoat raised the staff and motioned to the moon that had just peeked over the fortress wall. "I'll consider what you say, but for now, we must tend the gardens."

"The word calls you to action. None but you can see the way."

"What would you have me do then? Drink some of your witch's brew or charm some viper?"

"You must speak with Yod. If you can do that without my herbs, you're a great man indeed." She sprinkled some incense on the fire, grabbed the scepter from his hand, and pulled Chilgar to her side as she left the platform in a swirl of ceremonial robes and perfumed haze. The meeting broke up and left Chilcoat standing by the fire irritated by her arrogant demands.

Lannon took pity on Chilcoat's awkward appearance. "I think she's got you there."

Chilcoat turned to face him. "She's—oh never mind. Why aren't you out hunting?"

"I was just listening to the wife give me a ration about not being attentive. It's hard to be attentive if they won't leave you alone."

"*Bliss*—that's what us old guys call it, you'll get used to it in a few years."

"Yeah, well I can do without it."

Chilcoat reflected on his years of marital 'bliss'. *It wasn't always fun, but I miss it, nonetheless.* "You just need to go hunting. By the time you get back, she'll be glad to see you, and you'll be horny enough to screw a goat, so it'll all seem worthwhile."

Lannon looked unsurely at his weapons. "Speaking of which, why don't you come with me? We'll see if we can add a notch to your talking-stick."

"Weren't you listening? The princess wants me to go stumble around the altar with her barfing up my guts."

"I heard her challenge you to get off your ass. You've been moping around here long enough. You can mourn all you want, but at some point you have to move on or get out of the way."

"Harsh words from someone I call a friend."

"That's what friends are for… Are you coming or not?"

"I can't leave the kids."

"Let Charona take care of them. She deserves some bliss of her own."

"Alright, I'll do it. It'll keep Tarra off my back for a couple of days and do me good to get some exercise."

"That's the spirit. You can bring some smoking herb and maybe Yod will fill you in on what to do with her."

"Oh, I know what to do with her, but I'm not sure a public spanking would get us very far."

The trip down the cliff face was precarious in the dark, but it made him feel like a man again. His muscles complained at first, but soon responded with a strength he hadn't felt in months. The sweat poured down his chest as they trotted out across the savanna. The blue handprint ran in streaks down his stomach and soon disappeared into a vague smudge as it dribbled down his groin.

The hunt was moderately successful near dawn when they finally cornered a small herd of antelope. Lannon let Chilcoat take a young buck on the second shot. It wasn't a particularly clean kill, but it was good enough, and it gave him a boost that made him feel better about himself. *I remember how I had done a similar thing with Tangar. The old man lost three arrows trying to bring down an elk but he was finally successful while I tried to look busy doing something else. It gave the old boy a chance to brag around the fire again and no mention was made of his missed shots.* "Not like the old days, but I finally got him." He nodded appreciation to Lannon.

They laughed and smoked around the fire as they dressed the kill for transport. The conversation stayed away from Tarra and her mandate, but it still loomed heavily in Chilcoat's thoughts. The sun was starting to make itself felt as they gathered what they could carry and got ready to leave. *The remaining carcass will make a good breakfast for the scavengers,* he thought, as he pressed his hand onto the moist flesh. The blood was thick and sticky as he pulled it away and made a single handprint on his chest.

Lannon smirked at the gesture as the pair headed back across the savanna with their burden. By the time they reached home, the handprint had turned nearly black with dust and grime from the trail, but didn't lose its distinctive shape. They celebrated their kill around the fire with accolades going to the brave hunters. Lan gave full credit to Chilcoat for the kill, but Chilcoat tempered the tale with the truth that he had missed the first shot and nearly lost the prey with the second. It wasn't a necessary confession, but one that showed his acceptance of his age. A younger man, perhaps, would have relied on his companion to keep his secret, but he felt no shame in admitting that he wasn't the warrior he had once been. The humble gesture was largely lost on the crowd that gathered for the meal.

Tarra smiled knowingly at him and held Chilgar's hand quietly while he told the story. She brought him a cloth and water so he could wash up and said nothing while he washed his arms and face leaving the handprint for the last. He expected her to make a comment but was pleasantly surprised when she said nothing. She obviously took note of the marking but simply rinsed the cloth and handed it back to him so he could scrub his chest. When he had finished, she scrubbed his back vigorously while he held Chilgar on his lap playing keep-away with a game stick.

The feasting crowd ignored their little bonding ceremony, but he felt warmth in her actions that touched him deeply. He realized that he loved her despite the nagging grief over the loss of Caran. He couldn't imagine life without Tarra's... persuasion. *It's easier to face her when she's openly hostile to me. Then, at least, I don't feel like grabbing her and holding her close. I'm, somehow, more at ease if I feel like turning her over my knee.* "Thank you," was all he could think of to say.

"By your leave."

"Stop that. I don't want you to treat me like that. I'm your..."

"My what? My brother? My husband? My friend?"

"Yes. My friend... my best friend. What would you have me do, friend?"

"I told you. You must speak with Yod."

The contempt he felt for the unfeeling god that had taken his wife somehow seemed less as he gazed upon her angelic face. "OK . What are we talking about?"

"Let me go get the snake."

"All right, I'm sorry. I know you take this stuff seriously. I'm just uncomfortable with it. I never got the training you did."

"Papa trained you for what you do, so do it."

"What about the herbs and the snake? Can't we just sacrifice a goat or something?"

"You would force Vau to leave her chosen home to try to please Her? No. The sacrifice you must make is in your heart." She pressed her hand warmly on his chest. "Hea and Vau care nothing for you, they simply are... Yod is the only one that will listen to your supplication."

"You and your spirits... Tangar warned me not to go there."

"See, you do remember his lessons."

"I remember him sitting around talking to rocks. Is that what you want? You want me stay up all night and talk to the stars?"

"If it helps... You must talk with God, if Hea will help you, then you should accept the gift and be grateful."

"Are we back to snakes?"

"Why don't you start with smoking herb? You're comfortable with that."

"Will you be with me? I want that."

"Of course, it's my job." She gathered Chilgar and her other things and headed for her apartment. "I'll drop him off and we'll meet at your place. Bring some friends."

Lannon and Charona were the only friends he could think of, but he didn't want to impose on them. *I don't need an audience if all I'm going to do is sit around the house smoking and drinking. I pretty much have that down.* He sent his kids over to their friends and tried to clean up some of the clutter. *There isn't much hospitality I can offer, but I have an ample supply of wine and herb.*

She arrived in the late afternoon dressed in her ceremonial robes and carrying a small medicine bag. She had again stained her hands and arms. This time it was a rose color. He was speechless and bewildered. "Did I miss something? Do I have to dress up?"

"No. You're fine. You can wear whatever makes you comfortable."

She began clearing the large worktable and dusting the surface as she searched it for blemishes. A smile came across her face as she confirmed what she had suspected. She got a damp cloth and polished the platform revealing the great symbol in the center flanked by some decorative floral designs on either end. The drawings stained into the surface were light pink and didn't appear until the water soaked in.

"You sit here, and I'll sit here." She gestured to the floral designs. "That looks like tanasin, so I think you should sit there with the little man. This is kasis, the peacemaker." She climbed onto the table and settled onto her designated spot facing the center of the symbol.

"How did you know that this was here? I've been working on this table for years and never noticed it."

"This is the temple of the Shanare, so of course they have the symbol here."

"Temple? No. This is my shop."

"This is your shop in the temple of the Shanare, now sit and let's get started." She spread the medicine cloth in front of her and began arranging little packets on the cloth.

The delicate pink tears that stained her cheeks and the warmth that radiated from her partially exposed torso captivated him. He grabbed his herb pouch and flask of wine and crawled up on the platform. Straining not to grunt, he hoisted his considerable bulk onto the table and awkwardly moved to the center of his designated area. He loosened his robe and sat expectantly across the slab from her.

She kindled a small fire in the center hollow of the symbol and scented it with incense then looked up at him. "Aren't you going to smoke?"

"Ah, yeah, sure... I just thought you were going to say something or chant or something like that."

She looked at him for a moment then shrugged her robe from her shoulders exposing her torso. She raised her arms exhibiting the pink stains that ran down them and framed her breasts in almost perfect symmetry. She softly chanted a familiar song and made evocative gestures with her hands.

"Is that enough, or should I go on?" She asked as the song ended.

"No. I'm good." He bent to light his pipe with a twig that he returned to the fire. "I'm glad you came. I've missed having you around."

"I'm here for the asking."

"No, don't you see—I don't want to have to ask you to come. I want you to want to be here."

"You didn't invite anyone else?" She changed the subject.

"No. I don't really have any friends, except Lan, and he's probably sleeping."

"And Charona, you seem to be good friends with her."

"Yeah—she's probably sleeping too. No, I just figured if I'm going to do any spirit-walking, I'd rather do it by myself."

"Suit yourself. Here, drink this."

"What's in it?"

"Tea, you dolt—I'm not going to give you anything you don't ask for." She pulled her robe back on shaking her head in exasperation.

"So, what's next? Do we sacrifice the goat now?"

"Here, let me get the snake." She started rummaging through her bag.

He knew she was joking but was relieved when she extracted the two figurines she had brought. She had spent many hours carving the little figures to represent people more closely. Their stubby little bodies were nude with exaggerated sexual attributes and large flat feet. She stood them up on the edge of the symbol staring at the fire.

"Here, this is you. Place him." She moved the chubby little figure toward him. It had what he hoped was an exaggerated belly and a small but distinctively erect penis.

He picked up the figure and inspected it critically. "Thank you, I guess." He traced the protruding outline with his finger and looked curiously toward the other figure. "Is that you?"

"Yes, for now." She obviously carved the second figure while she was pregnant and showed her appreciation for the condition. The oversized breasts lay placidly on an equally oversized belly and the hips were excessively wide. She picked up the figure and scanned the symbol before her, delicately placing the doll in one of the arching elements of the diagram. "I am."

"You're what?"

"No, '*I am.*' That's what you say when you've decided where you belong on the symbol. Then someone will ask you to defend your choice. It's a game we play to help us understand our feelings."

She proceeded to explain the rules of the game, and they played several rounds with much dispute about where certain thinking had come from. He consumed several pipes of herb and most of the wine he had brought. They laughed and cried as they questioned each other's motivations and beliefs exploring the symbol.

Chilcoat stirred from the platform and retrieved their breakfast. "Will you live with me now?"

After a moment's hesitation, Tarra spoke softly. "No. I can't. We're two. See, you are tanasin and I'm kasis. We must stay apart to grow so that we can be brought together when we're needed." She gestured at the symbols on the table as she pulled her robes into place and hopped down.

"You and your damn weeds... I'm not a plant. I'm a man. I need you—not some mumbo-jumbo about signs and..."

"And God? The writings tell us that we are these things... We can't change that. We'll stay as we are." She kissed him lightly, took a small plum from the plate he had offered and left.

The fire she had kindled on the platform seemed to feel her depart, flickered once, and turned to a single aromatic wisp of smoke that trailed after her. "Damn her and her magic." He grumbled at the prospect of another night's work.

He normally didn't use the little fire pit in the table for his work. *I tried it a couple of times, but I found that it didn't draft well and left the shop smoky just as it is now. Maybe she's right. Maybe my workbench is an altar and I'm offending the gods with my menial labor.*

He swept the remaining ashes onto a plate and dumped them in the forge he had built at the far end of the room. They flashed to life in a shower of sparks that swept up the chimney.

"There, are you happy now?" He spoke to Tangar. "You and your witch girl... You make my life miserable with dreams and memories of how it was, but you give me no answers."

He stirred the embers and stoked the fire back to life. He was nearly finished with a shovel and needed to temper the blade. The work felt good in his hands and it pulled his mind away from the girl and her mystical ways. He couldn't help but linger for a moment on her as he remembered the song she had chanted so softly, and the way her arms seemed to writhe under the markings. *She truly is a witch.* He thought again of Tangar as his father. *I have to give you credit, you certainly trained her well.*

The fire chased the chill from the autumn evening as he moved the tool close to the coals watching it steam slightly. He remembered how the old man had taught him the process. *It was a day not unlike this one. I wasn't happy about the training lecture. I was going hunting with my friends and really didn't want to be bothered with such trivial things. After all, I'm a hunter. I don't need to know about garden tools. The training lasted far too long and my buddies left without me. I remember how Dad seemed to take pleasure in ruining my plans.*

Chilcoat spoke to the shovel as if it were his father. "You would give long boring sermons about the duty of being a man, and how important it is to provide for your family. You truly were stuck in your old ways. Maybe that's why you never taught anyone about the symbol." Tangar's words came to him as if just spoken: *"The secrets of Yod are for but a privileged few, common men should not delve into such things."* Chilcoat smirked at the thought. *Now your daughter is revealing it to everyone. I doubt you would approve of such a thing.*

Chilcoat prodded the fire and watched the sparks trail up and out the vent hole. "Is that it, old man? You want me to stop her from straying from your ways?" He thought about having Tarra as a submissive wife that stayed hidden from prying eyes doing his bidding in grateful servitude. A quick recollection of her standing over him with the spear he had fashioned disrupted the wistful vision. He shook his head. "If you're trying to tell me something, you're going to have to be clearer than reminiscing about your bigoted ways."

Lannon entered the shop. "What's that you say? She got you talking to yourself again?"

"Yeah, I was just finishing up this spade and trying to remember who I had promised it to."

"Yeah, sure—it's started to rain, and everybody's gathering in the plaza looking for some direction."

"Tell them to go home and be with their families. Rejoice in the coming of the rain. They don't need me to tell them that."

"They sort of want to know if Tarra's going to turn it into some kind of ritual."

"Of course she will. That's what she does. She turns everything into some kind of sacrament."

"Well, that's kind of what everybody wants to know—are you going to let her?"

"Sure, why shouldn't I? It's harmless unless she starts sacrificing children or something. It calls to some. It helps them mark their days."

"OK. I just wondered if you were OK with it. She has a whole bunch of people standing around in the rain waiting for you."

"What? Why didn't you say that?"

"I thought I did."

He considered his robes for a moment then opted for his sun cloak to keep the rain off. "Damn that woman. She's going to kill me."

Tarra stood on the altar stone with her spear planted at her side. The rain misted into the court and washed months of dust from the facade. Water bled down the walls of the plaza and flowed as a brown sludge in the gutters.

Most of the townsfolk had gathered around the altar stone in little family clusters. He strode to the edge and called up to her. "What is it now?"

"Hea calls to you. Will you speak with Him?"

"I'll speak with you. Why do you keep these people from their lives? Go home, all of you. The show's over." He barked at the crowd.

"Stand with me, Seer. Stand here on the great symbol and tell me what you see."

"I see a child playing in the rain and making a big deal about it."

Her robes clung to her torso and her hands dripped blood from the dye she had used. She held her spear aside and offered her hand to him. "Come and stand with us and worship the beauty of Hea. Perhaps then Yod will speak with you."

"I've spoken with Yod and He told me that you're starting to make Him mad. He said you've strayed from the path of your father and need to realize that you are but a woman with the healing gift, not the keeper of the divine word. You've fallen prey to the temptations your father warned us of... You seek to bargain with Hea, as if you can. He cares nothing for you. You're as the mud that pours down these gutters. You're here now, and tomorrow you'll return to the dust from which you came. You preach of things you don't know, to people who should know better." He gestured a sweeping motion to the crowd. "All of you should take measure of yourselves. Are you surrendering your will to a faith that has no answers? I would gladly accept Hea's dealings if I thought He would listen to me, but He doesn't. I've prayed for forgiveness yet He punishes us with heat and cold. The children go hungry, and the old go blind and die..." He hesitated at the realization of what he had said. "What has your god done for us? What can we do to make Him happy?"

"We can do nothing to make Him happy… We can only make ourselves happy with the knowledge that we *are* Him. He has given us life here in heaven—life to learn, to love, to feel."

"For life I'm grateful, for the strife... I'm not. If this is heaven, why are we tormented so?"

Tarra spread her arms wide holding her spear to the sky. "Feel it, learn from it, love it."

"You talk nonsense. Meaningless rhymes and riddles, chants and spells, games and puzzles. You have to grow up and face reality. These people need strength not dreams."

"Without dreams you can't know Yod. You say you've spoken with Him, but you hear only whispers from the darkness."

"Tangar has spoken to me. He tells me that you're a child who needs to learn her place as a woman and mother, not a priestess of things you don't understand."

"Are they whispers from Daddy, or is it a dark spirit that pretends—to fool you?"

"And you pretend to know?"

"What did you ask? Was it from your heart or your head?"

"That's what I'm talking about—riddles and games… I'm a warrior. I don't think with my heart."

"I am a warrior of truth!" She set the butt of her spear on the symbol with a resounding crack. "If you don't feel the truth with your heart, you'll be deceived by the spirits of darkness. They know your mind, and will trick you into believing you know what's right."

"I—oh never mind. You twist my words with your riddles. Look, the rains have come, that's good. They wash the misery of the summer heat from us and renew our fields. It's a time to celebrate, but it is nothing special, it's just that time of year."

"That's what's special, don't you see? Hea has smiled on us as He once did. This isn't the punishing rains of the cleansing. It's the rain of autumn as it should be. We should rejoice and give thanks so that He may hear us and continue to favor our ways."

"Has He favored us? It's just rain. He doesn't care one way or the other. It's just normal."

"Yes! That's right. You do see... It's a sign that things are getting back to normal. We need to thank Him for His wisdom. It may please Him enough to hurry the process."

"And how would you have me thank Him? What can one man do?"

"You are the *man foretold*. Come and stand with me on the altar."

"I'm not dressed for it."

"Stand here." She leaned over and extended her bloody hand.

He declined the offer and hoisted himself onto the platform in a single grunting thrust.

"OK, I'm here. Now let's get it over with."

"Look at the symbol below your feet. This is the arc of Vau, it curves up and joins Yod over there," she gestured. "Do you think you should be here, or over there?"

"What difference does it make? I just want to get in out of the rain."

"You tell me. Where do you think you should be to thank Hea? It is your choice."

He flinched at the silliness of her games but considered the platform and its strange markings. *It certainly must have meant something to someone, but to me it's just a bunch of meaningless lines.* He wandered across the naked surface. The few followers who remained on the platform stepped aside and let him view the symbol in its entirety. The intersection of lines leapt up at him through the film of water. He had never seen it so clearly.

"Where is Hea?"

"Here, this is his universe." She gestured at the circle with the butt of her spear. "Here He joins with Vau, and over there He joins with Yod."

"And what's this area?"

This is just pure Hea where He completes the circle of God."

"Well, that must be where I'm supposed to stand."

"If you wish, but why didn't you choose here with Yod? He's the spark of knowledge. Don't you think it would be better to appeal to His wisdom?"

"I thought you said I was supposed to talk to Hea, now you want me to talk to Yod. Why don't you make up your mind?"

"It's not for me to decide. You're the Seer. You must decide where you stand with God."

He looked at her angelic face and the cherub at her side and couldn't help but want to play her game in spite of the awkwardness he felt. He wondered if she would chide him for selecting the wrong move as he stepped into the center of Hea's circle. The rain fell harder as he stood quietly and surveyed the symbol around him. He looked at her for a sign but with none coming, he simply spread his arms and said, "Please Hea, smile on us again. Let this rain be your gift to nourish us."

Tarra pulled Chilgar up to rest on her hip. "You speak from your head. You say what you think is expected."

"I'm me. Yes, I do what people expect of me. It's who I am. I'm not ashamed of it."

"Good, you shouldn't be, but don't you feel the spirit of Yod pulling at you. Think of Daddy. Feel the warmth of Vau. Speak to those who will listen. Hea is magnificent in His glory, but He won't listen to your thoughtful plea. It means nothing to Him. You're but a single spark for an instant of time in His universe that is so vast, it is beyond our understanding."

"I thought you said I needed to talk to Him. Now you're telling me He's the wrong guy."

"I said you needed to thank Him, not ask Him for gifts. The only one that might listen to such supplication is Yod, and there you must be very careful. This is of what Papa warned—'don't speak from your head when you speak with Yod. Dark spirits will see your weakness and fill your thoughts with false dealings'."

"Tangar never spoke of such things. He said, '…stay away from what you don't understand…' and you don't understand this. You include all of these people. Tangar would never do such a thing. He knew that they would get it wrong and screw it up. Maybe that's why Hea's so angry. He's been punishing us since Tangar left."

"Daddy died in the first storms of the cleansing. I was there... remember? He spoke to me in his last days. He questioned the wisdom of his teachers, and lamented that he hadn't included me in on more of his dealings in the 'old ways'. He knew that the weak would think that Hea is angry and punishing us for our wrongdoing, but he wanted everyone to know that it was untrue. He didn't get a chance to tell them, so he trained me as best he could and begged Yod to smile on me... on us."

"He told you? Or are you dreaming now of things not said?"

"I talked with Papa and he told me that you need to know of these things. I am only the Keeper. I can't know the wisdom of what you see. You must divine the truth. I've shown you the spheres of God and how they intertwine… You must fit within their powers to see our way."

"I talked with Tangar too and he told me only that you're a child who's gotten lost."

"He was my father, he saw me always as his child. Do you see me as a child?" She stepped forward and pressed her hand on his chest.

Chilcoat stood transfixed as her hand burned a hole in his heart. "Yes—no, you know I don't. You're my—wife. Everyone knows that, everyone but you."

"I've known it for years. And, I tell you husband, you are the Seer, the one who must join with the spheres. I can't make you. You have to want it."

The First Rain

They stood silently facing each other, disturbed only by Chilgar's insistence that they get out of the rain. Tarra wrestled with him for a moment then released him to flee the platform. Looking in vain at Chilcoat for some sign of resolution she gave up and followed Chilgar to the shelter of their home. The audience had already grown tired of the bickering and left him abandoned on the platform.

He shuffled across the figure feeling oddly out of place standing alone in the plaza. The building surrounding him still radiated the heat of the day, but the rain poured a river of cool night air down onto the platform as he turned his face to the clouds and drank in the pure cold water.

"Dear God, I want to do the right thing, but I just didn't know how. She challenges me in front of the whole tribe... Now I'll have to resolve this matter or resign. Am I to just hunt rats?"

"You crafty old fart, you come to me now with your rats. What's the matter, old man—you need a good laugh? You tell me now of your mice... why don't you tell me of your daughter and her signs?" Chilcoat wandered around the platform looking at the crossing lines. "Well old man—you're not so talkative when it comes to important things. You used to bend my ear with your stories and riddles, why don't you talk to me now?" His answer came as a gust of cold wind that raced down the northern wall and sprayed rain in his face.

He recalled sitting around the fire with Tangar and wondering if it was all worth it. The old man would concoct some devilish brew and spend hours sipping it and muttering about the way things used to be. He never seemed to resolve anything during the ritual. He would just come around late the next day and lay down the law. "Is that what I'm supposed to do, get drunk on some of your daughter's poison and talk to rocks all night?"

He found himself standing in the center of the great symbol. The depression where Tarra had built her fire was now brimming with rainwater and bleeding a black ribbon of ash out across the platform and off the edge. He scanned across the stage at the symbol and realized... *This is the place I should be. Each of the circles spreads out away from me in symmetrical arcs that seem comfortable now. Could that be the answer to her silly game? I should stand in the center and declare myself in harmony with YodHeaVau. That's too simple. Surely, she would find fault in my arrogance. But, what other answer could* there be? If I accept her teachings, and this symbol is what she says it is, then there could be no other answer for where I should be.

"Is that it, old man? Has Yod spoken to me through you or am I kidding myself?"

The rain was beginning to fall heavily but he felt comfort in the realization that he wanted to accept her teachings. He wanted the symbol to be more than just a silly game.

He fled the downpour and warmed himself at home. The children were already in bed, so he sat by his work-hearth, drank warm tea, and smoked a small bowl of herbs. *He wondered if she was asleep but quickly put it out of his mind. I'm not ready to spar with her right now. Still, I long to hold her close.* He rose to go to bed and paused at the worktable. The pictogram again haunted him. *The Shanare certainly had a thing for that damn symbol.* He set his cup in the center of the diagram.

The tea kept him awake and the smoke jumbled his thoughts across all sorts of issues complicating his life. He kept coming back to her and her witching ways. He could feel her hand pressing gently on his chest. He couldn't get her out of his thoughts except through lecherous wanderings with Charona, but they always led back to her, her and her father. *That old coot certainly set me up,* he thought. *The old man set me on a path I never imagined. I grew up in an uncomplicated life among his family and friends. In the summer, we'd go to the lake, and in the winter, we'd go to the coast with the other tribes. It wasn't an easy life, but I loved it. Now, I live in a temple in the sky and talk with spirits.*

I long for the old days. Things were simple, the summer brought warmth and harvest, and the winter brought refreshing rains and renewal. Now the first rain brings the fear that it's the beginning of another harsh winter. If this winter is going to be as bad as the last, many will be lost.

Visions of the sky-fires from last season flashed across his mind. *They were different from those they had seen before. They were particularly hostile and strange. The ghost-like fingers grew until they formed a web of pulsing ropes of lightning trailing sheets of flame that twisted and strained across the southern horizon. The sky moaned in relentless strains of thunder and the ground quacked in response. The temple trembled and groaned as layers of stone flaked off the cliff face shedding the ladders and scaffolding in three places. The furor drew strength from the sun with the eerie pulsing web of energy overriding everyone's thoughts. Tarra and her followers chanted endlessly and she claimed it was the first bonding of Hea with Vau in heaven. "It's in the scrolls..."* she claimed. *"God yearns to begin a new cycle. He has learned all that He can from our foolish ways and desires to start anew with the children of Yod purified by His cleansing embrace."*

Chilcoat felt only coldness for the deity that would take his parents before he really knew them and his wife when their children needed her most. *Why would You torment so many so senselessly? These people are good. They've done nothing to provoke such unfair dealings. Have we unwittingly done something to anger You? Perhaps the elders are right. Perhaps we haven't walked as lightly as we should on Your world. We've done penance as the elders prescribed, yet the weather doesn't relent.*

"Tangar..., Dad, you didn't prepare me for such dealings. I wonder what you would do... Eat a bunch of herbs you shouldn't and spend the night talking to rocks?" *That's ironic*, he thought, as his voice echoed off the stone ceiling of his bedchamber. The spatters from the rain in the plaza whispered on the stones and the small flame of his work hearth flickered ghostly shapes on the wall.

He negotiated a more comfortable position and tried to clear his head of such things. He remembered the old man's words. *"Men aren't capable of offending God, they are of God, and play such a small part in the vastness of time that it is impossible for such a creature to offend Him."* *What then, can explain the harshness that has befallen us? Perhaps Tarra is right... It's simply His cleansing of those who are unfit.*

"It pains me to think that Caran was unfit. She had only done what she knew to do, but it just wasn't good enough. She's now with Yod just as Tangar and my parents and so many others. Isn't that enough? How many others must die to make You happy?" His eyes swelled with tears and his voice caught in his throat.

Tarra's words echoed through his head. *"We can only make ourselves happy that God has given us life in this heaven."*

I want more. I want God to care about me, to bring my loved ones back, to not take them in the first place. I want Him to be more like a man than an unfeeling sea of souls.

He realized, as the old text swam through his thoughts, that to be one of the souls of Yod was all he could hope to be. *"Kings, princes, and paupers are naught but one of these souls."*

*I selfishly want my life and my soul to be more than just one among countless millions, but I recognize that **is** the gift of life... It's my sacred duty to Yod to learn His lessons, to cling to this gift, this heaven, for as long as I can and to savor every moment of joy and pain. It'll soon be over and I'll be with Him to await His judgment on the execution of my duty. If He finds favor in my acts, He'll again allow me to rejoin Vau in this miracle of heaven.*

Chilcoat startled awake. He was sweating and his stomach was tight as if he had been running all night. He had dreamt of Caran. She was warm and comforting, but she scolded him about his robes. *I'm not sure why, but she was unhappy with my treatment of the garment. That's all I need. It isn't bad enough to have the old man visiting my dreams, but now my wife chastises me.*

The children were already up, and he needed to pee. He still felt perplexed by what had happened last night, but somehow his dreams seemed to settle his resolve. He knew he would have to make some sort of public announcement about Tarra's challenge this morning. *It's my duty to set things straight. I wonder if the weather will let up enough to permit a meeting.*

Considering his sun-cloak for a moment, he decided it was still too damp and opted for his work clothes. He shuffled across the plaza in his bare feet to avail himself of the facilities.

As he returned to his shop, he passed the altar platform and noticed a wreath of flowers left hanging off the far edge where the black stain from the fire pit ran down the face of the stone. He assumed it must be some of Tarra's doings but he had no idea what she was up to now. *Apparently, she's going to force the issue,* he thought as he got his children ready for the day.

It Is a Temple

Chilcoat walked slowly across the courtyard bantering with his friends. He noticed that the shrine had grown from a single wreath to several pots of flowers and offerings of fruit. He searched the crowd for Tarra and wasn't surprised to see her once again in her ceremonial robes. She was standing beside the platform near the decorative clutter. This time her hands were green and held the scepter in one and Chilgar with the other.

He wasn't sure he was ready, but his curiosity got the best of him. "What's up?"

Tarra looked solemnly at him and held the scepter out for him. "Ah, just in time. Here, take this and tell me what you see."

"I see you and a whole bunch of people that are very confused. What's the meaning of all of this?"

"I just wanted to celebrate the first rain, so I put a wreath to mark the day. The others joined in for their own reasons. Now it's your turn. Will you join us?"

"To celebrate the beginning of another winter of cold and rain?"

Tarra looked scornfully at him. "To celebrate the new beginning. It's time for the gathering. Are we going to go?"

"Some will make the journey—those who are of age. It'll be another year of hardship for those who feel they must go."

"Are you going to lead us?"

"I don't have much of a reason to go unless you're leaving me and want me to offer your hand."

"I'll think about it... I really need to speak with the elders about these writings."

"What writings? I see only little fat men doing things that are best left unsaid."

"Here, look—see, the water has drained here." She pointed at the obvious black stain pouring down the side of the platform.

"Yeah, so, it has to go somewhere."

"Look, see the little man is drinking the water that pours off the altar." She traced her fingers across the plump little figure.

She was right, the little man had his head turned up and his mouth was open acting as a drain spout for the gutter that serviced the platform. He, like the other carvings, was involved in a sexual escapade with an equally chubby female figure. The black stain ran down his neck and across his oversized belly before it flowed down his partner's head and down the side of the platform.

"So, the drain empties out here. It always drains out here. What's so special about that? He looks just like all of the others to me." Chilcoat gestured at the next pair of equally obscene figures in the endless stream of characters cavorting around the platform.

"No, see how pregnant she is? She's ripe and ready for harvest. For the first rain to come at this time of year is a good sign. It's as it should be—the first 'howler'."

"Howler?"

"That's what we called these guys with their mouths opened like that. They look like they're howling. See, there's another one over here, and here." She ran along the edge of the platform pointing out sets of figures. "There're more of them along here, and then they just stop over here." She ran around the side of the platform. "I think they count the rains of winter. And look, over here Hea is holding his hands up to the heavens, that was two days ago when you saw the season turn."

"Oh, now you've defrocked Hea and put Him in this debauchery?"

"Who else could it be? You see. This is Hea and this is Vau, and they mark the passing of time in cycles of birth and death. Here they join, here they celebrate, and here they mourn. And here they mark the coming of the first rain of autumn." She pointed to the stained figure. "See there's a pair for each day. It's a calendar that marks the season change. The women are skinny here, and they are planting seeds, and here they get fatter as the season grows."

"Skinny? They don't look very skinny to me." Chilcoat traced the outline of an obviously pregnant cherub.

"Well, sort-of skinny, that doesn't matter. Right now, what's important is that the first rain of the season has come at the right time. It's a good sign."

"If you say so, it all seems pretty silly to me. I mean, look at some of these, what are they doing here? And this pair—I don't think that's even possible."

"I don't know, maybe it's a ceremony or something. All I know is that I've spoken with Papa and he kept laughing at the figures. They made him happy and now Hea has given us this sign. The rain has come at the right time." She peeked out from under the hood of her robes. "What do you see?"

He searched her face for understanding then spoke in clear tones for all to hear as he raised the scepter to the west where the sun was beginning to poke through the clouds. "I see... I see, as never before, the wisdom of my father—of *our* fathers. I see that Hea has brought us the first rains. He cleanses the dust of summer and renews the soil. For that, we're grateful and humbly accept His gift. May Vau find favor in our harvest and bring new life to the temple." He lowered the scepter and held it out for her.

Her eyes clouded and a tear streaked the green stripe she had fashioned on her cheek. She took the wand and handed it to Chilgar. "Here, help me. Take this and try not to drop it." They strolled toward home.

"Do you replace me already?"

"He, at least, wants to hold the scepter."

"He was born to it."

"So were you. Papa took you as his son, just as you now take him. He'll grow in the ways of a leader and know the grace of YodHeaVau."

"And am I to lose you both to Shadoc when he calls?"

She stopped and turned to him. "Shadoc is very special to me... to us. He's given us the gift of Vau to join our tribes but he's not my husband. My husband is a great and powerful leader who will see his people through the trials of the new beginning. The scrolls have said this... 'The inheritor's of heaven shall know the wisdom of the man foretold'."

"Just when I was about to buy into it, you come up with something like that. Did that come from those old letches?"

"Don't call them that, they're just men like any other."

"Yeah, well, you just be careful with what they say. They're a bunch of old— scoundrels, just like Tangar." He hoped he hadn't already said too much.

"I'll not have you talk about my father... our father, in that way. He was only as clever as he needed to be." She resumed her walk toward home.

"I know. I just worry about you. I don't want you to get hurt by all this scroll nonsense."

"It's not nonsense. Everything that's written in the scrolls has happened, so why not believe that the other things they say will also happen?"

"Look, I don't know what the scrolls say, but I'm sure it's just a bunch vague clichés that any young girl would love to believe, and I think it's cruel of those old—'gentlemen' to encourage you like this. Have you actually read these scrolls or are they just more of their campfire fables?"

"Shadoc and I studied them together. That's why we…" She drew up short of blaming their involvement on the scrolls.

"OK, so what did they say about you?"

"They said the Keeper would 'know the word' and would 'nurture a new beginning as a warrior of truth', and that her mate would be the 'noble seer of the select few'. They said they will raise a son to 'herald the second coming and father the people who will walk proudly in the light'."

"Are you sure they didn't just slip you some of that magic in your tea to make you believe that everything is in the scrolls?"

"I'll show you at the gathering. The elders will probably banish me from their circle, but if you want to read them, I'll show you."

"It wouldn't do any good. I'm too dumb to understand all that flowery stuff. I just don't know what to do with—you. I'd like to believe you, but it just goes against everything I've ever been taught. Dad never spoke of such things, and now you say he knew all of this and just never got around to telling anyone."

"He was only a man. He did what he thought was right for his time. He knew many things that he never spoke of with any but his closest friends. It was the way of their school. He speaks to me now in ways I don't understand, but I know he's spoken."

"See, that's what worries me. It's not right for you to hear voices of the dead." He tried to pull her close.

"I don't hear his voice. I think his thoughts." She freed herself and sat on the floor near her table. "Papa's spirit gives me thoughts of stars, and worlds, and warmth that call to me."

"You think his thoughts—the thoughts are yours... The spirit of Tangar doesn't have anything to do with it. You think these things and you blame it on his spirit. His spirit has blended with Yod. He wants to move on. I've seen this in my dreams. He comes to me in the night and leaves only a feeling of unrest. Unrest in Yod isn't a good thing."

"Yes... It makes me sad. This is the way of Yod. He has more important things to do now and new worlds to see."

"Well, good riddance. I can do without his visits if I am going to sleep with his daughter."

"Who said I'm going to sleep with you?"

"Well, I just figured…"

"You just figured. Well, you just figured wrong. A man that hasn't faced his fears can't sleep soundly and doesn't make a good bedfellow."

"What fear would you have me face now? And don't tell me you finally found a snake."

"The fear of a loved one lost… I made enough lotion for three days, yet within two days, Caran was gone. Can you explain this to me?"

Chilcoat sat silently for several moments then spoke in a quiet tone. "She wept… I couldn't deny her. The pain was too much for her, for me… She—she begged me to complete her—life, our life—together. But it didn't. She lives with me still. At times, I wish she didn't, but at others, I can't imagine life without her. Did I do wrong? I would gladly face any penance that would take this guilt from me."

"There's no guilt in what you've done. You love her still, as you should. No one blames you for that. I made the potion for her. I knew what it would do. Must I share in your guilt? I did what I did because I loved her and it was the right thing to do. Just as you did."

"I don't blame you. God, I love you. It's just—I wanted to do more, but I couldn't. You didn't give me the right potion."

"You're wrong. I gave you the potion given by God. It worked just as it should. She sought comfort from you, and you gave it to her. She fulfilled her role proudly and should be respected."

"Is it just that easy for you? You can blame everything on God and just go on with your life? Well, I'm sorry. I can't." Chilcoat stood silently while Tarra began cleaning the stain from her arms and face.

"Did you act from your heart or your head? Yod already knows, so lying does you no good. If it came from your heart, you have nothing to fear. He'll comfort you. If it came from your head, then nothing I can say will lessen your burden before Him."

"How am I to just go on?"

She sat silently looking at him for several moments. "You do your duty as you know you should... Tonight we celebrate with the howler. Hea has blessed this day, so we must give thanks. Tomorrow we need to get ready for the gathering."

"Gathering, how did we get back to that?"

"I have to talk with the elders about what I've learned and I have to get the scrolls from them."

"Am I invited or are you going alone?"

"Oh, you have to come. You have to help me get the scrolls."

"You say what? What do you want with those old things?"

"I told you. I'm the Keeper. I need to get the scrolls and keep their knowledge for our children."

"And the elders are just going to give them to you?"

"Sure. They don't know it yet, but they have to."

"Let me guess, it's in the scrolls."

"See, I knew you'd understand. Besides, it'll give you a chance to lead again. That should be fun."

He knew that if the clan was to make this journey, he would have to lead it. "The harvest is poor, so the more people I can get to go this year; the better it will be for those who remain behind. It'll be a hard journey, but since we haven't gone in the last few years, there'll be many who'll want to go, perhaps, too many. Those who're too young will be the first to volunteer and some who're too frail will insist that they aren't. Have you gotten your people ready?"

Tarra removed her robes and began cleaning the stain from her torso. "My people? We've talked about it, everyone has. It's been a long time since they've seen their kin and they're excited about what they've discovered."

"Yeah, about that, I'm not sure we should make it sound too good. I mean, this place is nice for a small group, but the gardens are poor. If we make it sound too good, there'll be others who will want to come."

"It's the temple of the Shanare. All who come will bring gifts and visit only briefly. We'll grow herbs that we can trade."

Chilcoat considered her words and recognized that he needed to make big changes to assure the survival of his people. *Tangar had brought him to this place for a reason, and now it was clear that his quest was to discover the ways of YodHeaVau, not to build of a new village.* "Perhaps you're right. Perhaps we can make it work that way… It means we'll have to dress the part, and there'll be ceremonies to stage, but it might be the only way to keep these people alive. I'm beginning to understand why the Shanare abandoned this place. The medical herbs that you grow thrive in the skimpy soil, but the foodstuffs needed by the people struggle poorly. If the other clans will treat this place like the gathering village and bring gifts to trade, it might be possible for our people to survive. If this place is to become a temple, the people who live here will have to be those who believe in its powers."

Chilcoat stood in the doorway for a moment. "The rain's stopped. Will you do me a favor?"

"That depends, does it involve sex?" She grabbed a dry robe and held it to her chest.

"No. I've decided to rejoin the tribes. I want to hold an announcement ceremony. You know, dress it up, and make it a big deal. I'll dress too."

"By your leave, noble Seer of the Temple Tribe." She bowed submissively letting her robe fall away.

One Big Happy Family

The morning light was clean and sharp as people ventured slowly into the plaza in reverence of the freshly washed stones. The subtle tones of the colored rock leapt out in vibrant splashes that revealed the charms and ornaments of the architecture like never before. Tarra's chanting interrupted the normal breakfast shuffling of people and things. Her followers quickly dropped their tasks and started to assemble around the altar stone as she continued the chant descending the stairway. She had her formal ceremonial robes on and did her floating routine, brandishing her spear in wide sweeping arcs, which brought her to the center of the altar.

She called out above the din. "All are welcome. The Seer has called for everyone to attend. Spread the word, all who are able should come."

The fire pit in the center of the stone was still full of water, so she brought a small clay pot that wafted a ribbon of scented smoke across the plaza. She began chanting again and beckoned her followers to join in.

Chilcoat appeared in his doorway with his robes wrapped tightly around him. Walking slowly to the altar, he ascended the wooden steps that leaned against the platform. Tarra approached and bowed slightly offering the scepter to him from her now purple stained hands.

The crowd murmured with excitement as Chilcoat began to speak. "Hea has smiled upon us with this rain. It has come in the right season and now it has passed, just as it should. The time of the gathering is upon us again. I've spoken with Yod about this for many days now, and I believe the time has come for everyone to consider their future. This place is very special—but it isn't a plentiful table. We've struggled for years to make the gardens grow, but as you know, it provides for only a few. I think the time has come for us to rejoin our clans. We'll go to the gathering as we did in the old days. Everyone who is able, and willing, will return to their families. Those who are unable or unwilling to rejoin can remain here to tend the Sky Temple of the Shanare."

The murmur of the crowd grew to a general clamor of shouts and hollers. "What of our tents? We're not prepared to resume as we were."

"It's true we've lost some of what we were, but we've learned much and we've survived. I think that Hea will smile once again on our ways. We should give thanks that this refuge protected us during His wrath, but now it's time to once again live in the daylight. We'll still have to guard against his fury, but our children will grow to love the healing light."

A voice rang from the crowd. "It sounds to me like the witch has had her way with you."

Chilcoat turned quickly to face the challenger. "It's true that I've seen wisdom in Tarra's ways. If I am bewitched, so be it. It's my faith in YodHeaVau that captivates me, not Tarra's charms. I have felt His power here in this temple just as you have, if you will admit it. It has been our salvation and now you must decide if you are worthy of this gift."

He broke his gaze on the accuser to address the general crowd. "As I've said, this place isn't big enough for all of us. It is enchanted with symbols and carvings that no one yet understands. It's magic in its own way, but it will only sustain a few. Many fewer than we are right now. We'll journey to the winter village and meet with the elders. Tarra will again read the scrolls of knowledge and she'll return here to serve as the keeper of His wisdom. Perhaps others will visit and help provide for those who stay. If you're one of her followers, you may return with her, if you don't want to return, no one will blame you. The Shanare left this place. There is no disgrace in leaving."

The crowd continued to challenge his decision. "You would have us depend on the generosity others. What kind of a leader is that?"

"I'll not steal your dignity by having you depend on others. This place will support only a few, and our lives will be poor, but we'll not depend on anyone's charity. If the faithful come to learn and visit the sacred grounds and bring gifts to exchange for medicinal herbs, they will benefit just as we will. No. This place has served us well, but the time has come to rejoin the tribes and leave this place to those who feel the bond with YodHeaVau."

"Will you be one of them?"

"Yes. I'll return with my family." He gathered his children to his side and pulled Tarra and Chilgar under his arm. "And I want all of the bravest youngsters to join us. This place should not be a place for the old to die, like the winter village. It should be a place where the brightest can come to learn and teach."

"I, for one, don't want to leave my home here. You've stripped me of all that I have except for this patch of dirt and the cave I live in. I can't go back to my clan empty handed. They don't need another burden."

"I don't blame you for not wanting to return if your clan is so weak that they expect you to come bearing gifts to buy your way home. If you wish to blame me for your plight, that's your right. You can blame me, or Hea, or yourself. It doesn't really matter. It is what it is, deal with it." He turned to Tarra and spoke softly. "I think we're about done here."

She rolled her eyes meaningfully at the scepter.

"Oh, all right, the Seer has spoken." He shouted waving the wand first to the rising sun then to the west where it will set.

"Not very convincing." She admonished under her breath and began chanting the wedding song beckoning to all with gestures normally reserved for the newly joined couples. The crowd that had started to disperse paused to see what she was doing.

Chilcoat stood watching her graceful gestures then realized that she had captured the attention of everyone. As she finished the short verse, she again spoke. "All of you who are to be joined in the word and serve the temple, I want you to realize that you are wed to one another in a single family that must share their hardships and faith."

She smiled proudly and sang the short song again. Some of the skeptics wandered off muttering and giving scoffing gestures to those who remained. Those that stayed behind stirred nervously wondering if they were to partake in some sort of a bonding ceremony. Chilcoat wasn't sure if they were glad or disappointed that he simply held Tarra tightly for a moment then released her and descended the wooden steps. The general upheaval that followed included several arguments and much speculation about how the witch had woven her spell.

***

The trip to the gathering was slow due to the hodgepodge collection of carts they patched together, but Hea was kind and sent favorable weather. There was much adulation for their valiant effort, but the other tribes had no sympathy for their loss of goods and people. *All have suffered greatly through the cleansing and many have died from the sun-sickness.*

The elders held court to listen to Chilcoat, but had already decided that only their council would consider the mysteries and symbols of the temple. Tarra sat for many days talking and drawing figures for them but in the end, they dismissed her as a novice seeking approval for her fantasy. Talbot had passed away and Santos, of the enlightened school, dominated the council and found her interpretation of these signs blasphemous. The cherubs on the altar stone, however, were the subject of endless speculation and crude excursions through the memories of the old men.

Tarra excused herself after she had sketched representative figures and explained the numbers and seasonal variations she had observed. Nothing was resolved, but the elders had a great time reminiscing about their past exploits. She stocked up on herbs and seeds that could be found only at the coast, but her heart wasn't in it. She exchanged stories and recipes with the elders but they held her at a distance.

As the bonding ceremony drew near, Tarra dressed in her finest robes and brewed a batch of iridescent rose stain to dip her hands in. She called her followers together and they went through one of their ceremonies. They drew the great symbol in the sand and little clusters of people mingled and shifted from section-to-section arguing attitudes and perceptions. Some of the other tribesmen gathered to watch their antics and giggle at their expense. A couple of the onlookers showed interest in the dance and joined with awkward quips about their lives and dealings. The band welcomed them into the fray and tried to explain the significance of the symbol. The finer points were largely lost on them, but the opportunity to join in a social exchange with near strangers was too exciting to pass up. Most of the crowd soon drifted away, but a few new recruits lingered in heated discussions and quiet introspection. Tarra did her fluttering dance as she chanted the closing hymn. Chilgar joined in, scurrying around her in synchronized dashes and leaps that kept him just out of her embrace.

One of the elders stood by watching as the group dispersed. He approached Tarra as she laughingly gathered her son and started to leave. "You speak too freely of things you cannot know. You and your bastard son should be careful." The old man looked sternly at her and scuffed at the lines of the symbol as he left.

"It's written that my son will someday be the savior of your lost children. You would be wise to respect him, lest He find you unworthy." She called out for all to hear as she wrestled Chilgar into submission.

***

Chilcoat spoke with Lannon solemnly as they wandered across the clearing. "The elders called me aside today. They said Tarra's making trouble and they want me to stop her."

"Can you do that?"

"Probably not, besides, I don't want to... What she says makes sense to me now. She's just a little too—colorful for their taste."

"She does have a flare about her." Lannon reminisced about his snake tail and wondered where it had gone. *Charona has probably disposed of it.* "Are you going to talk to her?"

"Of course, I'm going to talk to everyone. We have to get a few things settled about our return."

"Talk to who?" Tarra approached.

"Oh, good, you're here. The elders have turned on you."

"I know. They sent a messenger."

"Why are you still dressed?" Chilcoat looked up from his pipe.

"The bonding ceremony, I'm officiating, remember?"

"Is it that time already?"

"You can't be that dumb. Get dressed. It's part of your job."

"I know. I just like to hear you ask." He smirked at her aggravation.

The entire tribe gathered along the path leading to the temple. They draped garlands and the children gathered in order. Tarra went to the head of the line of young women and began to chant softly at first, then rhythmically built to the traditional bonding call. She danced and gestured evocatively to the young men standing around as she pranced down the path toward the temple. The other girls followed in like fashion with varying levels of skill and confidence until the entire line of eligible women disappeared through the mysterious temple door.

Chilcoat waited for the entire entourage of families and friends to file in through the tunnel. Pulling his robes tight, he walked quickly to the center clearing, flanked by Lannon and a small band of friends.

Ironically, the stone of Hea stood draped with decorations before him. He leaned on Lannon and climbed to the top of the stone. "Can I have your attention?" He called out repeatedly across the crowd. "I've something to say before we continue with the ceremony."

The elders had already ascended their knoll and sat proudly on their pedestal. The eligible women sat quietly on their respective hill and the boys jostled each other on their platform trying to get a glimpse of what was going on.

"I'm sorry to interrupt the ceremony. I want everyone to hear this. You can go back to the party in a moment, but first I have something to say... My people, and I, come to you now with a problem. We've lived for several years in—the Sky Temple of the Shanare." He hesitated a moment considering his resistance to the concept.

"It's truly a magical place but it isn't able to support many. We, like you, have struggled under the trials of Hea. Many have died or grown old before their time, just as some of you have. It's been a hard time for us all but now there are signs that Hea is nearly finished with His cleansing and wants us to again live in the harmony of His ways."

"You speak of signs, but you have only the word of this harlot." Santos barked from his hilltop.

"I'll not have you speak that way of my wife!" Chilcoat proudly replied as Lannon and his band formed up a barrier around the base of the rock. "I've lost Caran, my wife and the mother of my children, to the cleansing. The sun-sickness took her and Tarra has consented to be my wife. She's not a harlot... She's as close to an angel as I've ever known. She has ways that heal and enchant and ways that make me question all that I am. I'm not here to argue her beliefs. They are what they are, just as your beliefs are yours to hold."

Chilcoat gestured to the crowd. "The cleansing has changed things. No one can deny that. Families have grown apart, torn by grief for old and young alike and some of us yearn to leave the misery of families torn apart. I think the time has come for the tribes to rejoin and bend to the way things are now. We need people of the right skills and age in each tribe, and the tribes need to be of a size that fits their village. Even the simplest mind knows that our communal ways of shared burden can support only a limited number of willing, hardworking, people." Chilcoat gestured to some of his tribesmen.

"As I've said, it's a meager table for those who live at our temple and many of our people wish to return to their families and friends, but that may not be possible without putting undue burden on the lakeshore tribe. Perhaps some can stay here in the winter village but it too is a delicate balance of skills and burdens. I ask the other tribes to consider their needs and perhaps come to a better mix of people and skills... That's all I have. I just wanted to let everyone know what I'm proposing." He started to climb down from his platform.

Santos barked from his pedestal. "This is a matter for the elders to consider not a public address?" He had moved from his throne to face Chilcoat. Several of the lesser council members descended the elder's mound and approached the stone where Chilcoat stood. Lannon's band of warriors drew weapons to stand guard.

Chilcoat returned to the summit of the stone. "I spoke with the elders when we arrived and they were only concerned with the images carved in their memories. They need the advice of the people on this. This goes beyond spirit-walks and herbs. Each of us needs to decide what is best for ourselves and not listen to a bunch of old men who have forgotten the ways of YodHeaVau."

"We've forgotten nothing! We guard the ways of Yod so that you, and others like you, don't make mistakes like this. You believe what this woman has said and now your people suffer. No! No, the tribes will not take your refuse. You've made your bed, now sleep in it."

Chilcoat stood defiant. "Show me... show me where it is written that 'the Keeper shall know the word and will be the mother of a new beginning'."

"How do you know of such things? You see, that's just what I was talking about, these are just half-remembered stories in forgotten scrolls and shouldn't be taken seriously."

"Then why do you fill a young woman's head with such things? You've told her she is the Keeper and now you say there is no such thing. Well, I think there is—and I think it's her. I am her Seer, and I see a bunch of old men that are worried about losing their jobs. I see a new people who don't need a bunch of herb smoking lay-abouts to stand between them and their god. These people want a real god. One they can talk to, one who cares about them, not a bunch of mysteries and drugs that lift you above them."

Tarra broke into a haunting rendition of the wedding song. Everyone stopped their grumbling and turned to see what was going on. She was standing on the steps of the women's platform with her hair flowing like flames in the breeze and her arms stretched out to expose the iridescent rose flesh of her stained skin. She beckoned all to gather in the joining ceremony as she finished the song. Some of the eligible candidates gathered on the platform behind her muttered in confusion. *The ceremony isn't finished so the song is out of place.*

Tarra stepped to the top of the stairs and spoke in a clear voice. "Look at the person next to you. You are all now married to each other. Some of you will be good husbands and wives, and some of you will not, but that doesn't change the fact that you are wed to one another in blood and spirit. You can choose to carry on in the ways of the enlightened council, or you can choose to seek the ways of God. Just understand that the ways of YodHeaVau will go on with, or without, you. They don't need sacred scrolls or magic herbs. They're simply the way it is. You are all part of it, whether you want to be or not."

With that, she broke into the wedding song again and slowly descended the stairs and walked down the hill toward the stone where Chilcoat stood.

Chaos broke out as everyone discussed what had just transpired. Tarra's followers gathered around her as she grabbed her spear and fought her way toward Chilcoat. He jumped down from the rock and embraced her warmly. There were supporters and detractors on all sides trying to talk to them as Lannon's little army struggled to keep hostilities to a minimum. The prime-elder also descended his hill with his entourage and the opposing forces met at the base of the sacred stone.

"There will be no violence unless you force it!" Chilcoat shouted out above the din. Lannon slowly eased his guard as the council members assessed their challengers and dropped their attitude. The leaders confronted each other. "We've come here in good faith and wish no harm, but this issue is resolved... My people will go wherever needed and welcomed. Some will return to the temple with Tarra and me, and any of you who wish to follow the ways of YodHeaVau are welcome. But don't think it will be an easy escape from your past."

The Prime looked disdainfully at Tarra's spear and resignedly barked at the crowd of onlookers. "Your people are welcome to join their families, but they must follow the ways of their tribe. We'll not have your blasphemy preached here!"

"Will you teach them from the scrolls?" Tarra challenged.

"Of course, we'll teach them of the scrolls as we always have."

"Then Hea will continue to punish you. The scrolls tell us this."

The prime-elder scoffed at her assessment. "What do you know of the scrolls? You're a novice and have only seen the scrolls briefly."

"Shadoc and I studied them. Have you ever read them?"

"Shadoc? I might have known he would be at the bottom of this. He teaches heresy and his people have suffered for it. Look around... You don't see any of his people here, do you? No. They're unable to come again this year. They are seldom able to come since the cleansing began."

"Are they unable, or unwilling? We studied the scrolls for many days and I know what they say. But, I don't think you do. You've chosen what fits your needs and let the rest waste away."

"We don't need to read them. We have studied them for many years and know what they say."

"Do you? What do they say of the Keeper? You tell me I am the Keeper, but you reject what I say."

Santos finally joined the quarrel. "It was Talbot's fantasy that you *may* be the Keeper, but now he's gone and the enlightened council has had an opportunity to consider it, and I doubt that you are *her*."

"The scrolls tell of the Keeper being the mother of a new people who will follow the true path and of others that fall from grace thinking they know the wisdom of Hea."

Santos nervously adjusted his hood to keep Chilcoat from seeing his eyes. "The scrolls say nothing of such things. You make too much of ancient fables. Those stories have outlived their usefulness, that's why we don't read them. They're full of flowery nonsense that doesn't work in the real world. We let you read them to get you out of our hair while we conducted our business."

"Your business of drinking spirit tea and smoking herbs? My father told me of the business that the council does at the gathering, and I don't want any part of it, but I do want the scrolls. You've said you have no need for them, and you obviously don't take care of them. You should let me take them to the Sky Temple of the Shanare where they will be away from the damp sea air. I'll transcribe them anew, as they instruct us to do, so that all who wish can read them."

"I'll not have the uninitiated gaze upon the sacred writings."

"Make up your mind. They are either worthless old rags or they are sacred. Which is it?"

"I'll not be spoken to in such a way by a common tramp. You and Shadoc defiled them by fornicating in their presence."

"How do you know that? Is that more of the business of the high council—spying on young people bonding?"

Santos flushed awkwardly at being discovered. Several of the council members looked at him anxiously. "Take the damn things. You and your heretics go back to the old ways. See if it serves you? We'll send a courier to your citadel in two years' time to retrieve them from your dead hands. By then you'll have starved waiting for your fantasy to come true."

Lannon made his presence known by stepping in and taking the ceremonial scroll from one of the council members standing nearby. "We'll welcome your visit, if you come in peace."

"How will we perform the bonding ritual?" He protested meekly.

Tarra pulled the scroll from Lannon's grasp. Fortunately, it was a recent copy of the bonding scroll and could withstand the tussle. "The scrolls play no part in the bonding, isn't that right Master? You said it would desecrate them to make love in their presence, so we'll relive you of its burden. As for the ritual, it is written here in this scroll that... 'At the turn of the season all are welcome to bond anew, seeking kinship with their fellows.' The bonding ceremony is to bring each together for another year, not a lifetime. Those who wish to bond anew are welcome to do so. Those who wish to renew their bond are celebrated. These are the old ways." She carefully unrolled the cloth and drew her fingers along a line of text. "In the name of the most sacred, all are welcome to seek bond with those willing to join him for a season. If the bond fails, Yod will be saddened and you must make amends by seeking bonds anew without fault."

Chilcoat placed his spear next to Tarra's with a resounding thump. "I also have read this scroll. Don't you see? The bond is a public declaration of your willingness to pair with each other, not a contract of obligation. Your only obligation is to Yod to honor without fault the person to whom you bound. You are to renew the bond each year as a sign of commitment and celebration. Yod rejoices in this bonding as a communion of the spirit within you, to reaffirm your commitment to others, a public acceptance of who you are and who is important to you."

"You twist the words of the sacred scrolls." Santos argued his point. "The council has long understood these words and built the foundation of our tribes upon them. Your vision would cripple our way of life. Women would be turned out to fend for themselves. No. It wouldn't work."

Chilcoat again struck the butt of his spear on the ground. "If anyone is turned out, the clan will judge what's been done. If the clan supports the act, then perhaps the offenders deserve the act and should change their ways. If the clan doesn't support the act, then it is up to them to shame the offended into doing right."

"You live in a fantasy world. Do you think men are so noble that they will do right because others judge them? We know better. We've served as high council for years and know that men will only do right if we direct them."

On the bottom of the little niche created by the stack of carpets there was a small prayer rug she recognized as the one Talbot favored for his evening prayers. She ran her hand softly across its delicate pattern of flowers and birds.

Holding her breath, she slowly rolled the carpet up revealing a plain brown pad that kept the rug off the dirt floor. Picking up the rug, she held it to her chest and turned to Santos with a tear in her eye. "What have you done? The people will suffer your ignorance for generations."

Chilcoat knelt next to her and held her warmly as the high-elder used the opportunity to sneak out the side door before anyone decided to assault him.

She sobbed loudly rocking the prayer rug in her arms like a child.

Lannon stood quietly watching the pitiful display for another moment. "You want me to go after him?"

"No." She spoke without hesitation as her tears disappeared. "Keep an eye out and be sure he doesn't come back." She began tugging at the edge of the brown padding lying on the floor. The hard-packed earth under the pad was smooth and without markings. She grabbed her spear and carefully dragged it across the patch of earth. On the third attempt the edge of a brown cloth peeked out from the scuffmark. Grabbing it firmly, she tugged it into view. The dirt fell away as she pulled a large package free and dusted it off. She un-wrapped it quickly and disgorged three ancient scrolls. Each had a simple cord holding it closed within a fine cloth pouch. "Praise God." She muttered repeatedly as she caressed each delicate package confirming that they were what they seemed to be. She looked back in the hole from where they come and started digging frantically looking for the final scroll. She knew there were six, and these three along with the two the elders had given her only counted five.

The words of Talbot returned to her. *"The Keeper must receive the scroll of heaven, freely given by the one foretold."* At last, she recognized that the sixth scroll was to remain lost.

She rolled the others tightly in the prayer rug, repaired the floor, and replaced the brown pad before moving some of the carpet pile back into place. No one questioned their departure as they made a grand exit carrying the two scrolls the elders had given them and the prayer rug she carried as if it was a keepsake from Talbot.

Tarra challenged the concept. "If they are so dishonorable, then perhaps the foundation you've built is not as strong as you would like to believe. I think people are able to know right from wrong without your 'direction'. They have God to tell them right from wrong. They don't need you to tell them what God thinks of their actions. The lost scrolls tell us these things."

"What do you know of lost scrolls?" The high-elder bristled at the challenge. "They are only fables spread by the unenlightened old fools of the past."

"My father was one of those old fools." Chilcoat interrupted hoping to keep Tarra from saying too much about the scrolls she had seen.

"I mean no offense." The elder quickly tried to defuse the situation before Chilcoat assaulted him. "I just meant, if there ever were any other scrolls, they're lost to us now and are only tales no one remembers well."

Tarra stepped up to confront him. "If you've destroyed them I'm going to…"

Chilcoat stepped between them again. "Easy there, dear. No need to get hostile. Right?" Chilcoat put his massive arm around the elder's shoulder and directed him toward the shaman's tent. "Why don't we talk about this in private?"

Lannon followed closely behind gesturing to his friends to keep the other council members at bay.

Tarra immediately headed for the high-elder's inner sanctum as they entered the tent. "Where are they?"

"Here, the death scroll is here." The high-elder pointed out a newly transcribed copy of the second scroll sitting on a table near the door.

"No! Where are the others?" Tarra stormed past him and pulled the drape aside peering into the private room.

"I don't know what you expect. I've told you, there are no others." Santos stood with his hand on the single scroll.

Tarra quickly moved to the pile of carpets at the back of the room. She pulled the top layers aside. Her heart sank as she gazed upon the empty hiding space where Talbot had first shown them to her. "Where are they?" She demanded, pulling at the carpets on either side.

As they made their way through the village commons Tarra proudly whispered to Chilcoat. "We're going to have a baby."

Chilcoat stopped and grabbed her arm. "We… you, whoa I'm too old for that kind of stuff."

"I'll remind you of that... She'll remind you." Tarra looked down and patted her belly gently.

"She huh? That's what you said last time."

"This time for sure. It's in the scrolls."

"You're going to force me to read these damn things, aren't you?"

"It makes a good bedtime story. Speaking of which, I need to drop this off with the high-elder." She pulled a small package from her things.

"What is it? It isn't going to bite is it?"

"It's the little man. I brought it to trade for the scrolls."